Praise for Previou

"a page-turner you'll talk about with your friends"
—Robert Liparulo, bestselling author of *Comes a Horseman*
and *the Dreamhouse Kings series*

"brewing with surprise"
—Brandilyn Collins, bestselling author of *Eyes of Elisha* and
Over the Edge

"a compelling tale"
—Ted Dekker, *NY Times* bestselling author of *The Priest's*
Graveyard and *Three*

"Wilson is an extraordinary writer"
—Gina Holmes, award-winning author of *Crossing Oceans*
and *Dry as Rain*

"His exploration of God's hidden workings and how they in-
vade human lives is as important as it is fun to read"
—Jeff Gerke, founder of *Marcher Lord Press*

"I am a big Eric Wilson fan"
—Tosca Lee, award-winning author of *Forbidden* and *Havah*

STEP 1 AWAY

STEP 1 AWAY

A Modern Twist On One of The World's Oldest Tales

ERIC WILSON

~ book one ~
By the Numbers Series

BAY
FOREST

One Step Away
Copyright © 2011
Eric Wilson

Cover illustration by Mona Roman Advertising
Interior Design by Bookmasters

Published by Bay Forest Books
An Imprint of Kingstone Media Group
P.O. Box 491600
Leesburg, FL 34749-1600
www.bayforestbooks.com

Printed in the United States of America by
Bay Forest Books

Library of Congress Cataloguing-in-Publication information
is on file.

ISBN 978-1-613280-14-0

Dedicated to four women who invested in my storytelling:

Patty Duncan,
for showing faith in me while I was in junior high

Betty Fletcher,
for encouraging me during my high school years

Nancy Kendall,
for sharpening me through creative-writing class

Betty Jean Glenn,
for challenging me in college to "do something with it"

"Where have you come from?" the Lord asked Satan.
Satan answered . . . "I have been patrolling the earth,
watching everything that's going on."
Then the Lord asked . . . "Have you noticed my servant, Job?
. . . He fears God and stays away from evil."

—*Job 1:7,8 (NLT)*

A Captured Eye

he roams
he patrols the earth
an accuser limited by time and space, he surveys humanity, the
young, the old, male and female, all spread out beneath indigo skies,
and he boils with the rage of ten thousand wraiths
  "these humans, these two-leggers, they're nothing special"
  the words rattle in his throat and spew forth in a roar
  again he roams, he patrols
  sweeping back and forth, his gaze pries at apartment curtains,
scales the proudest skyscrapers, plunders the filth of third-world bar-
rios, and rides the ocean swells where cruise ships cater to pleasure-
seekers and trawlers carry sun-baked fishermen
  the two-leggers labor and love, they suffer and cry, but does any-
one care? perhaps the almighty one grows weary of their voices
  whether the one does or doesn't, the accuser knows that the mo-
ment these whiny children are clothed and fed, they turn into mini-gods,
drunk on their own knowledge, vainglorious, forgetful, and pampered
  "why," he asks, "does the one even bother with them? why?"
  wandering another day, the accuser passes through forested hills,
crosses bridges, enters a city
  then something
  someone, somewhere
  captures his eye, and he moves in for a closer look

Chapter One

May 2008

THE VREELANDS WATCHED HER DIE.

The filly ran lean and proud, one step away from an out-of-the-blue, come-from-behind, Kentucky Derby victory over the hugely favored Big Brown. And then she buckled. A foreleg snapped.

Down she went.

Millions saw the chestnut horse sprawl on the raked dirt of Churchill Downs. Although an equine ambulance raced to the scene, the filly's courage and triumph gave way to sudden tragedy. Eight Belles would never rise again.

Together on the sofa, Bret and Sara Vreeland stared at the TV, both afraid to say a word. They too had fought the odds, put in long days, and lived in anonymity, nurturing quiet hopes and dreams. All their work had to count for something, didn't it? Their time would come. Of course it would. They were simply being tested, prepped, and purified.

And there the great horse lay.

Dead, just like that.

Bret muted the TV and mumbled that he had to fix the roof shingles loosened by last week's storm. Sara reached for him, but he was gone. She slipped into the kitchen. Soon their kids would be home from an afternoon at Adventure Science Center, and the family could sit down for dinner together.

She pushed aside the utility bill and the coupons clipped from Sunday's paper, set a box of spaghetti noodles on the counter, and turned on the stove.

Yes, their time would come.

Not in '08, though.

Nor in '09.

August 2009

Bret flinched. He looked down at the metal sliver poking from his thumb. With trimmed nails, he worked the object from his skin. A dribble of blood flushed the wound. He wiped the thumb against his jeans and got back to work, hanging cabinets in the bedroom of a luxury motor coach.

He'd been at Billingsley Coach Company for years and now pulled in $12.50 an hour. Not much, but they also had Sara's salary and they were frugal. Not much, considering this particular coach had just sold for a cool half-mil.

To a rising country star?

Nope, this one was going to the latest, local, rock god.

Nicknamed Music City, USA, Nashville was home to various celebrities. Nicole Kidman and Keith Urban lived here. Jack White, of The White Stripes, was a recent transplant from Detroit. With the metro population climbing toward the seven-figure mark, Nashville had hospitals, universities, and museums to go along with its friendly reputation.

So far, though, Bret and Sara hadn't benefited from this growth. Years had passed since Bret's last pay raise, and expenses were piling higher with their son going into fourth grade, their daughter into first.

Running a sander over a beveled edge, Bret offered up a silent prayer:

Keep their little hearts soft, Lord. All we can do is trust them to You.

January 2010

The city wore a shroud of dazzling white. With its rolling hills and narrow side streets, Nashville seemed to grind to a halt the moment five flakes of snow touched the ground. Many schools and businesses had closed, and customers had already ransacked milk supplies at the local H.G. Hill.

This unscheduled time off cut into the Vreelands' budget, but Bret and Sara shrugged off the stress and hit the slopes with their kids. A plastic garbage-can lid served as a sled, shooting them down the dip at the end of their street.

Who could predict that eight months from now, give or take a few days, their lives would change in dramatic, emphatic fashion?

Yep, $6,000,000 had a way of doing that.

Chapter Two

September 2010

ONCE OR TWICE A MONTH SARA VREELAND DREAMED OF ANOTHER LIFE AND, this part disturbed her, of another man. Though the dreams were never graphic, she couldn't shake her sense of guilt. She loved Bret. She loved his kisses. Sure, some days he smelled of sawdust and lacquer from the shop, but she couldn't fault him for that when he worked fifty- to sixty-hour weeks providing for her and the kids.

Hair still wet from the shower, she paused at the clothes rack in the walk-in closet and traced fingertips over the silk robe Bret had given her on the eve of their wedding.

Over eleven years ago.

Before student loans, medical bills, diapers, and the challenges of raising children.

"Sweetie?" Bret called to her. "You coming to bed?"

"Be there in a minute."

She rolled back her shoulders and took the robe from its hanger. What sort of God-fearing woman let her mind wander this way? She wore a wedding ring. They attended church as a family. She was a mother, for heaven's sake.

"Case you're wondering," Bret said, "I got Kevin and Katie tucked in and they're both fast asleep. It's just you and me all by our lonesomes."

She poked her head through the doorway, noticed the glow of candles on the dresser. "Don't you have to work in the morning?"

"They gave us this Saturday off. No new projects, and there's talk that some of the guys might get let go."

"What?" Sara's heart dropped. "They can't do that to you."

"Jason promises he'll keep me on till business picks up."

"He better. All these years, and you've never even called in sick."

"Can't afford to."

Sara slipped into the robe. "That place would fall apart without you. And aren't Jason and Zoe heading off to Cozumel again next weekend? The Billingsleys live it up while we scrape to pay the electricity. Really?"

"We do what we gotta do."

"And no matter how fast we paddle, we keep on sinking."

"Least we're paddling together." Bret's back was against the headboard, his green eyes twinkling. "You coming over here or not?"

"You deserve more, that's all I'm saying."

"You're my pay, sweetheart. You and the kids."

"I'm serious," she said.

His voice turned husky. "Does it look like I'm kidding?"

She knotted the silk sash around her waist, smoothed the material over hips that were fuller after birthing two babies, and stepped into view.

"Mmm," he said, toggling dark eyebrows. "Now that's more like it."

She smiled as she headed toward the hall.

"Where you going?" he asked.

"I just need to, uh, need to get a glass of water."

"Admit it. You're checking on Kevin, huh?"

"I'll be real quick."

"He's fine. Would you just get over here?"

"Be right back," Sara said. "Don't you go anywhere, Mr. Vreeland."

She felt his desire follow her from the room, nipping at her conscience. Despite financial difficulties and occasional differences of opinion regarding the kids, they shared a love most people dreamed of. How could she let herself think of the life that might've been?

She stepped past a pair of Katie's jeans and tripped over a LEGO fort. The house needed a thorough cleaning, but she was mentally and physically exhausted. She worked ten-hour shifts at Cumberland Sleep Clinic, from 7 P.M. to 5 A.M., Monday through Thursdays. Good luck getting a day shift when her duties involved testing patients' sleep patterns.

She eased into Kevin and Katie's bedroom, where a suspended sheet divided the space. Kevin said it wasn't fair since none of his friends had to share rooms with their "annoying little sisters." Katie insisted she wasn't annoying, and look how big she was now, "up to Daddy's belly button."

At the moment Katie was facedown, arm draped over a Care Bear she had decorated with Magic Markers. She looked so peaceful. Who would ever guess she was a force of nature by day?

Sara's attention turned to her ten-year-old son. His breaths were labored, sputtering like an outboard motor with only fumes left in the tank.

"Kevin? It's me, honey."

She felt between his lips and made sure his mouth guard was in place. The MAS, mandibular advancement splint, aided the flow of oxygen by keeping the tongue from becoming an obstruction. She eased him onto his side.

"That's right," she said. "Get some rest."

Kevin had obstructed sleep apnea, which meant his breathing stopped multiple times per hour while fighting to get oxygen during rest. Obesity commonly triggered adult apnea, whereas children with OSA burned so many calories in their nighttime struggle that they were often small for their age and ran risks of premature death.

Those two words.

They hovered over Kevin's sandy hair and squirmed through Sara's daily thoughts. She could think of nothing worse than losing her children.

Once her son's breathing had evened out, and only then, Sara headed back up the hall. The night was humid. She stopped in the kitchen for a glass of water. Through the window above the sink, she noticed an unfamiliar car, a sporty-looking thing parked across the street.

Here along quiet Groves Park Road, late-model vehicles were uncommon. The neighbors on the left, a middle-aged, reclusive couple, drove a faded green Ford Taurus. On the right, a trio of college students kept late hours and played loud music on weekends but were otherwise harmless. Rusty economy cars occupied their driveway.

So who did this vehicle belong to?

A large figure shifted in the front seat, a phantom in the darkness.

Sara set down her glass and moved away from the window. She double-checked the locks on the front and back doors, and headed toward the master bedroom. No need to act paranoid. If she mentioned any of this to Bret, she'd not only ruin his romantic mood but subject herself to questions about the car's year, make, and model. As if she had any idea.

Reaching their room, she heard a rumbling snore. Bret was face-up on the bed, mouth open, dead to the world.

She shook him by the shoulder. "Honey?"

He groaned. He was an infrequent snorer, but when he let loose, he did so with unsurpassed nasal orchestration. Sometimes in these moments, Sara gazed at her husband and felt love beyond words.

Other times, she wanted to smack him with a pillow.

She blew out the candles and told herself to forget about the person in the car across the street. Probably one of their neighbors' relatives in town for a visit. She closed herself in the walk-in closet, flicked on a night light, and stretched out on the single bed against the wall. This was her refuge when life got loud.

She peered up at the hangers, where garments read like a timeline of her early married years. The silk robe reminded her of her wedding night, and those *Under Construction* T-shirts hearkened back to both pregnancies. So many good memories.

And a few not-so-pleasant ones.

In a red hoodie from high school, she kept a photo hidden. She fished for the 3 × 5 now, brought its familiar image into view.

Alex Page. Her former fiancé.

The other man.

Despite years of faithfulness to her husband, she clutched the picture to her chest, burdened by dreams lost long ago, and by a nightmare that still lurked along the edges of the present.

Oh, God, I need Your help.

Chapter Three

Bᴿᴱᵀ ᴀᴡᴏᴋᴇ ᴀᴛ 1:24 ᴀ.ᴍ. Tʜᴇ ʙᴇᴅ ᴡᴀs ᴜɴʀᴜꜰꜰʟᴇᴅ ʙᴇsɪᴅᴇ ʜɪᴍ. Hᴇ ᴘʀᴏᴘᴘᴇᴅ. himself on an elbow, rubbed his eyes, and noticed the closet door was shut.

Shoot. He'd done it again, running his wife off with his noise.

"Sara."

Her name floated from his mouth, lingering, dissipating. Sometimes he was just too worn out to be all that she needed, a listening ear for her stories from the clinic, a handyman for another leaky faucet, both judge and jury for the most recent case of Katie's "artwork" on the bedroom walls. Tonight his tired bones had even cost him a few moments alone with his wife.

Only thirty-three, and already he felt like an old man.

He padded across the floor, peeked into the closet. Sara was still in her robe, asleep. In the darkness her short locks and high cheekbones gave her the look of some disheveled model in a black-and-white picture.

He carried her to their bed, where worn fitted sheets strained at the corners. He set her down, smoothed her hair. He covered her with a light blanket, wishing for the thousandth time he could treat her to new bedding and a new wardrobe. She deserved so much more than he could provide. She rarely complained, and yet he had sensed her pulling away these past few months, sensed her—

Hold it. What was that in her hand?

Bret eased the photo from between his wife's fingers, and the sight of a male face caused a throbbing in his temples. "I should've known," he mumbled.

Outside, a warm breeze blew, and tree branches tapped at the window over the dresser. He turned and saw a claw-shaped shadow roving to and fro, as though seeking entry into their home. His eyes shifted from that imaginary intruder back to the one in the photo.

Mr. Alexander Page. Dead and gone.

Bret had attended the man's funeral with Sara, acting as her friend and comforter, and all these years later she seemed to be still pondering the what-ifs.

He thought of waking her to ask what was going on, but her forehead was furrowed, her lips set in a line. She was a hard worker, always had been. She rarely complained about their limited resources, and she loved their children.

For now he'd cut her some slack. But they would definitely talk later.

Sara was dreaming again. She was a butterfly, fragile and weak. A child had grabbed hold of her, damaging one of her forewings by rubbing away the powdery scales that helped keep her membranes warm. Now she was losing altitude as she fluttered toward a daisy-thick patch of lawn in the shade of an old brick mansion.

The greenery absorbed her rough landing. Her tiny feet sought purchase on blades of grass. She tried to flap. So tired and broken, she tried to rise again.

Flap-flap-flutter-flap . . .

She refused to give up. Somewhere in the nearby shrubs her eggs were transforming into caterpillar larvae, and she wanted to live to see the metamorphosis of each one. They were what kept her going.

"Mommy . . ."

And now they were calling for her.

"Mommy, where's the milk?"

Butterfly dreams flitted off as Sara's eyes blinked open. She was only inches from the scrunched face of her little blond live wire. "Katie, what time is it?"

"I dunno. Me and Kevin're watching cartoons, but there's no milk."

"Where's Daddy?"

"Outside," Katie said. "You should see his boss's new truck. It's yellow."

"The Billingsleys are here?"

"Jason says he'll give us a ride sometime if it's OK with you." Katie hopped with both knees onto the bed and wiggled her nose against Sara's.

"Your breath smells like chocolate. What've you been eating?"

"Cocoa Pebbles."

"Dry?" Sara said. "From the box?"

"You said we could eat them on Saturdays. They're yummy."

"Not too much, though. That's a lot of sugar, and you," she said, touching her daughter's nose, "are already sweet enough. Now let me get dressed."

"Are we going shopping?"

"I, uh, we're waiting on my paycheck. How about waffles instead?"

Katie bounced twice, nodded, and darted off down the hall.

Sara sat up on the mattress, wondering how she'd arrived here from her spot in the closet. Her eyes panned to Bret's side of the bed, to the photo propped against his alarm clock. Digital numbers gave it an ominous red glow.

So her husband had found her memento.

She picked up the photo, cradling it in her palm.

Lord, You know I love Bret. But the way Alex died all alone . . . I should've been there with him. Why didn't You give me a warning? Something. Anything.

She chewed at a fingernail as she headed for the bathroom. Maybe she'd wanted Bret to find it. He tried his best, he really did, but years of shaky finances left her longing for stability. Was that so out of line?

She arrived at the front door in time to see Bret's boss behind the wheel of a monstrous, yellow Hummer. Jason Billingsley tapped the horn and waved a hand out the window as he backed from their driveway. The vehicle looked almost alien as it passed single-level, brick homes built in the 1950s.

"That's not like him to come by on the weekend."

"He was showing off his new wheels," Bret said, his back to her.

"While talking about laying guys off? He doesn't get it, does he? Did you talk to him about a raise? I mean, you shouldn't even have to ask."

Bret turned, hands shoved into the pockets of his University of Tennessee sweatshirt, tanned calves poking from calf-length shorts. His gaze ran past her shoulder. "Go back inside, Katie. We'll be there in a minute."

"Mommy's making waffles."

"Why don't you and Kevin set the table for us?"

"The plastic plates," Sara added.

A noisy spring yanked the screen door shut behind their little girl. Sara walked down the steps and faced her husband over a green sprinkler hose that snaked through the lawn.

"You've been thinking about him again," Bret said.

She dragged teeth over her bottom lip. There was no use denying it.

"For how long?"

"Bret, I don't know. It's just that—"

"How long? I need to know."

"What do you want me to say? It's not like I can just forget. You can't expect me to do that."

"Have I ever asked you to? Of course not."

"Then why do you sound mad?"

"Because . . ." Bret paced the grass. "Is it the house, the job? You think high-and-mighty Alexander might've—?"

"Alex," Sara corrected. "He thought 'Alexander' sounded pretentious."

"He said it. Not me. Listen, I know he could've put a nicer roof over your head with that fat bank account of his, but there's more to life than that."

"We were engaged to be married. I won't deny he had a special place in my heart, and I wouldn't expect you to feel any differently if things were reversed. None of that changes my love for you, not one bit."

"The accident was over twelve years ago."

Sara looked away.

"I'm not saying it'll ever go away, but when do I get to have all of you?"

"You do have all of me," she said. "That's ridiculous. We have the kids, and we have each other. You're the man I love."

"The other man."

"The only man. I gave you my heart."

He raised an eyebrow. "Last night I wanted to be with you, and instead I find you holding his picture."

"Wait a minute. If anything, I'm the one who should be complaining."

"How do you figure?"

"Well," she said, stepping closer, "the way I remember it, I came in for some hot lovin' and found Mr. Sleepy-Head sawing logs."

"Yeah, sorry about that. All my good intentions out the window." A worn-thin grin crossed his face. "I'm trying to keep up, Sara, I really am. With you. The bills. Kevin. Did he tell you he got shoved into the lockers again yesterday?"

"By the same boys? Hon, that is not acceptable."

Bret lowered his voice. "He's more embarrassed than bruised, but talking to the principal hasn't changed a thing at that school."

"Threaten to sue. That'll wake them up."

"If we had the money for legal fees, I just might. What I'm trying to do is arrange a meeting with the bullies and their parents."

"Will that help? I mean, who do you think taught them this behavior?"

"Hey," Bret said, "there's a part of me that'd just love to deal with this in some dark alley. I'm trying to take the high road here. We've got enough sue-happy people in this country as it is."

"So sue me," she said, trying to relieve some tension.

He coughed out a laugh.

For the hundredth time, Sara wished they could give Kevin a private education. He was a smart kid. What possessed bullies to pick him out of the crowd? What sick satisfaction could it provide?

"Thanks for stepping in, Bret. Really. Kevin's so tenderhearted, and I worry that—" Her voice caught. "I just don't know how much more he can take."

"We can't do it all for him. We've gotta let him stand up for himself sometimes. Yeah, he'll get knocked down, but he'll get up again. He's tougher than you think. And," Bret added, "I've got his back."

"What if you're not around, though? You can't always—"

"I've got his back, Sara. I'd do anything for my son."

"I know you would." She stepped over the hose and threaded her arms through his. "You're cold," she said. "Let's go inside for some breakfast."

"I was about to change the oil on the car."

"See there? What would I do without you? All that money, and Alex never even learned how to check the oil. Never needed to."

"The dipstick."

"Bret." She planted her hands on her hips.

"That's how you check it," he said. "Just stating the facts."

She groaned and spun toward the door, head full of images a sheriff described to her in short and her imagination filled in more vividly: Alex Page crouching beside his Infiniti along a rural highway, fumbling with a blown tire, working the lug-nut wrench in the setting sun, screaming out as a passing eighteen-wheeler caught and scraped him ninety yards over gravel and asphalt.

"Sweetheart," Bret called after her.

She waved him off and injected warmth into her voice. "Kevin? Katie? It's almost waffle time for all boys and girls with clean hands." Her words triggered a stampede toward the bathroom.

From behind, Bret slipped an arm around her waist and brushed his lips across her ear. "That was outta line. Am I still invited for breakfast?" When she shrugged, he added, "I should've kept my big mouth shut. You forgive me?"

"I forgive you. You and your big mouth."

She looked up, expecting warmth in his eyes, but his gaze had hardened and shifted down the street. Even as traffic moved along Eastland Avenue a block and half away, things here on Groves Park were quiet. Which made it even more conspicuous that a shiny black car was idling a few doors down. The one she'd spotted earlier? By daylight, it looked even more intimidating.

"Was that car there when my boss left?" Bret asked.

"I don't think so." She pressed her cheek to his chest. "But it looks like one I saw last night, while you were conked out. Could simply be a new neighbor."

"Driving a 2010 Dodge Charger? On this block? Don't think so."

"Honey, let's go inside."

"Look." Bret lowered his voice. "You see a man slouched in the front seat, hat hiding his face? He's just sitting there, watching us."

Chapter Four

Magnus Maggart patted the Charger's steering wheel. "Well, well, I have your attention now, don't I?'

Fifty yards away, the Vreelands faced him from their lawn.

Some said East Nashville had character, charisma, and charm. He thought it was all clatter and clutter. The boxy, brick houses along this street wore sagging carports and black wrought-iron porch railings. While trimmed shrubs and mowed lawns gave testimony to mindful homeowners, underground sprinkler systems were nowhere to be found. Low chain-link fences, not sidewalks, separated the yards from the road. And behind the eastern row of homes, two sets of railroad tracks carved out a littered, fifteen-foot gully.

Welcome to Rolling Acres Neighborhood.

Behind the low fence at 724 Groves Park Road, Bret looked irritated, and Sara nervous.

"Such a handsome couple," Magnus said. "Why the long faces?"

He knew the answer, of course. Intimidation was one of his favorite tactics, and blatant observation could rattle most nonmilitary types.

Civilians.

They were oh, so civil. So villainous.

Magnus believed all people had chinks in their armor, often gaping ones, and he took great pride in exploiting that fact. From corporate embezzlement to pastoral indiscretion to political corruption, humans found plenty of soil in which to plant their seeds of vice, and he had used such flaws to bring them down.

Eventually everyone reaped what they sowed.

And I, Magnus thought, tipping his ball cap at the couple across the way, *I am that reaper.*

He had no religious basis for this. He did not believe in God or justice, in heaven or hell. Fate did not exist, and if it did, he was the fate worse than death. His parents had divorced when he was seven, and he grew up with a mother who drilled into him these words: "Believe only in yourself, you hear me? I chose your name carefully. Son, you best live up to its meaning."

Counting himself a student of the natural sciences, Magnus knew humanity was the cosmic lottery winner, the species that evolved under the right conditions on the right planet at the proper distance from the sun.

There was no greater purpose, no grand design.

There was Magnus.

And Magnus, living up to his name, saw that he was great.

His ex-wife had disagreed, but then she was never as smart and strong as his mother. When she begged out after nineteen months, he obliged her.

Across the street, Sara Vreeland tugged at her husband's arm. Bret was following the advice of that classic Blue Oyster Cult song. He did not fear the reaper, and if he did, he showed no signs of it. His shoulders were wide beneath his UT sweatshirt, his muscles toned from his work at the coach company, where he was liked and respected by his coworkers. By all accounts, he was a swell guy. Paid his bills. Sponsored a family in Haiti. Spent Sundays with his family and his God.

It was amazing to Magnus that these types still swam about in the human stinking gene pool. They weakened the entire species.

Bret wasn't acting weak, though. Not at the moment. As Bret strode forward and called over his shoulder to his wife, Magnus touched his foot to the gas pedal, ready to give the Hemi V8 engine a nudge. He could come back later, since he'd been given orders not to engage. Not yet. This car was a purchase out of his $100,000 cash expense account, and he was the knight on his trusty black Charger, riding toward the fortress walls to identify weaknesses.

"And you do have them, Mr. Vreeland. Everyone does."

With Bret still coming forward, Magnus pulled a black box from his coat pocket and powered down the window.

Chapter Five

"Bret, please," Sara said. "The kids're waiting for their breakfast."

"Is that a smirk? I think he's smirking at us."

"Could be a bill collector. Some credit agency's been leaving messages."

"They can't legally stake out a house, can they?" Bret hopped their waist-high, chain-link fence. "Be back in a sec. I'm gonna see what this guy wants."

Sara pressed two fingers against her temple. She realized that backing down from a situation went against her husband's DNA. She'd known him since high school, when mental and physical toughness made him a linebacker on the football team, and some days he still seemed eager for something to hit.

"Bacon and waffles," she chirped, trying to lure him back.

"Sounds good." He never broke stride. "And put on the coffee."

Still in her robe, Sara eased up the front steps while tracking his moves. She would memorize the Charger's license tag if she could see the silly thing. She and Bret had grown up in Washington State where front and back tags were mandatory, but here in Tennessee only back plates were required.

Facing her through the car's windshield, the driver wore an arrogant expression beneath his mustache and baseball cap. His eyes were concealed, but Bret was right. That was a full-on, you-can't-touch-me smirk.

Well, who did this guy think he was?

"Mommy," Katie said through the screen door, "Kevin's putting out the fancy dishes. He's gonna break them."

"I am not. And you're not the boss of me."

"But Mommy told us the plastic ones."

"Katie, it's all right," Sara said. "Kev's trying to make things nice, that's all."

Down the street, Bret was ten yards from the Charger when its engine gave a throaty roar. Sara felt the vibration in her chest. She pressed back in the doorway, blocking the line of sight to her children, and Bret eased toward the embankment, torso still aimed at the car but ready to dodge aside.

"You got something to say?" he demanded. "Say it."

A longer roar.

"OK, then go away. In this neighborhood, we watch out for each other."

Tires squealed, smoke billowed beneath flared black fenders, and a fist rose from the driver's window. Sara's eyes fixed upon that hand in the suede glove, watched its fingers uncurl one by one.

A small object dropped onto the road.

Before Sara could identify it, the muscular vehicle lurched backwards through a haze of scorched rubber, its transmission screaming as it left the same way it came. Bret sprinted after it, for a moment close enough to reach out and slap the glistening hood, but the Charger whipped tail-first around the corner and accelerated from view behind a line of houses and shrubs.

Bret stopped and waited.

Around them, the area fell silent once more. Magnolia leaves quivered in the breeze, green and waxy. A calico cat arched beneath a gap in a fence.

"Mom?" Kevin's face appeared behind the screen. "How many scoops do I put in for the coffee?"

"Let me do that part, hon."

"Why don't you ever trust me? I already got the water filled up."

Thoughts spinning, Sara didn't have energy to fight. "Seven scoops," she said. "Dad prefers it a little stronger than it says on the bag."

Down at the corner, Bret turned as though reawakened by the mention of caffeine. He shrugged and gave her a smile. She smiled back. He marched along the pavement, stooped to pick up the object deposited by their intruder. Still coming toward her, he turned the thing once, twice, and shook it. It was a box, black and fuzzy.

"Be careful," she called to him.

Even as the words left her mouth, she realized how fearful they sounded. She could see from the porch that the box was nothing overtly threatening.

Unless it contained a noseful of powdery anthrax.

Or solar-powered, rotating razorblades.

Or brown recluse spiders.

Sara shivered, almost chuckled, at the thought of such highly improbable contents. She tried, really tried, not to be a drama queen. Her childhood in the Pacific Northwest had introduced her to random bugs and occasional rattlers. Here, though, near the Cumberland River, the creepy-crawlies were everywhere, particularly after the May flood swamped nearby homes. It was not uncommon to see large spiders, horned beetles, centipedes, and other creatures she had no interest in identifying. If Adam and Eve's sin in the Garden had introduced such evils, she believed it her right, if not her duty, to whip out a can of Black Flag and dispatch the invaders to the hell they surely deserved.

And if that's out of line, Lord, forgive me.

The clang of chain-link broke through her thoughts. Bret stepped into the yard, hooked the gate shut with his foot. Back on their property, he opened the box.

"What is it?" Sara said.

"I'm . . . it looks like. . . ." Forehead furrowing, he lifted his eyes. "You've gotta be kidding me. This should be sitting in my parents' attic."

"In Tacoma?"

"Get them on the phone."

"What?"

"I need to talk to my mom and dad. Right now, sweetheart. Please." Bret poked at the object, his eyes darkening. "Your cell's got free long-distance, and I gotta be sure that freak hasn't done anything to hurt them."

She pulled tight her robe. "They live over two thousand miles away."

"And that's where this should be."

Sara wanted to see what was in the box for herself, but the intensity in her husband's voice propelled her into action. "I'll get my phone."

Chapter Six

MAGNUS CRUISED WEST ON EASTLAND DRIVE, WINDOWS OPEN TO CLEAR THE cockpit of acrid smoke. He'd put on a juvenile display with all that Vin Diesel-like spinning of tires and screeching of rubber, yet it satisfied some visceral desire in him.

Oh, yes, let testosterone reign.

And where would this species be without it?

Cowering in a cave, that's where. Huddled behind a camp-fire, peeing their Cro-Magnon trousers while saber-toothed tigers prowled the woods outside. Sure, females were good for squeezing out babies and keeping the gene pool populated, but estrogen and pheromones were weepy chemicals in a stew dominated by male ingredients.

Tools? Thank the men.

Weapons? Thank the men.

Magnus threw his cap onto the floor and stripped away his adhe-sive mustache. So far there'd been no need for the Kimber pistol tucked into his waistband.

He replayed the last ten minutes, and saw Sara braced in the doorway of her home while her man confronted the threat head-on. For that, at least, the courageous hubby deserved the warning, the solitary item taken from his boyhood home and delivered to his current residence.

Did you think you would actually catch me, Bret?

Feeling smug, Magnus nearly ran a red light at the Gallatin Road intersection. If pulled over, he would take the ticket and say, "Thank you, sir." For a man of his prowess, though, such a lapse was inexcusable.

He was being paid handsomely to stay focused and dismantle Mr. Vreeland. Once his task was complete, Sara would shed her husband's last name the way a snake shed skin.

Chapter Seven

9:30 A.M. SUNDAY MORNING. THE TEMPERATURE HOVERED IN THE MID-80S AS Bret slid his guitar case into the family's sputtering Subaru hatchback. The interior was an oven, and he cranked open the windows. He tapped the horn lightly so as not to wake the neighbors. College kids liked to sleep in on Sundays, and he figured he should practice the Golden Rule with churchgoers and non-churchgoers alike.

"Katie, Kev, let's go."

"Mommy's still doing her hair," Katie said from the front door.

"C'mon out here then, so she won't be distracted."

Waiting, Bret studied the object found yesterday on the roadside. It was a padded black jewelry box, same as thousands of others. Except this one was last stored away in distant Tacoma, containing his high school class ring.

Pewter. With a red garnet. A ring loaded with shame.

Nearly a year had passed since Bret and his father last spoke, but Bret downplayed their differences during yesterday's ten-minute call and learned that his parents hadn't seen anything suspicious or noted any missing items. He was not about to make them crawl into their attic on S. Bell Street to double-check.

So what was his ring doing here?

And who was that man who delivered it?

Clomping feet signaled Katie's arrival. She hopped into the back of the car and giggled as she latched the seat belt over her dress. "I beeeat you," she said. "Not even close."

"I wasn't racing." Kevin folded himself into the seat behind Bret. "Dad, can you tell her to leave me alone? I'm not in the mood."

Bret tucked away the jewelry box, recalling the surliness attached to his own first hints of puberty. "You know, buddy, I never had a sister and I always wanted one. Katie's just trying to have fun."

"Yeah," she said.

"Hey." Bret caught her eye in the rearview mirror. "Enough."

"It's hot in here," Kevin said. "Turn on the air-conditioning."

"You'll get better results if you ask nicely instead of barking orders."

"Please, Dad. My pits are already sweating."

"Did you put on that deodorant I bought you?"

"It doesn't help."

"Did you put it on?"

"I was in a hurry," Kevin said. He pulled out the iPod he'd received last Christmas from Sara's mom and stepdad, and unraveled the ear buds.

Bret watched Sara lock the front door and float down the steps in fitted jeans and a white blouse. Her hair shimmered in the sunlight. He told her how nice she looked, and she thanked him with a squeeze of his arm.

"Any chance we can we turn on the air?" she said.

"Gotta say please," Kevin muttered from the back.

Pulling from the driveway, Bret shook his head. "Sorry, guys, but the AC'll suck up our last drops of gas. Least we don't have far to go." He turned left onto Eastland and crossed over Riverside. "Today we're relying on the Patented Vreeland Air-Flow System. Works best once we get this baby moving."

Groans became appreciative sighs as they coasted down a long hill and a breeze swirled through the windows.

"See?" he said. "Not so bad."

Tiny beads of perspiration appeared on Sara's forehead, and she massaged her temples. Bret knew she was frustrated. She didn't like arriving at a destination looking like a wreck, or as Zoe Billingsley called it, "a hot mess." Sara had foregone many luxuries that the Zoes of the world took for granted.

"Least next weekend we'll be traveling in style," he told his sullen crew.

Sara shot him a look. "Don't kid with us, please. Not right now."

"This is serious. I got an e-mail from the Billingsleys asking if we could drop them off at the airport next Friday. While they're in Cozumel, they want us to check on their house and feed their Yorkie and—"

"Really? That dorky Yorkie could go a week without eating."

"And . . ." Bret held up a hand. "They said we can drive the Hummer."

"The yellow truck?"

"Not exactly a truck, Katie. More like an SUV."

"Didn't they just buy that thing?" Sara said. "I don't want the liability."

"C'mon, sweetie, it's fully covered. And we can blast the AC all we want." He glanced over his shoulder to see the kids' responses, but Kevin was lost in his music and Katie seemed confused by the sets of initials. He said, "What that means is we won't have to sweat like little piggies."

Katie's eyes widened with a smile.

Bret rested his hand on Sara's. "I'll have my paycheck, and for a few days anyway we'll get to travel in style. No skimping on gas. And how about dinner together, just you and me? If I could afford it, I'd take you out every weekend."

"I know you would, honey." Sara laced her fingers through his.

"I'd treat you like a princess."

"You do."

He fixed his eyes on the road. He wanted nothing more than to spoil his bride, wine and dine his one and only, but each time he thought they would get ahead, another bill cut their legs out from under them. Kevin's clinic costs. Property taxes. A timing belt for the car. It was a parade that ran all year long.

In an alternate reality, with Alex, Sara would've been pampered beyond belief. Instead, tragedy had stolen away that chance, leaving

Bret to pick up the pieces, to comfort her as a friend. Somewhere in that process, romance had blossomed between them.

But am I her one and only?

The question was unfair, and he doubted even she could answer it. He knew that she loved him, and he could last a lifetime on that alone.

"Thanks for understanding, Sara." He braked, put on his blinker. "Sometimes, it just feels like things'll never change."

"But feelings shouldn't control us. Isn't that what Pastor's been teaching?"

"Hey," he joked, "I don't feel like hearing that right now."

"You don't have much choice." She laughed, pointing as they entered the church lot. She turned and ran a brush through Katie's hair.

"I'm sweaty, Mommy."

"It'll be cool inside. And guess who's playing on the worship team today?" Sara dabbed moisture from her own neck, gestured for Kevin to power off his iPod, and glanced at Bret. "Are you nervous?"

"It's not often Pastor Teman has me up on stage."

"You went over the chords and lyrics, right?"

He nodded, edged the car into a space.

"You'll do great then. Just sing from the heart."

"Sure, that works in the shower," he said, "but not always in front of other people. Just look at some of the *American Idol* tryouts, huh?"

"Are we talking worship here? Or idols?"

He winced. "OK. I think I'll shut up now."

"Daddy," Katie piped in, "it's not nice to say shut up."

He winced again. Even "off-stage," he remained on-stage as a father, one of those parenting facts never mentioned in the handbooks. He reached back and tousled her blond curls. "That's right. You're one smart girl."

Katie wrinkled her nose, the same cute way she had since the crib. The Vreelands had relocated from the Northwest while their son was still a toddler, making their daughter the only one native to Music City.

As Bret turned to the front again, the padded box flopped from his pocket, bounced off the e-brake, and rolled onto the passenger floorboard.

Sara reached for it and smoothed its velvety surface. "Honey, you know, it seems odd to me that I knew you in twelfth grade and never saw you wear your class ring. Not once. In fact, I wasn't even aware you had this ring until yesterday. Why'd you buy it if you never intended to show it off?"

"Who says I bought it?"

"You said it was yours, didn't you?"

"Yeah, but. . . ." He shook his head. "Listen, now's not the time."

She handed it back, her jaw muscles clenching.

Oh boy, Bret. Smooth going.

"You're right," she said. "Now's not the time. But after church, after the Rileys tell us again how to save money on gas and how to live on a family budget, as if our struggles are all due to some laziness on our parts, or after Jack Joiner reminds us how the storehouses of heaven shower down upon those who tithe without fail, as if we're some tight-fisted rich snobs addicted to the smell of money, after we get home out of this heat, I want you to talk to me. No secrets."

"Sweetheart, it's nothing like that."

"Then help me understand."

"Are y'all fighting?" Katie asked.

"Quiet," Kevin said. "It's none of your business. And don't say 'y'all.' It makes you sound country."

"I am country. I was born here."

"Guys, guys." Bret held up both hands. "Whoa, do you see what's going on? We have an enemy of our souls, and this morning he'd just love to keep us from praising God and being at peace with each other."

Kevin said, "If we resist him, he's gotta flee."

"That's right, Kev. And how do we do that?"

"Jesus," Katie shouted.

Bret met his wife's eyes and smiled. "OK, always a safe guess," he said. "Yes, Jesus came to destroy the works of the enemy, but when we're all mad at each other we give the devil a foothold. Now whaddya say we start fresh and walk through those doors arm-in-arm? We're the Vreelands, right? 'As for me and my house . . .'"

They joined him as one: "'We will serve the Lord.'"

A family motto borrowed from the Book of Joshua.

"Good." Bret fetched his guitar from the hatchback. "Now let's get moving. In this humidity, my strings, they're gonna be like wet noodles."

Sara was at his side, hooking her arm through his.

He gave her a wink.

"You're not off the hook," she whispered. "We'll talk when we get home."

Chapter Eight

MAGNUS TUCKED HIS CAR OUT OF VIEW BEHIND RIVERSIDE VILLAGE. THIS grouping of shops had an eccentric, earthy vibe, and Sip Café was his new favorite spot. It served good coffee and Mike's Ice Cream, and on this sweltering Tuesday afternoon a scoop of dairy goodness would be the perfect thing.

"Hola," the girl at the counter greeted him, although she wasn't Hispanic. She had hazel eyes above the glittering stud in her nose. "How ya doin'?"

"Great," he said. "And you?"

"Fine, thanks. Your usual?"

He glanced around. He was the only customer, save a frizzy-bearded forty-something on his laptop in the corner. Flyers on the wall announced a coming show by local band Eastern Block.

"Am I that predictable?"

"Most people are."

He winked. "You're telling me."

Her lips twitched into something resembling a smile. Good. She was softening. Her usual bored face was most likely a disguise for loneliness, perhaps even a broken heart. Not that he believed in broken hearts. If humans could be likened to chemical combustion chambers, their emotions were nothing more than dietary and environmental reactions.

Feeling blue?

Blame the barometric pressure.

Feeling smiley?

Blame that square of dark chocolate.

Anticipating his own chemical upswing, Magnus watched the girl scoop out Rocky Road and wiggle it onto a sugar cone.

"Thank you," he said. His eyes shifted to hers as he nibbled at the treat with parted lips. He stopped, dropped his gaze, and looked away. He'd found that females were easier marks when a man of his power and presence turned suddenly shy.

"That's my favorite too," she said. "They make it not far from here."

"Made with love. I can taste it. So, how much do I owe you?"

Hazel Eyes gave him a wink of her own. "It's on me."

"For free? No, I don't want to get you in trouble."

"Whatever. The owners, they're never around, and they expect me to run the register, serve customers, clean, sweep, mop, tear down. I do one thing wrong, though, and you better believe they're all over my butt."

"I hope you get paid well."

She raised an eyebrow. "Just enough to cover my college dorm."

"Here." Magnus tugged a dollar bill from his pocket and tucked it into the jar on the counter. "I'd put in a twenty if I had it."

Actually, overtipping her would make her feel indebted to him, and he didn't want that. Best that she feel equal to him, if not superior.

She curtsied and spouted her Spanish. "Gracias, senor."

He smiled. Yes, blame it on some Darwinian paradox, but it seemed that vulnerability enhanced the attraction between male and female. When Bible thumpers pointed out that "the two shall become one flesh," they missed something. In actuality, the balance between strong and weak, predator and prey, master and mistress always swung too far. The sharks were either decimating the oceans or being killed off in droves. Men were either dominating their wives or caving to their whims. To achieve perfect balance, a third agent was required.

Enter Magnus Maggart.

I am that great balancing agent.

He nibbled again at the ice cream, and the sugar compounds that crashed through his neural transmitters told his brain he was a happy man. Or maybe it was this girl's closeness. She smelled good. Looked good too.

"Mm-mmm, that's tasty." He leaned his hip against the counter. "Can I ask you something? You know those people who were in here a few days ago, a dad, mom, skinny little boy, and his younger sister?" "Skinny" was Magnus's label for weaklings who ought to be strained from humanity's stew.

Hazel Eyes shrugged. "Hard to remember everyone."

"The boy was wearing soccer cleats and a jersey, and the girl was—"

"The Vreelands. Yeah. They make it in every Friday for their family date."

"Family date? No kidding. Why, as a child I dreamed of domestic bliss like that, but my mother, she was bent on toughening me for the purposes she saw in me." A sharp laugh. "And she was effective, oh yes, even if not always kind."

"What? Like, she was abusive?"

The moment the girl asked, Magnus knew she was his—*I am that balancing agent.* Instead of answering, he clunked his knuckle against the tip jar and glanced toward the corner. Whatever Hazel Eyes imagined, it would barely scratch the surface.

"Sorry to hear that," she said.

He leaned closer. "Can I ask two more questions? Are you doing anything after work?"

She tilted her head, and strands of thick hair swept across her cheek. "That sounds like you're asking me out."

"Only if you're interested."

"I'm flattered, seriously. But let me think it over. It's not like we really know each other, do we?"

"Thus my request."

"Thus my hesitation."

Her banter further convinced him she would answer in the affirmative—*dominated by male ingredients.* Magnus said, "Either way, my second question remains the same. Next Friday, when the Freelanders come in for their—"

"Vreelands."

"Right. Can you give them something for me? Anonymously, of course."

"Sure." She brushed back her hair. "I guess so."

"Is that your answer to my second question or the first?"

"Hmm, let's say it's to both. And you can call me Natalie."

Chapter Nine

BRET HAD TALKED. SARA LISTENED.

Four nights later, she stood in the sleep lab at Cumberland Sleep Clinic. Thursday. 10:01 P.M. As she flipped back her patient's insurance form on the clipboard and ran her eyes down his medical and social histories, her thoughts were on her husband's explanation of the ring. That silly class ring.

"Ma'am?" her patient said. "D'ya think they got me misdiagnosed?"

"Uh." Sara looked up, cleared her throat. "What do you think, Theodore?"

Theodore Hart was in his mid-twenties, husky yet slouch-shouldered, with a brooding intelligence beneath his bashful smile and buzz-cut. "I think they were full of it, but Momma was convinced from the time I was in seventh grade. Each time I ended up in the principal's office, she told him she was sorry, acted all nicey-nice, and then the moment we got in the car, she slapped my head, told me to take my pills from now on and was I trying to give her a heart attack."

Sara read from his application. "I see you were diagnosed ADHD."

"All Day Hell and Damnation."

"Excuse me?"

"Pardon my language, ma'am, but that's what she called it. Day they told her, she laughed this weird laugh and said, yep, I was her little hellion."

Sara peered over the clipboard. Something about her patient seemed familiar. Wearing baggy shorts and a T-shirt for his polysomnogram, he looked like an overgrown child, and she had an urge to give him a hug.

"Momma liked to kid," he said. "She didn't mean nothing by it."

Sara pulled tight her white lab coat, wondering how some people survived their upbringings. She imagined Kevin's life if he were prescribed drugs that hid his actual sleep disorder. She thought of Bret's words four days ago, as he told her about the ring and the associated humiliation of his youth.

She said, "And you've always had trouble sleeping at night?"

Theodore nodded.

Why am I not surprised? Dear Jesus, help me show him some grace.

"Well, you've come to the right place. Some people's upper airway muscles collapse while they sleep, the way a shower curtain sucks in when you open the door. They snore, trying to get air, and this wakes up the brain multiple times each hour. No wonder they can't get quality rest. Did you know obstructed sleep apnea sufferers are nine times more likely to get into an accident?"

"I'm a good driver. Only one ticket so far."

"And we want to keep it that way, all right? By conducting a sleep test, we'll get a clearer picture of whether you were misdiagnosed."

She instructed him to remove his shirt and lie on the bed. She raised and locked the rails, noticed he bore thin scars along his thighs and calves. Signs of abuse? She scrubbed and lathered his chest, shaved the curly patches of hair, and attached sensors from head to foot. What fun she had for $1,950 a month, before taxes. A pulse monitor went on his fingertip, a respiration monitor on his nose. The jumbled wires ran to a large machine beside the bed.

"We call that the Spaghetti Monster," she said.

"Makes me nervous."

"Me too. I promise it won't bite, though. It seems awkward, but do your best to relax and get some sleep. This is one test you can't flunk. I'll go out, lower the lights, and we'll calibrate the system." She moved into the observation booth and communicated by intercom. "Look up. Yes, now look left. All right, blink ten times for me. Good."

Twenty minutes later, Theodore was snoring.

Listening to him, Sara had one of those rare moments when she'd give anything to cuddle beside Bret as he sawed logs through the night. She recalled his words to her after Sunday service, after she agreed to listen and not interrupt.

"I won't deny this was my ring," Bret had told her. They sat side by side on the couch. He twisted the heavy object and let sunlight play off the garnet. "But I never paid for it, never even placed the order. You didn't see me wear it in high school because I knew, even if none of my friends did, that it was stolen."

"Stolen?" Sara thought of her husband on the church platform only two hours ago, singing, strumming his guitar. What was he thinking as he worshiped God? What past guilts was he harboring?

He nodded. "Maybe I wanted it too much."

In the backyard, Kevin and Katie played badminton with plastic rackets. Sara watched them through the window and wondered how any parents could fail to provide for their little ones. Sure, the economy pulled the rug out from under some people, leaving them jobless, even homeless. A friend of theirs had job-hunted tirelessly without even a nibble.

But if at all possible, when times got hard you just worked harder.

Her own husband was an example of that.

"That's not like you, Bret. I don't understand."

"Just listen." He hung his head, made a fist around the ring, and pressed on. "I begged my parents to help me pay for it, but they were strapped for cash. I worked the next few weekends, odd jobs, anything I could find. I was still ninety-five bucks short, and Dad told me that was too bad. He wasn't running a charity here. 'A charity?' I yelled back. 'You don't do a thing for us. You gamble away your paychecks and leave Mom with nothing, that's what you do.' He'd been drinking that night, which was no surprise back in those days. He backhanded his bottle across the room, and it shattered against my knee, spraying me with beer."

Sara felt short of breath. "Honey, that's horrible."

"That was a first. He didn't usually get physical with me, big as I was. I almost stormed out the door, but I couldn't leave Mom with him, not like that."

"It's hard to imagine," Sara said. "I've never seen your dad that way."

"Believe me, he could be a real jerk."

"Was he an alcoholic? How come I haven't heard about this?"

"Dad's mellowed, hasn't had a drink in years. Gotta give him credit for that. He and Mom have worked through a lot of their issues, but he knows, we all know, that one drink could send him back into that hole. When you and I got together, I didn't wanna make him out like he was some kinda monster. Elder at the church. Part of Kiwanas. An all-around good guy, that's what most people thought. Mom always covered for him, said it was family business and it should stay that way. She told me I'd scare you off if I talked about his 'episodes.'"

"But you're not your dad."

"Like father, like son. That was my biggest fear."

"Did he ever hit her?"

"Sara, I don't think we—"

"Did he?"

Bret swallowed. "I was in grade school, maybe seven or eight, the first time I heard the thuds. Mom came tumbling down the stairs. I watched it all from the dining table, and swore I'd never again sit still while someone was in trouble."

"It's not as if you could do anything. You were just a kid."

He swallowed. Nodded.

"And your poor mom," Sara said. "I never knew."

"Sweetheart." He swiveled on the couch and took Sara's hand in his. "I will never hit you. Never. And if I ever did, I'd expect you to walk out that door with the kids. No. I would leave. Why punish you for something you didn't do?"

"Please, I'd rather not think about that."

"Me neither. I love you, Sara."

"I love you too."

"And that's why we're gonna make this last another eleven years."

"Why stop there?" Her eyes teared up. "Let's grow old and gray together."

"Gray and wrinkly."

"And bald," she added. She leaned into him, gripped his arm. "Thank you for telling me all of that. At least now I understand why you resorted to stealing."

"But I didn't," he said. "That's the thing. Dad, he would feel guilty for the way he treated Mom and me, and he'd buy us things as a way of saying sorry. Of course, it never lasted past the next drinking binge. He was up to his neck in debt, had loan sharks making threats. And then, snap, he made it all go away."

"How? What're you telling me?"

"He robbed a bank."

"You're serious?"

"Mom never knew, and he never got caught. After hitting me with the bottle that night, he barreled off in his old Chevy. Saw it on the news the next day, a bank struck within the hour down on the south end of Tacoma. They had a shot from a security camera, shadowy, hard to see, but I knew. The haircut. The angle of his nose. I just knew. Later, Dad showed up with this look in his eye. He said he got stuff worked out, did a side job for his pal Gabe, who lived in Kent to the north. 'What kinda job?' I asked. He got mad. 'What's it to you, Bretski?' But I wouldn't back off, so he said that he'd welded a winch and a tow hitch onto Gabe's truck."

"Sounds reasonable."

"Here's the thing, though. A coupla days later Gabe calls for Dad. I ask him how that hitch is holding up. He says, his very words, 'I can't solder worth a lamb's lick. I shoulda had your dad do it.' By the end of the next week, this was waiting for me." Bret lifted the class ring. "Yep, just sitting there in the school office, bought and paid for. But stolen, all the same."

"Did your dad ever mention it?"

"Once and that was it. He said he hoped I was happy now and I better cherish it the rest of my life. I told him I knew how he'd paid for it but wouldn't say a word, the Vreeland code of silence. He jabbed at my forehead twice with his finger and left me standing there. I never did wear the ring. Didn't even try it on."

"Has he ever apologized? For the drinking? The abuse?"

"He always said actions speak louder than words. Far as I know, he's stayed sober, so I'm sure he thinks there's nothing left to say."

Sara sighed. "That's not right, Bret. You deserved better than that. I love your dad, and your mom's an absolute doll, but I don't know if I can act the same around them now that I know about this."

"What I'm wondering is who snuck into their attic. Does that person know about the bank? Are we talking FBI? Is someone twisting Dad's arm for an old debt? Either way, bringing my ring here, it just doesn't make sense."

Chapter Ten

AT 4:22 A.M. THE CELL PHONE'S VIBRATION STARTLED SARA. ONLY FAMILY, close friends, and high-risk patients had her number. Who would call at this hour?

As Theodore rubbed sleep from his eyes and sat up on the bed in the sleep lab, Sara fished her cell from the pocket of her white coat and thought of that black car crouched in the darkness. She wondered if the kids were all right.

The caller ID read: *Ivan Storinka.*

She pictured Mr. Storinka, an elderly patient, and kept her voice low in the observation booth as she answered. "Sara speaking. May I help you?"

"Of course, my dear. That is why I called."

"It's awfully late, Mr. Storinka."

"It's early." His voice was raspy. "And I cannot breathe."

Sara liked the man. He was a dignified, silver-haired Ukrainian who bore his considerable girth on a large frame. He was in his early seventies, no immediate family. A lifetime of indulgence had taken its toll, and high blood pressure didn't help. Anticipating trouble, she'd told him to ring in an emergency.

"Should I call an ambulance for you?"

"Do not be silly," he said. "I can dial the phone. I have a crack in the seal of my CPAP mask. My throat gets very dry. A new seal and filter will give me better sleep, this I hope." He wheezed, coughed. "You finish your work soon, yes? I ask you to bring the items to my home, so I can sleep again like a baby."

"As a rule, we don't make house visits."

"Bah. You and me, we know each other for years. Seven, I think." Another fit of coughing. "I want only to breathe, my dear. Please."

"All right." She typed his info into the booth's computer. "We'll bill your insurance directly. Yes, here they are, the correct seal and replacement filters. Are you still at the Belle Meade address?"

"Buzz at the gate. My housekeeper will let you in."

"Give me forty-five minutes to an hour, and I'll—"

The phone went dead.

"So, ma'am, how'd I do?" Theodore pulled on his T-shirt over a face puffy and flushed from sleep. "D'ya think Momma was right about my ADHD?"

Sara met him at the bedside, fixed him in her gaze. "No, I don't. Our tests indicate that you've been exhibiting hyperactivity out of sheer exhaustion. Many sleepless nights, I'm guessing. You show all the symptoms of sleep apnea, and with a little patience we should be able to pinpoint the correct treatment for you."

"You mean . . . ?"

"I mean, Theodore, that hell and damnation are no more a part of you than they are of me. We all have our issues, but you've been created in God's image, and don't you ever believe otherwise."

"I . . ." He covered his eyes, his shoulders beginning to shake.

She touched his arm. "It's all right."

"I'm sorry."

"No need to be, none at all. Why don't I give you a few minutes so you can finish getting dressed?" She stepped into the clinic hallway and closed the door.

"Dad, I need the money by next week." Kevin slid into a seat at the kitchen table, dropped a packet beside his plate of buttered pancakes. He drizzled syrup over the short stack, took a bite, and mumbled through his mouthful. "The deadline's Tuesday, and I really wanna send

Grandma and Grandpa soccer portraits. I can even do different poses, down on my knee, dribbling the ball. Cool, huh?"

"Sounds like it." Bret turned off the griddle and picked up the pamphlet. "You're kidding me. Forty-nine dollars?"

"For the best deal, uh-huh. That's the one I circled."

"That's a lot of money, buddy. More than we've got in our budget."

"How much do we got?"

"How much do we 'have,'" Bret corrected. "Sometimes my English gets sloppy, hanging with the guys at work. I should've said, 'More than we have.'"

Kevin yawned. At a quarter after five in the morning, he was still in PJs and his hair was a mess.

"A budget," Bret said, grabbing pencil and paper, "is just a way of telling your money what its chores are. You make it work for you, or it'll go wandering off and get into trouble. See this line? Up here, you write down the money you make. Down below, you minus the things you need to pay for, big stuff, little stuff, and you—"

"Dad, I'm not really into math."

"Are you into having money to spend?"

Kevin seemed to know where this was headed but nodded anyway.

"Well, that's why we're talking about this. Thing is, you have to plan ahead or it won't work. See this date stamped on here? If you'd showed me this pamphlet when you first got it last month, I could've added it to our budget. But now? I wanna help you, Kev, but it's too late."

"What? That's not fair."

"Would it be fair to stop buying groceries for the rest of the week? Or what if we all stopped taking showers to save money on water?"

Kevin's forehead creased.

"Listen, we'll get the team photo. That's only twelve dollars, so we—"

"I don't want the stupid team photo. I want portraits, like everyone else."

Kevin's attitude set Bret on edge, and he tried to remember his own stress surrounding grade-school pictures. These days, there was more pressure than ever to get sports photos, club photos, and monogrammed yearbooks. Coca-Cola and Lay's weren't the only companies tapping school kids for big bucks.

Forty-nine dollars, though? He wished this weren't even an issue. It was play money to some. The Billingsleys, they spent that much on a chew toy for their dog. "You can't go overboard when it comes to your puppy's teeth," Zoe insisted. Speaking of which, this afternoon he would be taking them to the airport.

Today was also his payday.

"Kevin, don't forget God cares about even the little things in our lives. You want portrait shots? OK, maybe He has a way to help."

Kevin shoved another forkful into his mouth.

"My hours were cut short last week," Bret said, "but let me see how much I get on this check. If it's more than our budget, we'll see what we can do. If I were you, though, I'd pray. Ask God if there's a way for you to get those pictures. Maybe you'll find a mowing job. Maybe something else. He's a good Father, so it never hurts to ask."

"What if He doesn't?"

"Then you thank Him for the things He has done, and you move on."

Sara's patients had gone home. She clocked out for the night, stretched, and stepped into the dawn. She crossed the mostly empty lot to her car. Still minutes before sunrise, tall sodium lights created hazy cones in the gloom.

Was she being watched?

She hurried along and wiggled the key into the driver-side door lock. She touched the pepper spray in her purse.

She felt foolish as she cast a glance over the top of the vehicle, realizing she was the only person in a half-block radius. She shouldn't let the incidents of the past few days rob her enjoyment of this morning. In fact, she loved this part of her day. After hours of recorded snores, beeps of machinery, and hissing tubes and filtration systems, she relished these moments of tranquility.

Saplings lined the sidewalks. In the distance, the Nashville skyline reflected the first slivers of sun. It was so beautiful.

She quietly thanked the Lord for her life here, for her family.

As she climbed into the car, she left the door open and breathed in the morning air. This early it still tasted fresh, before the city's lungs got to work pumping out car exhaust and factory fumes. Soon, traffic arteries would start flowing and clotting along the three major interstates that crisscrossed the downtown area, and school buses and panel vans would slow things down on the surface streets.

She closed the door, praying the engine would start without any troubles.

All right, time to take Mr. Storinka his things.

Chapter Eleven

Magnus watched Sara exit the Cumberland Sleep Clinic. He once again wore the ball cap and fake mustache, but did not fear being spotted, not this morning. He was parked on the slope of an alley a block away, in an Avis economy car, simple and plain, paid for through the rest of the week. It was in sharp contrast to the black beast garaged back at his apartment in Nashville's Germantown.

Sara folded her lab coat and set it in the back of the Subaru, along with a blue and white plastic bag. She tossed her hair, her high cheekbones catching the blush of a sun still nestled behind hills and plateaus to the east.

She was a dainty little thing, a delectable little wifey. No wonder his employer had his sights set on her.

Enough with such thoughts.

I, Magnus, am better than this.

He tightened his grip on the steering wheel and sat up in the seat. He could not let some primal attraction distract him from his assignment. His sensory responses to this woman were unnecessary, even embarrassing. He'd felt this same inner weakness while talking to Natalie at Sip Café.

Oh, yes, I am better than either of these women.

He waited until Sara was two blocks away before pulling out to follow. She merged onto Ellington Parkway, but instead of taking her short jaunt home, she branched off toward the interstate. Circling downtown Nashville, with its distinctive Pinnacle building and the AT&T skyscraper he'd heard locals call the Batman Building, he tailed her from I-24 to I-65 to I-40 West.

Curious. A definite break from her routine.

He settled three cars back, choosing to investigate rather than intimidate. Reconnaissance was vital, and the more details he collected, the better he was equipped to overcome future obstacles.

Some mornings he watched young Kevin trudge through the doors at Bailey Middle School, and Katie bounce into Rosebank Elementary. Some afternoons he stood on the sidelines as Kevin's soccer team practiced, and as Katie left her after-school program, swinging her oh-so-predictable Care Bear pack on her way to the Subaru at the curb. He knew Bret's break patterns at work, a sack lunch, with very few splurges from the vending machine. And he knew Sara's clinic schedule.

All of this fit within the tasks on his list.

Investigate: Collect data, observe schedules, and identify weaknesses.

Intimidate: Apply pressure at work, home, and school.

Infiltrate: Access computer logs, snail mail, court and financial records.

Whereas most people in his line of work completed these tasks in strict linear fashion, he mixed and matched them. Only a person of his intelligence recognized such serpentine possibilities, and he pitied those who did not.

In the end, of course, the first three tasks led Magnus to his favorite.

Inflict: Cause emotional, psychological, and/or physical harm.

The very thought made him long for another clear view of Sara in the car that now chugged along at a quaint 57 mph. There she was. Her posture showed strength and confidence. Did she get it from her husband? From someone else? Whatever the source, it made her undeniably appealing.

And she was undeniably off-limits.

Hands off.

Despite great trust in his survival skills, Magnus did not dare touch her. His employer preferred to stay below-the-radar, off-the-grid, but he was known to have dangerous friends whom he could call upon at short notice. Not only might Magnus's contract be terminated and his accounts frozen, he would become the hunted. His own cell activity would be triangulated, his passport flagged to pin him down here in the States. He had an alternate passport, but even that might be known to his employer.

Bookman.

Magnus had never seen the mysterious fellow, but it's what the man called himself. Ha. As though he presented no more danger than a white-haired, bespectacled librarian. As though he buried his nose in the pages of classic literature and barely looked up to say boo. As though, in the last few weeks, he'd played no part in extortion and murder.

Stinking Bookman. No first name.

Whoever his employer was, Magnus loved this line of work, loved the power and money that came with it, and he would not stop until accomplishing his goal with the Vreelands.

Two short beeps from the cell phone on the passenger seat indicated he had missed a call. He checked the display, dialed back.

A man with a slight accent answered. "The woman is on her way here."

"To the estate?" Magnus said.

"By Mr. Storinka's request. He wishes to show her the place himself."

Curious and curiouser.

Magnus noted Sara's turn signal as she aimed toward the White Bridge exit. If she turned south, she may indeed be heading to Nashville's Belle Meade district. He maintained a two-car buffer. If she did turn into the Storinka estate he would be unable to follow, but this man on the phone would keep him updated.

"What is Storinka planning?" Magnus asked. "Why didn't you tell me about this in advance?"

"She's bringing him medical supplies. It may be nothing."

The Subaru angled south.

"Nothing? That seems highly unlikely. Either way, you'll find out soon enough, Viktor. I'm tailing her now, and she's only minutes away from you."

Chapter Twelve

A ROSE-TINTED DAWN SILHOUETTED MAGNOLIA TREES AS SARA REACHED THE swanky Belle Meade district. Her Subaru hatchback wobbled down the street, past pristine lawns and sprawling estates. Ahead, a Porsche eased between low brick walls, its headlights carving the shadows. Probably some doctor from Vanderbilt. Or a Music Row exec. A female jogger bounded by in a pink terry tracksuit, pulled along by a greyhound on a leash.

Sara rolled down the window, inhaled the cool, fragrant air. For one day, just one, it would be nice to know how the other half lived.

Her phone's GPS guided her around the next corner, where she followed a winding lane through stands of live oak and hickory, over a stone-sided bridge straddling a brook. The road curved up the hill to arched gates bracketed by limestone pillars that cradled flickering gas lanterns.

Leaning out her window, she was unable to reach the intercom. She stepped from the car, punched the Call button, noticed the closed-circuit TV camera eyeing her from high atop the wall. She shivered in the early chill.

"Hello?"

"Hi," she said. "This is Sara. I'm here for Mr. Storinka."

"Do you have his supplies?" said a male voice, slightly accented.

"I do."

"I'm Viktor. When you reach the house, stay in the car."

"That's fine. I can just hand the stuff through the window, and—"

"No, Mr. Storinka would like you to come inside. But please wait for me, Sara. It's the Dobermans. They're trained to attack."

"Oh."

The gates parted, welcoming her onto a crushed white-shell drive that meandered between crape maples and sycamores. She gave an appreciative whistle as she caught a view through the trees. Mr. Storinka had told her he owned a manufacturing firm, but never hinted at this aging yet impressive estate. Tendrils of ivy climbed the antebellum mansion's brick façade, and paned-glass windows reflected low clouds and the winks of a burnt-orange sunrise.

This was the place she'd seen in her recent dream. Or very similar.

How odd was that?

She followed the drive around a fountain to the front steps, where she parked behind a charcoal Maserati, a car most likely worth as much as her family's entire house. From the mossy pool, a family of geese statuary appeared to rise in flight as water cascaded down their stony backs.

A vision of serenity.

Waiting in the car per instructions, Sara felt dwarfed by the mansion and all it represented. Dreams or no dreams, she didn't belong here.

No. Not true. Why should material things make her feel less than?

She squared her shoulders, lifted her chin. She had as much right to be here as any diamond-encrusted socialite or stock-market millionaire. For heaven's sake, she had almost married one. Alex would have fit right in at this place, comfortable in his own skin, no need to flaunt his money. They would have been the couple others openly adored and secretly envied.

Was that what she would've wanted, though?

It seemed shallow, even cliché, to judge status by the cost of a woman's jewelry or the zip code of a man's beach home. Jesus Himself had no pillow for his head. Sure, a cushy savings account would be nice, but Sara relished the love of her children and her godly man.

For richer or poorer. Till death do us part.

And, Lord, she said silently, *the same holds true between me and You.*

A trio of dogs dashed into view, feet scrabbling on the crushed shells. A bit slow to react to her morning arrival, they made up for it now with snarls and flashing teeth. One positioned itself at the front of the Subaru, the others at the driver's door. Sara avoided their eyes. She knew her dear Katie would try to win them over with her optimistic charm, but she felt no such need. Let them bark.

How long was she supposed to wait here? She thought of honking the horn, but at last the thick front door opened to reveal a squat man with spiked black hair. Standing between huge flower pots, he gave a command that shut up the Dobermans and drew them prancing up the steps.

"Come," he called to her.

She opened the car door, hesitated. The dogs didn't budge.

"Good morning, Sara. I am Viktor, the housekeeper." He delivered this news without humor, and his black eyes dared her to receive it otherwise.

"Wish I could afford a housekeeper," she said, straight-faced. "May I, uh, come up to the door?"

"My girls won't attack unless I give the order."

"Nice girls."

"Come inside, if you will. Mr. Storinka is waiting."

She approached the entryway, holding the bag of supplies. CPAP, continuous positive airway pressure, was a good method for aiding sleep apnea sufferers, but worn-out parts led to irritated throats and dry mouths. She'd get this over quickly. Storinka would be thankful.

The Dobermans trailed her indoors, noses prying at the bag in her hand. She found herself in a foyer where polished hardwood flooring reflected the glittering lights of a massive chandelier. The corridor to her left opened into a dining hall and a separate sitting room with floor-to-ceiling bookshelves and fireplace, the one on her right to a coat closet, a washroom, and a white-tiled kitchen fit to serve a small army. And it might have, during the Civil War. Or the War of Northern

Aggression, as some Southerners called it. Straight ahead, dark doorways gave peeks into orderly bedrooms probably fitted for guests.

"Welcome, my dear."

Sara's eyes swept up the magnificent double staircase. Ivan Storinka stood at the top, propped against the mahogany rail in the center, his hair combed back from ice-blue eyes. He wore slippers, a black robe secured around his broad belly, and a gold religious medallion around his thick neck.

"Hi, Mr. Storinka. I brought your things."

"Let me see them." He gestured to the stairs. "Viktor, escort the lady."

Sara said, "I'm fine, thanks." The moment, though, that she started forward, the growling of the dogs froze her in place.

Accepting Viktor's offered arm, she felt rock-hard muscles beneath his sleeve. She scoffed at his role as housekeeper. Really? More like a personal bodyguard. He commanded attack dogs. He looked as Ukrainian as his employer. Though shorter than her husband, he was stocky and his sports jacket bulged on the left side.

A holstered gun?

It was like a scene from a movie. In which case, she was the hapless victim, the female without any sense who climbed the stairs to her grisly fate.

She brushed aside these fears. Mr. Storinka had never made suggestive comments or inappropriate queries. True, as their working relationship developed over time, they had talked about life, love, family, but never in a way that made her feel ill at ease. He treated her with almost fatherly respect.

"You have a nice place here," she said.

"Seven years," Storinka said, "and at last you visit. This is good."

She arrived atop the wide steps, feet sinking into burgundy carpet. Ah, that felt nice. She was tired, ready to lie down after her shift. Viktor fielded a nod from his boss, released her, and floated back down the stairs. With a single snap of the fingers, he led his trio of lovely "ladies" toward the kitchen.

"So, my dear, you like it here?"

"It's incredible, Mr. Storinka. I had no idea."

He gave a dismissive flutter of his fingers, but grinned in satisfaction. "It is too big, I think. I work hard, save. But what is this to me?"

"At least you have room for family and guests."

"Family?" His grin faded. "I am an old man with old-man regrets. I bought this place many years ago, a reinvestment when I moved to America. In Ukraine I was a rich businessman, but too busy. My wife, she found another man and stayed in Kiev. Only the last ten, eleven years I live in this house. Nashville is a good place, I think. Nice weather. Nice people." He ran a hand through his silver mane. "I make many travels for work, and this is a central location, yes?"

"Yes, we love this city. We came eight years ago. Things were tight where we lived, but my husband was offered a position here working on luxury coaches. I had no problem finding a job, since Nashville's such a health-care mecca. We miss the ocean, and certainly the mountains, but have no plans of going back."

"Let me guess. Northern California?"

"Washington State."

"Bah." He coughed. "Too wet and cold. Here it is better."

Sara opened the bag. "You don't sound too good. You ought to rest. I brought a pair of filters for your system, and the new seal should give your mask better airflow and cut down on the noise. Where's the machine?"

Storinka led her past a bathroom, where she glimpsed an old claw-foot tub. She dreamed of soaking in one of those, basking in bubbles and the scent of gardenias while reading poetry by Emily Dickinson. A foolish girlhood fantasy.

Darkness resided behind the next door, nicked only by a wedge of light from hooded lamps on the hallway walls.

A bedroom? For Viktor perhaps?

Her host hesitated, and pulled the door shut.

The final room was spacious yet sparsely furnished, with austere cabinets, a secretary desk, and a mini-bar. Persian rugs provided the only decoration. Daylight oozed through parted curtains and brushed the CPAP machinery and tubing beside the four-poster bed. Through the glass, Sara saw the circular drive outside and the wings of the fountain's uppermost goose, as though she'd glimpsed it in its moment of escape, a gossamer flight from the hunter's gunfire.

No. As she recalled, the statuary represented serenity.

She set to work at the bedside, attaching the mask's new seal. While used to long hours and shifts, she still sensed a lack of precision in her movements.

"Did you have a long night?" Storinka wheezed.

"It's the end of my work-week, and yes, I would like to get home soon. I try to have breakfast with my husband before he heads off to work."

"Bret, yes? I met him once at the clinic. He brought you flowers that day. Your anniversary, I think."

The memory steadied Sara's finger. Orchids. Her favorite.

"Does he still write and play his music?"

"When he has time," Sara said. "That's his release."

"It is rare, a man who works in a factory and is also creative."

"More than a factory. But yes, he's a good man."

"And your children?" Storinka said. "How are they?"

"Oh, they're our absolute treasures. After breakfast I take them to school, and only then do I get my turn to sleep. Which is what you should be doing."

He sucked in a deep breath. "Thank you. You are always good to me."

"It's my job."

"No, my dear." He touched his medallion with one hand and her arm with the other. His grip was firm, despite his age and deteriorating health. "Many people do not care, only work, work, work. You are different. You talk with me and listen. A big heart like yours is not easy to find. I wish . . ." He searched her eyes, as though deciding whether to divulge some private desire. "I wish I knew you, yes, many years ago."

She almost giggled. "I suspect I would've been too young for you."

"If I knew you," he continued, "maybe then I could see it."

"See what?"

"That I was wrong. Very wrong."

She felt a rush of empathy for him. His health was declining and he had few people close to him. In these situations, she liked to believe God had placed her in a person's life for a reason, be it large or small. Her eyelids felt heavy, her stomach empty, but right now this elderly Ukrainian man clutching her arm needed her to think more highly of others than of herself.

"Wrong about what?" she said.

She figured he might feel a need to confess, to remove some weight from his back. Everyone had secrets. Everyone carried guilt. Technically she was no priest, but she remembered words read only last week in her Bible: *"You are a chosen people . . . royal priests . . . As a result, you can show others the goodness of God."*

He gave no reply, only closed his eyes.

"Mr. Storinka, right now I'm off the clock, so it's just you and me speaking as friends. I know there is a God who cares about you, and He knows the things you've done. You don't have to carry those burdens to the grave."

He shook his head, pressed his lips to the medallion.

She said, "Nothing can separate you from His love."

"My dear, I am a bad man. Many, many bad things."

She waited as he fought off a fit of harsh, rib-rattling coughs.

"But," he said, catching his breath, "I have a plan, a way to settle matters."

"That's not necessary."

"Yes. Yes, it is."

"Well, it's good to put things in order. I don't know your past or the people in it, but if you ever need to get something off your chest, I will listen."

"It is my fault, Sara, that I lost those dear to me," Storinka's eyes clouded. "But the dead, they are always close to us, no? Only one step away."

She thought of the picture in her closet. "They're always with us in our memories, aren't they? All right, I really should be going. Now, uh, if you'll excuse me, will I be safe heading down those stairs? With the dogs and all?"

"Please, I will walk you out."

"You don't have to do that." She eased from his grip. "Take something for that dry throat of yours, and I'll close the curtains so you can get back to bed. I'll be fine, if you just call down to Viktor and let him know I'm leaving."

"Do not feel uneasy here, my dear. To you it is like home, I hope."

"Home?" She chuckled. "More like ten of my homes."

He popped a Hall's cough drop into his mouth, and the smell of eucalyptus washed over her as he barked into the bedside intercom. "Viktor, put away the dogs so the lady can come down. And you remember the item I set aside? She is the one. You will give it to her." Storinka patted Sara's arm. "My dear, do not refuse it, please. It is an old man's way of settling things."

Chapter Thirteen

THE NEW INTEL CHANGED EVERYTHING.

Off came the mustache as Magnus Maggart raced to his apartment. He gathered items in a briefcase, locked his Kimber Super Carry Pro and its ammo in a fireproof safe, and drove to Nashville Int'l Airport where he returned his Avis rental car. He bought a round-trip ticket to SeaTac. Although direct flights cost more on short notice, it would get him to the greater Seattle/Tacoma area in under five hours, under three if he converted Central to Pacific Standard Time.

With an hour and forty minutes until departure, he sipped a Starbucks coffee and nibbled on a sandwich. He could Skype his employer to discuss the recent changes, but that seemed insufficient. He texted Bookman, gave an abbreviated version of the new developments, and asked for a physical meeting.

Face2face, 4 pm?

OK@TM-OJ.

So, Bookman was agreeing to show his face? There was a surprise.

On my way.

Their plan was simple enough. Even a directionally challenged taxi driver could find the Tacoma Mall, and Orange Julius was a treat that couldn't be found in Nashville. A 3-Berry Blast smoothie would hit the spot after being cooped up on a plane with flatulent old men, harried mothers, and snot-faced kids.

At last Magnus boarded the aircraft, found his place, slipped his briefcase under the seat in front of him. A stewardess assisted passengers with small children. A steward, complete with nasally voice and guy-liner, demonstrated safety measures.

Buckled in, Magnus mentally replayed the earlier phone conversation that had sent him scurrying to the airport in hopes of salvaging weeks of work.

"You're certain, Viktor?"

"I gave it to Sara myself," the housekeeper said. "Following orders."

"From Storinka?"

"Yes."

"Explain to me," Magnus said, "why you think he would do such a thing."

"I cannot read his mind. My job is to protect him."

"What guarantee do I have, Viktor, that you didn't keep the gift yourself?"

"Mr. Storinka demanded that I take a picture with my phone to prove I had obeyed. I can send it to you, if you like."

"I'm waiting," Magnus said, and two minutes later he had the pic.

Now in his cramped seat, Magnus pulled up the image again on his cell. The screen showed Sara Vreeland on the lowest step of a grand staircase, eyes tired yet serene, a strand of princess-cut sapphires dangling a silver key from her neck.

"Sir?" Mr. Guy-Liner himself. "All electronic devices must be turned off."

What a blowhard. Magnus glared straight ahead and considered cataloguing the wide array of cellular frequencies that made such airline regulations utter folly. Instead he recalled a lesson from his mother: "Son, you've got a mind sharp enough to cut through people. Don't waste it. You jab a scalpel at junk metal, and all you'll do is dull the blade."

Pasting on a smile, he looked up at Guy-Liner. "Of course. Right away."

Best to keep this scalpel sharp.

Magnus put away his cell, leaned back against the headrest, and closed his eyes. He could still see Sara's form, her lovely form on that stairway. Could see that necklace clinging to her soft throat.

Why, look at her. The woman's entire life was about to change, and she had no idea.

Not. A. Stinking. Clue.

Chapter Fourteen

SARA TOOK KATIE'S HAND AS THEY HEADED TOWARD THE MIDDLE-SCHOOL soccer field. Katie skipped along in the late-afternoon heat, tennis shoes kicking up sprigs of grass. Kevin wore his home-team uniform, and Sara noticed his cleats were already laced. Thank the Lord. Perhaps her motherly advice was sinking in.

"After the game," Katie told her brother, "we're going to Sip Café for ice cream. That's what Daddy said."

"Big surprise. We always go there on Fridays."

"I'm getting peach-mango."

Kevin made a face.

"Kev, let's be nice." Sara let go of Katie's hand and touched her son's shoulder, but he shrugged away. "You know, your sister's here to cheer for you."

"Where's Dad? Is he coming?"

"He makes it to most of your games, doesn't he? He took the Billingsleys to the airport, but he should be arriving any minute." A blur of bright yellow turned her head. "See there? Just like I said."

"It's Daddy," Katie said.

Even Kevin grinned.

As the Hummer swaggered into the parking lot on large glossy black tires, Sara fiddled with the necklace in her jeans pocket. It was a gift from her patient, received off the clock and off the clinic premises. This morning she'd kept it to herself, deciding she would mention it to her husband only when they had ample time to discuss its ramifications.

She waved so that Bret would see her and the kids here on the grass.

Sliding from the Hummer's helm made Bret look awfully masculine to her. Call it shallow. Call it a victory for clever marketing. Whatever the reason, the moment he hopped down from the cab and locked the door, her heart skipped a beat. She went days, sometimes weeks, without experiencing a rush of physical excitement at the sight of her husband. After eleven years, the sparks had settled mostly into embers. But every so often, she found herself enthralled.

Those sparkling green eyes. That dark hair. His broad chest.

"Mmmm." She gave him a hug. "Honey, you look good."

"It's the wheels, isn't it?"

"No, of course not. You're just very debonair."

He kissed her. "And I don't look debonair driving the hatchback?"

"Stop it." She elbowed him. "You know, I'm trying to pay you a compliment. How'd everything go with Jason and Zoe? Did you get the house key and all the info about their Yorkie? Did their flight leave on time?"

"Yes, yes, and yes. And watch out, Mexico."

"Any money for my soccer pics?" Kevin asked. When Sara and Bret turned to him with quizzical looks, he said, "I figured maybe they would pay you for watching their dog. Maybe that would be God's answer to my prayers. It's only fair, isn't it? If you work, you should get paid."

"Sometimes," Bret said, "you do things just to help out your friends."

"Or your enemies. Says that in the Bible, I think."

Bret nodded. "That's right, Kev."

Sara wrapped an arm around her daughter and walked ahead, her ears still tuned to the father-son exchange. She never ceased to be amazed that the same boy who barked at his sister could dispense such words of wisdom.

Or, as his next sentence showed, such honest frustration.

"So," Kevin said. "My prayers didn't get answered."

Bret understood his son's frustration, having wrestled with similar issues. What was that verse in the thirtieth chapter of Proverbs? *"For if I grow rich, I may deny you and say, 'Who is the Lord?'" And if I am too poor, I may steal and thus insult God's holy name."* He clung to his belief in the Lord's goodness and provision, and yet their family's financial noose kept tightening. They were gasping for air. He often thought of that day two years earlier when he and his wife watched the gorgeous chestnut filly go down moments after the Kentucky Derby.

The horse gave all she had, and still came up short.

By a step.

A single stride.

"Hold on," Bret called, watching his son move away. He wanted to nip his son's negativity in the bud. David, in Psalms, had cried out with heart-rending emotion and doubt, but always returned to an attitude of praise. It was one thing to express feelings, and another to let them fester.

"Kev," he said, "let me talk with you."

"What? I should be over there with my team."

"Game doesn't start for another half hour. Right now it's more important that you get your heart in line." When he clamped a hand on Kevin's shoulder to restrain him, he noticed him wince. "Hey, what's wrong? You hurt?"

"It's nothing."

"Did something happen at school today? Those boys again?"

Kevin's chin dropped.

"Show me."

"Dad, not here. It's just a coupla bruises, mostly my ribs."

Bret wanted to slam his fist through a wall. *Lord, this is my kid. Your kid. What am I supposed to do, just stand by while he gets bullied?* He rolled his neck, fixed his eyes on the players clustering along the sidelines.

"OK," he said, "I get it. They're on your team over there, aren't they?"

"Two of them."

"Tell me which ones. I'll go talk to them this very second, find their parents and get this out in the open."

"That won't help."

"Sure it will. I'm not gonna let my son keep—"

"One of them's only got a mom, and the other one, he lives with his grandparents and they never show up for our games. I don't even know if they drive. I think he gets a ride with Coach. Can we just drop it? Please."

Bret stared across the grass.

"Don't worry, Dad. I'll keep turning the other cheek, the way Jesus said."

"Listen. It's good to take the high road, but you and I both know how boys can be, always looking for the weak ones to attack. Believe it or not, that's not all bad. God created us to be hunters, protectors, providers, and at one time we did need to be able to pick out the easy prey. He gave us testosterone and adrenaline, which is why we like our sports and Xbox and stuff, even if nowadays we find our meat in a Kroger aisle. Point is, we're men. And we still need to show what we're made of so that we can guard ourselves and our families."

"But, Dad, I don't even have a family yet."

"What do you call your mom, your sister, and me?"

"My family."

"That's right. And I bet you'd protect us if you had to."

"I'm ready. Let me get out and play, and I'll show you how I can kick."

"You can kick," Bret said. "That's a fact."

"Watch." Kevin ran forward three steps, lowered his weight onto his left leg, and swung his right using the full force of his hip. The instep of his cleat tore through dandelions and tall weeds.

"Do you trust me, Kevin?"

His son looked up. "I trust you."

"Good. Here's what I want you to do. Sometimes you gotta prove to the other guys that you're tough, that you're not gonna be pushed around. That doesn't mean you stop being a good sport, but you play aggressively, all caution to the wind. So your opponent's bigger than you? Big deal. The ball's about to nail you in the gut? Who cares? You lay it all out there and show no fear."

"But the ball does hurt."

"Not if you get to it first, it doesn't. Not if you're amped up and ready for anything." Bret shrugged, "OK, yeah, it may hurt for a few minutes, but you fight on. And here's the crazy thing, a lotta times your opponents will start backing off."

"Donelson's only lost one game."

"Which means they're not unstoppable. Will you do it?" When he saw Kevin nod, he said, "And if it doesn't work, play the way you want the next game."

"I'll do it, Dad. Just tell Mom not to be scared, OK?"

Fat, gray clouds rolled overhead and darkened the skylights in the Tacoma Mall. Magnus leaned back on a bench and hugged his briefcase to his side, scanning the walkways, storefronts, entries to the restrooms. He sipped his 3-Berry Blast within view of Orange Julius, and still no contact from the one who called himself Bookman, though their rendezvous time was ten minutes ago.

Magnus drew air through his mouth, exhaled slowly through his nose. He pressed his fingers to his wrist, measured his pulse.

Seventy-two beats a minute. For him, this was relaxed.

His cell told him the local time was now eleven minutes past four. He refused to be annoyed. No doubt this was an intentional ploy by his ultra-secretive employer to rile him and note his reaction.

Yes, Bookman was here. Oh, he better be.

Fighting a stiff neck from the flight, Magnus glanced over his left shoulder and swept the area with his eyes. He hesitated at each possibility.

What about that lean scarecrow of a man in the hooded sweatshirt? Or the fellow in the suit with the gold cuff links chomping on a

Dairy Queen burger and dripping ketchup? Or the elderly gentleman with the trousers pulled halfway to his chest and a pedometer clipped to his belt?

Perhaps Bookman wasn't here.

No, he's here.

Perhaps Bookman was a woman.

No, I heard his voice the day he called and commissioned me for this job.

Deciding to wait three minutes more, Magnus slurped up the last of his smoothie, wiped his mouth, and considered the diversity of the human species. Unlike the Bible thumpers, he found people neither marvelous nor miraculous. Stir up some genetic glue, toss in some chromosomes, flavor generously with any one of billions of possible DNA sequences, and you had yourself two-legged homo sapiens.

An ode to some divine spark?

Hardly, but an entertaining animal to be sure.

He set his cup on the bench and planted a hand on his knee, ready to go. Even without a zookeeper, the human animals were growing thick now, clustered this Friday afternoon here in a stone-and-glass habitat of their choosing, munching on goodies, and consuming, consuming, consuming. If these creatures represented the next step up the evolutionary ladder, Magnus dreaded what waited at the top.

His susceptibility to such depression further depressed him. Blame it on the drop after his fructose sugar-rush, but why let such things rule his mood?

He set his jaw. Logic was to be his ruler. Head over heart.

I think, therefore I am.

"Here, let me get that for you." A teen in a mall apron reached for Magnus's empty cup and slipped him a King County library card. "Magnus, right? The deal is, I just work here, but I'm supposed to tell you to take a cab into Seattle to the downtown library. Then ride the escalator up to the reading room."

"Who are you?"

"Like I said, I'm just cheap labor. But give me forty bucks and, hey, I'll pass on a message for you too."

Magnus stood, looked at the card. "Who gave this to you? Is he nearby?"

"I seriously doubt it. I mean, that was like an hour ago. He described you, said you'd be hanging by Orange Julius, and I should wait till a quarter past four before coming over to say a word."

"What'd he look like?"

"I dunno. Gray hair. Bushy eyebrows. In his fifties or sixties maybe, but I'm not good at reading people's age, especially when they're, like, over thirty. Wait." The teen scratched at his upper lip. "Oh. Uh-huh. He had a mole right here, right beneath his nose. Not big, but you could see it."

"You're certain?"

"Unless it was a zit. Do old guys get zits?"

Magnus thanked the young man and stalked toward the exit. Very well. If he was supposed to jump through a few hoops, he would start jumping.

Chapter Fifteen

Scared? Sara was a nervous wreck. Standing on the sidelines of the soccer field with hands cupped to her mouth and hair blowing in her eyes, she forgot about the next round of Kevin's medical bills, the rising cost of gas, the need for her annual doctor's exam, the past troubles between her husband and his father, the class ring and the Dodge Charger, and the sapphire necklace in her pocket.

And she screamed.

Of course, Katie screamed too.

By the time it was over, the Bailey Middle Bulldogs had defeated Donelson Middle 4–2. Kevin scored the final goal, and his team carried him across the field in celebration. He beamed despite scuffed elbows, dirt-caked shins, and a scrape down his left leg from a goal-saving slide tackle in the fourth quarter.

Sara turned to Bret. "Holy moly. What just happened out there?"

"Kevin realized that it's OK to be a warrior."

"That was amazing. It was fun seeing him play tough, don't get me wrong, but please don't turn him into something he's not."

"Sweetie, did you see him help up that kid from the other team? He's still got a tender heart, but today he learned how to protect it with an iron will."

"Daddy?" Katie tugged on his shirt. "I'm ready for ice cream."

"Me too," he said, scooping her into his arms. "Look, here comes your brother. Way to go, Kev." They bumped fists. "Now that's what I was talking about. Did you see the way they backed off when you got aggressive? That scrape, it'll heal up, but you won't ever forget that game, will you?"

"No way."

"Now carry that same confidence with you at school, OK? Other boys notice those things, and you won't come across scared or weak."

Kevin nodded.

"Let's go celebrate," Sara said.

"That's right," Bret nodded toward the Hummer. "I say we all pile in and head over to Sip. What do you think Natalie's gonna say when she sees us drive up in this yellow monster?"

Magnus rode north in the taxi cab toward Seattle. He looked up from the library card registered to a Gabe Stilman, and wondered if it was meant as a warning. He watched Boeing Field slide by on his left, the runway glistening from recent rain, and he recognized Safeco Field where the Mariners played baseball. He hadn't watched an entire ball game since the day his father walked out the door.

He tuned out the driver's music and ran through his last few weeks.

Investigating the Vreelands.

Intimidating. Infiltrating.

This morning he had been ready to inflict pain upon his principal subject, Bret Vreeland, when Mr. Storinka's unexpected gift to Sara flipped the script. Magnus was one of the lead actors in this play, and now he had lost his lines. Were his weeks of preparation wasted? He wouldn't know until tonight, when he got the revised script from Bookman.

"What's my motivation?"

It was a question he asked often in high school drama class. It wasn't for lack of intelligence. Quite the opposite. He didn't feel what his characters felt because he was more advanced in his reasoning. Emotions didn't push him around.

"What's my motivation?"

Of course he had no problem once the teacher explained the character's emotional arc. Once that was understood, he could act with the best of them.

Staring at his own reflection in the glass, he remembered his mother's words to him: "Magnus, you have no limitations except those in your own mind. Let no one stand in your way. You and I, we've learned the hard way, haven't we, that people are stone-cold liars. You've got to be colder if you want to survive."

He loved his mother. Why, then, had she done those things to him in that house? Why had she made him her whipping boy?

To make him colder.

You know she meant well, Magnus.

To sharpen the scalpel.

So quit your moaning.

The taxi halted at the curb of the Seattle Central Library. He put Mr. Stilman's library card in his wallet, paid the driver, and headed toward the doors. Swinging against his leg, his briefcase held files that represented weeks of fact-gathering and surveillance.

Oh, yes, Bookman would be impressed.

Magnus had stolen Bret and Sara's banking info from their home computer, along with employment records and résumés. He'd dredged up other pertinent details by visiting their workplaces, ever amazed at the loose lips and flapping gums of secretaries and janitorial staff. Enabled by the Freedom of Information Act, he sifted through military and criminal records of the Vreelands' relatives. Local courthouse documents were a gold mine, as were the National Personnel Records Center and the International Genealogical Index.

He was less sophisticated but equally effective in ripping info from Kevin's medical bills, thanks to a late-night forage through the family's garbage can. And he printed Katie's after-school schedule straight from Rosebank Elementary's Web site. All the info right there at his fingertips.

In addition, he pulled e-mails, phone numbers, and photos from Sara's Facebook page, and took hundreds of digital shots with his own camera.

All this hard work. Threatened by Sara's gift from Storinka.

Magnus entered the massive library, a modern display of steel mesh and glass, with escalators providing impressive views on their climb to the structure's apex. He rode to Level 10, where clusters of chairs graced the reading room. With the library closing in half an hour, patrons were few. He strolled about the space and waited for Bookman to make contact. Two young women tried to catch his eye, but he was used to such attention and gazed past them.

Nearing the end of his loop, he spotted a lone individual slouched in a chair, wearing a knit beanie cap, an oversized coat, and a pair of sunglasses.

Sunglasses? At night? It was like that old '80s tune.

As Magnus edged closer, he sensed sudden movement behind him. Even in a library he was on alert, and he pivoted, ready to thrust his left elbow into a solar plexus and follow it with a right hook to the chin.

"Now, now," said a man with a stubbled square jaw. "I'm not going to hurt you. Did you think that guy behind you was your contact? Some bum sneaking a few winks in the reading room? He's been in that chair for the past hour."

"Are you Bookman?"

"Is there someone else you're supposed to meet?"

"We're in a library, so I guess that explains your nickname."

"Actually," the man said, "I'll let him explain it for himself."

Before Magnus could ask who, a jolt of pain stabbed at his right buttock, causing muscles to turn numb. A needle? Some sort of poison? Why, it took some nerve to pull off such a stunt in a public place.

Liquid fire throbbed through his veins, coursing outward to his extremities. He stumbled, angled for a view of his assailant, realized it was Mr. Sunglasses-at-Night, and wanted to ask if he could borrow those shades because the lights were blinding him, chasing him, spinning about his head until nothing was left but a sense of gratitude that the pain was leaving, replaced by a glow of well-being.

"What're you doing, boyo?" said a flat male voice. "Get him into the elevator and make it quick. The car's waiting outside."

"How 'bout a hand? He's not exactly a lightweight."

Magnus wanted to disagree. He *was* light, light as a feather, light as a sunbeam, weightless as a white-cotton cloud. He was flowing like a river, to the stream, to the stream. He knew he was in trouble. Utterly defenseless, in fact. His legs weren't working. His arms were limp cords of rope. And the worst part was he didn't care.

Four hours later he would care. Care a whole lot.

Right now, though, he was just slip-slip-slipping away.

Chapter Sixteen

"O.M.G."

Even through the Sip Café window, Natalie's mouthed response was clear as the Vreelands parked at the curb. Sara saw the young woman hold up a finger to her male customer at the counter and hurry out the front door.

Sara helped Katie down from the backseat and turned to their drop-jawed greeter. "Surprised?"

"Is it yours?" Natalie said. "When did you get a Hummer?"

"We're borrowing it," Bret said. "It actually belongs to my boss."

"Least there's room for all of you. This has 'Vreeland' written all over it."

Sara liked Natalie. Although quiet at first, the girl had warmed to them during their regular visits and now came up to say hello at other locations, whether it be an aisle in H.G. Hill or beneath the trestles at Shelby Bottoms Park.

"Looks like your customer's still waiting in there," Sara said.

"Oops. I'm such a dingbat. You are coming in, aren't you?"

"Right behind you," Bret said. "We're celebrating Kevin's soccer game."

"He scored a goal," Katie exclaimed.

"No kidding?" Natalie turned, gave Kevin a jab to the arm. "Way to go."

Although he lowered his chin and shrugged, he was beaming.

Sara found Bret's hand, and they trailed Natalie inside. At the counter, the waiting man turned. His salt-and-pepper hair was combed back, and his clothing seemed to match his face, worn yet clean, and slightly wrinkled.

"Eli?" Sara said. "Hello, how are you?"

His gray eyes met hers. "Oh, fine and dandy. How 'bout you?"

Bret greeted the man with a handshake. "Good to see ya."

If Eli had a last name, no one used it. The man helped out around the church building, vacuumed rugs, scrubbed toilets, arranged classroom tables and chairs. He'd been part of the congregation for three years, working with Pastor Teman in exchange for a corner of the parking lot, where he lived in a Caribou camper shell mounted atop his old pickup. He was loyal and soft-spoken, his presence on the property a deterrent to graffiti artists and thieves.

"Eli," Katie gushed. She threw tiny arms around the man's legs. "Why aren't you at the church? Isn't that where you live? Kevin won his soccer game, but he hurt his leg. Are you getting ice cream? My favorite's peach-mango."

He chuckled at the rush of words. "Sounds delicious."

"Sip has the best, huh, Daddy?"

"They do. Now give Eli some space, OK?"

"She's no trouble," the older man said. "But you best do as your dad says." He leaned toward Kevin. "And to you, fine sir, congratulations are in order."

"Thanks."

While the Vreelands claimed a table against the wall, Eli ordered a house coffee. He filled his cup, gave them all a farewell nod, and slipped out the back door. The church was only a ten-minute walk from here.

Sara watched him go, wondering if he needed groceries. On more than one occasion, she and Bret had left a box of canned goods on his camper step.

Turning her focus back to her family, she noticed Kevin's cleats were leaving dirt clods on the tiles, and she told him to go kick them clean on the curb. When he returned, she handed him a wad of napkins from the sugar-and-cream station. He opened his mouth to protest, but chose instead to wipe up the mess and toss it into the garbage can.

She arched an eyebrow. Laced soccer cleats? Obedience without firing a word back? These were encouraging signs from their ten-year-old.

Standing at the espresso machine, Natalie said, "Thanks, Kevin. That makes you now officially first in line, you being the day's hero and all."

"It was only one goal."

"I meant you cleaning up after yourself. You know how many people come in, spill stuff, kick things under the chairs, and figure it's my job to pick up after them? More than will ever tip, I can tell you that much."

"Daddy always tips," Katie said. Her nose was pressed to the glass display, her eyes dancing over the bins of ice cream. "Don't you, Daddy?"

"I promise I will tonight. Wouldn't want Natalie mad at me."

"Sorry, I know I shouldn't complain. It's this semester, it's whipping my butt." A thick, college course book lay open on the counter. She bookmarked it with a coffee sleeve, slammed it shut, and leaned her elbows on it. Her nose stud flashed in the light. "I feel like I can let my hair down around your family. Is that a bad thing?"

"Absolutely not," Sara said. "Hair. Down. And we promise to still like you."

"Gracias."

The kids ordered cones of mint chocolate and peach-mango. Sara settled on almond fudge and a cup of decaf, Bret on espresso bean and the real deal. Sara knew he was a fan of Drew's Brews, the roaster featured here. As the amount of their order tallied on the register, Bret pulled a five and a ten from his wallet, the budgeted amount for their weekly family outing.

"O.M.G." Natalie gasped. "Wait right there. Don't move a muscle." She darted into the back, rustled around in a drawer.

Sara stepped up beside her husband, and he gave her a shrug.

The young woman reappeared with an envelope held high.

"What is it?" Bret said.

"It's for you. Man, I can't believe I almost forgot. It's a fifty-dollar gift certificate good for anything on the menu. Whatever's left, you just use it the next time you come in. There's this customer, he's seen all of you in here before and wanted to do something nice."

"Cool," Kevin and Katie said.

"He?" Sara's throat tightened.

"Yeah, but he asked me to keep it anonymous."

Bret pulled out the certificate. "Shoot. This should cover two visits—"

"Dad?"

"Maybe even three."

"Dad."

"Yeah, Kev?"

"That gives us more money on top of the line, right?"

"The line? What're you saying?"

"The budget." Kevin's voice rose. "You said if we had more on top, we could minus more underneath. And I prayed, didn't I? Maybe now we can pay for my soccer portraits."

Sara knew Kevin was set on giving photos to his classmates and relatives. She also knew the cost was more than they could afford, which apparently he and his father had discussed. Despite that letdown, he was attempting to keep his emotions in check. Maybe this *was* an answer to prayer.

Bret shrugged. "We'll be saving money on our next few visits in here, so yeah, what you're saying makes sense to me, bud."

"Does that mean I can get the portraits?"

Bret caught Sara's eye and she threw him a nod. Ruffling their son's hair, he said, "That means you can get them."

Kevin whooped.

Even in the midst of the rejoicing, Sara felt her throat muscles constrict and her fingertips tingle. What was it about this week that had her looking over her shoulder and fearing the worst? Nothing threatening had happened since the appearance of that car on their street.

There was still the issue of Bret's class ring from the Northwest, but that wasn't dangerous in any tangible way.

She tucked her hands into her pants pockets, where they bumped the necklace still stored there. Although getting a gift certificate from a stranger was odd, it was no less odd than an expensive gift from a patient. Considering the difficulties she and her husband had faced and the obstacles they'd overcome, it felt right and just that God would be smiling down upon them at last.

And honestly, who was she to question it?

Bret, though, seemed to share some of her concerns. He squinted, studying the gift certificate. "I bet I know who it was that left this for us," he said. "Pastor Teman."

"Pastor Teman." Sara nodded. Yes, that made perfect sense.

Natalie shook her head. "Nope."

"Nope?"

The young woman gave cones to Kevin and Katie, who wasted no time lapping up the drips. She handed Sara and Bret their coffee cups and assured them she would get their goodies once she reheated the metal scoop.

Sara clung to her hope. "Natalie, are you sure it wasn't our pastor?"

"I'm sure."

"Do you know what he looks like? He's short and, uh, slightly pudgy, and a bit older than us. He's—"

"Single?" Natalie said.

"What? No. He's married with three grown kids."

"Hate to say it, but that doesn't stop most guys these days."

"He's a pastor."

"Like I said," Natalie pursed her lips and tilted her head. "Nah, I'm sure he's a good guy. In answer to your question, though, this man definitely wasn't short and definitely wasn't wearing a ring." She met Sara's gaze. "OK, here goes. Since I know you, I'm just gonna say it. He asked me out."

"On a date?"

"He's cute. Well, maybe not exactly cute, but big and rugged. Got that look, like he used to be in the army. Yeah, just something about him. So we made plans to grab a bite a few days back, at the Village Pub, but the owners kept me here late that night. Let's not even go into that. But it's all good. He and I are making up for it next Wednesday night, since I get off early."

Sara's nerves still jangled. She turned, saw Bret's furrowed brow, and knew he was bothered as well. She wanted to press Natalie for more details.

As though reading her thoughts, the hazel-eyed girl said, "Nope, that's all you're getting out of me. He made me promise to keep his identity safe. He just wanted to do something nice. He says when he was a kid he always dreamed of having family dates, and seeing the four of you together, it inspired him."

"Inspired him, huh?"

"Si, senora," Natalie shrugged. "Guess he just wanted to bless you."

Chapter Seventeen

INSPIRATION WAS A TEMPERAMENTAL GUEST. IT DROPPED IN UNANNOUNCED, THEN left without so much as a goodbye, slipping out a window in the dead of night or sauntering out the front door, leaving the house empty, drafty, and cold.

Magnus felt no inspiration now.

He did feel warm urine seeping through his jeans.

Though his thoughts were fuzzy, he told himself he shouldn't be ashamed. He was immobilized, blindfolded, and sweating beneath leather straps that held his arms and legs against a thick wooden chair. All mammals had bladders, and all bladders had their limits, so it was only natural, biological, that an entire smoothie and two cans of ginger ale consumed during the earlier flight needed somewhere to go. Gravity helped direct the path down his leg.

Where was he? Was Bookman behind this? Or had someone else diverted him from the mall to the library so they could nab him?

Seemed unlikely. He'd texted Bookman only this morning, and no one else knew of their rendezvous. With this being their first physical meeting, he should've expected such a test, a shakedown from his elusive employer. Even now the man was surely close, orchestrating these events.

"Where's Bookman?" Magnus called out. "I want to talk to Bookman."

"Right here, boyo."

Coming from his left, the voice startled him. He considered himself a highly tuned creature, capable of sensing others within his electromagnetic field, but the sloshing of his thoughts and beating of his pulse had drowned out everything else. He tasted salt on his tongue. The world was tilting, swaying, and he felt nauseated. Probably the drugs in his system still dulling his senses.

He said, "Can we get rid of the blindfold?" The "we" was meant to establish camaraderie. "Whatever happened to a friendly face-to-face?"

"We're having it now."

Magnus licked his lips. "I can't see who I'm talking to."

"You thirsty, boyo?" Bookman said. "I bet you're thirsty."

The man's speech rang false, as though he were masking his true voice. Magnus said, "You want me to pee myself again like a little girl, is that it?"

"I'm trying to be polite."

"Some water would be nice."

Bookman snapped his fingers, apparently approving the request. Magnus detected light footsteps, felt a gust of wind tug at his hair.

A boat. That was it.

He imagined himself on the aft-deck of a yacht or in the cabin of a charter boat. Seattle boasted a number of marinas, and he could be at any one of them. No doubt he had been drugged, taken down in the library elevator, hurried out the doors to a waiting vehicle. Sixty seconds, seventy tops. Barely time for the thinning number of bookish patrons to react. Why, that taxi from Tacoma could've been part of the plan, still waiting down at the curb.

"Open wide."

Magnus heard the crack of a plastic seal. A water bottle poked at his lips, splashing moisture on them. He opened his mouth for more. The icy refreshment slid down his throat and began to cleanse his system.

"You can blame me," Bookman said, "for the chemical cocktail you received earlier. I mixed it myself, and one of the side effects is that it leeches water from the body. Taking into account your size and strength, I really thought I gave you the proper dosage, but you've been—"

"Mr. Sunglasses. So, that was you?"

"But you've been out for nearly three hours."

"My head's still fuzzy." Magnus said it in hopes of lowering the man's guard should he feel endangered and need to escape. On the other hand, it might be best to sit this out and prove he had nothing to hide. "Whatever you used, it worked quickly."

Bookman's tone lost its warmth. "What's your name?"

"Magnus. You already know that."

"A name can be changed. Faked. Made up. Bought. Borrowed. Stolen."

"What is your point?" Magnus said.

"Do you know my name?"

"You are Bookman. Is it because you lure your victims to the library?"

"Oh-ho, best if you don't pry to find out. Yes, your skills are well known in certain circles, which is why I hired you. You're not an easy man to track down, but Maggart is your real name. Your mother's maiden name, I'm told. There are other Maggarts in the phonebook, but I imagine you alone are the closest to a maggot and a braggart."

"Magnus means 'great.' I take pride in that."

"A braggart, like I said."

"You hired me. Are we in a place we can speak about the job?"

"Will anyone else hear you, you mean? No. Just you and me, boyo."

"And," Magnus added, "whoever went to grab me a drink."

"Very astute. Yes, we'll call him Waterboy. Speak."

Magnus blinked against the blindfold, but caught only glimmers of light. He sucked and swallowed the remaining moisture from his tongue. "I'm sure you looked through my briefcase," he said, "so you've seen the effectiveness of my work. Mrs. Vreeland is an attractive woman, so it's no great mystery to me that you want her husband removed from the picture. The timing is curious, in light of Mr. Storinka's interest in her."

"What's your point?"

"I want to know what's really going on. I called, flew here to share the most recent developments, and you take me captive. Is this meant to create trust between us? I wanted only to get your advice, being that it's your prize at stake."

"My prize?" Bookman said. "You think it's a game we're playing here? No, the Vreelands are more than a prize, much more. All I want is what should be mine, and I won't let you, or Storinka, or saintly Bret stand in my way. There is always a point of weakness. Always."

"And I will find it."

"Which is why I hired you. But let me be frank, Maggart the Braggart. I don't care if you trust me, and you will be safer if you don't."

Magnus stiffened. He flashed back to his wife's verbal abuses, so much like his mother's. So incessant, so very familiar.

Familiar. Family. Liar.

While he didn't appreciate being mocked, he refused to let such schoolyard name-calling distract him. He trained his attention instead on the aural and olfactory clues at his disposal. Bookman's voice gave little evidence of his age, an even tenor with a bit of gravel in the throat. A smoker, perhaps. Except he had cinnamon on his breath instead of nicotine.

Magnus committed these clues to memory. The more he knew about his employer, the more empowered he would be to counteract the man's threats.

And to know a person's identity was to hold the key to his or her secrets.

I will find that key, make no mistake.

Bookman continued. "You'll be safest of all if you don't sell me out." His voice was no louder than the water that lapped at the boat and rocked it against its mooring. "Have you sold me out, Magnus?"

"Why would I? No, I—"

The blow caught him in the ribs, just below the heart. It displaced the air from his lungs and cut short his reply.

"Have you?" his captor repeated.

"It would be foolish," he said, gasping. "You're already paying me."

"Well, that's what I keep telling myself. A hundred thou up front for expenses, another hundred deposited in your offshore account, and the remaining hundred once you've completed the task. Simple, right? No frills. Plenty of time to get things done."

Nodding, Magnus flexed his muscles against the constraints but sensed no give. Feet shuffled on his right, and he contracted his abs, anticipating another blow from the waterboy, probably the square-jawed fellow from the library. He knew this routine. Knew to isolate his mind from the pain. If he couldn't control certain bodily functions, he could at least master his emotions.

Just as you taught me, Mother.

"Do you have a problem with our arrangement?" Bookman said.

Magnus was shaking his head, when the second blow hit him in the ribs. He couldn't tell if he'd been struck by a fist or by the handle of a baseball bat. The energy dissipated over his conditioned muscles, painful yet manageable.

He was sucking in air when the next shot caught him in the liver. It felt like a railroad tie thrust through his innards, and the force momentarily shut down his organs and fired off multiple pain receptors. Another dribble of urine seeped through his pants. His head fell forward, eyes burning against the blindfold.

"This morning," Bookman said, "you spoke to Storinka's bodyguard."

He nodded. "Keeping . . . an eye on Sara."

"After browsing through your briefcase, it's clear you've been busy. Some nice work actually. But none of it changes the fact that Viktor is a patient little man who's going to get his patient little fingers caught in the old man's cookie jar. You know what I think? I think maybe he's talked you into helping."

"That's not tru—"

Agony bloomed along Magnus's left temple, a red-yellow ball of fire that exploded against his skull, leaving his brain-pan rattling, his eardrums ringing.

Are you watching? Do I make you proud?

Another bloom appeared at the crook of his jaw, jarring his teeth.

See how you made me strong?

He spit out blood, felt some trickle down his chin.

"That's only the first round, boyo." Bookman splashed his face with water and slapped his cheek almost playfully. "You're fully alert now, and I expect clear and concise answers."

The hand was rough and callused. Another detail to remember.

"I could save myself a lot of money," Bookman said, "if we just voided our contract now. There are other ways to get the task done, so don't think too highly of yourself, Maggart. I could end this here. By the time they found your body, you'd be barely recognizable."

"Why would I fly here if I had something to hide?" Magnus said.

I'm still of the mind that you came to wring more cash out of me, to play both sides of this deal. Explain to me, would you, why you're in contact with Storinka's bodyguard?"

"Storinka and I have a history. In fact, he's where I got my start, doing odd jobs for him here and there, back in 'ninety-seven." Magnus spit out another mouthful of blood. "All in the past now, but I still make use of those old contacts."

"Viktor, you mean."

"He's known Storinka longer than I have. Since their Ukraine days."

"And why would Sara's visit to the old man be cause for alarm?"

Magnus picked his words carefully. Here was the purpose for this trip to the Northwest, and he did his best to state those concerns, despite the split lip and pounding headache. When he was done, he drew shallow, controlled breaths to minimize the knifing pangs in his ribs.

"You're right," Bookman said at last. "This does change things, doesn't it? Excuse Waterboy and his workout, but I couldn't have any doubts about your loyalty. With what you've told me, I think we should dial down the aggression and let things cool a bit. There may be better ways to get at Sara and her dearly beloved. It'll take more finesse, though. You understand?"

"I'll need more money then."

"Oh-ho, so there it is. Playing me for the fatter paycheck."

"No. I won't sell you out for money, but it is what I work for."

"Maggart, we're both gentleman here, and I'll make sure you are compensated. You like that Charger? It drives nice? Good. But let's face it, nobody works solely for money. Put a rich man on a yacht or in a mountaintop resort, and you think he's still happy if he's all alone? No, we all want something. We work for power, companionship, freedom. Which is it for you?"

Blinking against the blindfold, Magnus turned his thoughts back to Music City and his upcoming date with the hazel-eyed girl named Natalie.

"What's my motivation?"

He was still trying to figure that out.

Chapter Eighteen

"Honey, would you mind tucking the kids in for me?"

"Sure." Bret kissed Sara's forehead, and she snuggled against him on the couch while the nightly news reported on a federal investigation into arms manufacturing. In their bedroom, Kevin and Katie were banging around. "But maybe we should give them a little longer," Bret said. "It's Friday, and it sounds like they're still having fun back there."

"It's late."

"They can sleep in. What a great day today, huh?"

"It was," she agreed. "But I'm ready to drop into bed, clothes and all."

"Go, sweetheart. Don't you worry about the kids."

"You sure?" she said. "I mean, you do have work in the morning."

"Should be a breeze. Jason told the guys I'm in charge of production while he and Zoe are gone. I'll just do like he does and kick my feet up on the desk, bark orders, and slurp down coffee."

"No, you won't. That's not your style."

"See, now you know why I'm not a manager."

"All I can say is I hope they had a safe flight to Cozumel. While I'm feeding their dog tomorrow, they'll be sipping drinks and dancing on the beach."

"Which, Lord willing, is what we'll be doing some day."

She nodded. "Except our wheelchairs'll be bogged down in the sand."

"C'mon. Sooner than that, I hope."

"Me too." She planted her palms on the cushions, and the couch springs squeaked as she pushed herself to her feet. "I'm calling it quits for the evening. This morning I could barely sleep when I got home from the clinic, and then we went to the game where I screamed myself silly, and then to the—"

"Sara. I got it covered."

"Don't wait too long, all right? And don't let Kevin forget to—"

"Put in his mouth guard. I know, I know. Do I get to be a dad here, or what?" He grinned and gave her a swat. "Go."

Bret watched her departure with husbandly admiration. He turned off the news, just more of the same-old, and picked up a novel from the end table. Though he wasn't much of a reader, he'd bought the book on a recommendation, and this Steven James guy sure knew how to keep the pages turning. The story provided an escape from the noise of TVs, cell phones, traffic, and barking dogs.

But not from Kevin and Katie.

Thummpp-thump.

Great. If they kept that up, their mother would never get to sleep.

He finished the chapter and saved his place with a bookmark. What were the kids doing anyway? Jumping from bed to bed? It was a favorite activity, one he discouraged even though it reminded him of happy moments from his own childhood. During seventh grade, Bret had shared his room with his cousin Darrell, who'd survived a family tragedy that no one wanted to talk about. Darrell, nicknamed Barrel, was only two months younger, and the two boys hit it off, getting into all sorts of shenanigans, fun-spirited and mostly harmless.

Thummmpppp.

That didn't sound right.

Protective instincts churned as Bret hurried down the hall. He thought of the half-hidden, thick-necked man eyeing them from the car a few days back. He smelled the burnt rubber of those spinning tires. He felt the cold pewter of his ring, a ring that belonged thousands of miles away.

Who was so interested in their family? Was someone breaking into the house this very instant, coming after the kids?

He knew the lone window in Kevin and Katie's room faced the backyard. Chain-link hemmed in the grass, while tangled vines and trees shielded the fifteen-foot slope to the CSX train tracks below. The light above the porch illuminated a rusty swing-set and Sara's flower garden, but a stealthy intruder still wouldn't have much trouble reaching the house undetected.

"Kevin?" Bret was almost to their door. "Katie?"

No answer.

"What's going on?" He burst into the room, found innocent faces staring at him from beside a dresser. Far off, a train whistle sounded. "You guys OK?"

"We were just playing," Kevin said. "Are we being too loud?"

"Your mom's in bed."

"Sorry, Dad."

Bret studied his son's expression. "Buddy, what aren't you telling me?" He ran his gaze along the window curtains, the ruffled blankets, the scattered LEGOS, toys, stuffed animals, and soccer ball. He paced toward the closet and came back to his children's position. "What was that thumping sound? Katie?"

"Kevin and me, we're just—"

"'Kevin and I.'"

"We're just having fun. He's showing me how to . . ." She shifted from foot to foot in her long, pink, pajama shirt. "How to do soccer stuff."

"Like how to kick a goal?" Bret said.

Her eyes brightened. "Uh-huh."

Kevin groaned.

"Well, that's nice of your big brother, but this isn't the time or place. It's been a good day, lots to be thankful for, and now you need to shut things down. I don't want you keeping your mom and I up all night."

"'Me,'" Kevin muttered.

"What?"

"'Mom and me.' Teacher says lotsa people get it wrong, but all you have to do is take the other person out of the sentence and see how it sounds."

"'I don't want you keeping *me* up.' Hmm, you're right." Bret pulled his son to his chest, clapped him on the back. "Pretty smart for a fifth-grader, aren't you? Soccer star. Ace at English. What can't you do?"

"He can't teach me to kick straight," Katie said.

"Ah-ha. So you're to blame for all the thumping in this house." Bret pulled her close with his free arm. "Family hug."

"But Mommy's not here."

"She's in bed, and that's where you two should be. Hop to it."

Once the room was straightened, potty breaks taken, teeth brushed, and dividing curtain drawn, Bret said bedtime prayers with each of his kids. Kevin thanked the Lord for money to buy soccer portraits. Katie prayed for the neighbor's cat, the one with the ear that "got chewed up in a fight." Bret turned off the overhead light, and in the dark they recited their family motto.

He moved to their window, peeked through the shades.

"What's out there, Daddy?"

That's what Bret wanted to know. Bugs were swarming around the porch light, and swing-set shadows crisscrossed the yard toward the back slope. A whistle sounded again, and moments later the nighttime freight train rumbled by, rattling houses, fences, and carports along Groves Park Road.

No signs of trouble, though. Nobody creeping through the grass.

"Everything's good," he said. "Just keep this window locked, OK?"

"I do, Dad," Kevin said. "Always, I promise. Sometimes it's just easier going that way when I'm playing outside."

Once Bret had assurances that his son would use the back door from now on, he told him to put in his mouth guard, then headed for the master bedroom where he expected to find his wife cuddled up, fast asleep.

But she was not.

"Hi, honey," Sara cooed. "I bet you thought this night was over."

She was reclined on top of their bedspread, showing no signs of the drowsiness that dragged her earlier from the living room. Her silk robe shimmered, and wisps of hair traced the curves of her ears and throat.

Despite the late hour, he was wide awake, his attention riveted on his bride. As he moved toward her, he noticed but didn't question the dazzling new necklace that caught each flutter of candlelight. She was his one and only, and the brilliant blue gemstones only enhanced her beauty.

"Well, hello," he said. "No Mr. Sleepy-Head tonight."

He was a man. Lost in the moment, he suspected no hint of a diversion.

Chapter Nineteen

Sara never meant to deceive her husband. Honesty between them was vital, always had been, and she convinced herself she was simply doing what other wives had done through the ages. She didn't gain an unfair advantage, did she, by using her womanly ways?

Of course not. Male and female were created equal, both made in the image of God, and that meant her husband had strengths of his own.

He was not powerless, after all.

Why, though, did she wait until he was suitably distracted to tell him about the necklace, about Mr. Storinka's extravagant gift? She'd done nothing wrong. In seven years of working with the Ukrainian businessman, she'd never asked for favors, tips, or presents. If the old man wanted to bless her, who was she to tell him no?

And just as Sara hoped, Bret agreed with her every word.

Yes, she should keep the necklace.

Yes, send a thank-you note.

Yes, have it appraised.

No, don't think of selling it, even if it was as expensive as it looked. It was meant as a gift, not some trinket to be pawned off.

Before leaving for Billingsley Coach on Saturday morning, Bret brought her breakfast in bed. Considering their sparse cupboards, the meal was a fine showing from her man of eleven years. She thanked him from her position against the headboard, and he kissed her goodbye.

"Don't you let any of the guys slide by at work today," she told him.

"Not even an inch." He handed her an envelope. "Here's the key to Jason and Zoe's, and the code to their alarm. You'll have thirty seconds to get it right."

"And what if I mess it up?"

"Expect the cops, helicopters, and all sorts of trouble."

"You know me. Trouble with a capital T."

"Sweetheart," he said, "don't remind me. I'll be late if I don't leave now."

Once he was gone Sara set aside the makeshift breakfast tray, a cookie sheet draped with a cloth napkin, and headed to the walk-in closet. She stood before the full-length mirror, admiring the strand of sapphires and the dangling key. She recalled the words that came along with the gift.

Storinka: *"She is the one . . . It is an old man's way to settle things."*

Viktor: *"Do not lose this key. It unlocks more than you know."*

She looped her pinkie through the necklace. The silver key was small and intricate, but hardly worth more than the sapphires. Did it access a safe? Perhaps a safe deposit box? Mr. Storinka didn't have anyone close to him that she knew of, particularly any women, and she flirted with the idea that he owned more jewels such as these, riches hidden away just for her.

But why her? What made her so special?

Storinka: *"You talk with me and listen. A big heart like yours is not easy to find . . . I wish I knew you, yes, many years ago."*

Stop.

This was foolishness to even entertain such thoughts.

Still standing before the mirror, Sara told herself to quit being covetous, to be thankful for the unexpected generosity. It was already enough. More than enough. After going so many years without, she now felt like royalty, and although she would never say it aloud, the jewelry looked good on her, accentuating her face structure and the almond shape of her eyes.

It was an answer to prayer really, a reward for believing even when times turned dark and money stretched thin. Why had she questioned the Lord's ability to fulfill the desires of her heart? Why?

A rush of tears surprised her. They spilled thin and hot down her face.

God, forgive me for ever doubting You.

She thought of Alex Page so many years ago, his confidence, his intimate smile, his financial security. He was guarded about his money and sources of income, but who wouldn't be when millions of dollars were at stake? He never introduced her to his family, worried that they wouldn't accept her and, even worse, wouldn't trust her motives for being with him. Of course, those worries seemed meaningless once his life was stolen away.

How many times had she blamed God for her fiancé's tragedy? Why that flat tire? Why that particular road? How many times had she pondered the life of relative ease she might've had as Mrs. Page?

She turned her thoughts to Bret, faithful, hardworking, young at heart. The strain of daily survival never seemed to let them go, yet he marched onward with her, pulling that burden for the sake of their family.

Thank You for such a good man. And for two sweet kids.

If, in fact, more gifts came from the hand of her Ukrainian patient, she decided she would decline them, politely but firmly. Here in this home, within these 1,400 square feet, she already had her true treasures.

"You look pretty, Mommy. I like your necklace."

"Morning, Katie." Sara placed a hand over the strand and turned to her daughter in the bedroom doorway. "What're you doing up so early?"

"We have to go feed the doggie."

"Not for another hour or two. What about your brother? Is he awake?"

Katie's chin moved up and down. "Uh-huh."

"Maybe we'll leave early then. Miss Zoe said we can help our-selves to whatever's left in their fridge." Sara hadn't grown up using "Miss" before a first name, but in the South, children used it while referring to an adult female friend. Sara, liking its tone of respect, had adopted the term around her kids. She added, "The food will go bad otherwise, so maybe we should make a big brunch while we're over there. How does that sound for my hungry little cutie-pies?"

"I'm not little," Kevin said, edging in past his sister.

"Of course not." Sara slugged his arm in the same good-natured way he did with his teammates, but it drew only a scowl. Had she hit him too hard? Too soft? She said, "Don't worry, Kev. Moms call their boys 'little' even when they're six feet tall and two hundred pounds."

"I'll never be six feet."

"You have your dad's genes, so you never know."

"You think so?"

"Absolutely. Now go get dressed and brush your teeth, both of you. The Vreeland Express leaves for the Billingsleys in approximately fifteen minutes. Dad took the hatchback, which means we're the ones who get to travel in style."

That was enough to hurry the kids from the room. Sara locked the bedroom door so she could get dressed, and faced the mirror, examining herself again from various angles.

By the light of day, the necklace looked almost gaudy next to her robe. She realized what she wanted now, what she needed, were shoes and a dress to match. Oh, she could already envision it. Best to save up and do it right. If she skimmed from her paycheck over the next year, she might just be able to afford something worthy of these sapphires.

"Ouch."

One of her hairs was tangled in the strand. She jerked it free.

After unclasping the necklace, she hid it away in her hoodie in the closet. It slithered from her fingers and curled up beside the 3 × 5 of her former fiancé, the photo she had put back here after finding it on Bret's nightstand.

She now eased it into view.

Wasn't it time to let go, twelve years after the fact? Wasn't that the lesson of these jewels? She could trust that God, by His grace, was working all things together for good, guiding her life around the obstacles and heartache.

Do it, Sara. Let it go.

She gripped the picture, began to tear at its edges, but her vision blurred behind another onrush of prickly hot tears. She swiped them from her cheeks, traced her fingers over Alex's face, and tightened her grip.

Do it.

She couldn't, though. Simply couldn't.

Sara touched his face again and wedged the photo back next to the necklace.

"You dressed yet?" her son called from the hallway.

"Don't rush me, Kev. Fifteen minutes, like I said."

"Why do you always do that?"

"Do what?"

"Act like you know what I'm gonna say."

"I . . ." Sara sighed. "You're right. That wasn't fair to assume, was it?"

"I was about to say there's a FedEx truck pulling up out front."

Delivery trucks rarely visited Groves Park Road, aside from one stop a week at an elderly widow's down the way. Miss Drake's boxes always bore logos from TV shopping networks, and she took each opportunity to chat with her deliveryman. Sara reminded herself that she and the kids should take cookies to the woman and let her know she was not alone, not forgotten. In fact, this might be a good day for it, once they were done at the Billingsley's Tudor-style home off Franklin Road. Goodness. Talk about a contrast in standards of living.

The doorbell rang.

"I've got it, Mom."

"Wait," she said. She couldn't shake the image of that man watching their place last week. What if the delivery was a trick to get inside the house? "Let me answer this, hon."

"I knew you would say that."

"For the moment, Kevin, I need you to be the man of the house, all right? Will you make sure your sister's not in the living room?"

"OK."

Sara hoped that was a brighter tone in his voice. So hard to tell.

She pulled on casual clothes and a sweatshirt, lifted her hair from under the collar, and hurried down the hall. The kids were in the bathroom, their voices echoing from the tub and tiles. By the time she reached the front entry, the FedEx truck was gone, its gears grinding in the distance.

She opened the door, found an overnight envelope tucked beneath the welcome mat and addressed to her. It came from Mr. Storinka's residence.

A Family's Name

the accuser paces, fidgets, slips uninvited into the mammoth hall, his lips dripping with venom and his eyes with accusation

"explain your presence here" the almighty one demands

he spits out a word, naming a family

"i know them well," says the one, "but you have no authority over them"

"do you think they are loyal to you, unswerving in their devotion?"

the one nods, obvious fondness softening his gaze

"well, why wouldn't they be? they think they need you, but let me put them to the test and we'll see if that loyalty holds"

"you tried such a thing before," the one says

"that was another time, another place, and all the troubles i set in motion only caused your weak and whiny child to go running back to you"

"but you still haven't learned, have you?"

"you think they have? they may bend their knees in adoration, but we both know there is still rot within their hearts"

silence follows, during which the almighty one folds arms as smooth as burnished bronze, as solid as the trunks of sequoia trees

"a test?" the one says at last

"i have things already in place, if you dare give me permission"

"just as before? a trial of misery, poverty, pain?"

"no, no, this time a trial of blessing"

"blessing?" the one's eyes narrow, and he says, "tell me what you have in mind, only remember that their power of choice must not be violated"

the accuser quivers in anticipation and outlines his plan, then, after a pause unfettered by the ticking of clocks, the one gives permission with a sage, somber nod

Chapter Twenty

"TUCK AND ROLL," BOOKMAN SAID. "THE SAME WAY YOU'D DO IN A FIRE."

Still blindfolded, Magnus heard the door open and grunted as he and the briefcase on his lap were shoved from the moving vehicle. He landed hard on his knees, rolled to a stop on the pavement. His hands were cuffed with nylon zip-ties, but he managed to rip away the confounded bit of cloth. Streetlights and passing headlamps blinded him, and he blinked against hazy spots in his vision.

Was the Escalade that now faded into Saturday's dawn the one belonging to his employer and captor? It bore Washington State plates, but that gave him little to go on, and its tag numbers were indistinguishable at this distance.

Who are you, Bookman? What are your stakes in all this?

A city bus blasted its horn, and Magnus crawled to safety on a sidewalk. He sawed loose his cuffs against the curb, rotated his stiff wrists.

Still unsettled by the night-long rocking of the boat and the dissipating chemicals in his system, he wobbled to his feet and gathered up the scuffed briefcase. He groaned. His ribs were sore, maybe cracked. His jaw made a popping sound each time he yawned, which was often, since Thursday was the last time he'd slept, disrupted most of the night by the sense he was being watched.

He steadied himself, looked around. A stone's throw away, white metal legs jutted into an overcast sky, and he realized it was the Seattle Space Needle.

So he was downtown. Very good.

Trivial as this seemed, it provided him some comfort. Now he had his bearings, and at least he hadn't been dumped east of here on some remote logging road in the Cascade Mountain Range.

He checked his pockets, found his cell phone and wallet still in place. His printed e-ticket was there, his ID, and a fresh stack of hundred-dollar bills. Bookman's way of saying sorry.

While the apology was appreciated, it wouldn't heal Magnus's ribs. Bookman talked about Magnus using more patience, more finesse, but apparently he didn't apply those new rules to himself.

At 7:45 A.M. Magnus splashed water on his face and cleaned up in the bathroom of a nearby McDonald's. The waterboy on Bookman's boat had inflicted damage, but aside from a slight split along his lower lip and a bruise at his left temple, which he hid beneath a tuft of hair, Magnus still looked decent. In recognition of this fact, he tipped an imaginary hat at his image in the mirror.

Battered, but still beautiful. A stinking specimen for the ages.

I, Magnus, am strong. And the strong shall survive.

He hailed a taxi outside, slid into the back. The dash clock told him he had a few hours till his flight back to Music City, time enough for a quick side trip. He scrolled through his phone's menu, found the exact address for the driver.

"Tacoma," he told the driver. "South Bell Street."

He settled into his seat and spit-shined his case. He checked his cell, and found a message describing the unfortunate, though not wholly unexpected, passing of Mr. Ivan Storinka.

Dead. Massive heart failure. Yesterday afternoon.

You had it coming, old man.

As the taxi butted into traffic on I-5 South, a truck's horn blared, a sound that triggered Magnus's own memories behind the wheel of an eighteen-wheeler.

In that first year of his failed marriage, he drove long-haul. His wife liked the money, but soon complained he was never home. The more she griped, the more he tried to toughen her up, to instill in her some backbone, yet he could not shut that mouth of hers. Each trip he took, she slipped a little more from his fingers. He used stimulants to keep him alert during the late hours he drove, fudging the numbers in his logbook. He found other stimulation too, in the back of his cab.

What the wifey didn't know wouldn't hurt her.

During the second year, Magnus's extracurricular activities ate away at his finances. Drugs and women did not come cheap.

In early 1997, he met silver-haired Ivan Storinka. He arranged shipments for the Ukrainian, doctored cargo manifests, proved himself handy with fists, knives, and guns. Yes, pain was a teacher he knew quite well, and there were always stubborn men and women who needed additional lessons. In Storinka's line of work, enemies were everywhere, close to home and in distant lands. The old silver fox paid well to eliminate such threats and foster loyalty, and Magnus never turned down a reasonable assignment.

He earned his largest chunk of cash when he killed a man in the spring of '98. It was early evening. He was headed west to Tacoma in his big rig. The sun flared as it sunk into the Pacific, blinding him, or so he claimed, as he barreled down the narrow state route. He told officers he never saw the man alongside the road, the man huddled in silhouette while changing the tire of his Infiniti.

Oh, but he saw him. Aimed for him and ran him down.

Turned him into fresh roadkill.

Magnus Maggart did his time, three years for vehicular homicide, out early on good behavior. Although Storinka never showed at the trial, he made good on his promise and deposited $750,000 in an offshore account. Twenty-six months and eighteen days later, Magnus walked out of prison a free man.

Free. Wealthy. And single.

His wife never visited him in the joint, and she vanished before his release. By his way of thinking, it was good riddance.

"Woman, you've got to be colder if you want to survive."

In the end, of course, even that could not save coldhearted Storinka.

◆◆◆

Magnus exited the taxi three blocks from his actual destination. He strolled the Tacoma sidewalk on this fine Saturday morning, a neighbor without a care. He'd been to the address once before, but this time he came unannounced.

He turned at the American-flag mailbox, which read: *Vreeland.* As he neared the house, he noted the unkempt lawn, the clouds reflecting off the windows of the Oldsmobile in the driveway, the yard gnomes peering from overgrown shrubbery. What was it about those things? He could square off with an armed man, but a knee-high plastic gnome gave him the shivers. Perhaps it was their round, pink cheeks.

Just like his mother's.

He mounted the uneven front steps with his briefcase, ready to stab at the black plastic doorbell.

"Good morning," a voice said. "May I help you?"

"Why, good morning." He turned, chiding himself for failing to spot the woman in the parked car. She poked a head of wispy auburn hair out the driver's door. "I'm sorry to disturb you," he said.

"You caught me just leaving."

"Well, I won't keep you. I was hoping to speak with the man of the house, Mr. Eddie Vreeland."

"Eddie?" The woman was middle-aged, her eyes wide and kind, despite worry lines that spread across her brow. "If I may, what's this concerning? Has he done something wrong?"

Magnus knew intimate details about the senior Mr. Vreeland, culled from local records, newspaper archives, and acquaintances. Eddie was no peach. Oh sure, he gave the appearance of an upright citizen, but he was known to brush shoulders with some unsavory types. Of late, however, it was rumored that he had changed his ways and that Tacoma's finest had lost interest in him.

Which meant one of two things.

Either he was a small-time bookie scared straight, or a big-time crook who avoided suspicion by throwing others in front of the bus.

"Something wrong? Oh no, ma'am." Magnus placed a hand over his heart. "No, it's a minor business matter, that's all. Shouldn't take long."

"He's not here."

"Do you know when he'll be back?"

"I . . ." The corners of her mouth fell. "I wish I did. He's been gone since last night, and I was headed out just now to search for him."

He weighed this revelation against another that still lingered. Yesterday, the delivery boy at the mall described a gray-haired man with a mole above his lip, a detail matching Eddie's description. Was Eddie the one who passed along the library card? And where was he now, after a night away from home?

"Listen to me, rattling on so," Mrs. Vreeland said. "There's no need to make a fuss. Eddie's Eddie. He's a grown man, and he can come and go as he pleases, can't he? Of course he can. But when he says he's shopping at the mall, well then, something just isn't right. That's not normal for him."

"If you want, I can help you search for him."

"How do you propose to do that?" Mrs. Vreeland looked both directions along S. Bell Street. "Unless you parked around the corner, I don't see how—"

"Just around the corner, yes, ma'am."

"I'll look for him myself, but thank you." She settled back into her vehicle and started the engine, no doubt torn between leaving her home unwatched and staying with this hulking stranger on her steps.

"I won't keep you," Magnus said. He drew a paper from his brief-case and trotted past the gnomes. "But if you'd be so kind as to give this to Mr. Vreeland when he gets back. I'll need it filled out before we can get things processed."

Mrs. Vreeland accepted the form. "Life insurance? Is that your line of work, Mr. . . ." She studied the letter head. "Mr. Hart? I'm sorry, but he should've informed you that he's already covered."

"Oh, it's not for him, ma'am. It's for you. He said you were under-insured. What am I thinking? All along I could've been talking to you about this."

"No. No, I think you ought to go. I need to find my husband."

"Is there any chance," Magnus said, "that he went to visit Gabe Stilman?"

"Gabe? Dear Lord, only fifty-seven years old and they find him dead in his place on Lake Meridian. The dear man. Well, yes, it's certainly possible. He was laid to rest just last week, and it shook Eddie up, them being the same age and all. He's visited the gravesite twice already. Yes, you may be right."

"There's more to this story, Mrs. Vreeland. Would you give me a few extra minutes of your time?"

Chapter Twenty-one

THE TEMPTATION WAS THERE. NO DOUBT ABOUT IT.

Bret was on his way home from work, elbow hanging out the window as he sang a worship song he'd written while messing around on his guitar, and all this was going through his mind, his heart flooded with a sense of God's mercy and majesty, when he passed the lottery billboard alongside the interstate.

There, in large, proud numbers: *$5,000,000.*

He saw that string of zeroes and wondered what it would be like to win. He heard guys at Billingsley Coach talk about buying their Powerball tickets. Sometimes they waited till it was "up there," till it was "a good one," rather than settling for a measly seven-figure jackpot.

As if $5,000,000 just wasn't enough. As if they needed a shot at $50,000,000 before deeming it worth their while.

Talk about good old American greed.

And still he couldn't help himself. Boy, he wanted to buy a ticket.

As Bret nursed the Subaru into a Mapco gas station, he spotted the state lottery symbol. It wasn't his reason for stopping. 'Course not. With his paycheck in the bank, he just needed to splash in a few gallons to keep the tank above E.

He stepped over a smear of oil and walked inside. He slid cash through the dip under the Plexiglas.

"Ten on number five," he told the clerk. He'd talked with her before and knew she was Kurdish, one of thousands who came to Nashville to escape Saddam Hussein's tyranny. "How're you today?"

"Hi, Mr. Vreeland."

"Do you ever play?" he said, nodding at the lottery kiosk.

She lifted a finger. "Once a week. You can't win if you don't put in."

"So I've heard. How much for a ticket?"

"It explains it all right there."

"Easy enough. Thanks."

Nearing the kiosk, he thought of those childhood nights when his father's car pulled into the driveway, and his mom, peeking through the living room curtains, told him to hurry to bed. Dad always came in wearing a flannel shirt, stinking of smoke from the casino, his eyes bloodshot and boozy. "Bretski," he would bark, "what're you still doing up?" When his wife asked about the squandered grocery money, he sometimes wept and begged forgiveness. Usually, though, he just stomped back to the car and vanished for another day.

"Did you want to play?" the Kurdish clerk asked.

Bret stared at the computerized screen, shook off those memories and any thought of following in his father's steps, and let the lines of his new song play through his head:

> *"A bed for a king, amongst donkeys and straw . . .*
> *You left heaven behind, and You gave us Your all."*

"Me?" He coughed. "No, I was just checking it out."

He pumped his ten-dollar's worth, glad to see it nudge the needle past the quarter-tank mark, good for a few more days of work. When he slid into the car, a text message from Sara winked at him from his phone on the center console.

Hurry home, hon. Important.

Probably something related to Kevin and Katie.

He rolled down the windows, sucked air from the Nashville humidity, and merged into traffic. He was only ten minutes away. No need to text back.

He continued with his chorus:

"Marched to the cross, like a criminal scorned . . .
You left riches in glory for a crown of thorns."

Hey, maybe he should run this song by Pastor Teman.

"I bow, I bow down, I bow down to the Servant King."

Bret had written dozens of songs, and prayed that someday he might share them with the congregation. Couldn't hurt to ask, right? If you put a guitar in his hands and let him sing in front of five hundred, he felt the expected nerves, but he also felt like a man doing that for which he was created.

Chapter Twenty-two

Sara scrubbed the sink while checking the street from the kitchen window.

Where were her reinforcements? She had texted Bret earlier but heard nothing back. Was he working late this Saturday afternoon? Despite the fact she needed time to change for tonight's coffee and dessert with some friends at the Rileys' place, she had more immediate concerns.

The FedEx envelope, for starters.

Since the start of the day, this had been top priority. The enclosed letter informed her of Mr. Ivan Storinka's death at 1:17 P.M., Friday, September 24, 2010, and requested her attendance during the Tuesday evening reading of the will at his Belle Meade residence. It was signed by Viktor Moroz, the executor of the will. Viktor the housekeeper? The bodyguard?

Intriguing as all this was, the final line took things up another notch.

"Please, Mrs. Vreeland, do not forget your key."

She could scarcely contain her anticipation. She thought of the sapphire necklace, the gift from her former patient, and knew she must have a significant part in his inheritance. Why else would she be summoned?

She debated keeping this a secret from Bret until she was certain, but that seemed even more dishonest than her actions of last night.

And for heaven's sake, why was she dreaming of riches when she hadn't even stopped to mourn? Storinka's death came as no surprise, considering his mounting health complications, but he deserved more than her money-grubbing.

Dear Lord, what's wrong with me?

After the early visit to the Billingsleys', Sara and the kids baked lemon cookies for Miss Drake down the street. The woman squeezed their hands, told them what dears they were. Later, Sara had Kevin and Katie pick up their room while she straightened the house and cleaned the kitchen. It seemed to be some nesting instinct, like those during each of her pregnancies, a sense that new things were about to be birthed and family affairs must be set in order.

She loaded the dishwasher, turned it on, but minutes later it emitted a burning smell. When she opened the door, steam hissed in her face, and she realized the machine wasn't getting any water.

What next?

Well, she thought, *how about new appliances, new carpet, a new home?*

Tuesday night couldn't get here soon enough.

In the meantime, she wondered how single parents did it, working, feeding, carpooling, and all the other things required within a span of twenty-four hours. Those hours formed days that formed weeks, months, and years. She doubted she would have the strength. And hoped she'd never have to find out.

Her day took another turn when she stopped for a late-afternoon break and checked her e-mail. One particular message was anonymous, but its subject line lent it a personal and chilling tone: *"the truth shall set you vree."*

While she wanted to shrug it off as the work of a hacker or a virus, neither of those explained its individualized content. Once more, fear burrowed through her head, causing her earlier hopes of fantastic possibilities to crumble.

Perhaps their recent stalker was aware of that will's contents.

Perhaps he wanted in on the deal.

Or wanted her out.

Still at the window, Sara continued scrubbing the sink with Comet, her wrists bleached white above yellow plastic gloves as she vented frustration on the aluminum surface. She checked the street again. Scrubbed. Checked. When Bret slid into view only minutes later than usual, it felt to her like an hour.

"About time, Mr. Vreeland," she grumbled.

With the Hummer dominating their driveway, he was forced to park the hatchback along the curb. He whistled as he grabbed the mail. He looked happy.

Good for him.

Sara peeled off her gloves, slapped them hard on the counter.

"Daddy's home." Katie's footsteps pounded on the floorboards, louder than seemed possible for a girl who needed a chair to reach the cereal cupboard.

"Tell him hi," Sara said, "and then you and Kev can go play out back, while I have a few minutes alone with your father."

"Are you mad at him?"

"Why would you say that? You know, people in England call being mad being crazy, and if Mom doesn't get time with Dad she just gets a little crazy."

"Like at lunch? When you yelled at Kevin?"

"When I . . . Really? I'm sorry. I shouldn't have done that."

"It's OK." Katie rolled her eyes. "Boys're mean."

"Sometimes, yes. But we can't let that get the best of us." Sara tapped the summer freckles on Katie's nose, accenting each of her words.

She accepted a hug around the waist, watched her daughter skip out the screen door and down the steps. Bret tucked the mail under his arm, swept up their six-year-old, and kissed her forehead. He threw a wink in Sara's direction.

"Where were you, Bret?"

"Had to stay and lock up, what with Jason being gone."

"Don't worry," Katie said, as he set her on the steps. "Mommy's not mad."

"That's good to hear."

"But she says she might go crazy."

"Hmm. Not so good."

Sara dodged her husband's second wink as he entered the house. She shooed Katie through the hall, nabbed Kevin on his way from the bathroom, and aimed them toward the backyard. She made them promise to stay inside the fence, where they could be seen through the window. She nibbled at her fingernail, squared her shoulders, and returned to the living room.

"Why didn't you call or text to let me know where you were?"

"I'm here now," Bret said. "C'mon, what's going on?"

"Oh, the day started well enough. We had a big breakfast over at Jason and Zoe's, fed their dog, and made some cookies for Miss Drake. After that, though, the dishwasher stopped working, just made this hot hissing sound, like it's not getting any water. My fingers are prunes from cleaning, my hair's an absolute disaster, and I'm supposed to be over at the Rileys' in an hour."

"Go," he said. "Get ready. I've got things handled on this end."

"Thanks." She softened a bit. "I also have some good news, I think."

"I'm all ears."

"But first I need your opinion on an e-mail I got this afternoon."

Squeezed between a living-room armchair and the adjoining dining table, the computer station was a black assemble-on-your-own-and-pray-the-diagram-is-accurate deal. It remained visible to all so that Internet access was less likely to be misused, but what it lacked in privacy, it made up for in function. It served not only as a homework desk, snack bar, and multimedia storage shelf, but as a collection center for junk mail, hair scrunchies, Nerf darts, and push pins.

Sara plopped down in the swivel chair, brushed crumbs from the Dell mouse pad. "Honestly, we need to make a rule about no eating at the computer."

"Didn't we try that before?"

"If you enforced it, instead of letting the kids do as they pleased . . ." She paused. "That's not fair of me, honey. It's this e-mail. It has me on edge."

"Anyone you know from your contact list?"

"No, I just have the sender's address. RT4104798@hotmail.com."

"That's not much help. Well, let's see what it says."

As Bret slipped behind her for a better look, she caught whiffs of paint thinner and stale sweat. She was about ready to put her concerns on hold, to tell him to go shower, when he rested his hands on her shoulders and started to massage. His touch was gentle yet firm, kneading the tension from her muscles. She leaned back into him, sighed. Perhaps her fears were for naught.

Bret froze.

"Don't stop, hon. That was perfect."

"The kids," he said. "Let's get them inside."

And with those words, he validated the worst of her fears.

"This e-mail's gotta be from that same guy, and he knows where we live. I'm calling Metro police," Bret said. "If they won't do something about this, I will."

Chapter Twenty-three

Bᴿᴱᵀ ᵀᴿᴵᴱᴰ ᴵᵀ ᵀᴴᴱ ᴼᴸᴰ-ꜰᴬˢʜᴵᴼNᴱᴰ ᵂᴬʸ. Hᴱ ˢᴬᵀ ᴬᵀ ᵀʜᴱ ᶜᴼᴹᴾᵁᵀᴱᴿ ˢᵀᴬᵀᴵᴼN, thumbing through a Nashville phonebook. When he turned to the government blue pages, the book flopped from his lap and landed on his foot. He made another attempt, found a list of police-related numbers.

He dialed the first and got a recording.

Tried the second. Another recording.

He bit his lip, tapped the cell phone against his forehead.

"Nothing?" Sara said.

"Maybe they take weekends off."

"As if criminals take weekends off. Keep trying. I already called Jeannie Riley and told her I won't be making it out there tonight. She sounded disappointed, but that'll give the ladies more to talk about. They can sit around and judge my lack of commitment, add it to the list of my obvious shortcomings."

"You think that's really the way they are?"

"I know it is," Sara said. "I've been to these functions before, and I'm telling you, the gossip's so thick you could stir it with a telephone pole."

Bret ran his finger down the next column of police numbers, seeking the best option. No wonder 9-1-1 got overworked. At least a real person answered, which was rare nowadays. That old phrase about the customer always being right had led to spoiled consumers who vented at service agents who in turn waved the white flag and let digitized voices and people in India take over.

And that, as he told his kids, was why it paid to be nice.

"Dad, what about TBI?" Kevin sat cross-legged on the living room carpet. He and his sister were playing Battleship with the old-school plastic units. "Did you know their HQ is right here in Nashville?"

"At this point, that's probably not necessary. Look, this might work."

Bret dialed Metro's Investigative Services and heard it ring three, four, five times. The automated messages usually kicked in on the second ring, so this was a glimmer of hope. It might be an actual phone on an actual desk, where a living, breathing person filed reports and sipped coffee.

Six. Seven. Eight.

Bret tapped the cell against his head, harder this time, and doubted his own advice. Being nice? It often meant getting left behind, run over, taken advantage of, ignored, treated like dirt, and—

"Metro Police. Detective Meade speaking."

"A real person. Finally."

"Real as can be." The detective's tone was droll. "I hope you're my excuse to take a break from filing reports. What I really need is a cup of coffee, something strong enough to curl a few more hairs."

Bret grinned. "I know what you mean, about the coffee anyway."

"It's my own fault," Meade said, as though discussing this with an old acquaintance. "I usually grab a drink on my way in, over at Black's Espresso, great place if you've never been there. But I didn't leave myself enough time this morning."

"This is Investigative Services, right?"

"Yes, it is."

"OK," Bret said. "I get it, Detective. You're trying to put me at ease, and I appreciate that, but right now I'm worried about my family and just need to know if I called the right department."

"Let's start with your name and address, sir. If I can't help, I'll connect you to someone who can. None of that phone-tag stuff. Sound fair enough to you?"

"Thank you, yes."

"Name?"

"Bret Vreeland. That's with a V. My wife's Sara, and we live on Groves Park Road over in East Nashville. It's normally pretty quiet on our street."

"You have a family, you said."

"Two kids. Boy and a girl."

"I have a daughter of my own, Mr. Vreeland, going into sixth grade now." Again, the conversational tone. "Hard not to worry about them, isn't it? Tell me what's got your feelers up."

"I think we're being watched."

"Watched?"

"A few nights ago, a man parked outside our house just eyeing the place. The next day he was there again, or maybe he never left, sitting down the street in his black Dodge Charger, one of those two-thousand-tens with the Hemi."

"The V-eight? Nice."

"Not when it's staring you down all morning."

"What morning was this?"

"Week ago last Saturday."

"Did you happen to get the tag numbers? I can run them and see if he has any priors, warrants, anything that might give cause for concern."

"We tried," Bret said. "But we never got a look at the back of the car."

"Did you recognize this individual? Could you identify him?"

"Maybe. Big guy, mustache, but he wore a baseball cap down low where we couldn't see his face. He'd still be sitting out there if I hadn't confronted him."

"Confrontation is not something we advise."

"He wasn't gonna leave any other way."

"I know where you're coming from." Detective Meade cleared his throat. "Fact is, though, even in a residential neighborhood, the roads are public access, and only a restraining order would bar him from parking along your curb. Did he say or do anything threatening?"

"Besides watching our every move?" Bret skipped the bit about the class ring, realizing how sketchy that part would sound. "Listen, I'm not gonna let just any old clown prowl around my property, not when I have a family to protect."

"Let's think through the options here. Does your wife have an ex?"

"No."

"You have any enemies at work?"

"No."

"School? Church?"

"Church?"

"Have you watched the news lately?"

"I'm not naïve," Bret said. "It's just our congregation's a pretty relaxed bunch. The whole idea, well, it's almost comical, if you know what I mean."

"School?"

"My son, he goes to Bailey Middle where he's been getting harassed by some of the boys, but I doubt there's any connection."

"Mr. Vreeland, not to downplay your concerns, but you're not giving me much to work with here. Is it possible last Saturday was an isolated incident? Have you seen this fellow with the mustache since?"

Bret cupped a hand over the phone, turned to Sara who was on the couch with arms wrapped around herself. "Any signs of that guy in the Charger again?"

She shook her head. "But honestly," she said, "I'm not sure I'd recognize him, especially in a different vehicle."

"No," he told the detective.

"Of course, he could've shaved the facial hair," Meade said. "Or for that matter, the mustache might've been a fake all along."

"Which is why we didn't call earlier." Bret wiggled the cursor over the message on the computer, hit Print, watched a sheet of paper scroll from the printer. "Today, though, my wife got this e-mail full of strange references and threats. Anonymous, of course. Through Hotmail, which means it could be bogus. The sender's not anyone from her contact list, and there's nothing we can pick out as obvious clues from the address itself. RT4104798@hotmail.com."

"The initials don't match those of anyone you can think of?"

"Not offhand."

"The seven digits, they could be a phone number."

"I tried it just before I called you. Some teenage girl named Rachel something-or-other, working at Sonic." Bret rolled his neck. "What about the IP address? Is there a way to track down where it came from?"

"Could be time-consuming, if the sender made any effort to redirect it."

"And if not?"

"Sure, an IP address could help. Once I've heard the contents of this message, I'll know better how to proceed. Now if you would be so kind, Mr. Vreeland. Otherwise, I have work to do."

"Filing papers?"

"Takes longer than it does on the TV shows."

"So here it is." Bret steeled his voice, gulping down anger and fear as his gaze ran over the text he was about to read aloud.

> *Oh, Sara, all alone . . .*
>
> *But you're not alone, are you? Not anymore. Don't think for a minute I don't know that. No matter how painful your past, you've taken on a husband and small children. So tell me, how deep is your love for him? How strong is that family bond?*
>
> *Everyone has their price, and everything comes at a cost. How much are you willing to pay? Don't make the mistake of thinking you'll get the truth for vree.*

After delivering the words in a monotone, he said, "And that's it, Detective. There's no signature, no fancy lettering. Except he spelled that last word with a V, like our family name."

"And we know it's a 'he' how?"

"I guess we don't. Just figured it must be, considering the other stuff that's gone on around here."

The detective's silence left Bret shifting in the desk chair. Metro probably got wacky calls every day, paranoid nut-jobs who saw demons under bushes and killers lurking in the broom closets. When Bret first read the e-mail over Sara's shoulder, it pumped cold dread through his limbs, but reading it aloud to an officer of the law made it seem melodramatic if not downright hokey.

Like something from the suspense novel he was reading, or a scene from a late-night, made-for-TV thriller. Or long-lost evidence from the Zodiac case.

Well, there you go. That case was the real deal, an unsolved mystery, which meant his concerns weren't so far-fetched. There were actual sociopaths in this world, always had been. Blame it on nature. Blame it on nurture. Since the days of Cain and Abel, sinful human *nature* had *nurtured* more of the same.

Detective Meade was talking. "We don't know yet if this e-mail is someone's idea of a joke, but now I understand your concerns as a father and as a husband. Our families mean everything to us, don't they?"

"That's a fact."

Sara looked up from the couch.

"I'll put in a request," Meade said, "for more patrols in your neighborhood. Ramp up the police presence, and that alone might scare off any pranksters."

"I appreciate that. My wife does too."

"What?" Sara mouthed.

"Extra patrols," he whispered.

"But try something for me, if you will, Mr. Vreeland. You still have that e-mail up? All right then, you see a small box in the right corner, on the same level as the sender's address? Click on that Reply button and it should drop down a menu. You tracking with me here?"

"I think so." Bret followed the instructions. "Yeah, I'm at the menu."

"You should see a 'view message source' option. That'll open a box with all sorts of garbled numbers and code. In there, you'll find something that says 'received from,' followed by seven or eight numbers broken up with periods. Have I lost you yet? Stop me if I'm going too fast."

"I'm good. Yep, here it is."

"Now highlight and copy those numbers, then go to IP2location. com and paste them in the search window. You'll find out the country, state, city, even the service provider the e-mail was sent from."

Bret followed instructions and tapped the Search button. He was amazed at the simplicity of the maneuver, all this info only seconds, only clicks away. Then his eyes widened. His throat tightened. Although the details on the screen eased his immediate worries, they stirred up other troubling suspicions.

Who was behind this? Was his dad involved?

Enough, Bret. Don't go there.

"You still tracking with me?" Detective Meade wanted to know.

"Yeah, I . . . it's all right here in front of me."

Sara slid over from the couch. She rested a hand on his arm, and shot him a look when he flinched. "What is it, hon? What's wrong?"

Meade said, "What are you seeing there on the screen?"

"The message, it . . ." Bret shifted in his chair. "It came from Tacoma, Washington. From the city library."

"A public-access computer, most likely, which makes it nigh-near impossible to pinpoint the responsible party. But now you know that it was sent from thousands of miles away. That should give you some level of peace."

Bret grunted, unable to trust his own voice.

Sara pressed her ear next to his against the phone.

"Unless," the detective added, "you know someone in that region."

"I grew up there," Sara said. "Both of us did."

"Hello, Mrs. Vreeland."

"Hi, Detective. We've been meaning to fly back and visit our relatives ever since we moved out here, but with the price of airfare these days and time off work and all, well, it simply hasn't happened."

"I'm sure they understand. As for the e-mail," Meade said, "it could be some old friend of yours giving you a hard time, maybe some-one you went to school with. I'll still send a patrol car through your area, just to ease your minds. Overall, though, I don't see much reason for Metro to pursue this any further."

Chapter Twenty-four

SARA AND BRET THANKED THE DETECTIVE FOR HIS TIME AND DISCONNECTED the call. Sara turned, catching the concentration on her husband's face. Clearly these events unnerved him. He liked answers. Options. Solutions.

During the call, her initial concerns about the threatening message gave way to admiration for this man at her side. He was always there for her, offering comfort and rising to her defense.

In sickness and in health.

Through every step of Kevin's sleep therapy, not to mention the bills.

For richer or poorer.

Mostly poorer.

She now allowed herself to hope that all of it was about to change, some relief at last from their burdens, a reprieve from their stress. It was just the sort of thing God would do in answer to her years of prayer.

She nudged Bret's shoulder, gave him a half-smile.

"What?" he asked. "What is it?"

Her smile widened.

"Should I be worried?" he said.

"If you recall, when you got home I told you I also had some good news." She waved the FedEx envelope into view. "This came this morning, letting me know that one of my patients died yesterday. "You remember Mr. Storinka, the one who gave me the necklace?"

"Yeah, but how is that good news?"

"It's not." Sara sagged back onto the couch. Throughout the day she had avoided facing this alone, but with her husband now by her side she accepted the full weight and finality of Storinka's passing. Tears brimmed in her eyes. "I was with him only hours beforehand," she said. "I took over some supplies. He was a lonely man in this amazing old mansion, but always kind to me. He seemed to carry a lot of guilt, and I tried to share with him God's forgiveness, tried to. . . . Oh, Bret, I had no idea that was the last time I'd see him."

He knelt beside her, clutched her hands in his.

She squared her shoulders. "I should've said more to him."

"Least you tried, right?"

"He wasn't interested. He told me not to worry since he'd already found 'a way to settle things.' Those were his words."

"And this was only hours before he was gone?"

"Yes, that's the odd part about it. Obviously his dying isn't good news, and I feel awful for even getting my hopes up, but it's only natural, don't you think? Considering how tight things've been for us?"

He let go of her hands. "You lost me. What're you saying, sweetie?"

"Here. See for yourself."

"The death certificate?"

"Read what it says." She pulled the one-page letter from the envelope. "And please, Bret, if I'm being silly about this, don't try to soften the blow. Shame on me for even letting my mind wander."

He perused each line. "OK, now my mind's wandering too."

"While I was out there, I met Viktor in person. He's the executor, the one who signed that letter and divvies out the estate according to Mr. Storinka's wishes. Why would he request my presence at the reading of the will, unless—?"

"Hold it, Sara. Playing the what-if game could get us in trouble."

"Honey, this could be big for us. For the kids."

"Don't get too caught up in it. You were only his therapist, after all. If he left you anything, it's probably something small, some trinket he knew you liked."

"That's just it, honey. That necklace, the one I wore last night, it's the key to his safe. I'm fairly certain of it anyway. From the get-go I had this feeling, and I suppose I should've told you more about it when you weren't so distracted, but I needed you to agree to me keeping it. Don't you see now? It was no accident. He gave it to me. I hold the key."

Chapter Twenty-five

"WHAT A SWELL DAY," MAGNUS SAID.

He had arrived the previous evening at Nashville Int'l Airport, and this early Sunday morning he stood in striped green and black boxers at his Germantown apartment window, appreciating the view of Music City.

Bicentennial Mall Park rolled out carpets of emerald grass and budding flowers toward Capitol Hill, where the state capitol gazed upon skyscrapers, honky-tonks, upscale lofts, and symphony halls. In the distance, somber church bells clanged for religious busybodies with pious faces, a stern contrast to the cheery waltz of the sun into a clear blue sky.

By Magnus's way of thinking it was one more hypocrisy that those who believed in a creator were the last to celebrate and protect the fragile ecosystem. While they put their hopes in the hereafter, more useful individuals dedicated themselves to prolonging life in the here and now.

As he swiveled toward the breakfast bar, ready for his protein shake, his left leg buckled. He braced himself against the glass, and took stock of his injuries. The soreness only made him chuckle.

"Oh, it's a swell day, all right. A little swelling in the ribs, above the eye, and in my knees."

He felt no ill will toward Bookman for this. In fact, he respected his current employer even more for his craftiness, for protecting his assets and checking on his investments.

A few years back, Magnus had parted ways with Storinka for the very reason that the old Ukrainian had turned soft, becoming like many

Americans who relied on the basic goodness of their fellow man, on some naïve sentiment birthed from puritanical ideals. Paradoxically, the same people lived in perpetual fear, news junkies using the world's travails as an excuse to hide away, gobble up sugars and nitrates, and pray for escape in the glorious Rapture.

Good luck with that.

Magnus wished that the Bible thumpers would, in fact, find their stairway to heaven. While they hoped in something that did not exist, the strong prowled the streets and took their places in seats of power.

He reached for his shake, took gulps of the gritty sludge. His thoughts turned to Eddie Vreeland.

Eddie was a former alcoholic, former bookie, former lawbreaker. Magnus and Eddie had crossed paths in years past, in the way two-bit players often did, taking handoffs from each other, making payouts under the table. What now, though? Was Eddie a man with actual juice? Or just a washed-up, strung-out has-been? Had he arranged the delivery of Gabe Stilman's library card as a warning? Be careful or you'll end up dead like dear Gabe.

Either way, the fact that Eddie knew to find Magnus at the Tacoma Mall implied he was linked to Bookman.

Again, the obvious question. Who was Bookman?

Magnus had run out of time before his departure on Saturday, unable to find and question Eddie. Instead, on the flight home, Magnus checked his phone for the latest online information and found a *Seattle Post-Intelligencer* article about the discovery of Mr. Stilman's body in his lakeside home in Kent.

Visible blunt-force trauma. A missing portable safe.

No signs of forced entry.

The authorities listed no suspects or persons of interest, but Eddie's name was sure to pop up at some point. Eddie and Gabe were shady individuals with a shared history, and early on Magnus guessed that blackmail between them was a probability.

Eddie might've said: "You make payments on my boat, and your old lady'll never know about that woman you got tucked away in Olympia."

Gabe might've thrown back: "Who cares about the statute of limitations? Those douche-bag Tacoma cops get one look at a certain missing security tape and they'll be stuck to you like glue. You'd best step up when I need an errand boy."

All things considered, Eddie seemed a likely murder suspect.

Magnus stepped into a pair of jeans. He loaded .45 ACP ammo into his Kimber, pushed it into his waistband, covered it with a Vanderbilt Commodores T-shirt. Go 'Dores. Supporting the local teams was one way to curry favor.

He grabbed the keys to the Charger, and padded down the outside stairs to his locked garage. Ten minutes later he prowled the streets near Riverside Village, waiting for Sip Café to open its doors. Since Bookman had temporarily limited his tactics with the Vreelands, Magnus would use his testosterone to pursue prey of a different sort.

Hazel Eyes, to be exact. Dear Natalie.

She arrived a half hour early, parked and locked up her Vespa behind the building. He pulled in behind her, but she didn't turn. She wore an iPod on her purple belt, ear buds running up into her '70s-style flower-power helmet. Clearly she didn't hear him, and this lack of caution disappointed him.

Strike one.

He rolled down his window now, and gunned the big V8. In nature, some predators attacked before giving even a hint of their presence, while others fed off their victims' fears, teasing and toying with them. Though he'd been known to use both tactics, he preferred the latter.

When Natalie shook her hair free from the helmet and turned his way, a half-smile tugged at her lips.

"I was wondering when you'd notice," he said, turning off the engine.

"How ya doin', Teddy? That your car?"

Teddy was the name he'd given her, one that sounded less threatening. Just one big teddy bear. So huggable, squeezable. "You like it?" he said. "I hope you're not going to ask for a ride, since that would be so cliché."

"Just nice to know you can take care of yourself, that's all. Not always the case with some of the guys I meet. 'Course, you could always catch a ride on my moped, but being as big as you are, your knuckles might drag the pavement."

"I'll stick with the car, thanks."

She rested her helmet on her hip. "Aren't you early?"

"I can wait till you're open," he said. "I won't get in the way of your work."

"I was talking about Wednesday, dingbat."

"Our date, you mean."

"So," she said, "it's a date now, huh?"

"Me, man. You, woman. Dinner together sounds like a date to me."

"Si, no problemo. Just wanted to hear you say it. Heck, if it wouldn't land me in hot water with my bosses, I would let you come in right now and I'd put you to work." She nodded at the café's rear entrance.

Strike two.

"You know, you ought to be more careful."

"I'm not dumb, Teddy. I do keep my eyes open. Some guys, I wouldn't let them get within ten feet of me before pulling out my pepper spray. One squirt of that stuff, and they'd be whimpering on their knees."

"Like I said, I won't get in your way."

"Here's a little hint for you. Today's first customer through the door gets a free cup of coffee, just to make sure it tastes good." Keys in hand, Natalie pivoted toward the café's back patio and shot Magnus one last look over her shoulder.

Strike three.

It was her fault their date would be canceled, her fault she would suffer. Not only was she careless, she was flirtatious. Even after she stepped inside, he could not shake the image of those seductive hazel eyes sparkling above her nose stud. How foolish of him to believe she might save herself for only him. He couldn't have her running around with other guys now, could he?

No, Magnus Maggart settled for nothing less than full ownership.

"We work for power, companionship, freedom. Which is it for you?"

All three, he decided. But on his own non-negotiable terms.

He climbed from the Charger, glanced around the empty back lot, slid his hand along his waist. The pistol was there, loaded and ready to go. The lot was empty, the streets quiet on this early Sunday morn.

Time to nab himself a captive.

If he played this right, the Vreelands would still get the message loud and clear that he was near, he was watching, and he would not be denied.

Chapter Twenty-six

"Pastor?" Bret caught the shorter, stouter man in the church parking lot. "Can I talk to you for a minute?"

"Bret, you're still here. Where's your car?"

"Our rust bucket? Home getting a much-deserved break."

Morning service was over, the sun blazed overhead, and Eli's camper-pickup huddled beneath a cottonwood tree. The lot had already emptied, but that was no surprise with NFL football underway. Many Southerners, men and women alike, treated it like a religion. Wear your colors, drop your cash into the coffers, and hope the wayward super-stars found redemption come playoff time.

The Tennessee Titans usually did battle at LP Field along the banks of the Cumberland River, but today was an away game against the New York Giants. Bret thought of his own high school exploits on the gridiron. Later he might call his parents, but the broadcast would provide an escape from his questions and suspicion, not to mention his curiosity about Mr. Storinka's will.

"Listen," Pastor Teman said, "if you need a lift home, I'm happy to help."

"Appreciate it, but I'm good."

"You sure? That's a bit of a walk, isn't it?"

Bret heard an engine, and he grinned. "Who said anything about walking?"

Pastor arched a bushy eyebrow that matched his thatch of jet-black hair. He rubbed his tummy, maybe to assure it that lunch wasn't far off, and said, "I get the distinct impression there's a punch line on the way."

"And here it comes."

The engine revved, and Bret watched Sara swing the Billingsleys' vehicle around the building. She wore large white-framed shades that looked fantastic on her, despite being eight-dollar fashion rejects from a nearby truck stop. She had her own touch of class that made even cheap look chic.

How she did it, Bret did not know. But he wasn't complaining.

"Good gravy," Pastor said. "I guess you do have a ride home."

"Yeah, we parked it in back to avoid attention."

"It's bright yellow."

"Hard to miss, huh?"

The man raised a hand in greeting as Sara pulled alongside with the kids buckled up in the backseat. "She sure looks happy up there behind the wheel."

"I won't be able to pry her fingers loose."

The pastor laughed.

Sara powered down the window. "Good word today, Pastor."

"The question being, will anyone remember it next week? That's always the true test."

"Some of us will. I mean, I don't remember what I ate for dinner three nights ago, but it sustained me for another day."

"See," Bret said, "she's the brains of this operation."

"Not that there was ever any doubt."

That made Sara smile. "I'll let you men finish talking."

The window went back up, resealing her and the kids in cool luxury. Against the glass, Katie puckered her lips and puffed her cheeks, crossing her blue eyes in an attempt for a laugh. Bret responded with a wink.

"So." Pastor Teman gestured at the Hummer. "Who won the lottery?"

"Not us. We're just borrowing this thing. Being real honest, I did almost buy a ticket yesterday, but just couldn't do it. Of course, the irony is that the more we need the money, the less we can afford to play."

"Who can? Like God's Word tells us, 'Wealth from get-rich-quick schemes quickly disappears; wealth from hard work grows over time.'"

"Proverbs thirteen, verse eleven," Bret said.

"You know your Bible better than most."

"All I know is Sara's loving that AC."

"And why not? It's one thing," the pastor said, "to chase after riches, but good gravy, there's certainly nothing wrong with enjoying the good things in life."

"Like gravy?"

The man seemed perplexed.

"Yeah, uh, biscuits and gravy," Bret said. "Mm-mmm."

"I'm more a butter-and-grits man myself. What I mean to say is that food, clothes, cars, all of them are gifts the Lord loves to lavish upon His people."

Bret imagined God on the Hummer assembly line, snapping the vehicles together like children's toys. He kept that thought to himself, thinking it might sound disrespectful. For him, though, it wasn't. He loved serving a God who made Himself known, who had walked the earth as a man, wiped sweat from His brow, and pulled slivers from His fingers. Bret could relate to that.

"Your family's waiting," Pastor said. "I don't want to keep you, brother, but you did say you had something to talk to me about."

"Just a little thing."

The pastor was rubbing his stomach again. "Nothing's too little."

"Yeah." Bret tried not to stare.

"And I'll admit, some things aren't little enough."

"Huh?"

"My weight, for example. Trust me, it's an issue I'm working on, since the Lord won't let me slide when it comes to my health and eating patterns. There now, that's out in the open. Confession is good for the soul. So tell me what's weighing on. . . . Let me rephrase that. What's pressing on your thoughts?"

"I wrote a song."

"Good to hear. You're quite the guitar player."

"Thanks. I've been putting together a collection. Mostly worship stuff, lyrics based on Scripture. I don't really talk about it much." Bret looked off over the man's head. Since when did he get nervous in a one-on-one situation? He plucked a sleeved CD from his shirt pocket and forged on. "OK, I know I sound like a cliché, being here in Music City where every other person thinks they got a hit record in them. Well, not a record, I guess. Maybe a CD. Or MP3. Anyway, you get my point. But I did it anyway, burned a copy of the song."

"And more power to ya."

"If you'd at least listen to it." Bret handed it over.

"I've always admired your passion. This city does have its share of wannabe superstars, but I've never seen you attach ego to your music."

"I try not to. I just want to inspire and challenge people, to peel back the blinders and let them see God's presence all around them." He hooked his thumbs into his jeans. "So that's it, that's what I wanted to talk to you about. Sara says it's wrong to bury my talents, that I've gotta bring them into the open and let them multiply. Like in the parable. So I'm trying to step out here. Not that I have to explain the principle to you. Being a pastor, you know what I'm talking about."

"I do, indeed."

"If it fits in one of these Sundays, I could even sing it for the congregation."

"Great, Bret. I love to hear your heart."

"Is that a yes, then?"

"It's . . . Not exactly. With nearly seven hundred people in attendance at Sunday service, we do get multiple requests like yours. There's a procedure, a process, submitting the lyrics, getting the song screened in advance. That all runs through the Rileys, since they oversee our music ministries."

"Sure. That makes sense."

"As you pointed out, this is Nashville," Pastor Teman wore a wry smile, "where trick-or-treaters get demo CDs in their candy bags, and every other person in Starbucks plays on a worship team or an up-and-coming band."

"So it's a no."

"I'm saying you need to go through the proper channels."

"Got it. OK."

"And if it is a no," Pastor said, shaking the CD, "God is still pleased to hear the praises of your heart. There's nothing that means more to Him."

Bret nodded, convinced of the same thing.

So why do I feel shoved aside?

"Quick question," he said. "Someone left us a gift certificate over at Sip."

"I steer wide of their ice cream. Fleeing temptation, you might say."

"We all have our areas, right? Our family, we love stopping in there, so we wondered if you were the one who left the gift."

"Wasn't me. But trust me, brother, I know things've been tight for you and yours, and Rhonda and I keep you in our prayers. We had our struggles early on, same as most newlyweds, but God is faithful, isn't He?"

"We're not exactly newlyweds anymore. We have eleven years under our belts, and it'd just be nice to get some breathing room. You know what I mean?"

"I do. Tell me, how're things at work?"

From the Hummer's cab, Sara met Bret's eyes, and he knew she read the tension on his face. Her window inched down.

He kept his tone even and answered the pastor's question. "Am I showing up, earning a paycheck? Yes, I am. Am I a hard worker? My boss, he'd have to answer that, but I do my work as unto the Lord. Have I got a raise in the last couple years? I've asked a number of times, done everything but begged, but it's just not happening in this current economy."

Pastor Teman cupped Bret's arm. "Understand, my job is to watch over my flock, and obedient sheep rarely have trouble finding the trough."

"The trough?"

"I must ask." A pause. "Are you being faithful in your giving?"

"You should know," Sara cut in, eyes intense and glowing, "that my husband is the last person to think of himself. He goes above and beyond."

"I mean no offense, Mrs. Vreeland."

"None taken. I'm simply setting the record straight. Whether it's tithes, offerings, missions, he gives faithfully and generously. Half the guys down at Nashville Rescue Mission are wearing stuff he's donated, and I doubt he has more than five or six shirts in his own closet."

"Sara," Bret said.

"He needs to know. It's not like we throw our hard-earned money at frivolous things. We live on a tight budget, rice and beans, and generic brands."

"As your shepherd, I was only asking," Pastor Teman said.

Bret slipped free of the pastor's hand. "Listen, I know it's rough taking on the burdens of so many people. I've got a lot on my own plate just providing for a household of four. Seriously, thanks for your work around here."

"Rhonda and I are glad to do it. This flock is our family."

"Yep, well, as long as we don't forget who the Good Shepherd is, I think we'll all be OK. Speaking of family, we're gonna head home now. Thanks again."

Bret uttered a farewell, climbed in next to his wife, and fixed his gaze straight ahead. Kevin and Katie, seeming to recognize his mood, kept quiet in the back, but Sara cast him a sideways look as they edged onto the street.

"Tell me what you're thinking, honey."

"It just gets old, being judged by the size of my wallet. Gets real old."

"Did he give you the usual runaround about your song?"

"Maybe I'm being prideful, Sara. Do you think that's what's going on here? If it's all about me, I don't wanna be the one who's—"

"That's not at all what I think. And you know, things could be changing for us come Tuesday night." She turned onto Stratford Avenue. "You, Bret, are a gifted man, and it's only natural, or I should say spiritual, that you want to give birth to this dream God's given you."

"A man giving birth?" He tilted his chin. "You lost me with your metaphor."

She grinned, "You are such a dork."

"A pregnant dork, don't forget."

When she slapped his chest, he caught her hand and gave it a kiss.

"Pardon the metaphor," she said. "Yes, you're big and tough, but if you don't give birth to this thing soon, if you're told not to push, it's going to end up stillborn or deformed. I don't want that to happen to you. You are full of God's Spirit."

He kissed her fingertips.

"I only wish," she added, "others would recognize that too."

"Hey, you do. And that's what matters."

At the junction of Stratford and Porter Road just ahead, noonday sunlight glanced off a polished black chassis and curved glass. It was a Dodge Charger.

Bret jerked upright, broad shoulder straining against the seat belt. "Sara."

"I see it. Dear Jesus," she cried out, "what are we supposed to do?"

"Go after him. Now. Go, go, go."

Chapter Twenty-seven

Sara Vreeland was driving. Magnus tipped his cap and smirked, well aware of this woman's law-abiding, toe-the-line attitude. 57 mph in a 55 zone? That was her version of walking on the wild side.

He flashed through the intersection, checked his rearview, and wondered if the Vreelands had got a good look at him.

The Hummer pulled in behind him.

The bright yellow of that military-vehicle-turned-suburban-status-symbol stirred an old contempt in his gut. Civilians. These oh, so civil villains, were nothing but moochers and posers in a land paid for by the blood of U.S. troops. He'd done his own time in Bosnia, in early '96, keeping the peace among gun-toting towel-heads. Most people had no idea what that meant.

Despite his disdain, Magnus focused on more pressing concerns.

First: his license plate.

Its numbers could lead to the Germantown rental, forcing him to relocate. He hit his brakes and peeled the tires, sending up plumes of black smoke.

Second: his hazel-eyed darling.

Although Natalie's disappearance would be noted soon enough, he didn't want his movements backtracked to her location in the nearby Quonset hut. He had staked out the site in previous weeks and knew it to be abandoned since the May flood, but the convenient location could turn decidedly inconvenient if she were found.

"Very well," he said, casting another glance at the mirror. "Let's race."

He shifted gears, stomped down on the gas pedal, felt the Charger shove him back in his seat. His pulse throbbed in his fingers on the wheel. The car tore west on Porter Road, screeched hard to the left at Riverside Drive, and rocketed to 60 mph, widening the gap between it and the Hummer.

He laughed, "Come on, Soccer Mom. Show me what you've got."

Chapter Twenty-eight

"Mommy," Katie said, "you're scaring me."

Sara was scaring herself. This vehicle was unfamiliar to her, and even though its wide wheel-base gave solid traction, she felt precarious propped this high above the pavement. Not to mention that her heeled shoe hovering between the gas and brake was all wrong for this task.

"Don't back off now," Bret said. "I need the rest of that license number."

"It's KSW-something."

"There was also an eight, I think."

"An eight?" She picked up speed on the straightaway. "It was hard to tell through all that smoke, but I thought it was a six."

"Mommy, please."

Katie's voice, so warm and tender, roused mixed emotions in Sara's breast. She was an angry mama bear, ready to do anything to protect her little ones. She was also cautious, willing to be ridiculed for her slow-poke ways if it meant safeguarding her six-year-old girl and ten-year-old boy.

Kevin urged her on. "Go, Mom. Go. Don't let him get away."

"Slow down," Katie said.

"You're such a scaredy-cat," Kevin said.

"Am not."

"Are too."

"Cool it, both of you," Bret ordered.

Ahead, the Charger roared past the stop sign at Eastland. The driver paralleled the train tracks, the same CSX tracks that ran behind the Vreelands' property and teetered along rusty trestles high above the Cumberland River.

"He's gonna get a ticket," Kevin said from the back.

"He's headed for Shelby Park. Should I just let him go?"

"No," Bret snapped at her. "As long as we're this close, I wanna get the rest of that license plate. Just in case."

"This, uh, isn't working. I can't do it like this." Sara kicked off her right heel and the vehicle lost momentum, until she found the pedal again with nylon-wrapped toes. "I wish you were driving. That car's too fast for us."

"By the time we switch he'll be gone, and if we don't nail him now, he'll keep messing with us, watching the house. Maybe this has to do with that will. Who knows? Put the pressure on him and eventually he's gonna drive past a cop or get caught in traffic or lose control. C'mon, Hummers are made for this stuff."

"It's not even ours." She scanned both directions, saw no other cars, and groaned as she accelerated through the intersection. "What am I doing? What if I'm the one who wrecks?"

"Sweetheart, this is our guy."

"Where're the police when we need them? He could have a gun."

"You were right," Kevin said. "He cut into the park."

"Good job, Kev." Bret leaned forward in his seat. "Help me figure out which way he turns, otherwise we might lose him in all the hills and side roads."

Avoiding a mountain biker who exited Shelby Park, Sara edged through the narrow two-lane opening that dipped beneath the train tracks. Further south, the slope dropped away and left the trestles towering seventy feet in the air. Beneath those ironworks, the Shelby Bottoms Nature Center offered area information, and miles of greenway served dog-walkers, joggers, and cyclists.

"Where is he?" Sara cried.

"Kev, you see anything?"

"There."

Sara twisted her head. "Where?"

"Left. See? Off through those trees."

"Got it."

She spun the Hummer in a sharp half-turn, climbed the rise, angled down again. The floorboards burned beneath her nylon. Her daughter whimpered in the backseat, while her two men egged her on.

"Go, Mom. You're gaining on him."

"Sit back," Bret warned their son. "You still got your seat belt on?"

"Dad, I'm trying to help."

Sara careened along the winding pavement, caught glimpses of black through the foliage. Perhaps she could do this, actually catch up to the slimeball. Adrenaline pumped through her arms and legs. It was heady stuff. Even though she pushed harder on the accelerator, she was no thrill-seeker. Absolutely not. When her husband talked about striking out in search of adventure, she wrote it off as a symptom of the deranged male mind.

Skydiving? She liked her feet on the ground.

Cliff-climbing? She liked her feet on horizontal ground.

Bungee-jumping? She snapped hair-ties just helping Katie put up a ponytail, and she wasn't about to trust life and limb to some glorified rubber band. No thank you.

"Don't lose him," Bret said.

The sleek car vanished around an outcropping, and from Sara's visits to the park she knew various paths split off beyond there, increasing its chances of escape. She gripped the wheel, felt another spurt of adrenaline, and took the corner with barely a tap on her brakes. Each of her senses stood on high alert.

"Sara!"

Rounding the outcrop, she understood the reason for her husband's yell. The Charger was at a dead stop, nudged against the right embankment and only halfway on the pavement. It was a crude yet clever tactic, presenting enough of an obstacle to force a split-second reaction.

She cranked the steering wheel, felt tires carve into grass off the left side of the road. The vehicle leaned, the rear end swiveled downhill, and the shadows of hovering branches slapped at the windshield as she overcorrected and spun everything the other way, almost flipping the wide machine.

Katie was crying. Kevin screamed. Bret reached for the wheel, but his seat belt snapped him back.

"Jesus," she prayed, bearing down on the brakes. "Dear Jesus."

In what seemed like slow motion, the Hummer skidded backwards into a maple tree. The rear passenger-side bumper absorbed the impact, and airbags deployed in one explosive sound that masked her gasp of terror.

My children. What have I done to my kids?

"Katie?" She fought the airbag. "Kevin?"

"Mommy."

"Are you all right? I'm so sorry, so sorry."

"Why'd you do that?" Kevin wanted to know, his voice shaking.

"I had no clue that he'd . . . he'd be stopped right there. I was trying to. . . ."

She heard her husband's door open, which meant he must be okay. She managed to release her own seat belt and turn toward the back, where airbags formed a cocoon around her most precious treasures. One look at their frightened faces and she could no longer contain herself. She took hold of their hands, sobs welled in her throat, and she decided she would never let go.

Never.

"I love you, Mommy."

"Love you, too, honey. I love you both so much."

"Sara," Bret called from outside the vehicle. "Everyone OK?"

"I think so. How am I going to explain this to Jason and Zoe?"

He opened her door. "You weren't going more than five, ten miles an hour when we hit. This, it's nothing. I can drive it outta here." He cradled and kissed her cheek. "Main thing is nobody's hurt. But that man in the car, he watched the whole thing, the sick freak. I pegged his back window with a rock as he drove off, and I got the rest of that license number. Believe me, we're gonna bury this guy."

Chapter Twenty-nine

Bᴙᴇᴛ ᴘᴜsʜᴇᴅ ʙᴀᴄᴋ ғʀᴏᴍ ᴛʜᴇ ᴍᴀssɪᴠᴇ ᴅᴇsᴋ. Hᴇ ᴡᴀs ᴀᴛ Bɪʟʟɪɴɢsʟᴇʏ Cᴏᴀᴄʜ Company, seated in Jason's office, where usually he enjoyed the smells of the padded leather chair and the teakwood. At 10 ᴀ.ᴍ. Monday morning, while the rest of the crew gathered in the break room to trade jokes, homemade jerky, and opinions on the Titans' victory, Bret was on the line with Metro's Investigative Services.

"I wish it were that simple," Detective Meade said through the phone.

"Just go by the numbers," Bret shot back. "You've got it all right there on your screen or whatever you're looking at. This car belongs to a known felon."

"A Mr. Hart, yes."

"So, what if we put out a restraining order on him?"

"On what basis?"

"This guy's not gonna leave us alone. You realize that now, don't you?"

"I'll take your word for it," Meade said.

Earlier, Bret had called Jason in Cozumel about the fender-bender. Jason sounded already slightly inebriated, but took it in stride, said what was insurance for, and kidded that it would come out of Bret's next check. He insisted, for security's sake, that the Vreelands stay in his home till his and Zoe's return. Even now, Kevin and Katie were hidden away with Sara on the Billingsleys' property, playing with the dog, watching movies, and cooking, while monitored cameras and alarms guarded the premises. Must be nice. Such security measures weren't even an option in the Tightie-Whitie Vreeland Budget.

"Take my word for it?" Bret said, rubbing a hand over his forehead. "What is that supposed to mean, Detective?"

"Mr. Hart's past offenses establish a pattern of behavior, yes, but they do not implicate him in any new crimes. The way this works? A proposed order of protection is submitted, the opposing party is given notice, and the court sets the date for a hearing for a temporary injunction, during which you present documents supporting the claim that you are being stalked. If the case ends up being dismissed, though, you pay a hundred-and-seventy-five dollars out of your own pocket."

"Shoot, we don't have that kinda money lying around."

"It's one way of keeping fraudulent orders from being filed."

Bret planted work boots on the floor, fixed his gaze on a framed 5 × 7 of Jason and Zoe during their last trip to Mexico. They wore white smiles and golden tans. Jason lifted a half-empty Dos Equis, while his wife sported a red bikini that showed off recent implants and glittery, dolphin-shaped, belly jewelry.

The jet-setting couple. Not a care in the world.

He tugged his eyes from Zoe's figure, focused instead on a brass bull paperweight. "OK," he said into his cell, "what about that e-mail I read you? Doesn't that count as—?"

"An e-mail from Tacoma, from a public library computer? Let's face it, Mr. Vreeland, it seems a bit far-fetched. And are we even sure this is the same fellow you saw last week?"

"Same guy," Bret said. "Guaranteed."

"You got a clear look at his face this time?"

"I . . . well, yeah, he was wearing the same ball cap. Pretty sure of it."

"'Pretty sure' doesn't fly. A judge would laugh you out of circuit court."

"So what're my options? I can't just let this go. My kids are already hiding out at our friends' house, skipping school for the day, and my wife works a late shift tonight at Cumberland Sleep Clinic. She'll be practically all alone."

"Has she been getting harassed at her workplace?"

"Not that we're aware of, but—"

"She may be perfectly fine then," the detective said. "Since she's currently at an unknown location, it's not likely she'll be tailed from there to her job, right? And if she drives an unfamiliar car, she could further avoid detection."

"I don't like it. Who says this guy doesn't know where she works?"

"I'm sure the clinic keeps its doors locked after-hours."

"That doesn't help when she's out in the parking lot."

"Remember," the detective said, "we're both fathers here, both husbands. You're not alone in your concerns, but will you let one person shut down your entire lives? Have you considered maybe that's the very thing he wants? Power over you? Intimidation? A bully, same as those your son's faced at school."

That thought tightened Bret's grip on the phone.

"Did I lose you?"

"See, that's just it," Bret said. "I don't want this guy playing his little games. I'm not afraid for myself, used to play linebacker, but I don't want him harassing my family. I'd rather deal with him face-to-face than wait for his next move."

"If you recall, I advised against confrontation."

"Yeah, well, the pretend-he-isn't-there thing isn't exactly panning out."

"We first need to know if you've even got the right person. Fact is," Meade said, "there are dozens of two-thousand-ten Dodge Chargers registered in Davidson County, probably a third of them black."

"What's your point?"

"It is possible, isn't it, that you and your wife chased some unwitting stranger through a city park, disrupting his Sunday afternoon?"

"I don't believe that."

"But it's possible."

"You said yourself he's a convicted felon."

"Who's done his time. He's had a clean sheet for over five years."

Bret huffed. No wonder domestically abused women had trouble getting help. Sure, the laws aimed to protect all parties involved, but what happened when the only supporting evidence was a fired bullet or the drawn blade of a knife? Too late then.

"So that's it," he said, slamming his palm on the desk. "I guess your hands are tied, huh? Which leaves me to do this on my own."

"Do what?"

"Protect my family. Whaddya think?"

Detective Meade's tone shifted. "Answer this for me. Did you give vent to the same anger yesterday by throwing a rock at one Dodge Charger?"

"What? Where'd you hear that?"

"Yes or no."

Bret bit his lip. "Yes."

"That would explain why he placed a call of his own to Metro, complaining that you cracked his rear window. He wanted to file an order of protection against you, Mr. Vreeland, and the physical evidence would seem to lean in his favor."

"I only meant to scare him off."

"By damaging his personal property?"

"My anger took over," Bret said. "I was wrong. Shouldn't have done that."

A measure of warmth returned to Meade's voice. "I appreciate that, but it's always easier to be sorry once you've been caught."

"Because of him, we went sliding down a hill into a tree. What if there'd been kids playing there? Or lovebirds on a picnic blanket? And here's the part I don't get, Detective. How'd he know my name? If this were some random owner of a Charger, somebody with no clue about our family, he wouldn't know who to report unless he stuck around to trade information with us."

"Would you stick around if a stranger threw rocks at your car?"

"You better believe I—"

"Hold on there," the detective said. "We haven't even met in person, but I should've anticipated your answer. You have a valid point, of course, about him knowing your name, and I'm personally inclined to believe your version of this story so please don't take our conversation as a reason not to call again. I'll give you my cell number. But do not, I ask of you, take matters into your own hands. Now that his name's on record, I doubt he'll be bugging you."

Bret hefted the paperweight. "If he comes onto our property, I'm gonna defend it."

"And you'd be well within your rights. Don't go looking for trouble, though. This fellow's sheet is clean now, but his prior convictions suggest he is not someone to mess with."

Chapter Thirty

BEST TO BE CAUTIOUS. NOW THAT THE CHARGER WAS MARKED, MAGNUS wouldn't be able to use his apartment or conduct activities as Mr. Hart. He parked his newest rental car in the darkness and walked five blocks through the sweltering heat. He removed a padlock, entered the rusty Quonset hut with his flashlight slicing.

The beam found Natalie's face, reddened and wide-eyed, and he fed off her fear, let it fill him like a hearty meal. He was the caveman, the strongman, the superman at the evolutionary apex, and his eyes drank in her sweat-drenched locks and the dried drool that whitened her lips. A rolled red cotton gag cut into the corners of her mouth.

Why, look at her, thin and shriveled in this late-summer heat.

She looked oh, so pitiful. So full of the pit.

Oh, not that he believed in anything so crass, of course. If there were such a thing as eternal judgment, it would be a place like Guantanamo, a filthy little hellhole reserved for do-gooders who forced their morals and absolutes upon those who never asked for them. While he and fellow social Darwinists fought for mankind's betterment, the pew-sitters and pulpit-pounders stood in their way.

At least Natalie was no pew-sitter.

No poo-sitter either. He gave her too much respect for that.

Here, shackled to an interior rib of the structure, she crouched near a five-gallon paint bucket provided for her excremental needs. Whoever thought he was cruel did not know the lengths he went for those in his care. He understood that a prisoner treated too harshly might have a physical or psychotic break.

Learned it from the best, Mother. You were never too harsh.

Magnus tilted Natalie's head back and dribbled bottled water through the gag. "My little coffee bean," he said, "how're you this evening? You don't mind if I call you that, do you? Considering our relationship started at the café?"

She sputtered, coughed, but the moisture brightened her eyes.

He said, "This isn't quite the date you had in mind, is it?"

She rose to her feet, the tendons in her thin arms twanging like guitar strings as she strained against her shackles. She threw a kick at him, though in her weakened condition it was too slow to catch him.

"Well, well, you still have some fight in you, Natalie. Very good. Don't think I mean to break you. Not at all. Muscles grow large through repeated ripping and healing, and a human responds much the same. I'm here to make you stronger."

Her grunts turned angry and questioning.

"Why, you ask? Because we can be partners. You're better suited to infiltrate the Vreeland family. They know you. Trust you. Sure, you've probably lost your job for failing to show up yesterday, but once you are free and show your wounds, no one will doubt your traumatic circumstances."

Natalie fell silent.

"Wounds?" he said, continuing his role play. "We'll get to them soon enough. It's not that I want to hurt you, but who will believe you if we skip that part? They'll think you got fed up and just walked out on the job."

She slouched again, her back against the metal rib.

"Another drink?" He raised the bottle. When she shook her head, he said, "You sure, my coffee bean? I doubt anyone else will be coming to your aid."

This hut, Magnus knew, was one of five that once housed small aircraft here at East Nashville's Cornelia Fort Airpark. Cut from foliage along the Cumberland River, the private airfield was named after a native Tennessean, a female pilot from the 1940s who followed in the ways of Amelia Earhart. The site was deserted now, ruined by the May flood, during which the waters rose nearly twelve feet above flood stage in less than forty-eight hours.

"Pain has its benefits," he said. He pulled a retractable antenna from his back pocket and extended it to full length, causing silver to flash in the moonlight through the dusty windows. "Look here." He tugged on his pant-leg, revealing stripes of scar tissue on his own hairy calf. "And I'm all the better for it. Now sit yourself down, all the way down, and stretch out those pretty legs of yours."

Chapter Thirty-one

"A BABYSITTER?" BRET SAID, FACING SARA IN THE LARGE VANITY MIRROR of the Billingsleys' master bath. "Kev and Katie are good kids. Why don't they just go with us?"

"To the reading of a will?"

"They'll be quiet. C'mon. How long can the whole thing last?"

"If you're worried about paying someone, the Rileys said not to worry about it. I promised them I'd help out later with some weeding around their place." Sara turned from the counter, elbows close to her sides to avoid jabbing him in the ribs. It was a habit from their small bathroom on Groves Park. In here, though, she figured they had room for a game of volleyball.

"Sweetheart, I don't like it. What? Now you're their gardener?"

"And now they're our nannies?" she fired back. "You're not making sense. They're trying to do us a favor, and this could be a very important night for us."

"Keep the expectations low. Don't forget."

"I know." She kissed his neck. "I'm trying to stay calm."

"You sure look nice, anyway."

That earned him a kiss on the lips before she spun away in a light-blue summer dress graced with white butterflies. From K-Mart. Not that she cared, but Jeannie Riley was the type to turn up her nose at a Jaclyn Smith label. As for Sara's sapphire jewelry, it was too opulent for anything hanging in her closet and she chose to wear a faux-pearl necklace instead. She hid the more expensive jewelry in her small white purse.

"Zip me up?" she said.

"Mmm. So you've got the night off work and we have ourselves a sitter. What if we just skip everything and enjoy the house all by our lonesomes?"

"You, Mr. Vreeland, are a bad boy."

"But a good husband."

"Zipper. Please."

"That's a no, I take it?"

"You better not start moping."

He zipped up the back of the dress, buttoned his own collared shirt over clean jeans. "Just don't ask me to carry your purse."

"Tonight? Absolutely not." She slapped his chest. "But you know, Bret, it's not like it makes you any less of a man."

"You have no idea. I shrink an inch every time I have to hold that thing."

The very memory of it seemed to chase him from the bathroom.

Sara grinned at herself in the glass. No matter how she tried to contain these expectations, she sensed an impending shift in her family's axis. Where their spinning world was now only brushed by the rays of a distant sun, it would soon be basking in a radiant glow. She could feel it already seeping into her skin.

Mr. Storinka's words ran on Shuffle and Repeat through her head.

"You are always good to me."

"I wish I knew you, yes, many years ago."

"Remember the item I set aside? She is the one."

These recollections cooled as she descended the scalloped steps to the rust-edged Subaru. She was certainly no Danica Patrick. Thanks to her, the Hummer was in a body shop that honored the Billingsleys' insurance, and although it would be good as new by the weekend, this meant they had only the old hatchback for this momentous occasion.

Keeping me humble, I suppose? Well, whatever it takes.

◆ ◆ ◆

Bret drove. The Subaru chugged along Franklin Road, hiccupping exhaust and nearly stalling each time he came to a stop. Tomorrow, he vowed to himself, he would deal with this fuel filter on his lunch break. Least it should be a cheap fix.

As they followed the interstate back toward East Nashville, his mind toyed with this evening's upcoming possibilities.

A silver key?

An old man's will?

Truth be told, the thought of piles of money scared him.

Didn't I Timothy 6:10 say that *"the love of money is at the root of all kinds of evil"*? The Bible was full of cautionary tales about men and women corrupted by their riches. Ecclesiastes, written most likely by King Solomon, one of the world's wealthiest men, put it this way: *"Those who love money will never have enough. How absurd to think that wealth brings true happiness!"*

"Dad," Kevin spoke up from the backseat. "Why do we even need a babysitter? The Rileys are OK, but it's not like I'm a little kid anymore."

"You're definitely growing up. But not tonight."

"I'm big too," Katie said.

"Yeah," Kev said, "and I could take care of her."

"Not with that guy prowling around our neighborhood, you can't. We're not gonna let him bully us, but that doesn't mean being stupid."

"I'm not afraid, Dad."

Bret caught his son's eye in the rearview. "It's good to see you standing up for yourself. I like it. There's a time for everything, though. When you can, it's best to avoid a fight and steer clear of trouble, right?"

Kevin pressed his lips together.

"We shouldn't be too long," Sara said from the passenger seat.

"Where y'all going?" Katie asked.

Sara cleared her throat. "A, uh, a patient from Mommy's clinic died, and we're supposed to meet with some of his friends and family."

"Sounds boring."

"Kevin." Bret shook his head. "Apologize to your mother."

"Mommy?" Katie said. "Was he a nice man?"

"I didn't know him too well, but he was always nice to me. He was getting older and his breathing difficulties put a lot of strain on his heart."

"Kev."

"Sorry, Mom."

Bret pulled into a long driveway. Only a mile or two from the Vreelands' place in East Nashville, the Riley residence was one of the historic, vaulted-ceiling homes now part of the urban renewal. Such addresses catered to new-money hipsters in retro clothing and laid-back baby boomers. To Bret, it seemed both groups lived with a calculated lack of pretension. Was anything more pretentious than pretending not to be pretentious?

Of course, that could be his envy talking.

"Bret," Derek Riley greeted them at the front door. "Miss Sara. I know you two are running late, so—"

"Not really," Bret said.

"So we won't keep you. And don't you worry about the children. Jeannie's in the kitchen as we speak, pulling cookies from the oven."

"Cookies?" Katie's eyes couldn't hide her excitement.

"Snickerdoodles."

"Yum." Sara nudged Kevin inside. "Don't they smell good?"

"Come on in, kids." Derek stepped back from the doorway. "Shoes off, if you don't mind. We're sticklers about the hardwood, all original flooring, resurfaced, and freshly waxed."

"Beautiful," Sara said.

Bret watched their daughter kick off her shoes and prance down the corridor in search of goodies. His son dashed after her, caught her at the arched entry to the kitchen. Jeannie waved them in with an oven mitt, her hair pulled back so tightly that her plucked eyebrows formed a stiff V.

"How're you holding up these days?" Derek joined Bret beneath the porch light. "Pastor gave me your CD. You have a nice quality to your voice, some real potential there."

He felt Sara's hand slip around his waist. He said, "My song, you think it's worth sharing with the church?"

"Certainly possible," Derek said. "I'm sure there'll be a time and a place."

"You can't be any more specific?"

"All right." Sara gave Bret a restraining squeeze. "Remember, Derek, no drinks past nine for the kids. We ought to be back by ten or thereabouts."

"Take your time. And truly, Miss Sara, we're sorry for your loss."

"Thanks. Please tell the kids we love them."

"OK." Bret took his wife's hand. "I guess that means we're outta here."

Magnus Maggart cleaned the blood from the antenna, collapsed it, and put it back in his pocket. He left the bottle of water for his captive, figuring if Natalie took hold of it with chapped lips, she could guzzle warm liquid during the long night ahead. Alone in the metal hut, she would have to deal with tiger mosquitoes and the shrill sound of insects in the lush vegetation around the property.

"Be strong, coffee bean." He waved a hand around the hut and gave her a dose of her own introductory Spanish. "Mi casa es su casa."

He padlocked the door, tuning out her moans of protest. He slinked over the low fence where metal signs warned against trespassers, and he scoffed at such restrictions, designed for fearful simpletons.

He stayed vigilant on his way back to the car, wrapping himself in shadow. Once behind the wheel and moving away, he speed-dialed his phone.

Viktor picked up on the second ring. "You're calling too soon."

"You haven't opened the will yet?"

"They're on their way, but we can already guess the contents, don't you think? The old man wouldn't give his reasons, but he was very fond of her. Just last week, he privately revised the will."

"With no witnesses?" Magnus said. "Is that allowed?"

"In Tennessee, holographic wills are legal. He sealed it in an envelope in his safe and told me I would be the executor. I am bound by its provisions."

"Any chance that I'm in it?" Magnus dredged up a sharp laugh. "Of course not. We both know I fell out of favor long ago. But you'll be in there, Viktor, considering your years of service. Proof that if you kiss up long enough, you will get your reward. I actually admire your cunning."

"You are wrong. He was like a father to me."

"Why, there's a scary thought, knowing how he dealt with family."

"Either way, I'll call when it's over."

"That'd be swell."

"And after this," Viktor said, "you and I will be done with each other."

Chapter Thirty-two

THICK PILLARS BRACKETED THE FRONT GATES OF MR. STORINKA'S BELLE Meade estate. Bret marveled as he drove over crushed shells, between rows of trees, toward the antebellum mansion where paned windows glowed in the night.

Were battles fought on this land?

Did this sprawling terrain hide spilled blood and the relics of war?

He circled a fountain and parked behind a line of cars, two BMWs, a vintage Jaguar XKE, and a Maserati Granturismo. He tried not to gawk. Could their hatchback seem any more out of place? He straightened his shirt.

"I thought you weren't nervous," Sara said.

"This is more than I expected. You sure we're supposed to be here?"

"I know I am. I mean, I'm the one with the key and all."

"See there?" he said. "Already getting snooty."

"That's not the way I meant it, you dork."

"I can wait in the car, if you want."

"Hon, don't be silly. Let's get this over with. And Viktor promised he would lock away 'his girls,' so we should be safe."

Bret went around and opened her door, treating her as though they had arrived in a Rolls-Royce. "Milady." He offered his arm. "Allow me."

Arm-in-arm, they met Viktor Moroz at the wide front door. Arm-in-arm, they took a thirty-minute tour of the mansion's 5,575 square feet. Arm-in-arm, they were introduced to two lawyers and an accountant in the ground floor's corner study, where red leather sofas, built-in bookshelves, and an antique desk lent the space a comfortable yet somewhat stale feel.

Like a museum. Or mausoleum.

"This was Mr. Storinka's favorite room," Viktor said, his accent slight. "We're told that during the Civil War it was used sometimes as a hospital."

Bret nodded. Seated with him on one of the sofas, Sara tugged at the hem of her summer dress and scooted closer. The leather squeaked.

"But this is not the reason we're here." Viktor stood behind the desk, arms stiff at his sides, black hair spiked and at attention. "The letter I sent told of my employer's passing. He died in his bed. The death certificate lists heart failure as the cause, and in light of his preexisting condition, the doctor believes an autopsy is unnecessary. Does anyone here disagree?"

No one disagreed.

"While he was alive, Mr. Storinka did name me as his executor. I've acted on that assumption, but we will soon see if I was wrong. Thank you for coming."

"Is everyone present who should be?" one of the lawyers asked.

Sadly, Viktor assured them, this was it.

He explained that Storinka's ex-wife lived in Kiev, remarried for many years. Storinka himself was an orphan of the Second World War, a ward of the state until he reached adulthood. He had worked hard and built an arms-manufacturing empire on no-nonsense practices born from his survivor mentality. With unprecedented success, Storinka Defense Systems was poised to compete in the U.S. market. The silver-haired mogul moved to America, where he cut his Eastern European ties, fended off former associates and rivals, and vied for military contracts. Of course, this move earned him no shortage of enemies.

Bret took it all in, a single life condensed into a ten-minute history.

Nothing more than a blip on the screen.

Viktor wrapped up his summary by turning his attention to Sara. "Mrs. Vreeland, you put a sparkle back in his eyes. You knew nothing of his past or his riches, but you listened and you cared."

"I liked him," she said. "Perhaps he softened with age."

"Yes, there was a clear change in him. We all saw it."

"I hate to sound callous," the accountant huffed, "but I'm sure there'll be time for a memorial soon enough. Let's not drag this on any longer than we must. It's late already, and my wife and I like to catch *The Apprentice* together."

Nothing more than a blip.

"Of course." Viktor braced his hands on the desk. "Sara . . . Is it all right if I call you by your first name? Good. Would you bring forward the key I gave you?"

"Here." She fumbled in her white purse. "Uh, just a sec."

Bret noticed her trembling fingers and clipped words. If necessary, he decided, he would help her search the purse, sacrificing his male dignity for this whole stilted charade. Did the accountant or these lawyers care at all about their former client? Or was Storinka only a name on a large retainer? A way of paying for their fancy cars out front?

"Got it," Sara said, lifting the necklace and its dangling key.

Viktor produced a similar key. "Come over. We must do this together."

Bret squeezed her hand and let go.

The spiky-haired man pulled a hinged frame from the wall, a depiction of battle between the smoking cannons of a Union ironclad and the rifles of uniformed cavalry onshore. From behind the painting, a safe stared at them.

Viktor inserted his key. Sara did the same.

They turned them in unison.

Whirrr . . . clickkk.

According to the grandfather clock in the corner, the matte-finished silver door swung open at 7:46 P.M. Even from the sofa, Bret could see stapled papers atop a cigar box. They were handwritten in flowing black script. His heart pounded. His mouth turned dry. Sara returned to his side, the necklace clutched in her fingers like a strand of rosary beads, the key shining like a religious icon.

A reverent silence filled the study.

Viktor scanned the document. "As I said, I'm the trustee and executor."

"We'd like to verify that for ourselves," one of the lawyers said. "Of course."

After the suits-and-ties put on a show with perfunctory glances and grunts, they handed the papers back.

Viktor's black eyes peered across the desk, and when he opened his mouth, his voice failed him. He tried again in a monotone. "With the five of you as witnesses," he said, "I will now read the last will and testament of Ivan Storinka."

A Matter of Time

the accuser considers the steps already taken, the players put into place, and convinces himself the plan will work if he is given enough time to erode the trust and confidence of his targets

time is the issue, always time

why this fickle measurement, fencing in the lives of the two-leggers and hemming in his own efforts as well?

a cloud of doubt hovers in his thoughts, but he turns that doubt into unholy inspiration, and with new possibilities taking shape, approaches once more the chambers of the almighty one

"you dare show your face again?"

"i do not fear you," the accuser says

"if you did, you would have the beginnings of wisdom, and yet even as you claim this lack of fear, your cohorts believe and they tremble"

"fear is the crudest of tools," the accuser fires back, "and while it has its place, your beloved two-leggers are alert to it, which is why i and those who serve me often use tools more subtle and sublime"

"have you come only to list your accomplishments?" the one says

"the family we spoke of before, they are positioned for the test, but if I don't have a few months to carry this test to completion, your joy over them will be meaningless and weak"

"my joy is their strength"

the accuser shrinks back, tastes bile in his throat

"so it's time that you want," the almighty one says

"yes, since you are the one to blame for putting it all into motion with your spinning planets and gaseous, blazing suns"

"six months," comes the answer

"i can do it in even less"

Chapter Thirty-three

October 2010

THREE NIGHTS EARLIER IT BECAME OFFICIAL. SARA VREELAND WAS RICH.

Filthy rich.

The will identified only two beneficiaries. The first was Viktor Moroz, faithful companion and gun-toting "housekeeper." He would receive Storinka's $1,000,000 life-insurance proceeds, paid in a lump sum, exempt from income tax. He would also get Storinka's old house back in their homeland, appraised at $250,000 in U.S. dollars. Viktor could inhabit the property on the outskirts of Kiev, rent it out, or sell it for a profit. As for the Mercedes convertible garaged here on this Belle Meade estate, its title would transfer to him directly.

His last directive was to care for the Dobermans, to do everything within reason to keep them healthy into old age. It was this that made Viktor smile.

The second name belonged to Sara Vreeland, devoted mother and sleep therapist. Storinka had established for her a testamentary trust. It included his domicile, which was the legal term for his antebellum mansion, five wooded acres, stable, pump house, and triple-car garage. Bought outright seven years earlier, the place was now worth $2,750,000. Also listed was a Lexus. The Maserati. And shares in Storinka Defense Systems.

Overall value: $6,000,000.

This trust agreement would be managed by Viktor, the trustee, until being cleared through probate proceedings. Not to worry, though. With a signature or two, Storinka's checking balance at First Tennessee Bank would be hers.

This gave Sara another $181,021. Give or take a few nickels.

Following these revelations, Bret remained matter-of-fact. He pressed the lawyers for details, asked the accountant questions about taxes and how long this would be mired in probate court. Sara admired Bret's calm demeanor. He was a cool customer, acting as if the evening's news was nothing surprising.

Then again, his name wasn't the one on the papers, was it?

No, Sara didn't expect him to understand. Not fully.

Her own response in the quiet corner study was less calculated. For days she had kept a tight rein on her emotions and expectations, promising herself to remain poised no matter what. But the moment she heard the details of the will, the enormity of the whole thing ripped those reins from her fingers. Seated on the sofa, she forgot about the stern men in attendance, about the threatening e-mail and the dents she'd put in the Hummer, about her makeup and hair.

She collapsed into her husband's chest and she sobbed.

The years of struggle, of scraping by . . .

The grief of a fiancé taken from her, of what might've been . . .

It was all there on her shoulders, everything she'd tried to ignore, tried to carry, tried to count as joy because such trials produced endurance. These burdens were part of her, boulders in a backpack. She could barely remember a day not carrying them.

Was it any wonder she ended each evening so depleted? She went without name-brand shampoos to make sure Katie had school lunches. She shopped for clothes at thrift shops and Walmart, scraping pennies together so Kevin could play soccer. On Bret's end, he chipped away at their son's medical expenses and never talked about bigger TVs, newer vehicles, nicer tools.

Sara knew that billions around the world would consider her lower middle-class lifestyle a fairytale, but this only added to her guilt.

Wasn't she a good enough wife? A good enough mother?

Although she prayed regularly that her family would find financial relief, she knew deep down it would not come. Why should it? What made her more worthy than anyone else? She didn't deserve one dime more than she had already, not when some nights she dreamed of a man named Alex Page.

No. Not worthy.

And then, the will was read and her name was spoken: *"Sara Vreeland."*

There on the red sofa she clung to her husband, tears dampening his shirt as the years and the fears seemed to tumble away.

Oh, Jesus, it's so much more than I deserve. Thank you. Oh, thank you!

Storinka's last will and testament was the shout that started the avalanche.

In nature, Bret knew, something as small as the snapping of a tree branch could trigger a deadly onrush of snow, capable of uprooting boulders and bedrock, demolishing households, swallowing bodies. During their first year of marriage, Bret and Sara saw just such a display while on a camping trip in the Cascades of northern Washington. The ground shook beneath their sleeping bags as thousands of tons of frozen precipitation plunged down a mountainside that faced them across a wooded valley. No one was hurt, but they never forget the beautiful yet terrifying sight.

Of course, this current avalanche of theirs was a force for good.

"Six million? What else could it possibly be?" Pastor Teman exclaimed during a private meeting at the church office. "I'd say that's very good."

"It just feels, shoot, I don't know, almost unethical."

"It's a gift, Bret. Rejoice in it and be glad."

"Oh, we'll take it. Believe me. But in my head I've got all these pictures of droughts in Africa, tsunami victims, even the families in our own congregation who can't find work. Is it wrong to take more than our share while others starve?"

"Let me apply some basic logic and unpack this for you."

"Unpack away."

Pastor leaned back in his chair, hands linked across his belly. "In God's Word, we read of a Heavenly Father who wants to bless His children. On the flip side, we find a devil who wreaks havoc and destruction. When we consider these two options, the source of your blessing is clear. In the same way God showered down manna from heaven to feed His people in the wilderness, He is pouring out love upon the Vreeland family."

"Why us, though?"

"Well, you must be doing something right. The Lord rewards those who seek after Him. Brother, my counsel to you is this. Use it wisely, tithe from the first fruits, and take care of your precious children. Allow God to be the judge. He decides these things, and who are we, after all, to question?"

Chapter Thirty-four

ACROSS FROM BRET, SARA RESTED HER FINGERTIPS ON THE SAPPHIRES AT HER neck. She was more beautiful than ever, her cheekbones accentuated by the flickering candle on the table. The hair that hugged her ears also brushed her throat's delicate curves, and he imagined his lips landing there.

She was his princess.

And this? This was Bret's dream, a chance to wine and dine her.

Sara still had to work tonight, making up for her time off on Tuesday, but when she suggested they skip ice cream at Sip Cafe, get a sitter, and discuss their new life over an early dinner, he knew what her destination of choice would be now that the documents were signed and the bank funds transferred.

The Melting Pot. The restaurant they could never afford.

While gift shops, dance clubs, B.B. King's, and Hard Rock lined downtown's Second Avenue, steep steps led down to the restaurant often voted Nashville's most romantic. Dark wood, secluded booths, and low ceilings set the mood for a leisurely fondue meal. The food was first-class, everything from fresh bread, veggies, platters of meat, and simmering pots of melted cheese and various sauces, to the finale of rich dark chocolate in which to drown fat juicy strawberries.

Bret tried not to think of the price. For over a decade, he and Sara had supported foreign missions, with $28 a month able to cover a month of food for a family in Haiti. He felt decadent slapping down a hundred for a meal for two.

Especially when he had to cook his own food on tiny forks.

"Skewers," Sara had corrected him.

"Tiny forks."

Not that any of it mattered. They were here together, and in light of recent events the bill was the least of their concerns.

"Still feels unreal," he said. "When do we wake up?"

"I know, right?"

"What's our next step? Have you told anyone besides Pastor?"

"Jeannie may've noticed my excitement the night we picked up the kids, but I could hardly hide that from her, could I? I mean, my makeup was ruined."

"Did you talk specifics? Dollar amounts?"

"Absolutely not." She adjusted the neckline of her blouse. "Just that we might be getting some unexpected money, enough to ease the load. That was it. It's big news, Bret. I'm doing my best to keep quiet, but I'm practically bursting to call my mom and stepdad, all my old friends, everyone who's pointed fingers and judged our piece-of-junk Subaru and—"

"Sara."

"Well, it's true. Just last Sunday, Pastor acted like you were to blame for our financial troubles. I know you better than that. I respect your integrity. And just wait till next Sunday." She grinned. "When he sees the check that drops into the plate, he'll think you're the most righteous man around."

"Even regarding our giving we need to talk about things and make decisions together. The lawyers told me probate should go quicker than normal, since Storinka didn't have any debts and there aren't any relatives clamoring for their share. Still, this could drag out for a few months." Bret dipped a finger in the chocolate, popped it in his mouth. "We need to take things slowly."

"Hon, your fine-dining manners could use some work."

He wiped his hand on his napkin.

"I know it's not your thing," she said, "dressing up and sitting still this long, but thank you. It means a lot to me."

"It's not that bad."

"You know what's odd, honey? Last week, Mr. Storinka made it sound as though he bought his estate ten or eleven years ago. Why do you think he would lie about that?"

"Who knows? Could've been a senior moment. Listen, we need tax advice, investment advice. We've gotta figure out how to handle this for Katie and Kevin so that it's a blessing on them and not a curse."

"A curse. Really?"

"How many times do you hear about this sorta thing in the news? M.C. Hammer. Nic Cage. Even Ozzy and Sharon Osbourne. One minute you've got money coming out your ears, next minute you're filing for bankruptcy."

"Honey."

"Or posing for a mug shot in the county jail."

"No matter what they say, I loved Lindsay in *The Parent Trap*."

"Or running from the IRS."

"Bret, I get what you're—"

"Like that guy, the world chess champion who ended up as some tax fugitive and died up in Iceland somewhere."

"Bobby Fischer."

"What I'm saying is it can happen to anyone."

Sara giggled. Actually giggled.

He would have been mad if it weren't so cute. It stirred memories of their engagement, when the loss of her former fiancé was still fresh, her guarded heart still hesitant to express joy. The week before their wedding, Bret and Sara had spent a day alone at Port Defiance Park in Tacoma. They strolled along the promenade, climbed on the driftwood, and when he tackled her on the pebbled shore he heard her burst out in genuine laughter for the first time in over a year.

Dear God, I don't ever want to steal that away from her.

"What?" he asked now. "Did I say something funny?"

"Oh, Bret, don't you think you're going a bit overboard? It really is all right if we savor this for a few minutes, even a few days. You know, we could get so caught up in worrying about our millions. . . ." Her eyes flitted toward the neighboring tables, and her voice dropped a notch in volume. "So stressed that we miss out on some of this new freedom God's giving us."

"OK. I hear what you're saying. But if anything, we need to be more responsible than ever before, otherwise this money could just slip through our fingers like it talks about in Ecclesiastes. We've still gotta keep on budget."

"On budget."

"Same as we always have," he said.

They had lived on a budget since those patchy first few months as newlyweds, and he believed these good habits laid the solid foundation for a new life ahead. Nothing extravagant. Nothing decadent. Just more freedom to do things they enjoyed, buy clothes that actually fit, and drive cars that didn't smoke, backfire, slip out of gear, screech their brakes, or die at every other intersection.

"Bret, please tell me there'll be room for some adjustments," Sara said.

"Of course."

"I mean, I don't want to walk around with a poverty mentality, feeling guilty if I buy Kraft macaroni and cheese instead of generic. I want to be wise, of course. And responsible, absolutely. But if we're pinching pennies every time Katie needs a wrapped gift for a friend's party, or shopping for days to save a few bucks on new cleats for Kevin, we could reach the point where having the money becomes as much of a shackle as not having it."

He wadded and set aside his napkin, took both of her hands in his. "I don't want that, Sara. I love you."

"I know you do."

"I love our kids, our life together. Even with all its ups and downs."

"I do too."

"God made you the way you are, nurturing and caring and beautiful. He made me logical and protective and—"

"Oh, so you're the logical one?"

"And," he pressed on, "it's in my nature to look out for our family."

"Which I appreciate."

"Sweetheart." He fixed his gaze on hers. "I don't ever want to rob you of the joy I see in your eyes right now. You hear me? Not ever. You've waited so long for something like this. Forgive me for being such a dork, such a man."

"I love that about you. The being-a-man part."

"The truth is maybe I haven't been trusting the Lord the way I thought. Every day at work I think about how to save, how to eke out another mortgage payment. I skip buying a Snickers from the snack machine and even feel a little proud of myself, like my piddly little sacrifice should earn me a gold star. I'm just tired of carrying the weight, trying to do it on my own."

Bathed in candlelight, she nodded and her eyes turned moist.

"Maybe I've been relying on my own wisdom instead of the Lord's."

"No," she said, "I don't believe that. You're human, and our motives can get awfully clouded, but look at us now. Maybe this is your gold star."

He gave her a half-smile. "It was your name in that will."

"Don't be silly, hon. We're one."

"So you're not gonna take the money and run out on me?"

"Where would I go without you?"

"A good point. A very, very good point."

"Plus," she added with a wink, "I'd like a man to carry my bags when I take my trip to Cozumel. Turns out, we won't be needing wheelchairs after all. And what if we just took everyone? Kids, friends, family. One big celebration."

When the waitress came with the bill, they paid her on a debit card, figuring it wouldn't even put a ding in their newly bloated bank account. When they climbed the stairs to Second Street and found a parking ticket under their wiper, they shrugged. That, too, could be paid. When a panhandler with layered shirts that smelled of smoke asked for help, they pooled their cash and gave him four dollars along with a "God bless you" and a pair of smiles.

Although such behavior was nothing new for Bret, this time he felt no sense of sacrifice or favor earned. Just one good deed for their fellow man.

He turned the car onto the Woodland Street Bridge, determined that this time they would pay the Rileys for watching the kids. "Speaking of Cozumel, Sara, can you believe Jason and Zoe get back tomorrow? It's been nice staying in their house the past few days, for safety reasons, but we need to shift back to our place. I'm planning to do that with the kids tonight while you're at the clinic."

"Sounds good. And Eli's giving me a ride there, to help me keep a low profile. I know, I know, but his camper's so conspicuous no one will even notice."

"I hope not. I don't want anyone messing with my bride."

She touched his arm. "I'll be fine."

Chapter Thirty-five

MAGNUS MADE HIS NIGHTLY VISIT TO THE QUONSET HUT. IT WAS FRIDAY already, and his trussed-up, hazel-eyed captive was stronger than he thought. She had endured the insect bites and sweat, the loneliness and degradation, the whipped legs and meager meals. She reasoned with him, resisted him.

Showed. Some. Stinking. Backbone.

He could respect that.

So far, the disappearance of Natalie Flynn was nothing but a thirty-second news clip on Channel Two, a page-five-article in *The Tennessean.*

Her roommate at Trevecca Nazarene University, a chubby blond with dark mascara, said Natalie had left for work last Sunday morning, but hours later the café was still locked up and her Vespa nowhere to be found. Please, if anyone had information about her whereabouts, call the number provided. Natalie's employers were contrite, admitting their initial anger was now only deep concern.

Metro's finest were on the case, and Magnus knew to be careful.

He had toppled the Vespa from his Charger into the murky Cumberland. The airpark was off the beaten path, unlikely to attract attention. And he wouldn't be tracked from his Germantown apartment now that he was using a different name for the rental car and for his stay at InTown Suites.

Despite his male urges, he made no advances at his captive. Sexual contact would leave his DNA behind and threaten the success of his larger task.

Clearly, though, Natalie was a survivor. Far as he was concerned, that was a rarity among her gender and generation. Nature had a way of weeding out the weak, and even Bible thumpers talked about good seed choked out by thorns and weeds, stealing the concept from the world around them, a world that rewarded the ruthless over the selfless.

Pluck those weak weeds.

But Natalie was not weak. His little coffee bean was still useful.

Sara and Bret climbed the scalloped steps of the Billingsleys' home and stepped into the foyer. While Sara disarmed the alarm, Bret rubbed the Yorkie's ears. Kevin and Katie dashed past Sara's legs and shoved their way down the hall. She called after them to slow down, but they were out of sight.

Ah well, Sara thought, it was time to switch duties for the evening.

Mr. Mom: Bret Vreeland.

Working Woman: Sara Vreeland.

"How does it feel coming home to a place like this?" she asked him, gesturing at the tall double doors.

"Where'd the kids run off to?"

"Don't worry. They love it back there with Jason's big screen and the Wii."

"Oh."

"So," she tried again, "you think you could get used to this?"

As though awaiting his answer, an oil portrait of the Billingsleys, lifelike and impressive, gazed down from the wall in a large gilded frame. Jason wore his usual jaunty smile beneath wavy black hair. Zoe's full lips were slightly parted, her eyes direct and beguiling.

"I don't feel like I belong," Bret said, untucking his shirt.

"Honey, look at you. You're my handsome prince."

"Aye, milady. Our trusty steed died twice today at the red lights, and I'm thinking it needs a new fuel filter. My tools, they're all back at the house."

"Good thing Eli's coming for me." She gave him a playful jab. "He should be here any minute."

"Make sure," Bret said, "that he drops you at the front of the clinic and waits till you lock that door behind you."

"You sound like my mother."

"And he is picking you up afterwards, right? Door-to-door service?"

"You know him, a regular night owl. He told me he's looking forward to something other than another evening alone in the church lot. Bret, thanks again for a romantic dinner together. That food was fantastic, and I loved being alone together, just you and me."

"Technically speaking, it was on your dime."

"Stop that."

"You're right, Sara. It was nice." He pulled her into an embrace. Although he did the same thing when he got home from work each day, this time he didn't smell of grimy sawdust and perspiration. He smelled good. "So tell me," he said, "do you really want to live in Storinka's mansion?"

"He did give it to us."

"We could sell it."

"In this economy?" She stepped back, hands still linked behind his neck. "Even if we found a buyer, we'd probably get less than it's appraised for. No, I'd rather enjoy the place for a while, wouldn't you?"

"I'm not sure."

"We both love East Nashville, the community, the whole vibe. But let's face it, there is a crime element that isn't the best for the kids. And the schools, well, they're wonderful, but Kevin needs something different, someplace without the bullying, where his quick mind and creativity can be challenged."

"What would we do about our house?"

"I've thought about that, and I have an idea. I mean, I'm certain you'll, uh, think it's crazy, but it could benefit all concerned."

"What're you talking about?"

The intercom buzzed on the bottom of the alarm panel, and the CCTV camera showed an older man's salt-and-pepper hair as he leaned out his cab window. Reduced to black and white pixels, he appeared almost ghostly.

"Hi, Eli." Sara touched the button to open the gate. "Be right out."

"He's even a few minutes early," Bret noted.

"Him," she said. "Eli."

"What?"

"He could take our house. Why not? Either he could rent it from us, or, I don't know, perhaps own it flat-out."

Bret's dark eyebrows lifted into his hairline. "Wow. OK."

"We can talk more about it later. Love you. I'll call to let you know when I've made it safe and sound." She gave him a peck on the cheek and hurried down the steps toward the old Caribou camper-pickup at the gate.

Eli lifted a hand in greeting, leaned over and opened the passenger door, washing the cab in the pale glow of the dome light.

She climbed inside. The seat was springy, the aroma that of pine trees.

"Thanks for doing this," she said.

"Sure thing." He pulled on the column shifter. "Buckle up."

The kids helped Bret load the hatchback and they headed from the Billingsleys' back to their house on Groves Park. Tonight, they would sink into their own beds. Tomorrow morning, while they and their mother slept in, he would pick up the repaired Hummer en route to the airport for Jason and Zoe's return.

The Subaru sputtered and died as they pulled into the driveway.

"Well," he said, "least we made it all the way home."

"I liked it better at the Billingsleys'."

"Can't blame you, Katie, but we're supposed to be content whether sleeping in a tent or a palace. 'No matter what happens, always be thankful. . . .'"

"'For this is God's will for you,'" Kevin said, completing the verse.

"Nice job, Kev."

"That's an easy one."

With the children in tow, Bret circled the perimeter of the house. Inside, he searched each room and closet, under each bed, behind the doors and shower curtains. Found no signs of thieves, intruders, or a smirking, ball-capped man.

After tucking Katie in and checking that Kevin put in his MAS, Bret settled down to catch the news. It was the piece about a missing college student, a female barista at Sip Café, that jarred him.

With his new Blackberry, he speed-dialed his wife at the clinic.

Chapter Thirty-six

S<small>ARA STOOD IN THE BOOTH AT</small> C<small>UMBERLAND</small> S<small>LEEP</small> C<small>LINIC,</small> <small>PULLED HER</small> white coat tighter to ward off the vented A/C, and gazed through the glass. At 10:28 P.M., her patient stirred on the bed in the sleep lab. His pulse rate jumped on the monitor, and his cortisol readings seemed all wrong.

Was he still asleep?

As if to answer that question, the large man sat up on the mattress.

She spoke through the intercom. "You all right in there, Theodore?"

He turned toward her, his nose and mouth covered by a CPAP mask, and shook his head. Big as he was, he still looked to her like a forlorn child.

"Is it the mask? It does take some getting used to."

A vigorous nod.

Sara made a note of his response on his chart. This pressure device kept the airway dilated so its wearer could sleep, and many found it life-changing. However, some found it claustrophobic, and others claimed it was plain too creepy. Kevin tried the contraption once and refused to give it another go, saying he sounded "like Darth Vader."

"I'll be right there," Sara told her patient.

He lowered the side rail, swung his legs over the edge of the bed.

"Please wait, Theodore, until I can get you unhooked."

Even as she entered the laboratory, her thoughts returned to Kevin. Adult sleep apnea sufferers had no surgical solutions available, but sometimes younger OSA patients could be cured by a tonsillectomy. The Vreelands' health-care provider was reluctant to cover the procedure since there was no guarantee it would cure the problem, but Sara now had the five or six thousand dollars to remove that dagger of premature death dangling over her son.

It was good news. Great news. She'd talk to Bret about it in the morning.

"Take this off," Theodore gasped.

"You poor thing. Hold on a sec."

Sara turned off the machine, removed the straps. Theodore slouched on the side of the bed, eyes darting back and forth, hands jittery. Again, she thought he seemed familiar, but every day she saw strangers who looked like someone she knew. Barely visible in the dim light, the scars on his legs still hinted at an abusive past.

"There's nothing to be afraid of," she said. "It's just me."

He looked at her from the corner of his eye.

"Don't worry. CPAP was simply our first option for your sleep disorder, but there are others. Did that, uh, bring back some bad memories?"

He shrugged a shoulder. "Momma just wanted me to be strong, ma'am."

Sara wondered what sort of "All Day Hell and Damnation" this man's mother had put him through. She said, "I'm a mom, Theodore. I want my children to be strong, but I'd never do anything to harm them. No child deserves that."

"My daddy, he was weak. Not me."

"I'm sorry to hear that, but you have nothing to be ashamed of."

He sat up taller, peeled the sensors from his body, pulled his T-shirt over broad shoulders. "Are you strong, Sara?" His down-home drawl seemed suddenly less pronounced.

"I'm . . . Well, yes, in many ways I believe I am."

In the booth, her cell phone vibrated on the desk.

"And your boy?"

"Theodore," she said, "this is my workplace. Let's stay focused on—"

"Is Kevin strong like his daddy?"

A chill raised goose bumps on her arms, while her feet edged her toward the insistent phone. "Hold that thought, all right? This could be an emergency."

She felt the big man's gaze follow her into the booth. She eased the door shut, turned the lock. He remained on the bed, forehead furrowed, eyes hooded. How on earth did he know Kevin's name? She'd never divulged that to him. And what'd happened to his drawl? Or his shy, I-don't-mean-to-be-a-bother posture?

Sara turned sideways, cupped the phone to her mouth. "Bret?"

"Sweetheart, if you've got a minute, I need to—"

"Oh, I'm glad you called." She blurted out her thoughts. "I have this patient here, this guy sitting in the other room, and I was trying to help him, to talk him through some past issues that might be related to his sleeping difficulties, but then he turned the questions around and wanted to know stuff about our family. His voice changed. His posture changed. It's like, I don't know, like he turned into this other person all of a sudden."

"Where are you right now?"

"In the booth. With the door locked, thank God."

"Saaara," Theodore called to her.

"And what's he doing?" Bret said.

"Staring at me, calling my name from the bed."

"Ignore him. Is there anyone else in the building? Any security?"

"Saaara."

She did her best to tune that out. She said to Bret, "We have an elderly guard who patrols the front, drinks coffee, and chats up our lady technicians. It's mostly for show, though. I'm not even sure he carries a loaded gun, and my pepper spray's in my purse, in the office down the hall."

"Well, don't go back out there. On the news they just talked about Natalie, the girl from Sip. Did you know she's been missing since Sunday? Scary stuff. All I can think about is the guy she was supposed to meet, the one who gave us the gift certificate. What if he's that ex-con, that Mr. Hart who owns the Charger?"

Sara ventured a glance at the man on the bed. She let her imagination pencil in a mustache and a ball cap over his buzz-cut. "Did you say Mr. Hart?"

"Yeah," Bret replied. "That's what Detective Meade called him."

"Honey, I know you try to protect me from this stuff, but I need to know those types of details upfront. This patient of mine? His name's Theodore Hart."

"He's there in the clinic with you? Sara, listen. You got a chair? Wedge it under that doorknob. Duck down out of view if you can, and stay on the phone. I'm gonna call Meade on the other line, tell him to rush someone over there."

Theodore Hart was his birth name. After his father deserted them, Magnus severed those ties by combining his middle name with his mother's maiden name to form Magnus Maggart. "Theodore" still served as a handy alias, though.

Perched now on the bed, hands gripping the mattress, he knew he would never forget Sara's face as it morphed from bewilderment to realization to fear.

He sang softly: "Oh, Sara, all alone . . ."

Still on her phone, she turned and vanished beneath the lip of the viewing glass. Soon enough, he guessed, the police would be notified of this situation. Friday nights were often busy for the city's public servants, but the threat of a hostage situation or something worse would have them tripping over themselves for a piece of the action.

Of course, they weren't much of a match for a combat-seasoned pro.

For a clean-up artist of his caliber.

I, Magnus, fear no one.

"Sara?" He stood from the bed, retrieved his loaded Kimber Super Carry from his night bag. He tapped the barrel on the glass. "What happened to my sleep therapy? Did I scare you off, little woman? You must admit, I had you eating out of my hand, worrying about my childhood, and nearly tearing up when you saw my scars. Very sweet of you."

Nothing moved in the booth. Was she talking to the cops even now?

"Just to be clear, though, my mother never let me call her 'Momma.' No, that was too casual for someone of her authority. As for you, you're quite the beneficiary, aren't you, raking in Storinka's riches? Yes, I know all about that. Rumors, rumors. Millions of years of evolving communication skills, and homo sapiens still have this nasty habit of flapping their gums."

No response.

"Do you know why Storinka chose you, Sara?" Magnus tapped again, although he had no intention of using the weapon. Not yet. For now, dear Natalie was the object of his aggression. "The old silver fox felt guilty, that's why, and tried buying your forgiveness on his death-bed. What do you say to that?"

Chapter Thirty-seven

SARA SQUATTED BENEATH THE DESK, HER KNEES PUSHED INTO HER CHEST. SHE shifted her weight to a more comfortable position, repositioned the phone. She was still on hold with Bret, while her patient in the adjacent room knocked on the glass and uttered haughty words through the intercom. She told herself not to pay any attention to Mr. Theodore Hart. He was an actor. He had drawn her in with his aw-shucks attitude, bashful grin, and stories about his momma.

She remembered her own words to him: *"Hell and damnation are no more a part of you than they are of me."* So much for her good intentions.

ADHD? She had a new definition for him: *All Day Hiding and Deceiving.*

"Don't pretend you can't hear me," he said to her now.

That was the problem. She could hear every word.

"Even millions of dollars can't buy forgiveness for a man like Ivan Storinka," he continued. "He sold arms to black-market dealers in war-torn countries. He financed terrorists in Chechnya, when it suited his aims, and helped Moscow's politicos when they needed reliable weapons. He was ruthless. If someone defied him, why, the things that man could do with a cigar cutter. Not that I believe in it, but if hell existed, he'd be there now manning the gates."

Don't pay him any attention. Don't trust a thing he says.

Sara tucked her head between her legs, rocking on her heels. The longer the man jabbered, the greater likelihood he would be cornered by the police.

Bret came back on the line. "You still there?"

"This guy's scaring me," she whispered.

"I had to wake Meade up, but he's talking to Metro right now. I love you. Hold tight, OK? I'm gonna check and see what sorta time frame we're on."

The line went flat again, as her patient rambled on.

That's right, wise guy. Keep chatting.

"True enough," Theodore said, "Storinka moved to America and turned a new page, so to speak, but only to avoid his growing list of enemies in Eastern Europe. When they hunted him down, he struck back to safeguard his company and his life. He even killed someone you knew, Sara."

She tried to block out the voice.

"Someone close to you."

You're a liar.

"Not that he did the actual killing, though that's only a matter of semantics. Over twelve years ago he arranged the accident, that unfortunate affair along Route Four-Ten. It was an April evening, just east of Tacoma. Ring any bells? Any wedding bells? Only later did I learn the victim was your groom-to-be."

Sara's stomach twisted. Momentary shock squelched her fear, and she peeked from behind the desk to see her patient waving a gun around the shadowed room, talking like an orator on stage, a mad dictator at his podium. She ducked back down, repulsed by this man only feet away from her.

He said, "Yes, old age causes some men to go soft in the head, even blowhards like Storinka. Six million dollars was his way of buying absolution. The police are no doubt on the way, so I'm going to make my exit before I'm forced to hurt any one of them unnecessarily. Please give your husband my greetings, tell him he owes me a car-window repair. Oh, and ask him why his father took a phone call from Storinka on April seventh, nineteen-ninety-eight."

Eddie Vreeland? How is Bret's dad involved in this?

"Enjoy your millions, Sara."

She heard the outer door click open, heard footsteps pad down the hall. She looked over the windowsill into an empty room. She eased the tightness from her knees, hoping the elderly security guard was on smoke break. He would be no match for Theodore Hart.

"Sara?" Bret was back on the line. "The cops should be there any minute."

"Too late. He's already gone."

"Did he hurt you? Sweetheart, tell me you're OK."

"I'm fine," she said. Then she broke down and cried.

Chapter Thirty-eight

DETECTIVE MEADE ENTERED THE SLEEP LAB, DARK EYES ROVING THE MACHINERY. He stepped over a cord, joined Bret and Sara beside the hospital-style bed. He was a tall man, maybe late thirties, skin as smooth and dark as motor oil. His hair was short and coarse above tired yet alert eyes.

Bret shook his hand. "Bret Vreeland. And my wife, Sara."

"Detective Reginald Meade."

"Good to meet you in person. Is it Reginald? Or Reggie?"

"'Detective' will do."

"Sure thing," Bret said. "Over there, that's Kevin and Katie zonked out on the chairs. Least they don't have school tomorrow."

"Hmm. I feel their pain."

"Yeah, I bet you're kicking yourself for giving me your cell number."

"Here to serve and protect, right?"

"Thank you," Sara said. "I can't even begin to tell you."

Bret wrapped an arm around her, pulled her close. Her whispers on the phone had torn at him. He'd felt helpless, miles away, unable to leave while his children were asleep in their beds. He could only imagine the fear she had faced.

Meade said, "You can breathe easy now, Mrs. Vreeland. We have officers searching the building and clearing the perimeter. They did wake up an older man in his camper-pickup, ID'ed him as Eli Shaffokey. He claims he knows you."

"Eli who?"

"So you don't know him?"

"Yes, he . . . Shaffokey. I never would've guessed. He was my ride home."

"The man seems harmless enough, but always best to check." The detective shifted gears, his gaze circling to the booth window. "This is where it happened, these two rooms? Did your patient leave anything behind?"

"He had a night bag, but it's gone."

"I'm not going to step on any toes regarding private medical histories, but if I could get his basic contact info that would be handy."

Bret watched his wife switch into work mode, standing, buttoning her jacket, and retrieving the patient's info from the booth. Though her knuckles were white against the clipboard, she was no longer trembling as when he first arrived.

She handed it over. "Here you go, Detective."

"Hmm." He eyed the forms. "Looks like the same name and address we already have on file. I'll have a cruiser drop by Mr. Hart's apartment, but I doubt he's going to make it that easy for us. Some perps, they're not exactly the sharpest tools in the shed, but we suspect he's used other identities."

Sara seemed to mull that over, gnawing on her lower lip.

"Let's sit down," Meade said, "and you can tell me what happened."

For the next ten minutes the detective listened, nodded, prodded with occasional questions, and made notes on a pad pulled from the pocket of his black leather coat. Bret wrapped an arm around his wife's shoulder, felt her tense as she spoke of Storinka's possible connection to the death of Alex Page. She paused, hugged her arms over her tummy, and hunched forward.

Bret wondered if she was withholding info. What could she have to hide?

"Any other details you'd like to add, Mrs. Vreeland?" The detective looked her way, but her face stayed down. "Large or small?"

She shook her head.

Meade switched his gaze to Bret and tapped the pad with his pen. "Is it true, Mr. Vreeland, this part about your family receiving an inheritance?"

"Still in probate actually. We're not sure how the word got out."

"Probate proceedings are a matter of public record, giving the relatives and creditors a chance to swoop in for their share. Whenever money's involved, things can get messy, and millions of dollars provide a mighty strong motive. As for Mr. Hart, it could explain his reasons for stalking and intimidation."

"Is there a way to, uh . . .?" Sara pushed a strand of hair from her eyes. "To check his claim that Mr. Storinka planned that accident outside Tacoma?"

"Was there ever a conviction?"

She blinked, chewing on a fingernail.

"It was ruled vehicular homicide," Bret said. "A truck driver. He did three years, got out early on parole."

Bret would never forget those long days in the courthouse providing moral support to Sara. He could still see the defendant hunched and broken in the witness stand, a bulky, shaggy-haired man accused of a tragic, split-second mistake. He was found criminally negligent for the deed, since he had put in more than his limit of over-the-road hours and falsified logbooks to cover the fact.

"I feel sick." Sara stood, pressed her fingers to her temple. "I don't understand. Am I that blind? I mean, yes, Theodore looked vaguely familiar, but the thought never crossed my mind he was the man harassing us. I should've at least. . . . For heaven's sake." She shuddered. "I even shaved his chest while putting on the sensors. He sat right there, Bret. Slept right on that bed."

"And you're safe, that's all I care about. He fooled us with a hat and a fake mustache. I don't even think I'd be able to pick him out of a lineup."

"The sheer audacity, though. He had me feeling sorry for him, like he was some sort of victim. But he's not a victim, is he? He's a known felon. And what about Natalie? You said she's missing, and he could be the one behind it."

Detective Meade sat back. "Is there something else I should know?"

"She's that missing college girl. We think he had contact with her at Sip Café," Bret replied. "They were gonna go on a date this week, but I guess that didn't happen. Least not in the way Natalie thought. We're just praying she's OK."

"Did she ever describe him to you?" When the detective got nothing in return, he said, "Until now, our department's had no evidence in this case, and we thought it could even be a voluntary disappearance. This changes things. And it makes that e-mail from Tacoma seem that much more ominous. I need to verify Mr. Hart's actual identity, and see if he had any ties to Mr. Storinka. I still wonder what he hopes to gain. Does he think you'll just hand over your money to him?"

"He, uh, did say one other thing."

Bret stared up at his wife.

"Yes?" Meade prompted her.

"He told me to pass along a message." She offered Bret an apologetic smile. "For you, hon. It sounds crazy, probably certifiably so, which is why I didn't mention it earlier. I mean, are we going to let this guy play head games with us?"

"C'mon, Sara. Let's hear it."

"As he left, he said that whole piece about you owing him a repair for his window, and then he told me to ask you a question. He wanted to know why Mr. Storinka would call your dad on April seventh of 'ninety-eight. The day of Alex's accident. I would write it off, except for the way your class ring showed up from your parents' house. That was more than a little odd. Almost as if. . . ."

"What?"

"As if he knows them."

"Or broke into their house," Bret shot back.

"And climbed into their attic for a ring boxed up in storage?"

He wanted to deny the very notion, but his wife made a point he had tried to brush off. He knew firsthand his father's character flaws and spotty past. Eddie had changed, though. Cleaned up his act. At least that's the way Bret's mother told it. According to Claire Vreeland, Eddie was a regular charmer now that he was sober again. Bret wanted to believe it for his mom's sake, if for nothing else.

"OK, I'll call him," he said. "Try to feel it out."

"Thanks, honey. I'm sure it's nothing."

Detective Meade was scribbling something on his pad. He considered his work, turned it so they could see letters and numbers separated by dashes.

RT410-4-7-98

"Look familiar?" He tapped with his pen. "Do I have this correct?"

"Yeah," Bret said. "It's part of that e-mail address."

"And what else?"

Sara's voice went flat. "Route Four-Ten. April seventh, 'ninety-eight."

"Mr. Hart not only has knowledge about your current situation but about that past event. While we don't know his motive, I do have a few theories. As for the e-mail, was he the one who sent it? Or was it Bret's father?"

The accusation rankled Bret, yet he couldn't ignore the possibility.

"What should we do, Detective?" Sara closed her eyes. "We're all ears."

"It's nigh-near one a.m., and you're emotionally exhausted. I'm sure your kids would like to be in their beds. All things considered, Mr. and Mrs. Vreeland, I suggest you spend the weekend in a hotel. Get some family time away."

Bret almost commented that was out of the question, but realized money was no longer an obstacle. He nodded. "I think we'll take you up on that."

"As for the inheritance? In my line of work, I get regular reminders just how fragile this life can be. This is a rare opportunity you have. Don't let one man's vendetta or another man's guilt steal away your joy. These are bullies we're talking about, out to rob, steal, kill, and destroy."

"Words from Scripture," Sara said.

Meade nodded. "So you're hearing what I'm saying. Good. Enjoy your kids. Enjoy each other. Store up treasures that you know will last."

"Thank you. We'll certainly try."

"Before you go, I'd like to collect some quick DNA samples, even a hair or two that I can submit for analysis." The detective moved toward the bed. "By cross-referencing state and federal databases, we may come up with a hit."

"Usually," Sara said, "I strip the bedding after each session. I didn't notice until just now that Theodore must've wrapped it up and taken it with him."

"Easy to miss. It's been a long night for you."

"But that leaves you with nothing to work with."

"No, not true, Mrs. Vreeland. What I'm looking for is the razor you used to shave the patient's chest. And this sink here, is it the one you rinsed it in? Was there a towel you used? Trust me, there's DNA just begging to be collected."

"So the cheap shave was worth it after all?"

"Better believe it." The detective poked his head into the hallway, tossed his keys to a younger officer. "Evans, grab me an evidence kit from my trunk, if you would. And while you're out there, tell Mr. Shaffokey he's off the hook. He can go home."

"He has no home," Sara said, catching Bret's eye. "Not yet anyway."

Chapter Thirty-nine

CLAIRE VREELAND SPREAD ANOTHER DOILY ATOP THE PIANO AND PROPPED HER grandson's soccer portrait on it. Kevin was such a little man now, his eyes so serious. Although she missed her grown son and daughter-in-law, she felt particularly robbed of the time with her grandchildren.

Economic hard times were to blame for Bret and Sara's relocation, and she had no right to hold that against them. By no means. But aside from a weeklong trip to Nashville after Katie's birth, Claire never saw her grandbabies and wondered if they would even recognize her on the sidewalk.

This newest picture was something, at least. It came in yesterday's mail, framed and bubble-wrapped with an enclosed note from Sara.

Claire was so happy for them.

$6,000,000? That was hard to imagine, wasn't it?

Bret and Sara announced that they had big plans for Christmas, still to be revealed, and Claire supposed they might be flying out with the kids. How delighted she would be to see her grandchildren.

"It will be wonderful," she said aloud to herself. "Just wonderful. We'll pull down the old comforters and cuddle up by the fire, just as cozy as can be."

Upon hearing the good news, Eddie's musings had turned philosophical.

"All these years I claw and scrape to get by, and my son reaps the rewards. Where's the fairness in that, huh? Tell me, Claire. Where?"

"It's plenty fair," she said. "Since you've never given him a leg up."

"You watch your mouth. I've done things you don't even know."

Oh, but she did know.

She drew back the living room's damask drapes, ushering in pale light that washed the sofa and love seat, the rocking chair, and the oil paintings by her mother. She gazed out at S. Bell Street as she had for decades with hair done, makeup applied, and a brave smile that said all was in order, no need to fret.

Claire's marriage was her private burden, and she carried it as though on pilgrimage. Oh, sure, she'd taught Bret there was nothing he could do to make himself worthy in God's eyes, only the sacrificial love of Christ could cover his sins, but her Catholic upbringing urged her toward acts of penitence.

And for her, fretting was one such act.

"Darling Claire," the church folks called her.

If only they knew the truth about her.

About her husband.

She wished she could go back to those few good years while Bret was in high school. Not only did her son stay out of trouble by venting his teen angst on the football field, earning a spot as first-team all-district linebacker, but her husband stopped his drinking and gambling for nearly two full years, living out his own failed dreams through their only child. During Bret's senior year, though, Eddie slid back into his black hole.

Bret graduated, worked for a local motor-home company, saved his money for an escape into his own apartment. He took courses at a community college where he dated two or three girls, but he always had eyes for Sara. When she got engaged, he was heartbroken.

And then the accident happened.

In her grief, Sara turned to Bret. She found in him the strong man to carry her through her darkness. He found the love of his life, a woman with whom to start a family. Although he feared being like his father, he defied the odds and proved himself a good husband and dad.

For this, Claire was eternally grateful.

Despite suffering verbal and physical abuse over the years, Claire never left Eddie's side. Never let on about their troubles. By sheer stubbornness, she held their small family together, and Bret's current happiness was one thing she pointed to that made it all worthwhile.

Of course, Eddie was Eddie. And recently more the Eddie of old.

He wouldn't even return his grown son's calls. Claire told Bret everything was fine, not to worry, and no, they hadn't sent him any recent e-mails. She barely knew how to use the computer, since that was a freedom Eddie forbade, but she knew things weren't right.

A few weeks back, Eddie's life insurance agent had stopped by, catching Claire out front in the Oldsmobile. Mr. Hart, according to his letterhead. He pressed her for information about Eddie, about Gabe Stilman. When she invited him in for morning tea, he told her he was actually a fraud investigator, weeding out those who wanted to capitalize on the deaths of their friends or family.

How well did Eddie and Gabe know each other?

Was Eddie under financial pressure?

Did he show signs of violence?

Any recent strange behavior?

The questions overwhelmed her, and she shooed the man out, but the suspicions circled as though a fly had planted eggs and let the little rascals hatch. Questions. Buzzing about her head. Giving her not a moment's peace.

She thought back to the day of Gabe's death. She remembered Eddie going out early and coming back late. Yes, he had acted strangely.

She retreated now from the picture window, from the view of the world outside. She found it tiring to wear the smile. She sank into the old recliner, and she remembered exploring the bedroom closet after Mr. Hart's departure.

On the left, she found her flats and white soft-soled sneakers lining the floor. On the right, she found her husband's slippers, tennis shoes, and loafers mingled in one large heap. Buried in that heap, a pair of steel-toed boots looked normal enough, but she knew they were the ones Eddie wore the morning of Gabe's death, and upon closer inspection she found tiny telltale splatters.

"Blood?" she gasped. "Good Lord, Eddie, what've you done this time?"

The insurance man's suspicions were correct, and there was no use pretending otherwise. She was a practical woman, traditional in her views, and it was her job to help cover her husband's faults, same as always.

But this wasn't just another "episode," was it?

It wasn't just another suffered black eye.

Claire Vreeland blotted her lipstick on a napkin and picked up the phone.

Chapter Forty

"Natalie," Magnus said, removing the shackles, "you're free to go."

She cowered against the hut's metal ribbing, thin arms wrapped around her knees, hazel eyes shrouded by matted hair. After ten days in captivity, she was weak, but if she didn't pull herself together soon, he would put a bullet through that skull and walk away. He didn't have patience for weaklings.

He nodded toward her toilet bucket. "You can dispose of your waste, if that matters to you." He toed the bottled water on the dirt. "You can wash your hands and face, or even bathe your wounds."

She worked her jaws and mouth, free at last from the gag.

"Sing 'Zippy-doo-dah,'" he said, "for all I care."

She was conditioned now to get her food, attention, and instructions from him. He hadn't broken her, though. He made sure of that. He never sexually assaulted her, realizing it was a surefire way to break the spirit.

Why, though?

Sex was a basic biological function for the species' survival, so where did it get this influence upon the spirit? As far as he was concerned, all the religious talk about souls and spirits was a load of crock. Yet they got broken all the time.

"If you want, Natalie, you can take a walk to the nearest neighbor's house and call the police."

She clambered to her feet.

"But," he told her, "don't forget the—"

Emitting a growl, she bowled into him. Her small head drove into his gut, her nails tried to claw at his arms, and she drove him back a step or two. He belly-laughed before tossing her aside and watching her land hard on her knees.

"Ha. A valiant effort."

She whipped around, flung clods of dirt at his face.

He sidestepped her attempt and drove her onto her side with a straight-kick to her hip. "A show of toughness. Now that's what I like to see."

Groaning, she curled into a ball, and his pleasure over her display gave way to bittersweet memories.

Magnus was back in his childhood bedroom in the military housing at Fort Lewis-McChord, on the south end of Tacoma. He was a fatherless boy, a lonely boy. But he had his mother. She was worldly wise, combat ready, and wouldn't send him into adulthood without the necessary toughening and conditioning.

He was gritting his teeth. Mother set down the metal stick.

He was fighting back tears. Mother clapped her hands.

"That's what I like to see, Magnus. Be my little man."

He was great and he was strong. Hooah.

Standing now in the Quonset hut, Magnus stared down at Natalie. "You do realize you're not my captive anymore? Go. Be free. But don't forget our agreement. You keep that cell phone of yours handy. When I call for your help, you will give it without question. If you fail to do so, I'll choose a smaller, younger captive next time around. Katie Vreeland, perhaps. I will break her, and it'll be your fault, because you didn't keep your promise to me."

Natalie wiped her face with the back of her hand. She rose to one knee.

"What is our word?" Magnus said. "Just so you'll know that it's me?"

"Antenna."

"Easy for you to remember, I should think."

He stalked from the hut, through the grass, up over the fence. He waited for her to exit. There she was. She stumbled into the moonlight on cramped, feeble limbs. Soon the cops would come to her aid.

Very good. The trap was assembled, the levers and gears set in motion.

And the Vreelands were his prey.

Hunting, he knew, was a primitive art form, an instinctual behavior within the male race, and such instincts felt like personal guidance to Magnus. Whereas the extinct T-Rex had been mighty, Magnus was subtle and sublime.

He threw Natalie a farewell wave. "Keep those antenna up."

Chapter Forty-one

For the second time in as many weeks, Bret weaved through the Belle Meade district, over the stone-sided bridge, between hickory and live oak trees, toward the lantern-topped pillars guarding the Storinka estate.

Nope.

The Vreeland estate.

On this fine autumn morning, he felt almost guilty calling a place like this home. The property alone could contain dozens, if not hundreds of refugees. The mansion was large enough for multiple families. Why, he wondered, would God favor them and let others suffer? Not just people in faraway lands, where Haitians dealt with earthquakes and Sudanese faced genocidal maniacs with machetes, but even those on the streets of America?

What about the recent flood victims here in Music City?

The people still displaced by Hurricane Katrina?

The laid-off autoworkers in Detroit?

Bret did understand that it wasn't within his power to hold off disasters natural, economic, or political, but it seemed unfair that his family's fortunes had changed so drastically while many of their friends still struggled.

Maybe "unfair" was the wrong word. In a "fair" world, each person would receive equal income, matching homes, identical vehicles. But would that be fair to those who busted their backs at work while others dragged their feet?

No, that didn't seem right either.

Verses came to mind:

> *"Good people leave an inheritance to their grandchildren,*
> *but the sinner's wealth passes to the godly." —*Proverbs 13:22
>   *"True humility and fear of the Lord lead to riches. . . .*
> *Do you see any truly competent workers? They will serve kings."*
> —Proverbs 22:4, 29

His thoughts flipped through the various monies he and his family had given over the years to missions and ministries. They offered their resources to the Lord with open hands as opposed to closed fists. Even when on the brink themselves, they reached out, whether with a few dollars to a homeless man, canned goods on Eli's camper step, meals cooked for a pregnant woman's family, or cabinets sanded and stained for a single mother on welfare.

And it was no different now.

A couple weeks back, Bret and Sara had rounded up the amount from Storinka's account, and dropped a $20,000 tithe into the plate at church, using a personal check for tax purposes. They thought it would be hard, but it wasn't.

It was liberating. They were giving back.

Maybe Sara was right about this inheritance being a "gold star" for their work well done. If so, who was he to reject the rewards promised in Scripture?

Bret's latest song played through his head as he neared the estate:

> *"A bed for a king, amongst donkeys and straw . . .*
> *You left heaven behind, and You gave us Your all."*

At the wheel of a U-Haul truck packed with all of his family's earthly goods, he checked his mirror. Sara was behind him in the Lexus, beaming in her big white sunglasses. He waved his arm out the window, and she tapped her horn.

Boy, he couldn't wait to take that sleek Maserati for a spin. Just how fast was the thing? There was no question, though, that they would sell it and buy something more reasonable, a year-old Camry or a Chevy 4 × 4. The money saved could go to better things.

Beside him in the cab, Katie bounced on the bench seat while Kevin rode with an elbow on the door like his dad.

"We're really moving?" Katie said. "For good?"

"For good."

"'Cause it's not safe at our old house?"

"That's a big part of it. It's also why Mom's taking extended time off work. We don't want that guy in the black car messing with us anymore, do we?"

"Nuh-huh. I don't wanna crash."

"That was scary, wasn't it?" Bret pulled her close, caught a whiff of her apple shampoo. "We still need to be careful, but at least at this new place we'll have security cameras and an alarm system."

The estate offered a safe haven. Every time he thought of his wife cornered by that pistol-waving freak, he knew this was the right decision, but the two of them had sought the feedback of others just to be sure.

Pastor Teman insisted once again it was a sign of God's favor.

Bret's mother encouraged him to pay the blessing forward.

The Rileys saved them seats in last Sunday's service, with Derek kidding that he and Jeannie wanted to be close "the next time the Spirit stirs the waters."

"Well, someone must be looking out for you," Jason said, high-fiving Bret at the airport that first weekend after the will's reading. The Billingsleys had no financial need or ulterior motives, and so their celebration seemed genuine.

"Couldn't happen to a more deserving couple," Zoe agreed. She pulled Bret into an exuberant embrace and kissed his cheek. "And Sara? Is she just jumping out of her skin? Oh, she has no idea what she's in for, not even a smidgen. I know every shop owner between here and Manhattan."

As far as Bret was concerned, wealth was fickle, but as a father he loved to bless his own kids. And wasn't God's heart a thousand times larger?

"Marched to the cross, like a criminal scorned . . .
You left riches in g.lory for a crown of thorns."

How could he refuse this good gift when his Heavenly Father had sacrificed so much to make it possible?

"I bow, I bow down, I bow down to the Servant King."

"Daddy?" Katie was tapping his arm. "Why didn't we bring our swing set?"

"That old thing?" Kevin huffed. "It's so rusty, Mom says if we scratched ourselves on it we'd get blood poisoning and need tetanus shots."

Katie shook her blond curls back and forth. "I hate shots."

"It's just a needle."

"I hate needles."

Kevin sneered. "Even the Seattle Space Needle?"

"Whoa now," Bret said. "She's never been there, and you were too young to remember. You were barely two when we moved here from Washington."

"I remember."

Bret stopped at the limestone ramparts, punched in the code on the keypad. As the arched gates parted, he gave his son a look. "Kev, it's really OK to admit when you're wrong. What's Proverbs say? 'Fools think they need no advice, but the wise listen to others.' That's one of the signs of growing up."

"Wow." Kevin deflected the attention. "Look at this. Is it for real, Dad?"

"Pretty cool, huh?" Bret pulled ahead, waited for the gate to close behind Sara in the Lexus. "You're gonna meet Viktor in a minute. He's put down money on his own property out in Kingston Springs, plenty of room for his dogs, so he's letting us move in early."

As executor and trustee, Viktor Moroz had already petitioned the court to open probate and admit the will, but on the phone with Bret and Sara he also listed his other responsibilities, such as obtaining a performance bond, inventorying assets, and managing properties during the process. Creditors had a six-month window in which to file claims. If the will survived probate, estate taxes would come out of it, with the inheritance tax at a higher rate since Sara was a nonlineal heir. From there, Viktor would distribute and/or liquidate assets as stipulated.

"Legally," he explained, "the mansion and the cars are still held by the trust agreement, but it's my job to make sure they are taken care of during this process. Someone needs to watch over these things. So why not you?"

He meant Sara, of course.

Bret kept thinking how it was her name in the testamentary trust, and even in community property states, rights to an inheritance were not automatically shared with a spouse. When he told her his fears, she assured him there was nothing to worry about. They were in this together.

As the U-Haul rolled beneath the canopy of branches, Kevin said, "So, Dad, how many square feet are we talking?"

"Listen to you, Mr. Realtor. Over five-thousand-five-hundred."

Katie wrinkled her nose. "All I see's grass and trees."

"Keep your eyes open. In about thirty seconds we'll be pulling up to our new home, except it's not really new since it's from the days of the Civil War."

The long drive broke free from stippled shadows, depositing them at the front of the mansion. Sunlight winked from ivy-framed windows, water burbled in the fountain, and stone geese rose in perpetual flight from the mossy pool.

"Coooool," the kids shouted in delight.

Bret saw Kevin reach for the door. "Nope. Wait till we're parked."

Moments later, the four of them gathered around the steps and stared at the door that would usher them into a whole new existence. This went above and beyond anything they ever dreamed of. It was more than they needed. More than ninety-nine percent of the world ever experienced.

Bret again felt humbled by such extravagance.

Why us, Lord? What've we done to deserve this?

He realized, with a touch of irony, that he had prayed these exact same words in times of hardship and desperation.

"I wanna go inside," Katie said.

"Absolutely." Sara lifted sunglasses onto her forehead. Her eyes glowed. "You two'll love it. You three," she amended, hooking Bret's arm with her own.

"We should pray first," Kevin said. "You always tell us to say thank you before we start playing with our birthday presents."

Sara tilted her head toward Bret. "Out of the mouth of babes."

Kevin stiffened. "I'm ten."

"Go ahead and lead us," Bret said.

They joined hands. Kevin prayed. Once he was finished, they faced the mansion as a family. Bret started them off, and with one voice they declared: "'As for me and my house, we will serve the Lord.'"

The door opened. Viktor invited them in. He introduced himself to the kids, and gestured toward the sweeping double staircase and the chandelier.

"It's all yours," he said. "Your fortunes are about to change."

Chapter Forty-two

AND CHANGE THEY DID.

After the children got the tour and chose their own rooms, Bret led them out back to see the stable and garage. Sara suspected he wanted another look at the Maserati before he put it up for sale. With Viktor at her side, she entered the spacious kitchen, where cabinets and a walk-in pantry had been skillfully refurbished to join antebellum appeal with the needs of a modern chef. The appliances were top-notch European, glistening and barely used.

"Viktor," she said, "this is amazing. Thanks for letting us move in early. You don't even know what a big deal this is for us right now."

He dipped his chin in acknowledgment. "Mr. Storinka would be happy. If you don't mind, I packed my own kitchen supplies to use where I'm going. The furniture throughout the house will stay here, yours to keep. As for the room upstairs, the one beside the master suite, I boxed up the contents but they are of no monetary value. One day I will show them to you."

"Sure. I trust your judgment."

Sara did remember Storinka's privacy about that particular room. Although she gave it little attention then, her curiosity was now primed after Theodore's recent accusations about the old man and his blood money.

"All of this, Viktor, it's far more than I ever expected. But this kitchen? My goodness, it's immaculate. Did you ever cook in here?"

"Every day. Who do you think fed Mr. Storinka?"

"You're kidding. Well then, give me the name of your cleaning service."

"I was the housekeeper. I told you that when we met."

"Yes, you did." She grinned. "You know, I figured you for a body-guard. The morning I came by, I was certain you had a gun under your sports jacket."

"I still do." He flashed it for her to see. "A Walther PPS. Very reliable."

"Goodness, is that thing even legal?"

"I have a carry permit, yes. When I first moved to America years ago, I studied law at University of Washington and made sure I walked the proverbial line. Does it surprise you that not all Ukrainians are criminals?"

"Was Mr. Storinka?"

Viktor stepped back. "Please, Sara. He's no longer with us."

"I don't mean to be disrespectful, but I've, uh, caught wind of some rumors about his arms manufacturing, that he wasn't always so easy to get along with. This is important to me. I need to know."

"What have you heard?"

"Did he arrange for people to be killed?"

"You Americans." He wagged his finger from side to side. "You fill your heads with scenes from your blockbuster action movies."

"Fine. I'm being a silly woman. Answer me this, though. Did he have business dealings in Washington State? Did he know we moved here from the Northwest? Was he watching my family?"

Viktor faced her over the enormous kitchen island, his eyes passive. He was the trustee, the man not only managing this property but also extending a favor by handing over the keys, and she was risking his wrath.

So be it. She needed the truth.

Was Storinka's gift a form of blood money? The price for her forgiveness? She recalled his words: *"I was wrong . . . I have a plan, a way to settle matters."*

"Storinka Defense Systems," Viktor replied, "is an international business, with holdings in a dozen countries. Years ago, yes, he had offices near Seattle's shipping yards. But he wasn't watching your family. He knew you came from that region because you spoke of it during your visits at the clinic and more recently here at the house. Was it a secret to be guarded?"

"Not true," Sara said. "He even tried to throw me off, guessing that we might be from northern California."

"If there's anything suspicious, it is the way you stepped in and won him over in his final days."

"You think that was calculated on my part? I had no clue he was rich."

"Please, no. Don't worry." Viktor clapped a hand on the island. "My dogs liked you, yes, even with all their barking, and I trust my girls. I only mean to show you how easy rumors arise. Now, have I answered your questions?"

"One more," she said. "Did he know a man named Alex Page?"

Viktor lifted his chin, his spiky hair like the plume of a centurion's helmet or the feather's of a combative bird. "It's sad. The man leaves you millions, and here you try to desecrate his memory and punish him for his sins."

She wasn't letting go of this. "So he knew Alex?"

"They were business associates. After the unfortunate accident, accusations haunted Storinka and he lived with them the rest of his days. But I assure you, he did not kill Mr. Page. He mourned his loss."

"So did I," Sara said. "He was my fiancé."

Movement at the window turned her head, and she saw Pastor Teman pull up in a church van. Bret greeted him as men piled out, representing the weekly Bible study group that Bret hosted at Portland Brew, another of East Nashville's coffeehouses. They must be here to lend a hand.

She said, "I meant no disrespect, Viktor."

"I understand. And please, I'm sorry to hear how you were affected by this tragedy. At least you found a good man in Mr. Page's absence."

"Absolutely." Her throat muscles constricted. "Bret's the best."

By the time Sara reached the front door, she had regained her composure. She welcomed in the moving crew, thanked them for coming, and directed the assembly line of boxes from the U-Haul into bedrooms, bathrooms, guest rooms, study, living room, sitting room, landings, family room, dining room, and entry hall. The belongings from Groves Park barely dented the space here.

She was most excited about her new kitchen, but this soured as she peeled open each box. She'd never given much notice nor been able to address the chipped, warped, scratched, and discolored state of her kitchenware. The pots and pans were a gift from her wedding day. The salad fork and spoon wore spots of rust. Viewed against this backdrop, it all seemed hopelessly out of place.

Surely, she told herself, Bret would agree to a shopping spree.

On budget, of course. Always on budget.

"The guys're about done," Bret said, sweeping past her. "And the kids, they're bouncing off the walls in their rooms. You'd think it was Disney World."

"Perhaps we can take them there, once probate closes." She caught his hand. "Thanks for calling for help. What a blessing."

"Wasn't me. Pastor took that upon himself."

"That was thoughtful. Do you think we should, uh, pay them something?"

"They'd be insulted. This is church family, not a moving company."

"In the past," she said, "we would've scraped together change for some chips and Dr. Pepper. I don't know. Doesn't that seem a bit inadequate now?"

"Whaddya mean?"

"You know."

"What? Just say it, Sara.'

"The guys. Pastor Teman. They all know."

"About the money? Listen, you think I don't struggle with this too?" Bret's green eyes met hers. "Jerry, he's been looking for work since last Christmas. The Campbells, with their five kids, they're scraping just to feed the mouths at their table. Boy, do we know what that's like. And now look at us, sitting pretty."

"What? Are we supposed to refuse God's gifts? I don't think so."

"No, me neither."

"I believe God's blessed us and wants us to enjoy it," Sara said.

"And get this." Bret stepped closer. "Pastor pulls me aside and tells me Derek Riley likes my songs and is arranging a meeting at Desperado Artist Development. We're talking producers with Grammys. It's where Johnny Ray Black records his stuff. This could be huge."

"Desperado? On Music Row? Hon, that's unbelievable."

"Yeah, we'll see what happens. Listen, you're right," he said, reaching for his wallet. "It's not like we're gonna solve all the world's problems by midnight. We're still figuring this out ourselves. Here. Take a twenty and go grab a couple dozen Krispy Kremes and some coffee. The guys'll be thrilled."

"You certain twenty's enough?"

"Forty better?"

She nodded, accepted the bills, and recruited Katie to join her in the Lexus, knowing a six-year-old could get trampled in the house. The "house"? While that sounded too casual, anything else sounded pretentious. She couldn't exactly go to work or church and invite friends over for "dinner at our mansion."

Sara was unfamiliar with the Belle Meade area, but she used her cell to track down a nearby donut shop. She and her daughter made their selections from shelves of fresh goodies, and within twenty-five minutes they were back at their front gates. In Katie's lap, the donut boxes nearly reached her button nose.

Sara was tapping in the gate code when an American-built sedan appeared in her rearview. She squinted for a better look.

Was that Detective Meade at the wheel? And who was that beside him?

Katie turned, nearly toppled the tower of donuts.

"Watch what you're doing there, cutie."

"Look, Mommy," Katie squealed. "It's Natalie. Natalie's alive."

Natalie was alive. She was also terrified.

"She escaped, but she's been through quite an ordeal," Detective Meade told Bret and Sara in their study. "Assault, deprivation, isolation. Mr. Hart is our primary suspect. The one bit of good news, there was no sexual contact. She's young and she'll bounce back, but she's afraid of being in her dorm at Trevecca Nazarene, same thing with her job at Sip. Can't really blame her, can you?"

"He beat her with an antenna?" Sara clung to her husband. "How could anyone do such a thing? That's just evil. Our family loves her, the poor thing."

"And she's expressed her love for you. Her own family's in Idaho, parents divorced, says she doesn't have much connection." Meade folded his arms. "I haven't mentioned this to her yet, so there's no pressure, but I do have an idea."

"Yeah?" Bret said. "Let's hear it."

"With Mr. Hart still on the loose, you have your own worries for Kevin and Katie. Natalie tells me she loves kids and has college credits in child education. Why not take her on as a live-in tutor? Seems it could work well for everyone."

Chapter Forty-three

Bᴏᴏᴋᴍᴀɴ ɪɴɪᴛɪᴀᴛᴇᴅ ᴄᴏɴᴛᴀᴄᴛ ᴡɪᴛʜ ᴀ ᴛᴇxᴛ ᴍᴇssᴀɢᴇ.

Latest info? Call 8 a.m.

From his pillow, Magnus Maggart heard the cell quivering on the nightstand and spotted the message. When it vibrated again with all the fervor of a hornet in a jar, he heaved himself to a sitting position and slapped the thing to his ear.

"What?"

There was no voice on the other end, of course, and he sneered at his own mistake. His time in the military, his tour in Bosnia, had taught him that sleep deprivation hampered even the most conditioned soldiers. Tonight he'd tried sleeping on his side, his back, his other side, and nothing worked. Sara Vreeland was right. Although his appointments at her clinic were a ploy to toy with his prey, she had convinced him he needed therapy.

Sleep therapy. Just to make that clear. When it came to therapy for the mentally disturbed, he figured he ought to be the one dispensing the advice.

"Suck it up," he'd tell them. "Embrace your pain. Be strong."

He erased Bookman's text along with its Washington State prefix. A cell's position could be triangulated, its conversations intercepted. These basic precautions had saved him in times past while doing cleanup for Storinka.

He shuffled to the safe in the hotel closet, one of those deals with a reprogrammable security code, and retrieved the docs, pics, and clippings related to the Vreelands. He spread them on the lopsided table, took a seat in a cheap metal chair, and dialed his newest boss from memory.

"M-and-M," Bookman answered. "You in a good place to talk?"

"Which am I, the rapper or the little chocolate-coated candy? If that's meant to protect my identity, it won't work for long."

"Bookman's not exactly a brainteaser either." His employer mocked him in that gravelly tenor voice, poking at him the way a bully poked a stick at a dog in its kennel. "But don't you think M-and-M's better than B for Braggart?'"

Magnus stiffened. He wasn't some canine to be messed with.

"You still there? What's the latest, boyo?"

Magnus sensed once again that the man was disguising his identity, tacking on "boyo" as an afterthought. Was this his standard precaution? Or was he someone Magnus knew already, someone trying to remain anonymous?

"One moment," he said. He thumbed through his documents. This old-school paperwork could be destroyed forever, whereas computer files had a way of coming back to bite the careless. "First, you should know that the family has moved onto the estate, driven there early by fear. I've backed off, per your instructions. As for the will, it's still in probate. No way around that. The county courts and their jesters are slow to act."

"It's true, then? The old man gave her everything?"

"Almost everything. His longtime 'housekeeper' also got a share. I had the very same man on my payroll, my eyes and ears at the estate, but that pipeline's dried up now that he no longer needs my cash."

"Have you put another pair of eyes into place yet?" Bookman said.

"My dear Hazel Eyes."

"Who?"

"She's tutoring their kids." Magnus leaned back, drawing a groan from the metal chair. He was still strong as an ox, but gradual weight gain had triggered his sleeping difficulties. "Even so, I bet she can't stop thinking about me."

"Your ego knows no bounds, does it? Tell me this, my chocolate-coated candy, have you caught wind of any troubles with the probate process? And debtors? Any greedy little relatives crawling out from their hidey-holes?"

"Storinka had no family to speak of. And his company was in the black."

"So no troubles?"

Magnus closed his eyes. "What're you getting at?"

"I don't want complications. The old man picked this woman for a reason."

"As you told me earlier, it's never just about the money."

"That's right. Power, companionship, freedom.

Magnus chuckled. "You missed one."

"I doubt that."

"Guilt."

"Oh-ho," Bookman said, "guilt's just an obstacle to one or all of the above."

"Whatever you call it, the old man wanted absolution."

"He wanted freedom."

Annoyed by his employer's smugness, Magnus jabbed the cracked remote in the direction of the TV and changed the channel to the morning news. On Mute, the newscasters were nothing more than voiceless puppets. He wondered again about the true identity of this man on the phone.

A former Storinka employee? A rival?

Someone linked personally to the Vreelands?

"Very well," Magnus said. "He wanted freedom from guilt. He stole something precious to her, a person she loved, and he didn't want to carry that to his grave. Look it up. It filled your local headlines back in April of 'ninety-eight."

"And you know he was responsible? You have proof?"

"There was a funeral, and it's hard to argue with a corpse. I should know," Magnus said. "Why, I'm the one who was paid to carry out the deed."

Gravel rumbled in Bookman's voice. "I'm well aware."

"And you're upset? You knew the type of man I was when you hired me."

On the TV, the news flashed a photo of dear Natalie, safe and sound, while nighttime security footage showed a hunched figure, head down and face indistinguishable, entering Cumberland Sleep Clinic.

"Relax," Magnus said. "I'll make certain you get what you're after. And don't pretend that money's not a part of it. You knew about the will, didn't you? You knew of the old man's connection to this family. That's why you targeted them before anyone else realized they were beneficiaries."

Bookman changed the subject. "Is it true you were married years ago?"

Magnus dropped his chair legs back onto the carpet. "Excuse me?"

"My own wife, she's a real piece of work. Sweet as pie, her friends would tell you, but they aren't the ones living with her day in and day out, are they? It makes a man wonder. Makes him think about what he might do under different circumstances."

"With a different woman?"

"Why not?" Bookman said.

"Ha. So it's companionship you're after."

"Or the power to get it on my terms instead of someone else's."

Magnus coughed out a laugh. As far as he was concerned, marriage was a ball and chain. Although it provided a sense of security and teamwork during the early stages of mankind's development, it now did nothing but hinder the species' advancement. Best to shed it like a vestigial tail.

"Hear me now," Bookman said. "The only way you'll get the rest of your contract is by clearing the path so I can get what I'm after."

"I won't disappoint you. The trap's already set, just waiting to be sprung. I have the young woman in position, and I've recruited some other people as well. Not to mention, the family members themselves have weaknesses I can exploit."

"Don't we all, boyo?"

"The things people turn to in times of trouble tell a lot about them. Even more telling? Things they turn to when the pressure's off and times are good."

"Athletes in the off-season. Churchgoers on a weekend in Vegas."
Magnus grinned. "Exactly."

"Soldiers on leave."

His grin flattened, and his pulse quickened.

"So tell me," Bookman said, "is that what happened to you? Bosnia. 'Ninety-six. Dishonorable discharge for aggravated assault and insubordination."

"Oh, they regret it now. I was one of their best."

"B for Best? I think you've got that wrong."

Magnus told himself to breathe deeply, to remain calm.

Bookman kept pushing. "Don't you let your own weaknesses jeopardize my goals, you understand? You've already been caught on camera, blown a cover, and been forced to abandon your apartment and vehicle."

"I've since switched names and locations."

"Wonderful. You keep it that way. Now here's the thing, I need you to fly out to my neck of the woods. There's a potential problem, something that could throw a monkey wrench in all our plans. You come on out. Do what you do best. Investigate, intimidate, infiltrate, and inflict. If we hold off these problems till the dust settles in probate, we can both cash in and walk away untouched."

Untouched? No, Bookman, you'll pay for trying to shame me.

"Check your e-mail," his employer said. "The tickets should be there, already paid for from your expense account."

"Why should I trust you? My bruises just healed from my last visit."

"Nothing like that again, I promise."

"But I can't leave now," Magnus said. "Especially with—"

"You work for me, right? And didn't you just say that you're backing off for the time being? Trust your recipe. Let them cook in their own juices. Your flight's scheduled to take off tomorrow morning, so you better get packing."

"Si, senor," Magnus mumbled. "No problemo."

Even as he said it, he thought of Natalie. Was she enjoying her privileged life on the Vreeland estate? Were her wounds healing? He had shown her respect by showing restraint. It was no wonder, despite the pain and panic in her eyes, that she looked to him with a tinge of adoration.

"What's my motivation?"

He wanted to know what new troubles brewed in the Northwest. Wanted to know Bookman's identity. Wanted to carry out orders, collect his paycheck, and teach a few lessons to this smug, gravel-voiced man.

Most of all he wanted to see *her* again.

My Natalie.

Chapter Forty-four

November 2010

Bret walked along Radnor Lake. Nestled in the hills of Nashville, this wildlife area offered gorgeous late autumn vistas, and he marveled at trees crowned in yellow, orange, and gold. He veered from the main path, climbed a ridge, and spotted eight deer munching on the undergrowth. The ninth was a six-point buck, head up, eyes alert.

Bret slowed to a stop. He watched the small herd wander off and felt a deep appreciation for God's creation. This was why he came here.

As he continued his walk, he thought of how much things had changed. For eight years, he'd spent every Tuesday morning sweating in a warehouse, but this Tuesday he was taking the day off and seemed to have the park to himself.

Yep. All that work finally paid off.

How many times had he and his wife heard sermons telling them if they were faithful in the little things they would be put in charge of greater things? If they sowed good seed they would reap the rewards? If they invested their talents wisely they would see them multiply? They were children of the King, after all.

It all sounded good.

But to those digging ditches along the Yellow Brick Road, such words felt like stinging rain, and after a decade of faithfulness and seed-sowing and claiming rights as heavenly heirs, the Vreelands had still lived paycheck to paycheck.

What about the American Dream?

What about the "pursuit of happiness"?

On a regular basis, they read Apostle Paul's words in Philippians 4:12: *"I know how to live on almost nothing or with everything. I have learned the secret of living in every situation, whether it is with a full stomach or empty, with plenty or little."* Either way, they decided, their goal was to be content.

And here, at long last, they were reaping the rewards.

With the riches at their fingertips, Bret and Sara had a multitude of decisions to make, each one weighted by a variety of factors. While their freedoms seemed greater than ever, so did the consequences of failure.

How'd the old saying go? "The bigger they are, they harder they fall."

As Bret rounded the northeast corner of the lake, he thought back to his college days when financial decisions had to do with used course books versus new books, fast food versus on-campus meals, city buses versus his gas-guzzler. He thought of those early years of marriage and parenting when health insurance cut deeply into their monthly income, when a date night meant playing backgammon at Taco Bell, chowing down dollar burritos and free refills of Coke, while the babysitter raked in the majority of their evening's budget.

It all seemed laughable compared to the numerous concerns and choices they now faced. Not that he was complaining. Far from it.

Circling the lake, he ticked off some of the items on his mental list.

Theodore Hart?

Weeks had gone by without a sign of him, his Dodge Charger, or his unique brand of intimidation. Regardless, abduction and aggravated assault were serious offenses, and Detective Meade vowed this case would not slip off his radar. He was still waiting on DNA results from TBI's lab.

With price no longer standing in his way, Bret bought a Glock 23, a 9mm semi-automatic. Best to be prepared.

The detective told him it was one of the world's most trusted handguns and helped him through the concealed-weapon permit process.

Kevin and Katie?

Despite the lull in Mr. Hart's fear tactics, Bret and Sara decided to pull the children from their schools and keep them close by. No need to get careless.

And Natalie?

They worked with her to find suitable curriculum, and as a family project turned one of the mansion's guest rooms into a schoolroom, replete with desks, rolling blackboards, oak lockers and shelves for supplies. In a nod to the future, they bought iPads for the tutor and her students. No more spine-breaking packs full of books. Now it was all at their fingertips.

Sara?

For reasons of safety after her confrontation with Theodore, she extended her leave from the sleep clinic. She received regular invitations to coffee and scones at Atlanta Bread Company with some of the church ladies. Zoe Billingsley dropped by daily to keep her company, and promised to sweep Sara away on a shopping spree of "just us girls, to the Big Easy, the Big Apple, or maybe both."

Sara taught Katie how to cook basic items. She taught Kevin how to shovel out a barn, an important task now that they were renting the estate stable to a neighbor girl with a horse needing space to gallop and graze.

Bret?

For reasons of sanity, he kept punching a clock at the coach company, needing stuff to do with his hands and his time. Regardless, his shop hours decreased while his tee times with Jason Billingsley increased. Bret discovered he had a killer golf swing, even if his short game failed him more often than not.

His old crew kidded him regularly about his new situation.

"Wha's wrong with you anyways, Vreeland? You one of dem workaholics? Stay 'round here too long, and you gonna lose a finger in the table saw."

"That's right. Me, I'd be on G6 flying a straight shot outta here."

"What?" Bret said. "And leave you clowns to run the asylum?"

"Dude, your old lady's loaded. I say, milk that long as you can. You wanna buy yourself a flat-screen? You do it. New wheels? You pick top of the line."

"You gotta wear da pants, Vreeland. You tell her wha's what."

"You guys have it all wrong," he said. "It's not like Sara's some sorta nag or spy. These boundaries, they're just our way of keeping on top of things."

"Call it what you want, dude. You done turned in your Man Card."

"Been upgraded," he joked back. "To full-on Family Man."

Some afternoons Bret spent father-son time with his ten-year-old, hitting golf balls together on the back end of their property. Kevin talked a lot about the girl with the horse. Her name was Hannah. She was also in fifth grade.

"I told her that next week's my appointment for a tonsillectomy, and she didn't even know what that was. Pretty dumb," Kevin said, "if you ask me."

"Seems kinda harsh, buddy. You only know because you're getting one."

"But don't you think girls are weird? She's always playing with her hair."

"Hmm. I think girls are just glad you're thinking about them."

"Dad, that's not even . . . I wasn't . . . forget it."

Thanks to Derek Riley's connections, Bret put in studio time at Desperado, bringing to life song after song from lyrics and chords that for years lay dormant in his lined notebook. These were his heart cries to a God who collected the tears of His children, who inscribed their names on the palms of His nail-scarred hands. Pastor Teman said his music was "anointed," and if the CD got into the hands of the right people it could "really take off."

Bret was more concerned about his passion coming through. In the studio, worship with his voice and guitar sometimes felt strained, especially after the seventh or eighth take. Sure, in front of a crowd he was more likely to tense up, but that tension demanded his humble reliance on God.

The Subaru?

They gave it to a needy family in the church. The husband, an auto mechanic, said he could whip it back into shape without much trouble.

The Lexus?

They kept it as Sara's runaround car, comfortable but not too flashy and rated high on collision safety.

The Maserati Granturismo?

Even in Belle Meade the vehicle turned heads. Bret drove it to work once or twice at the request of his crew, but the thing was ostentatious, costly to repair, and even costlier to insure. Sara told Bret he looked absolutely dashing behind the wheel, but Bret told Viktor to put it up for sale.

The house at 724 Groves Park Road?

They met with their bank manager and paid off the mortgage in a lump sum of $51,304. They'd forgotten what it was like to walk without that burden on their backs, and they felt younger, lighter, stronger.

On Sunday afternoon, Bret and Sara stood in their old driveway and handed their keys to Eli Shaffokey. Sara hugged the older gentleman, and his eyes glistened.

"You sure you wanna do this?"

"Definitely," Bret said, shaking Eli's hand. The grip was firm, the skin dry and rough. "We've watched you work hard, helping out around the church. Pastor vouches for you, says you're as deserving as they come."

Salt-and-pepper brows arched over Eli's gray eyes. "Don't know 'bout that. Don't know that any of us is deserving, but that's what makes grace so amazing."

"Eli, you're a wise man," Sara said.

"That's old age for ya. Wrinkles, white hair, and wisdom out the wazoo."

"OK." Bret laughed. "We'll take your word for it."

"It's a mighty big step, giving up your home. You know, I don't talk about it much, but it's not like I never had me a nice place. Lotsa good memories there."

"What happened?" Sara said. "I mean, how'd you end up in a camper?"

Eli shrugged, his eyes twinkling. "God and His mysterious ways."

"Listen," Bret said, "if you saw the new place we're living, you'd know not to worry. You will have to fix the dishwasher here, but you're good at that stuff and it's not like you'll pile dishes as quick as the four of us. Sara and I, we've talked this over with Kev and Katie, and we all agree this is what we wanna do."

"What can I say? Thank you kindly, Mr. and Mrs. Vreeland. Your family's always been good to me. 'Course, if anything changes, you just lemme know. Never can tell when you might need the place back."

"I doubt that's gonna happen."

"Look," the older man said, "if it's my camper you're after, it's not up for grabs. Makin' that clear right now."

"What?" Bret grabbed his chest. "I'm crushed."

"But," Sara said, "you'll still give me rides every now and then, I hope."

"That I will do. Either way, I'm keeping your names on that mailbox."

"Just in case God forgets our address, huh?"

"He never forgets," Eli said. "We're the ones who do that."

Chapter Forty-five

THE AVALANCHE OF BLESSING CONTINUED ITS ROARING, CLIFF-CLEARING, white-majesty descent through the lives of the Vreeland family. Two months after the reading of the last will and testament, Bret was still amazed by their shift in fortunes.

Seated in the dining room, he inhaled the Thanksgiving aromas of oven-roasted turkey, homemade rolls, mashed potatoes, yams, stuffing, cranberry sauce, and green bean casserole. He was joined at the long table by Eli, Natalie, Pastor Teman and Rhonda, Jason and Zoe Billingsley, Derek and Jeannie Riley, and the members of his own family. Pastor led the gathering in prayer.

Yep, Bret thought, there was so much to be thankful for.

They had five acres of property, shaded, well-tended, protected by tall limestone walls and cameras guarding the perimeter 24/7.

They had a huge home in which to raise their children, a place full of history, mystery, and character.

They had a live-in tutor.

They had vehicles to drive.

They had millions of dollars of stock in Storinka Defense Systems.

They had updated medical checkups, with clean bills of health all around, and their son's tonsillectomy had gone without a hitch.

They had six figures socked away in a checking account, an amount that seemed almost obscene, considering ten weeks ago they were worried a $49 portrait package might overdraw their account and incur subsequent bank fees. As throughout their marriage, they shared joint access to the funds, and they agreed to purchase large-ticket items only on consensus. "Large-ticket" used to mean anything over $100, but that figure now stood at $500.

They had a financial consultant, a man from their church who had the heart of a teacher. He advised them on tax liabilities and investment options, in anticipation of the day a circuit judge closed probate. They intended to diversify their stock portfolio, increase their term life insurance, and establish college trust funds for the children.

These blessings ran through Bret's head as the prayer dragged on. Bret ventured a peek at Sara. She was fidgeting, clearly concerned that the food was getting cold.

"Amen," Pastor Teman said at last.

"Amen." Bret lifted fork and knife in opposing fists. "Let's dig in."

Kevin and Katie followed orders, while Sara shot him a look from the far end of the table.

"Bret," Zoe said with a grin, "you are such a caveman."

"Caveman want drink." He pointed at the bottles of Carriage House White, brought from Belle Meade Plantation by the Billingsleys for this joyous occasion.

"All yours." Zoe handed over the wine along with a corkscrew.

"Who wants some?" he said, popping the cork. "We got lots to celebrate."

Two hours later, he was so full he could barely lift a finger. The Rileys said farewell, still planning to visit their son over in East Nashville. Eli caught a ride with them. Bret, feeling droopy-eyed, plopped into a rec room armchair beside Jason to watch the Saints-Cowboys game. Natalie and Kevin battled out some mean air hockey. Zoe and Katie rang up points on the *Pirates of the Caribbean* pinball machine. Sara played the arcade Ms. Pacman.

Amidst this activity, Bret's suspicions circled back to Tacoma. He wanted to shove them down for now, but they seemed to pop up at the worst of times.

His pewter class ring.

Theodore Hart had delivered it in its little black box, but how did he get a hold of it? Was it stolen from his mom's attic? Handed over by his dad to avoid a string of old gambling debts? How many times had Eddie and his pal Gabe Stilman disappeared for a few days and come back with emptied pockets, boozy breath, and bloodied lips?

And the e-mail sent from the public library.

Mr. Hart could've written it, but what about this idea that Eddie was in contact with Mr. Storinka on the day of Alex Page's death? If Eddie once robbed a bank to buy a mere ring for his son, was he capable of arranging a deadly accident so the same son could have the one woman he loved?

That was crazy. There was no way.

Yet the strands of intimidation kept twisting back to that period over twelve years ago, and Bret felt as though the noose were tied about his own neck.

On the one hand, he wanted nothing more than to look his father in the eye and demand the truth. On the other, he wanted to treat his mother to all the goodness she deserved, all the things she'd been deprived of through the years by a man often more interested in feeding his addictions than his family.

Most of all Bret wanted to protect his wife.

She had suffered enough back in '98, and he wouldn't let anything rip from her the joy and freedom of their new circumstances.

"Sara?" He waved from his reclined position. "You ready to do this?"

"Like Brutus."

He smiled as she came over from the wall of video games. "Glad to hear you sounding less stressed. And thanks again, sweetheart. That dinner rocked. I'd give you a great big hug if I could pull myself outta this chair."

"So much for all that caveman talk, huh?"

"What Zoe said? Hey, my table manners, they're still a work in progress, but at least she didn't seem to mind."

"Yes. Awfully magnanimous, isn't she?"

Magna-what?

Still drowsy, he wasn't sure he had that definition nailed down, and the image of his boss's wife in her heels and tight capris further clouded matters. She was magna-something, and he didn't want to think too much about that. "Whaddya say? We'll call our parents later, but do you wanna be the one to deliver the news now that we got everyone fed, relaxed, and in one room?"

Sara glanced at the HDTV. "What about that?"

"The game?" He hit the remote's Off button. "Halftime, so it's all good."

The sudden drop in volume caused every head to turn. They'd been told an announcement was coming, and their eyes widened in anticipation.

Chapter Forty-six

"COZUMEL? FOR CHRISTMAS?" CLAIRE VREELAND CLASPED ONE HAND TO HER heart, while holding the phone with the other. "Oh, Bret, you can't pay for that."

"Sure we can. And we did."

"Who's all going?"

"Thirteen total. Our friends, Jason and Zoe, they helped arrange it all since they're the big-time Mexico fanatics. We're staying in a private villa, five full days, entire place to ourselves. It's them, you and Dad, me and Sara, her mom and stepdad, our pastor and his wife, and our live-in tutor to help with Kev and Katie."

"My grandbabies? I . . . I'm so pleased, dear. So very pleased."

Claire peered down the hall toward the kitchen, where Eddie was ransacking cupboards. This Thanksgiving Day, they had no guests. She loved serving others around her table, but it took too much effort masking the pain in this place. Just covering for short periods in public left her plumb worn out.

"Cozumel," she repeated. "My, it's hard to even imagine. Will it be warm?"

"Peak season. Bring lotsa sunscreen."

"Sounds delightful. You know how miserable the weather here will be."

"Rain for nine months outta the year. No thank you."

"Really now, dear. Was it all that bad growing up here?"

"With you? Mom, I wouldn't trade that for the world."

She beamed out the living room window as headlights zipped by in the gathering dusk. Falling rain beaded on the glass and on the painted caps of her yard gnomes. She heard Eddie still fumbling around. He said he wasn't interested in her store-bought stuffing, pre-sliced turkey, and cream of asparagus soup, said he wanted a man's meal of meat, potatoes, and cold Rainier beer.

Claire wondered if she should confess to Bret what she'd done. If she was wrong, well then, good. And if she was right, well then, let the chips fall as they may.

"Bret, please tell Sara how delighted I am. You're sure it's not a bother?"

"A bother? C'mon. You're my mom."

"And I couldn't be an ounce prouder of you."

"Thanks. Is Dad around where I can talk to him?"

"One moment." Claire hoped her husband was in the mood to accept a call. "Eddie?"

More fumbling.

She took cautious steps toward the kitchen. "It's the phone."

"You deaf?" he barked. "Or just ignoring me? Where'd you hide the salt?"

"Your cholesterol, dear."

"Don't 'dear' me. I'm a full-grown man."

"Try the cookie jar."

Eddie, his flannel shirt unbuttoned, tore off the ceramic lid and flung it to the floor. It exploded into white-edged shards. Claire tried to hide her flinch, since outward shows of fear only roused deeper anger from her husband.

She steadied her voice. "It's your son," she said, holding out the phone. "Calling all the way from Nashville."

"What's he want?"

"He has good news. Won't you talk to him, Eddie?"

"'Course I'll talk to my son. What? You think you got exclusive rights to him, is that it? You know, Claire, you're not the only parent 'round here." Eddie grabbed the phone from her, covered it with his hand, and nodded at the mess on the floor. "Best clean that up or you'll cut yourself."

She nodded. "I'll have it done in a jiffy."

"Bretski," Eddie called out. "Happy Thanksgiving."

Claire swept ceramic fragments into the dustpan, gentle swishes, gentle swishes, trying to catch the father-son conversation. She heard in her husband's voice a desire to please. That was not like him, and it underlined her fears.

Eddie had changed since Gabe's death. He came and went with scarcely a word, and some nights she heard him moving about in their garage. She pretended to be asleep for fear he would accuse her of spying on him, but when he came in, he pulled a blanket from the closet and grabbed a few winks on the couch. In the morning she found him snoozing with their shotgun cradled against his chest.

"Cozumel, you say? In Mexico?" Eddie's voice rose. "Well, hot dog."

Swish-sweep-swish.

"Your mother? Sure, I'll make sure she's got everything she needs. So how's this work, Bretski? OK. Yep, yep. And that's it, huh, just show your ID? We got our passports a coupla years back. For our cruise to Alaska, remember?"

Bent over the dustpan, Claire remembered. While her husband threw away their savings at the ship's blackjack tables, she wandered the decks and took in the majesty of glaciers, whales and dolphins, and rustic towns crouched against misty mountainsides. She returned lonelier and poorer than ever, but her memories were richer for it.

Swish-sweep.

"That's big government for ya," Eddie said. "Using IDs to watch our every move. Pretty soon those buffoons'll be carding us for a box of Cocoa Pebbles. Liquor. Gas. Cigarettes. So why not sugar next? Regulations up the yin-yang."

Swish.

"Cocoa Pebbles? You let my granddaughter eat that junk? Say, she's cute as a button in those last pictures you sent. And Kevin, he's quite the man now, huh? No, no. 'Course we're gonna come."

Claire breathed a sigh of thanks for that, at least.

"Fun to be had by all. Hey," Eddie added, "can you hold on a sec?"

Sensing danger, Claire got to sweeping again, but her Eddie was sharp. He didn't like her hanging on his every word. He swiveled back her direction, eyes ablaze, hand cupped over the phone, and reached for the heavy cookie jar.

Huddled on the floor, Claire awaited impact.

It was her fault. Yes, she realized that. She shouldn't hide his salt from him, shouldn't stick her nose into his business. Her hope, though, was that it would all be over soon. Lord help her, she was done covering for him.

I beg of You, don't let Eddie hurt another soul.

Chapter Forty-seven

MAGNUS MAGGART WAS RUNNING SURVEILLANCE. HE SAT AT THE CORNER OF S. Bell Street, barely able to see the small house down the block. Amber light spilled through the front window onto the bushes and lawn, but the *Vreeland* on the mailbox was unreadable in this weather.

Another damp night in Tacoma. Another typical Thanksgiving.

No offense, Mother. Our Turkey Days together were never typical.

Hunched in the front seat of a Dodge Caravan he'd purchased for $2,500, he rubbed his hands near the heater vent and peered through rivulets of rain on the windshield. This vehicle wasn't his first choice, but now that his cover as Theodore Hart was burned, he couldn't risk swiping his card at an Avis and thus alerting authorities through some federal computer network.

At least I blend in this way. I am Magnus, Master of the Minivan.

His cell lit up with a text from Bookman.

Any movement?

Nada.

Stay alert.

I'm FBI, Magnus replied. I report every fart, burp, and itch.

ROFL

He smirked at the lingo. Did anyone actually roll on the floor laughing? Could grown adults seem mature while typing abbreviated messages? What was the purpose of this surveillance anyway?

Bookman claimed he had received threats from a person capable of triggering a federal investigation and undercutting all his plans. It was someone local, he believed. Someone with previous connections to Mr. Storinka and/or his arms manufacturing. Of course, Magnus had done side jobs for Storinka in years past, as had Gabe Stilman and Eddie Vreeland.

Gabe was dead.

Leaving Eddie as the obvious suspect.

None of this came as a surprise to Magnus since he kept up with the local news. Two months ago he even waved doctored evidence in Eddie's face and coerced him into handing over a personal item that belonged to his son Bret.

Why yes, that old class ring worked quite nicely.

Investigate and intimidate.

Magnus also used Gabe's murder to plant seeds of suspicion in Claire Vreeland's mind. It was another level of infiltration, and the woman was weak.

Pluck those weak weeds.

Nonetheless, Eddie remained an enigma. He attended Kiwanas every Thursday, Mass every Saturday, and sneaked from casino to tavern to pool hall the rest of the week. Tacoma's finest knew him as a gambler, a drinker, a lowlife, and yet the slippery little weasel seemed to avoid most legal troubles.

Was he smarter than he let on? More powerful?

What dangerous secrets might he be guarding?

Why did he keep rummaging around in that rinky-dink garage of his?

Magnus shivered in the driver's seat and cranked the heat another notch. He wondered if the middle-aged Vreeland couple was seated around their table even now, sipping eggnog and supping on Thanksgiving dinner.

His stomach knotted at the thought. He recalled his mother's yearly lessons in thankfulness, her holiday meals that seemed normal until he took that first bite. As his teeth were sinking into dark turkey meat, she mentioned the neighbor's missing dog. As he was chewing seasoned mashed potatoes, she pointed out that the flakes of oregano looked like ear mites from a cat.

"Son, are you thankful?" When he nodded, she patted his hand. "That's good. Never show your emotion, and be sure you don't ever flinch."

Magnus observed movement down S. Bell Street as a blurred figure drew the curtains at the Vreelands' front window. At 10:27 P.M. on the van's dash clock, lights turned off throughout the house.

He told himself to ignore the cold, to wait a while longer.

Ninety-three minutes later, he sent Bookman a text.

Going in.

Magnus stepped into the drizzle, pulled a rain parka over his head. He checked the safety on his Kimber and wedged it into his waistband. He'd brought his favorite handgun on the flight, emptied of ammo and locked in his check-in luggage, but his employer warned him not to use it unless in danger of losing his life. The less collateral damage the better.

With no traffic coming from either direction, Magnus darted along the sidewalk and cut behind the fence that bordered the old garage. On this side, he was invisible to those in the house. Wood-slatted walls wore a coat of chipped paint. Narrow windows ran beneath the eaves, painted over in white. The structure was small, too small for the couple's Oldsmobile, but suitable for mowers, tools, and bikes.

He tested the lifting garage door. The handle squeaked and turned loosely. A faulty mechanism? Or purposely disconnected?

He shook the rain droplets from his hood, moved around the corner, and noted a thin door hidden from the house and bracketed by overgrown shrubs. Was he wasting his time? Why was this garage not better protected?

Well, at least there was a padlock on the door.

As he stepped forward to deal with this obstacle, he stubbed his boot into something. He glanced down. A stinking yard gnome lay on its back, mocking him with a rosy-cheeked grin.

He raised his boot. Stomped down. Crushed that painted face.

"Don't ever show your emotion"? Ha. So much for that.

As he removed his foot from splintered plastic, a glimmer of glass caught his attention. He crouched and saw the cracked lens of a security camera. He lifted the object, discovered a cord running from its base into the dirt. Before he could stand again, lights flashed on from the other side of the garage. The house door slammed open, followed by the metallic sound of a shotgun being cocked.

That was his signal to retreat.

Curious and curiouser. So there was something worth protecting after all.

Chapter Forty-eight

On the first day Sara moved into the mansion with her family, she intended to tear up her old 3 × 5 of Alex Page. The abundant life before them seemed a sure sign of God's favor, and she told herself it was time to embrace these rewards. Time to let go of the past. Here in late November, though, her commitment to this plan was still derailed by her sleep-lab confrontation with Theodore Hart.

Were his accusations true?

Was Mr. Storinka's gift nothing more than a guilt offering?

Was her former fiancé, even in death, the reason for her new riches?

Her blur of thoughts and feelings and memories stirred the heartache anew. Each time she tried to bury the past, it seemed to crawl up from the grave.

Please, she cried out. *I need to know the truth.*

She called Viktor at his place in Kingston Springs. He told her he could be over in an hour, and added that he had a buyer for the Maserati Granturismo. $94,000? Wasn't that low? Yes, he admitted, but in this market it might be the best they could do.

"In that case," Sara said, "perhaps we should hold off on it till later."

"Are you telling me you want to keep the car?"

"For Bret. He'd never take it for himself, but I know how much he loves it."

Viktor said, "None of this is the reason you called, Sara. I'll bring the boxes like you asked, but are you certain you're ready to do this?"

"It's been over twelve years. Yes, I think I'm ready."

"Mr. Storinka would be glad. He left it to me to share with you in the right time. I'll carry the boxes to the upstairs room. That's where he kept his shrine."

Sara could hardly breathe. "I'll be waiting."

And she took up position in the silence of the spare bedroom.

"Mommy, why're you in here?" Katie said, peeking through the door.

"I'm thinking."

"Wanna play Candy Land with me?"

"Not now, cutie pie. I'm waiting for someone. Where's your brother?"

"Playing Xbox in his room, but he won't answer the door."

"What about Natalie?"

"Watching *Jersey Shores*, but she says I'm not allowed."

Sara groaned. "Yes, she's right about that. Sounds like the rec room's the best bet at the moment. You can put in *Monsters, Inc.* till I come down."

"No one wants to do anything with me," Katie said. "I miss my swings."

"Like I told you, I'll be down in a little while."

"You promise, Mommy?" She snuggled next to Sara. "You won't forget?"

"Katie." She tapped her daughter's nose. "You know how cats run away if you try to grab them? Even though they like it when you pet them, they can't be forced or rushed."

"I like kittens best."

"Kittens are cuddly, aren't they? Just like you. As people get older, though, they often need more space. If you force yourself on them, they'll avoid you."

"Like Kevin?"

"He loves you. Honestly, he does. He's just learning how to show it. And as for Natalie, after her classroom hours she needs an occasional break." Sara lifted Katie's chin and looked her in the eye. "You've seen the scars on her legs, haven't you? Some days Natalie still feels sad and needs time to process what happened. That's why she meets with Pastor's wife each week."

"If you have scars, that's when people help you."

"They should, absolutely. But we should all help each other, and it's best to give attention instead of trying to get it. You know, even when people are hurt, like Natalie, they heal quicker while helping others."

"Like her teaching Kev and me?"

"That's right. She says you remind her of her little sister."

Katie's lips and eyebrows arched in opposite directions, producing a wide-eyed, heart-melting smile. Sara pulled her close, heart swelling with affection.

Katie threw both arms around her. "Love you, Mommy."

"Love you more."

"Nuh-uh. Love you more."

The boxes arrived at 4:30 P.M. and contained an astonishing array of memorabilia, all of it centered around Alex Page. There were photographs, newspaper articles, even an old *Wall Street Journal* piece, titled "The Man with 10,000 Arms," about this fast-rising player in the arms manufacturing industry.

Seated on the bed, Sara's eyes misted over as she searched the items spread out around her. So much about her former fiancé was a mystery. She was only nineteen when the sharp-dressed twenty-six-year-old proposed. He told her he was a well-to-do businessman. Caught up in the romance of bouquets, fancy dinners, and nice cars, she didn't question it. She now learned he had been chief operating officer at Storinka Defense Systems, a Fortune 500 corporation with military contracts and a penchant for secrecy.

When Alex died along Route 410, rumors swirled that Mr. Storinka had eliminated the one man most likely to topple him from his throne.

"Tell me," Viktor said, "is this the collection of a man guilty of murder?"

"I, uh, I don't know what to think. Why would he save all this stuff?"

"Mr. Storinka was Alex's mentor. He took him under his wing, grooming him to take over in the years to come, and he felt responsible for his loss."

"Mr. Storinka told me he'd done bad things," Sara said. "Explain that."

"He was not always a nice man. His past, his life in Ukraine as an orphan of war, hardened him. This was one reason for his success. When he moved his operations to America, many overseas contacts feared he would reveal their secrets. They felt betrayed."

Hands cradling a yellowed news clipping, she met his eye. "How does that tie in with Alex?"

"It is the truth you're after? The driver of this semi-truck that killed Alex, he had done previous contract work for Mr. Storinka. When Mr. Hart took a bid from a competitor and arranged Alex's 'accident,' Storinka blamed himself for creating such enemies and for training Mr. Hart to begin with. He turned this room into a memorial for the man he once hoped would fill his shoes."

After Viktor's departure, Sara dragged herself to the dining room for supper with Natalie and the kids. Natalie said something about an incident of Kevin's misbehavior at the stable earlier in the day, but Sara barely registered it. She told Natalie to mention it to Bret in the morning.

"Where's Daddy?" Katie asked. "At the studio?"

"I know he's late, but won't it be fun to hear his CD when he's all done?"

Natalie cleared her dishes and headed to her room. Her cell phone was to her ear, and she looked upset. Was she feeling lonely? Overwhelmed?

"Thanks for all your work with the kids," Sara called after her, but she was already gone. "Kev, don't you have some homework to do?"

Nodding, he stacked his dishes with his sister's. "From my field-trip to the zoo. You shoulda seen it, Mom. The keepers threw in these dead rabbits for the Siberian tigers, and this one tiger, he got a head in his mouth and he—"

"All right, all right. Go put it all in your report." As he darted off, Sara turned to her six-year-old. "That leaves just us girls for dish duty."

At the kitchen's wide double sink, Sara rinsed and handed over items for Katie to load into the dishwasher. Later they read a story in Katie's bedroom, where Katie confessed that she didn't like being alone and wanted a room with Kevin again. Sara told her it was all part of growing up and becoming a big girl.

In Kevin's room, Sara brushed fingers through the hair of her son conked out on the covers. He was dressed, mouth opened, Nikes pointed at the ceiling.

Not a hint of a snore.

The surgeon called his tonsillectomy an LTA, a laser tonsil ablation, during which a handheld laser vaporized the unwanted tissue. Kevin bragged for days that he was "shot with a laser and survived." Sara was simply glad to have her son's risk of premature death diminished. She didn't have to panic anymore that the constant strain on his heart might end his life without warning.

Sara climbed the grand staircase to the upstairs bathroom, filled the claw-foot tub, and took a long hot bath. This was her girlhood fantasy, and she enjoyed every luxurious minute of scented bubbles, dancing candlelight, and a book of romantic poetry. As she imagined her upcoming shopping with Zoe Billingsley, the Thanksgiving banter between Zoe and Bret jostled for her attention. Goodness, how could she compete with Zoe's brazen beauty?

She sank beneath the water's surface, cocooned in the stillness, alone with her thoughts of boxed photographs and memorabilia.

When she was done, she wrapped herself in a large, fluffy towel. She'd donated the old threadbare ones to Goodwill. She combed her hair as she walked down the hall to the master suite.

Still no sign of Bret. Really? While she hoped, truly hoped, the music thing worked out for him, a part of her resented his absence in this vulnerable moment.

Suspecting he might later snore up a storm due to exhaustion, she slipped into the spare room and snuggled into the full-size bed. She held Alex's photo in her hand. Any other spare rooms would've worked, that's what she told herself, but she knew it wasn't true. In this room, her life had come full circle.

Was Mr. Storinka the one who arranged Bret's job transfer here?

Did he know who she was before becoming her patient at the clinic?

What were the odds of them meeting here in Music City of all places?

She realized these could be the reasons Storinka lied to her about when he bought the estate, trying to hide the fact he actually came here later to watch and evaluate her for his own guilt-relieving purposes.

Sara woke the next morning to the growls of the Maserati. With Alex's 3 × 5 in hand, she moved to the window and spotted her husband down by the fountain. Just arriving? Or leaving again so soon? He looked so debonair climbing from the car with his sunglasses on. Her darling. The man she loved.

She told herself this was it, time to tear up the photo from the past. The good life she'd missed with one man was now the good life she had with another.

But it was her name on that will, wasn't it?

And these blessings were, in part, because of Alex Page.

Oh, maybe it was never meant to be, but I can't just toss all that away.

Chapter Forty-nine

"Hey, Bret?" Natalie called. "Wait up a minute."

Cradled in the Maserati's bucket seat, he barely heard her over the fountain's babbling waters. He powered down the window and waited for her to descend the mansion's steps. These days he showed his face at work for social as much as financial reasons, but this morning there was a company meeting.

Natalie moved gingerly in his direction, her hand on the rail. Though her leg wounds had almost healed with regular cleansing and antibiotic cream, the scars would remain, thin white lines across her shins and calves.

How stupid can you be, Bret? What're you thinking?

He hopped from the car and whipped off his sunglasses.

"You're fine," she said. "It's not like I'm an invalid."

When he reached for her hand, though, she took it.

Natalie Flynn was a pretty girl, with her wide blinking eyes and tiny nose stud. All clues pointed to Theodore Hart as her abductor, and although Bret had expected her ordeal to make her more cynical, she proved to be a gentle and competent tutor, seeming to find new purpose in her work with Kevin and Katie.

Bret liked her. He had a soft spot for the wounded and the abused, and he would never forget his mother tumbling down those stairs in his childhood home, nor his vow to fight the abusers in this world. Right now that meant getting his hands on Mr. Hart. Given the chance, he'd show the man there were other, more creative ways to inflict pain with a metal rod.

"Taking the sports car?" Natalie reached the bottom step and let go of his hand. "Sweet. Of course, Sara thinks you should keep it, and I have to agree. It really does fit you."

"Thanks. She hasn't said a word to me about it."

"She says it's no use, that you're probably right anyway."

"What'd you stop me for, Natalie? I gotta skedaddle."

"Skedaddle." She tilted her head. "Definitely not Spanish."

"Is it the kids? If they're not doing their homework, we'll—"

"No, everything's good with their studies. It's Kev."

"Yeah?" Bret said.

"Yesterday, after he finished his American History early, I let him go outside. Sara says that's fine so long as they stay on the property, and I swear, I had no idea she was out there."

"She?"

"Kevin's normally such a good kid." Natalie swept her hair from her eyes. "Even if I knew, I wouldn't have expected trouble between him and a girl."

"What girl? What happened?"

"Hannah. The one who stables her horse here."

"Ah-ha." Bret folded his arms. "Yeah, he could be developing a crush."

Natalie leaned back. "A crush? Don't know anything about that. From what I understand, though, she went out to the stable to see him, and she—"

"To see Kevin?"

"Her horse."

Bret put his sunglasses back on. He still had songs playing through his head from last night's studio session, and he wondered what was on this morning's agenda. Late Thanksgiving bonuses? More likely an announcement about the luxury coach they'd been commissioned to build for Kings of Leon.

Music City, USA. Gotta keep those rockers rollin'.

"Hannah found Kevin feeding her horse an apple," Natalie continued, "and when she said not to spoil him, Kevin told her he could do what he wanted since this was his property. When she tried to argue, he shoved her down."

"Kevin? You're sure?" Bret was shocked that his son who suffered at the hands of bullies would use those same strong-arm tactics against others. Especially a girl.

"Hate to even bother you about it, but when I tried talking to him he ignored me. Sara told me you're the one to deal with him."

This explained his wife's strange behavior last night. He'd arrived home at a quarter past midnight, after recording his twelfth and final song at Desperado. He was excited, bursting to tell Sara that his CD was ready to be mixed and mastered, but found her sound asleep in a spare bedroom down the hall. She must've taken a late shower, based on her damp hair spread out on the pillow.

But why a separate room? Why that bed?

No wonder, Bret. She needed you while you were off doing your thing.

"Where's Kevin right now?" he asked Natalie.

"Working on the biology report he owes me from yesterday. Rhonda and Pastor Teman took him on a field trip to the Nashville Zoo."

"Thanks for your good work with him. He and I, we'll have a talk."

Bret marched back to the sports car. Gunning the engine, he heard the tires spit crushed shells against the stone fountain. He threw a glance in his side-view mirror and caught a glimpse of his wife at an upstairs window.

Gotta run, Sara. I'll make it up to you later, OK?

He picked up his Blackberry to give her a call, but it rang in his hand.

"Bret, you headed this way?" Jason said.

"Yeah. Just had some, uh, trouble here on the home front."

"Listen to you, big guy. Whatever happened to the always-on-time clock-puncher I used to know?" Jason chuckled. "The way you come and go as you please these days, you'd make good manager material."

"You wish," Bret ribbed him back. "You wanna promote me so bad, quit with the idle threats and pull the trigger."

"Well, wise guy, why do you think I called this meeting?"

"What? Are you serious?"

"Stop your yakking and get down here, would you? If you show up much later, I'll have to promote you to part owner, and that is not happening. Not today. For now you'll have to settle for chief production manager. Act surprised when we announce it in the boardroom."

"It won't be an act, Jason. I'm not even sure what to say."

"Next time we're on the links, shank every tee shot and we'll call it good."

Bret's new salary package provided him $110,000 a year, the potential for $84,000 more in bonuses, and a Belle Meade Country Club membership. On the boardroom table, an envelope contained all the details, and he rested his hand on it as though swearing an oath upon the Bible.

"All yours, Vreeland. If you want it."

"Wow, Jason, I don't know what to say. Yes, of course. I accept."

"Good." Jason gave his understated shock a slight nod. "You've earned it."

"Well yeah. And after eight years, I'd say it's about time."

The others around the table tensed.

"Watch it," Jason said, hooking a thumb toward the crew at the end. "Or I'll snip your eagle wings and toss you back in with these turkeys."

Everyone laughed, and even the guys Bret was leaving behind applauded the news. He was their poster boy. If he could fly the coop, if he could rake in unforeseen riches, there was hope. And, more immediately, he was one of their own, a man who could voice their blue-collar gripes.

Perched in his new office an hour later, Bret gazed through tinted windows at the production floor spread out below him. Even here in his eagle's nest, he was not so far removed from those sweaty "turkey" days.

Yep, he had busted his hump for this place.

The promotion felt good. Felt right.

"Lookie what I found," Jason said, knocking and entering.

"What now? I can only guess."

Jason toed the door shut and produced a square, squat bottle, capped with two upside down shot glasses. "Some Gentleman Jack for the occasion?"

"C'mon. You know I'm not much of a drinker."

"Who said anything about drinking?" Jason tapped the bottle twice with his knuckle, sloshing the deep amber liquid. "This here is sipping whiskey. You sip."

Bret loosened his top button. He drank wine with dinner every now and then, but refused to tread his father's path through casinos, basement poker games, and six-packs of cheap Rainier. There was no class in that, no dignity.

"Look, Vreeland, we're just two grown men, honoring the occasion."

"OK," Bret said, rising to his feet. "A few sips."

"Now that's what I like to hear."

He watched his boss serve the drinks and hand a glass across the desk. Before they could clink glasses and tilt them back, he had to know something. "What was it, Jason? What finally qualified me in your eyes?"

"What're you talking about? I've always liked you."

"Six months ago I couldn't get a raise to save my life. Not that I'm complaining, but here I am, not really needing the big bucks like before, and that's when you decide to come a-courtin'. What gives?"

"Success breeds success. We all know that. I see a winner, and sure as there's rain in the Amazon, that's where I'm going to place my bets."

"And I wasn't a winner before?" Bret said.

"You're looking at this all wrong."

"How am I supposed to look at it?"

"It's just a fact that some people are lightning rods. They've got the Midas touch. Whether you're talking basketball, business, or bear-hunting, they're the ones you want on your team. So you and Sara, you hit it big. What's that tell me? Tells me you're doing something right, you got someone smiling down, and it's only natural that others are going to want in on the deal."

Bret wasn't sure how to respond. Jason had a point. It sure seemed they had rounded a corner and reaped the benefits at long, long last.

"Would you stop your navel-gazing, big guy? Time to celebrate."

"You're right." Bret lifted his glass. "To winners."

"Attaboy. To winners."

Clink, clink.

"And this," Jason said, "is only the beginning. Coupla weeks? Christmas in Mexico? I know it's your treat this time around, but just you wait. Zoe and I, we've always liked you and Sara, always thought you two deserved something special. We'll show you the best beaches, all of the hot spots. You better believe we will celebrate in true Billingsley style."

Chapter Fifty

Time for a little golf practice on the estate. Bret watched his son heft a Callaway golf bag nearly as large as his own body. Kevin hugged the thing and walked it forward, his nose getting batted by a sock-covered driver. He wrangled the bag at last onto the back of a bright red golf cart with a white canopy.

"Just a runaround," Bret told Sara, while convincing her it was worth the expense. "It'll be great for Kev and me, a little father-son time hitting balls."

And it was great. Many mornings Bret took the cart out on the back acreage while Kevin studied. He chipped shots one direction, ran them down, and did the same thing back. After weeks of practice, he was a force to be reckoned with around the country club greens.

"Now if you can get my bag," Bret said, "we'll be good to go."

"Not fair, Dad. Why do I have to do everything?"

"You're this week's caddy, remember? That's the breaks. Hey, think of it like this, you learn to work without complaining and you'll be like gold to any boss."

"Done." Kevin gestured to the loaded bags. "Can I drive now?"

"Sure thing, caddy."

They slalomed through the trees to an open stretch of grass, where Kevin parked the cart, stabbed a tee into the turf, lined up with his 3-iron. Once he was done hitting, Bret asked him about the incident in the stable.

"So what's this I hear? You shoved Hannah to the ground?"

"She was trying to boss me around."

"It's her horse, Kev."

"This is our property, not hers."

Bret took a practice swing. "OK, so you think I should shove Mom if she bosses me around?"

Kevin hung his head. "That's not the same."

"You're setting patterns for life here. One day you'll be married and—"

"Gross."

"And that's all part of the deal, showing love even when you don't feel like it. I think Hannah deserves an apology. Sure, you can be aggressive on the soccer field and stand up to bullies. That's all good. But you don't wanna turn into a bully yourself, do you? We're talking about power under control."

"Like Jesus," Kevin said.

Bret figured it was a generic answer, a way to get out of trouble.

"On the cross," his son added, "He could've called down angels to fight for Him, but He just stayed there and took it like a man."

"Like a man," Bret agreed.

The Blackberry cut short their conversation. They both turned toward the object in the cart's cup holder, and the race was on. Although Bret was bigger and faster, the call caught him while he was squaring up over his tee shot. He dropped the club and lunged toward the cart, but his ten-year-old darted under his arms, slid across the front seat, and nabbed the phone.

"Got it, Dad. Too slow."

"You think you're real slick, don't you?"

"Slick like a booger. I won."

"By just a nose."

Kevin giggled at that. "Next time you have to caddy."

"Yep, that's our deal." Bret pointed at the phone. "So who called?"

"This is supposed to be our golf time."

"Could be important. C'mon, bud, let me see it."

Kevin surrendered the cell and flopped into the driver's seat.

"See, good thing we checked," Bret said, hitting the Send button. "Looks like a call from Detective Meade."

"Dad, ever since we moved, you're always on the stupid phone."

Bret turned to address this comment, stunned by his son's pre-adolescent angst. Almost eleven years old. What would he be like at thirteen or fourteen?

A droll voice caught him before he could speak. "Mr. Vreeland, thanks for getting back to me."

"Detective, what's up? You gonna come hit some golf balls with Kevin and I? Uh . . ." Bret threw a glance at his son. "I mean, Kevin and me."

"Sounds tempting, but you know how it goes for us working people."

"Hey, I'm just sharpening my game so that I can beat the pants off my boss the next time we go eighteen holes."

"You haven't quit your job yet?"

"Nope," Bret said. "Can't seem to get it outta my blood. Anyway, loafing around like some lazy, rich person, who wants to do that?"

"Lots of people. You'd be surprised."

"What's the saying? 'Idle hands are the devil's workshop.'"

"Here in Investigations, I see evidence of it daily. Speaking of which, I got back some DNA results and dug up some other info you might like to hear regarding your wife's patient at the clinic."

"OK." Bret stretched an arm over the golf cart seat. "I've got Kevin sitting here with me. You mind if I put it on speaker? He might find this interesting."

"I'll trust your judgment," Meade said. "Has he ever watched *CSI*?"

"He's played the computer game. He likes that sorta stuff."

"It's not a rosy picture, but I'll give the edited version."

Bret activated the speaker. "We're all ears, Detective."

"I'll start," Detective Meade said, "with a quick overview of our DNA testing process. Last month we declared your wife's sleep lab a crime scene, collected evidence, and submitted the DNA samples through our department to TBI's headquarters here in Nashville."

Kevin looked up. This was one of his areas of interest.

Winking, Bret gave him a fist-bump.

"They're backlogged for months out," the detective continued, "but we pushed this through fast as we could. We had no follicles or roots to work with, but the hair strands provided mitochondrial DNA, which is very stable. This confirmed Mr. Hart's identity, meaning the man who confronted your wife is in fact the man who owns the Dodge Charger you encountered. That's nothing new to you, but it establishes a pattern of stalking and intimidation, which would earn you an order of protection in court."

"Would it do us any good?"

"In legal terms, yes. In practical terms, probably not."

"Is he still in the area?" Bret said. "Do we know that much?"

"I'm working on that, but I have reason to believe he flew into SeaTac a few weeks back."

"Under his own name? He had to show ID at the airport, right?"

"That's where this gets interesting, Mr. Vreeland. Criminal DNA evidence not only stays in CODIS, the Combined DNA Index System, but also gets catalogued in NDIS, the national system. Mr. Hart has quite a history, much more than turned up from his car registration. His full name is Theodore Magnus Hart, born in Renton, Washington, in 1976. His parents, both army folks, divorced when he was seven years old. He lived at Fort Lewis-McChord with his mother and had behavioral issues throughout his schooling. Medical records show he was first prescribed ADHD medication at twelve years old, though your wife might argue his diagnosis."

"Yeah, she mentioned something about that, didn't she?"

"Doctors also thought he might be a victim of parental abuse, but he denied it. Swore up and down that his leg wounds were a biking accident."

"I feel for the guy, but that doesn't excuse him harassing my family."

"Agreed," Meade said. "In ninety-five, he followed in his parents' footsteps and joined the army. He did a short tour in Bosnia in early ninety-six, but got dishonorably discharged. Within a few months, he was back in the Seattle, King County area. He married. Divorced a year and a half later. His ex-wife relocated to Florida, about as far away as she could get from him. That's no wonder, considering she placed domestic abuse calls three times during their short relationship."

"This guy's a real winner, isn't he? Some of this came out during the trial for vehicular homicide."

"It gets worse."

Kevin leaned forward, and Bret wrapped an arm over his shoulder.

"You already know about the deadly results of his truck-driving, but what you don't know is that his mother, Patricia Maggart, went missing in two-thousand-three. Her strangled body was found three months later, in a wooded area around Lake Washington. Her legs bore multiple lacerations. Do you detect a pattern here?"

Kevin's eyebrows jumped. "Natalie," he said.

"Why isn't he in prison?" Bret asked.

"Lack of evidence. He was a person of interest, but he faced lie detectors voluntary and beat the things twice. A sociopath lacks remorse. He feels little empathy. He fails to conform to social norms, even laughs at them. This fellow, if he has any relationships, is in them only to satisfy his own needs."

"What causes it? An issue from birth? A response to environment?"

"Nature versus nurture. The classic question. Percentages are much higher in children born prematurely and in homes without a father, so that early affection and validation is important. When it comes to these types, though, I don't know that anyone has it figured out. We do the best we can."

"Good thing," Bret said, "that God can renew our minds. I know I need it."

"I hear you. Of course, people have to make their own choices."

Kevin gave Bret a nudge. "Where's this guy now? Ask him, Dad."

"Good question, Kevin," the detective cut in. "When I ran Mr. Hart's full name through federal databases, the combination 'Magnus Maggart' kept creeping up. I speculated that it might be an alias. Wouldn't be difficult, since it contains portions of his birth name."

"Magnus Maggart." Kevin scrunched his nose.

"A few weeks earlier, as I alluded to, a man used that name and caught a flight into SeaTac. A one-way ticket. Here in Nashville, there's record of him checking into hotels, renting cars, but nothing so far in Washington State. I've flagged him so that we'll know right away if he books a return trip."

"What if he drives?" Bret said.

"We'll do our best," Meade answered. "Even the police have limitations."

Chapter Fifty-one

SARA LOVED THE TIME WITH HER CHILDREN.

To her surprise, she loved the time away almost as much.

Today's shopping spree with Zoe was a case in point, even more fun than expected. While Natalie tutored the kids, the two ladies headed for the mall. Sara planned on updating both her kitchen and her wardrobe, and the Mall at Green Hills was an upscale dream where shoppers were as likely to bump into Taylor Swift or Sheryl Crow as they were to spot Faith Hill and Tim McGraw.

"Tim's a cutie," Zoe said, "I'll give him that. But take off the hat, and half his appeal goes with it. Now, Faith? In person, she's just stunning."

"Really?"

"Oh my, yes. Her and Nicole. I'd kill for looks like that."

"Don't be silly," Sara said. "You're gorgeous."

"Like Dolly Parton says, 'It takes a lotta money to look this cheap.'"

"Zoe." Sara swatted the woman's hand. "Give yourself some credit."

"Look. At. This." Zoe held up a black Max Azria dress. "Wouldn't this look fabulous with your sapphire necklace? Try it on, Sara. You must."

Despite her change in zip codes and tax brackets, Sara couldn't help but flip the tag over and gasp. "Holy moly. Look. At. The. Price."

"Oh, don't pay that any attention. Try it on already. I am the queen of hard bargaining. You find yourself a matching pair of shoes and a clutch, and with a few bats of the eye and a flash of platinum I'll have them knocking thirty percent off the deal. Viola."

"You can do that?"

"You have no idea, babe. Fitting room's back over there."

When Sara reemerged, Zoe feigned a swoon and dropped into a stuffed armchair. Ten minutes later they exited the store with bags in hand.

"What'd I tell you, Sara? A third off without even breaking a nail."

"Where to next?"

"Soma Intimates," Zoe cooed. "Time to turn up the heat."

Although neither woman spotted a celebrity during the visit, neither one cared. Sara felt like a free-spirited college girl, practically skipping through the mall from trendy retro shop to hot new boutique. People always told her she had an innate sense of style and looks to go with it, and here was voluptuous Zoe to lend her complementary knowledge and shopping experience.

"Why didn't we do this years ago?" Sara asked, as they rounded off this splendid day in a cookware aisle at Williams-Sonoma.

"Didn't seem like your thing."

"I'm a woman, aren't I?"

"With two kids." Zoe examined a berry colander. "Those first few years, you were busy being a mommy. Don't get me wrong, I respected the heck out of that. Certainly not for the faint of heart. Oh sure, Jason hinted about being a father when we first got married, but I'm not cut out for motherhood. I'm just not."

"You never even considered it?"

"Children? My goodness, no. They're cute, but from a distance. Is it terrible of me to say so?" Zoe batted smoky eyes and dropped her gaze to silicon enhancements. "You tell me, do I look like a woman aching to change a diaper?"

"We're all different, Zoe. I mean, who am I to write your story for you?"

"So there you have it. That's why I never invited you shopping, that and the fact your hubby was pulling extra hours to make ends meet.

He asked for a raise how many times? Jason lost count. It would've been tactless of me to drag you along while I bought dresses with steeper price tags than your family car."

"Am I ever glad that thing's history." Sara flicked a fry pan with her finger.

"Oh, me too. I was so embarrassed for you."

"Embarrassed?"

"You just deserved better, that's all. Look at you now, babe. I can't wait to hear of Bret's reaction when you parade before him in your new ensembles. A man like that, you'll be lucky to get the door locked before he attacks."

A man like what? What's that supposed to mean?

Sara added the collection of pans to her cart and headed for the register.

Bret sat at the secretary desk in the master bedroom, travel books and itineraries spread before him. With a shot of Gentleman Jack from the mini-bar, just a little for sipping and relaxing, he tried to focus on the good times ahead instead of on the unsettling details about Magnus Maggart. As he looked over plans for their upcoming trip, the purr of the Lexus in the drive signaled his wife's return.

He moved to the window and frowned. Oh, boy. Not good.

Bret tried not to count the colorful, logoed bags that Sara lifted from the trunk. Earlier he'd checked their online banking and swallowed hard when he saw the hole left by the cleared payments for Cozumel flights and accommodations. Storinka's original $181,021 transfer was already slashed in half by mortgage payments, tithe checks, and vacation plans.

The positive thing, according to Viktor, was that probate should close quicker than usual. Once that happened, the Vreelands could liquidate stocks and sell off some of the estate's more frivolous items.

He finished off his drink, tucked away the glass, and popped a piece of gum in his mouth while returning to the books on the secretary desk.

Sara whisked into the bedroom minutes later, arms loaded. She flooded him with the accounts of her day, and insisted that he sit tight while she changed into an outfit "absolutely made" to go with her necklace. She rushed into the alcove that branched from the master bath. Padded benches and a row of hangers made it a perfect changing room. Not that Bret used it much.

"You ready out there, lover boy?"

"Mm-hmm," he said.

She stepped from the alcove, a small purse in hand. She wore black ankle-cuff heels and a matching dress that ended just above her knees. The side was cut out, accentuating the curves where her hip and waist met. The lines of the sleek material highlighted her strand of princess-cut sapphires.

"What do you think?" she said. "Isn't it incredible?"

"Wow, sweetheart." Bret pushed aside the travel books. "Wow."

"You like?"

"I like."

"You know, I picked it out with you in mind."

"Your trip to the mall with Zoe," he said. "Yeah, that was today, huh? How much does a dress like that cost anyway?"

"Honey, honestly. Can't you simply enjoy it for a minute?"

"I'm enjoying. Very much. But how much're we talking?"

"Zoe bargained and got like thirty percent taken off. You should've heard her. That means that I, uh, basically got the pumps and the clutch for free."

"Pumps, meaning heels." He nodded. "But the clutch, that's where you lost me. The only clutch I know of belongs in a car. Preferably something fast."

She strutted toward him, hips swinging. "You are such a man."

"Thanks."

"This," she said, lifting the purse. "This is a clutch."

"I'll take your word." He pulled her close. "So, how much altogether?"

"Somewhere around nine. Is that whiskey I smell?"

"Nine hundred? As in, dollars?"

"After tax. Are you avoiding my question?"

He took a step back. "I could ask the same thing, Sara. What happened to our large-item limit?"

"Please." She squeezed his hand. "You know how long it's been since I really shopped for myself? Is it so out of line if, on my first big shopping day, one particular dress catches my eye?"

"That's not the point."

"What is the point, Bret? You're always so 'budget this' and 'budget that,' and for once I wanted to have a little fun without stressing over every dollar. If that makes me the wicked witch, I don't know what to tell you."

"Hey, don't put words in my mouth. That's not at all what I think."

"So why'm I in trouble?"

"You're not in trouble," he said. "It's the fact we didn't discuss it. That's always been part of our deal, so it's not like I've turned into some jerk here."

Sara lifted a foot and reached back to slip off her shoe. "You have no idea, do you, how freeing that was for me?" Off came the other shoe. "Zoe kept telling me to try this on and try that, and I couldn't believe I was finding things that fit me so well. I've never had a day like that, where I could buy what I really liked regardless of the price. Will it become a habit? No. But I was willed this money, and I think I have the right to enjoy a bit of it, don't you?"

"Long as we communicate. The golf cart? I talked to you about that."

"And I wanted you to have it, same as I want you to keep the Maserati."

"Sara, I—"

"I insist. You love that car. It fits you."

He stepped to the window, his movements deliberate.

"I understand," she said, "what you're telling me. A lot's changed, though, and I think we ought to get a little wiggle room every now and then."

"Wiggle room." He bit his lip. "So we're gonna be that guy?"

"What guy?"

"The NFL draft pick who goes wild once he gets his hands on a little fame and fortune. Or the actor who goes from nice to major jerk faster than you can say 'Extra, extra.' Or CEOs taking huge bonuses while their companies post record losses. Somewhere it gets twisted. I just don't want that for us."

"Honey, we're hardly on that scale."

"Do you hear yourself?" He gestured over the treetops that lined the drive. "We don't have to own an island to be considered rich. Isn't it more than enough that we have running water, AC, and a stocked refrigerator? Not to mention a freezer full of steaks, shrimp and salmon fillets."

"I hear what you're saying, hon." She joined him by the window. "I do."

"Listen, five years down the road, I wanna be the family that still loves each other and looks for ways to help those in need, not the lottery winners who threw it all away, who can't even go out to eat without people pointing and whispering, and who get hounded by long-lost nieces and nephews."

"Did Natalie tell you about that, the mail from my second cousin?"

"Hmm, let me guess. A request for college money? Rent money?"

"Someone stole their food stamps."

"See there, that's how easily we could mess this up. We've got a chance to change our family tree, not just for the kids but for our grandkids too."

"Were you drinking, Bret? You never answered me."

"Not even a full shot, OK?"

"I just know how much you try to avoid making your father's mistakes."

"This has nothing to do with him. What? That's who you think I am?"

She nudged his leg. "You're my big-hearted man, and I care about you."

"Listen," he said, "can we agree to talk about how much is gonna be spent the next time this happens?"

"Of course. And can't we up the limit just a teensy weensy bit?"

He faced her, rested his hands on her hips.

"We'll keep giving," she told him. "I mean, we've always been generous. We were content with small things in the past, weren't we? So why not enjoy the bigger things now that we have them? It's not as if we randomly guessed the winning Lotto numbers. We've worked hard for this, Bret."

He cupped her cheek with his hand. She was right. They weren't going overboard. They were simply learning to be responsible with the more they'd been given.

"Sara, thank you for all the sacrifices you've made."

"And you too. You're a good man."

He kissed her, lingering until her lips yielded to his. He pulled back a few inches and said, "Milady, you are worth every frivolous penny."

"And you, my handsome knight, belong in that Maserati."

"C'mon. It seems kinda selfish, doesn't it?"

"Don't be silly, honey. It's my idea. And if you don't drive that car, someone else will. What difference does it make? Think of it as my gift to you." When he nodded, she said, "Really? You'll keep it? Oh, that makes me happy."

"So," he said, "whaddya think about fifteen hundred dollars?"

"As a new limit?"

He nodded.

"Sounds more than generous. Thank you." She lifted on tiptoes for another kiss. "All right, Mr. Vreeland, I suggest you hang onto your hat. I haven't finished modeling for you, and the best is yet to come."

Chapter Fifty-two

7:33 P.M. WEDNESDAY. ALREADY DARK ALONG THE PACIFIC COASTLINE. MAGNUS tailed Eddie Vreeland north of Tacoma on I-5. He was tempted to stay back at S. Bell Street and search the garage, but Bookman wanted Eddie kept in sight at all times, believing he might turn over info that threatened their goals.

Magnus stayed a half mile behind the Oldsmobile's taillights, chugging along in the minivan. He missed his encounters with Bret and Sara Vreeland, not to mention his face-to-face times with Natalie. He missed his mother too.

Why, she was the one who made him who he was.

She gave him the strength to do what had to be done.

Like you taught me. Pruning the weeds so the strong can grow stronger.

It was true he had strangled her. How could he trust a jury to understand his motives? They were shallow in their understanding. As for the cops, he'd given them a chance, hadn't he? They nearly peed themselves when he agreed to take their lie detector tests. They thought they could crack him like a nut.

But killing her, that didn't qualify him as being nuts.

When psychologists tried to label those who lacked a conscience, he laughed. Who were they to decide right and wrong? When they categorized certain people as antisocial, he wanted to ask them why the masses spent half their waking hours watching TV, texting on cell phones, sitting at computers. Their notions of social interaction were pathetic.

Of course, weak minds always wanted labels. They tried to cram life into boxes and categories.

While I cram gory cats into boxes.

No, Magnus admitted to himself, that was an exaggeration.

There was little to gain by hurting creatures lower on the food chain. The true challenge, the true pleasure, came from mastering an apex predator, and homo sapiens sat at the top of the list.

Currently, his kill count stood at three.

The first was Alex Page, there along Route 410. Following orders, Magnus let the wheel slip through his fingers and watched his big rig do the messy work. He did his stint in prison, collected his pay.

The second time around, he wanted to feel that power at his own fingertips. Months after his release, he paid his mother a fateful visit.

The third victim was not far from here either, along the shores of Lake Meridian. Bookman ordered the hit, and Gabe Stilman was easy pickings. He was a dockworker at the Port of Seattle, a gruff, middle-aged divorcé whose grown son had died years ago in a freak mishap on those same docks.

Magnus used a fireplace poker to kill Gabe, but beforehand he made Gabe call his old pal Eddie and beg for help. Eddie, oh so predictably, rushed to the scene only to find a ransacked house and a corpse on the blood-wet floor.

For Magnus, this unsolved murder provided blackmail opportunities.

With Eddie?

"Do as I ask," Magnus told him, "and I won't turn over evidence implicating you in Gabe's death. Considering your history, it wouldn't take much."

With Claire?

"As a fraud investigator, I have suspicions about your husband, Mrs. Vreeland. I'm sure you've read that Mr. Stilman's portable safe went missing, and it suggests a possible motive, doesn't it?" Actually, Magnus himself had taken the safe, paid someone to open it, and found only a pile of smutty magazines, but she didn't need to know that.

"If Eddie is innocent," he told her, "I'll do my best to protect him, but I may need some information from you. Call me at this number if you agree to help. And please, let's keep this just between us. Clear enough?"

But now none of it was clear to Magnus.

Ahead, the Oldsmobile peeled off the freeway and followed signs for Muckleshoot Casino. It looked like Eddie was itching for a round of blackjack.

Another dead end. Another cold night in the van.

Claire stood at the front window. Eddie was gone for the time being.

"Gotta run an errand," he'd told her. He propped their shotgun by the front door. "You keep an eye along the street, and anyone so much as steps foot on our property, you fire a shot in the air. One warning, that's all they get."

He was one to talk, wasn't he?

For years she had hidden his faults the best she could. She applied face powder and makeup to conceal the abuse from Bret. She did weekend yard sales to buy groceries while her Eddie threw their money away.

Covering sin.

Yes, indeed, wasn't that the Christ-like thing to do?

But she could not excuse murder. My, it was almost too much to believe that he could kill his own friend, but there was no arguing with the fraud investigator or the blood droplets on her husband's boots. How could he murder a man and march right back in here with those same boots on? She knew she must go tell the authorities and, as Eddie was so fond of saying, let the chips fall where they may.

It would be the hardest thing she ever did.

But only after our trip to Mexico, Claire decided. *Bret and his sweet family deserve that much at least. Anything else would be hurtful.*

The garage now beckoned.

Was Eddie hiding evidence out there?

His key to the padlock sat under his boxers in his clothes bureau. She'd found it while putting away his laundry. Her hand shook as she retrieved it, but if she was going to go to the police she needed to be armed with all the facts.

She cradled the key to her belly, biting her lip as she slipped out the side door to the garage. The yard gnome was still upended, and Eddie was none too happy that his security camera was destroyed. She entered the dark garage. Pulled the string for the overhead bulb. Dug about in the tools and paint cans.

One can seemed too light to be worth keeping. She thought of tossing it out, but took note of fresh scrapes along the metal rim.

She pried at the lid with a screwdriver.

Chapter Fifty-three

MAGNUS WAS MISSING SOMETHING, SOME VITAL PIECE OF THE PUZZLE.

Slouched in the van in the casino parking lot, he sipped lukewarm coffee from his Thermos and ran through the past months.

Bookman believed there was a potential leak in their operation, and he feared it would draw the attention of federal investigators. He admitted using Eddie in the past for local jobs, and suspected Eddie was their problem. Magnus was beginning to agree. Eddie did seem to be hiding something in that garage.

Damaging info on Bookman? Who was Bookman anyway?

What was his real goal with the Vreelands?

Magnus's original task from Bookman was to undermine the Vreelands through fear and force, but Storinka's will changed those parameters by removing financial hardship from his box of tools. Nevertheless, Magnus continued his intimidation tactics, using his car and his computer and the clinic to great effect, while never touching the hairs upon the Vreelands' heads.

Even if delectable Sara did shave some curlies from his chest.

Hold on. His grin faded. *How could I be so foolish?*

His own DNA, he realized, could've been harvested from the sleep lab, his identity uncovered. He could no longer risk credit card purchases or plane flights. Thanks to Bookman, he at least had the cash from his expense account.

Seated in the van, Magnus realized he needed to take a leak after all the coffee. The Muckleshoot Casino lights flashed along its façade, but shadows dominated this edge of the lot. He hopped out of the van and emptied his bladder in the grass. As he scrambled back inside, his cell vibrated against his chest.

His heart jumped when he read the display: *E & C Vreeland.*

"Hello?"

"Mr. Hart?" said a tentative female voice.

"Yes. Is this Claire Vreeland?"

"My Eddie's out at the moment, but I really ought to make this quick."

Magnus glanced toward the casino entrance. No movement. The Oldsmobile was parked four rows over, visible between the vehicles. "Take your time," he said. "Why, I'll understand if you need to hang up suddenly."

"Oh, I do hate to even call. We have a vacation coming up, and I want him to enjoy that before the police come knocking. I love Eddie, despite his faults."

"Do you have something new for me, Mrs. Vreeland?" When she said nothing, he added in his official tone, "Look, you are doing the right thing here. And I assure you, this conversation is confidential. Please proceed."

"Thing of it is, I found a can of secrets."

"A can?"

"Hidden in our garage, that's right. An empty paint can. Inside, papers were rolled up in a plastic bag. Don't know right off what it all means, but there's receipts, manifests, photographs. Most of it's dated years ago, even paystubs from the docks where Eddie and Gabe loaded ships."

"Do these stubs list the employer?"

"Storinka Defense Systems."

He sat up in his seat. "Why would your husband hide this information?"

"That's what has me worried, Mr. Hart. If he wants this stuff kept hidden, I have to wonder . . . has he done other unlawful things? Oh, he has a nasty temper. That much I won't deny. He's had his share of episodes at the bars and whatnot, got into a tussle here and there, but that's just Eddie being Eddie."

"Unlawful things. Could you please clarify that for me?"

"But what if he . . . he finds out I told you?"

"Do you have reason to believe he would harm you?"

"Yes, I—" She stifled a cry. "It's just . . . Judging by these papers, I don't think Gabe's the only one Eddie's killed to cover his tracks."

Magnus leaned back, a theory forming about Bookman's real identity.

A Sad Old Song

the accuser roams
he patrols the earth
is there no end to this roving to and fro?

oh yes, the air is his realm and provides swift access to various corners of the globe, but he cannot be everywhere at once, cannot see all things, cannot know all things, and he rails against these limitations

the one, the almighty, he alone possesses such abilities, flaunts them for his sniveling two-leggers, and even so he fails to get their attention, which only underscores his ineffectiveness

given the same abilities, the accuser would rule with an iron fist, whereas the almighty rules by granting freedom and grace

it's a sad old song, experimented with throughout the ages, but freedom's bells always toll the demise of the peacemongers as the strong and the mighty march in to conquer once again

grace is weak
and freedom, it's a hoax

the accuser halts his roaming, considers the progress of his latest test, and although the outcome remains to be seen, he spots cracks in the family walls, flaws that could bring the fortress crumbling down

he recalls the one's insistence that "their power of choice must not be violated," and he scoffs at the idea this will limit him somehow

those given wings to fly, may they soar into the path of his arrows
those given legs to run, may they plunge headlong into his snares
those given eyes to see, may they gaze on things perverse and profane

"it's freedom you want for them, is it? it's power of choice you give? very well," he roars at the heavens above, "let them choose"

Chapter Fifty-four

December 2010

KEVIN SPOTTED IT FIRST AS THEY PULLED INTO THE CHURCH PARKING LOT. IN HIS best radio announcer voice, he read aloud the words from the marquee beside the road.

Bret Vreeland
Worship w/ Passion
10 A.M., Sunday, December 12

Katie cheered for her daddy. Sara, behind the wheel of the Lexus since the sports car would be a bit much in this East Nashville setting, reached for his hand and squeezed.

An hour later the sanctuary's eight hundred seats were nearly filled, and the crowd buzzed in anticipation. Word of the Vreelands' inheritance had made the rounds in the preceding weeks, and Bret heard whispers that if God was showering down money on Bret's family, then imagine what He might rain down through Bret's voice and his guitar.

Only last week after worship practice had Pastor Teman decided Bret was ready to lead the congregation in praise and worship. The first of many good things to come, he said. God coveted the praises of his people, and He raised up anointed individuals who could lead others into His presence with passion.

Bret nodded, "That's my desire."

"I know it is. And this is how congregations across the country, even across the world, are growing. Passionate music fosters passionate people."

"Let me guess. I'm supposed to do my new song, 'Passionate People.'"

"Not just do it. Teach it. It'll be on CD soon enough, in stores and maybe even on the radio, and I want it to be part of our worship rotation."

"Wow. Sure."

"I'd like very much for you to join our music ministries."

Bret had to know, just as he had with the promotion at Billingsley Coach. "Why now, Pastor? Is it because of the money?"

"Are you suggesting Rhonda and I are after your family fortune?"

"Just checking," Bret gave a wry grin. "You'd be surprised by some of the calls we've got recently."

"I like it. A direct question from a direct man. But no," Pastor said, resting a hand on his belly. "As you can see, I'm well taken care of."

"Guess what I really mean is, did the money validate me somehow?"

"I wouldn't say so. Money's an amoral thing, a tool for good or for evil. It's no mere coincidence, though, that those who give freely often worship freely."

Bret raised his eyebrows. "What about Jack Joiner, loaded to the gills, but short on musical ability? You ever heard him sing?"

"Can't say that I have."

"He doesn't," Bret said. "Can't carry a tune to save his life. So instead he drops checks into the plate, closes his eyes, and mouths the next song to spare those around him. Shoot, if he had it his way, he'd be belting it out."

"Did he tell you this?"

"Watch him from the stage. He's as into worshiping God as anyone I know. Singing's just not his thing, not the thing of most guys I know. But you can see it on Jack's face. He's singing his heart out, even without making a sound."

"I'll watch for it." Pastor stepped closer, took hold of Bret's elbow. "To answer your question, brother, when I look for men to lead our congregation I look at the way they lead their marriages, their children, their finances. When cash is tight, it's often a sign of something off-kilter."

"But that seems easy to misread. You could have a businessman throwing chunks of change your way while ripping off customers during the week. That makes him more worthy? He's in a suit and tie, so we assume he's OK, but the guy in jeans and a flannel shirt, oh, he's the one probably dealing with porn. It seems too shallow, Pastor. Where's the gift of discernment? We've had our backs to the wall since Kevin's medical issues started, even before that, and without changing a thing this inheritance has dropped into our laps."

"God's memory is long. You've been noticed and rewarded."

"Well," Bret said, "I just don't wanna be held up as the next poster boy."

"Does this mean you're not interested in leading worship?"

"That's not what I'm saying. Not at all."

"What are you saying?"

"I'd love to." Bret shook the pastor's hand. "More than anything."

Bret now stood at the stage curtain. 10 A.M. About time to do this.

He looked out across the wide platform. In the church's front row, his wife corralled their daughter's ponytail with a scrunchie, while their son swung his legs beneath the chair and almost toppled someone's travel mug onto the carpet.

Guitar strapped over his shoulder, Bret stepped to the mic.

Lord, help me not screw this up.

The crowd quieted. Katie looked up and gave him a wave from close to her chest. Kevin extended an imaginary fist bump. The lights dimmed as Sara lifted her chin, and he wasn't sure if she caught his smile.

Rather than give introductions or throw out some early humor, he launched into his solo acoustic version of "Servant King." The lyrics appeared on screens left and right of the stage. During practice earlier, he watched the graphics that accompanied the words, images of a desert road and a crown of thorns and knees dropping to the ground amidst a slow motion swirl of dust. All of these layers added to the worshipers' experience.

Eyes closed, he picked out the melody and strummed through the refrain. The crowd joined in with increasing fervor.

> *"Marched to the cross, like a criminal scorned . . .*
> *You left riches in glory for a crown of thorns . . .*
> *I bow, I bow down, I bow down to the Servant King."*

The final time through he put it into the plural form.

> *"We bow, we bow down, we bow down to the Servant King."*

As the guitar's resonance faded, applause began. He patted the air with his hands to silence it. On cue, the worship band filled positions on the stage.

"This morning," Bret said, "let's not just clap at every song. I'm not here for a performance, and I know God's more concerned with our hearts."

"That's right," someone called out.

"He doesn't need your empty applause. Maybe at this very moment your mind's on a situation with your teenager daughter. Or some bad news from a doctor. Your marriage could be falling apart." He scanned the crowd. "Who knows, maybe you're where my family was a few months ago and you need a financial miracle."

"Amen," a chorus of voices called out.

"Whether or not those things happen today or tomorrow or next week, we're called to bring a sacrifice of praise to our Heavenly Father. Some days it sure feels like a sacrifice, doesn't it?"

The responses turned more somber, introspective.

"Every word hurts."

Behind him, the band started playing.

"Every song cuts deep."

The music's volume picked up.

"And this," he said, "is when we cry out, 'Daddy, we need You.'"

For the next thirty-five minutes, Bret led the congregation through newer songs, '90s standbys, and a traditional hymn. At times he stepped back as other band members took the spotlight. Halfway through the set, his throat tightened. He could barely speak. He dropped his head, struck by the responsibility and privilege of leading hundreds of hurting people into God's transforming presence.

"Now," he said, "now that our hearts are turned toward the Lord, now that He's seen our sacrifice and knows that we want Him more than anything, let's give Him the shouts of praise He deserves. C'mon, people. Now."

The last restraints came off, and applause thundered through the building on a swell of jubilant cheers. The floor quivered beneath Bret's feet, and for a moment he believed he could shoot through the roof and join Jesus in the clouds.

At last an associate pastor walked forward and took the mic. He thanked Bret and the band while they exited stage-left and stood just out of sight.

A hand clasped Bret's arm from behind.

"Yeah?" He turned. "Oh, morning, Pastor Teman. Time for us to go back out already? I thought we waited till after the announcements and offering."

"That's right. Start back up at the end of the thirty-second meet-n-greet. If I could, though, I'd like to speak with you and your wife after service."

Bret thought of his name on the church marquee. He hoped he hadn't done anything to misrepresent the pastor or this congregation. These people were like family. Even through the glare of the lights, he'd spotted Eli's salt-and-pepper hair on the left about ten rows back.

"Is something wrong? Is it something I said, Pastor?"

"If only it were that simple. Sure appreciate it if you could both be in my office, say ten minutes after you wrap things up."

"We're gonna wrap things up," Bret told the congregation, "with a song I wrote six weeks ago. The words are pretty simple, and Pastor wants this to become our cry for the year ahead. Do you want to be a passionate people?"

A burst of cheers. Some clapping.

"Why don't you stand with me, and let's declare this with one voice."

Bret started it off on guitar, the bass and drums kicked in, the keyboards added texture, and the gathering joined in as lyrics appeared on the screens.

> *"This is my cry, in the midst of pain*
> *This is my cry, when life wears me down*
> *This is my cry, God, this is my cry, God,*
> *These are my hands, letting go of my sin*
> *These are my hands, reaching out to You*
> *This is my cry, God, this is my cry, God,*
> *Make us a passionate people . . .*
> *Make us a passionate people . . .*
> *We need Your touch, need our Daddy's love*
> *Make us a passionate people."*

The real test of sacrificial praise came after the service.

Chapter Fifty-five

SARA INSTRUCTED HER KIDS TO PLAY TOGETHER NICELY IN THE YOUTH ROOM, and followed Bret into the pastor's office where they found places in cushioned chairs. Wooden blinds, mahogany shelves, and the scent of old books created a subdued atmosphere. She knew this was the room where Bret sought spiritual advice the day after the reading of Storinka's will.

Pastor Teman waved a hand from his tall chair behind the desk. "Thanks for coming in, the both of you."

Standing at his side, Rhonda offered Sara a closed-lipped smile. She had violet eyes, wide cheekbones, and wore a floral print dress that masked a stout Germanic build. Rhonda set her hand on her husband's shoulder. Jewels glistened on three different fingers.

The Temans were the sort of couple, Sara decided, that could blend in with Saturday shoppers at Cosco or the fans at a baseball game.

"Bret," Pastor said, "I must tell you, that was a fine job you did this morning. Nothing but good feedback so far."

"Always nice to know. Thanks."

"Unfortunately, the news I have to share is not so pleasant."

Sara's gaze darted to Bret, but his face was fixed forward. Whatever the problem, she could see the old linebacker in him was ready to tackle it head-on.

"For legal reasons," Pastor said, "we need to be certain this remains between us for the time being, but a few weeks ago we realized money was being skimmed from the church account. Our annual budget runs close to two million dollars, and to facilitate our various departments we have four people authorized to access funds and sign checks. We've never had an issue before."

"This doesn't sound good. Let's hear it," Bret said. "Don't drag it out."

"He's getting there, honey."

"This last Friday, we . . ." Pastor reached up, resting his hand on his wife's. "We confronted Derek Riley about the missing money and he confessed."

"Derek? You're kidding," Sara said. "Does Jeannie know?"

"She knew all along, yes," Rhonda said.

"Derek had authorization as the music minister," Pastor added. "None of us realized he was buying personal items and embezzling funds. You knew the Rileys made a recent trip to Fort Lauderdale? It seems the whole thing was paid on a church debit card. Our bank manager tells us she thought nothing of it, assuming there was a district conference or something of the sort."

"So," Bret said, "it took weeks for someone to notice a problem?"

"Much as I hate to say it, yes."

"How much?"

"What?"

"How much did he steal? Embezzle? Whatever."

"The exact amount is yet to be determined by a judge, but it's safe to say it was around twenty thousand dollars."

Sara's mouth dropped. Upset as she was by the Rileys' actions, she was more horrified at the ease in which her entire first tithe check could be obliterated. She'd signed that check personally. Bret dropped it in the plate.

"Twenty thousand." Bret folded his arms. "What are the odds? The Rileys, they better read the story of Ananias and Sapphira. Dangerous stuff, messing with God's money."

Pastor Teman and his wife exchanged a look.

"What?" Bret said.

"So that you don't hear this elsewhere, we should tell you Derek blames part of this on the fact that he and his wife weren't included in your Mexico plans. All the help he gave you getting into the studio, getting hours to record, he figures they had the right to go along."

Sara rubbed two fingers against her temple. "That's ridiculous."

"No one's saying he's right, but it's part of his rationalization."

"Of course he's not right."

"As for your CD, Bret, let me assure you this in no way interferes. In fact, the mastering's already completed. Of course, Derek will no longer be on the project, and he's been asked to step down as music minister. If I may be frank, you're a better fit anyway for where our church is headed."

"I . . ." Bret looked toward the ceiling. "Listen, I appreciate that. But the timing, isn't it like pouring salt in Derek's wounds?"

"He made his choices. I see no reason you should be punished for them."

"That's right, hon," Sara said. "Perhaps God knew this was about to happen and brought you to the forefront at just the right moment."

"For which we're all thankful." Rhonda's violet eyes shone with sincerity.

"Hold on," Bret said. "Are we suggesting God gave us this money so that the Rileys could be offended so that I could become a worship leader? Sounds pretty twisted to me. I'm not sure that's how He works. Am I wrong, Pastor?"

"Who am I to say? We can't always understand His ways."

Bret barked out a laugh. He ran both hands through his hair, leaned forward, and said, "C'mon, let's hear the real reason you called us in here. Why us instead of hundreds of others? The way this looks to me, you're doing damage control by easing the fears of your large tithers."

"Honestly," Sara shot him a look, "I can't imagine this is easy for them."

"I'm not saying it is. But why us?"

Sara turned toward the Temans. She envisioned these new opportunities being crushed underfoot by her well-meaning but brusque husband. "I think what he means to say is we don't want to be treated any differently now that we have the resources to play a larger part in what God's doing here. We hate to hear of this situation with the Rileys. I mean, we all have blind spots, right? Regardless, we don't want this to sour our experience here or our relationship with you two."

"We don't want that either," Rhonda said.

"We want to be good stewards of our money and talents," Pastor added.

"Let Bret and I sleep on this. Talk it over. I'm sure it'll all work itself out. Don't you agree, honey?"

He gave a tight nod, but the earlier passion had seeped from his eyes.

Chapter Fifty-six

GABE STILMAN'S LIBRARY CARD RESTED IN MAGNUS'S LEFT PALM. IN THE OTHER hand, he held a briefcase and waited at the counter for an assistant here in the modern Seattle Public Library. Slushy rain beat upon the soaring levels of glass, and he watched the escalators climb toward Level 10 where months earlier he felt the jab of a needle and the numbing effects of the Bookman's chemical cocktail.

Who was Bookman?

Magnus figured that was only part of the question. If he was going to test his theory, he needed to examine this from a new angle.

Who was Eddie Vreeland?

Eddie was a married man, a father, a character who lived a double life. Decent citizen. Dirty scoundrel. He worked as a bookie for small-time gambling operations. He and Gabe both worked the docks to pay bills. His wife now believed he had killed his friend, but Magnus knew that wasn't the case since he had done the deed himself.

What, then, was Eddie trying to hide in an empty paint can?

Magnus rapped his knuckles on the library counter. He wondered if the young woman had forgotten he was here.

Still waiting, he played out his theory . . .

Eddie Vreeland was more than a dock worker for Storinka. He did cleanup work for the old man just as Magnus once did. Eddie knew months ago about the old man's last will and testament, and hoped to tap the large fortune given to his son and daughter-in-law. He knew Magnus's background and hired Magnus to manipulate the events in Nashville, since Eddie's own face would be recognized. He also ordered the hit on Gabe Stilman, silencing a man who knew his identity and secrets, some of which were now hidden in Eddie's garage.

Could Eddie be Bookman be Eddie?

"Eddie being Eddie," as his wife would say.

Magnus still had some puzzle pieces to put into place, though. True, his theory gave a clearer picture of recent events, but Eddie's reasons for flying Magnus back to this area again seemed murky. Why would Eddie, as Bookman, order surveillance on himself? Was it an attempt to throw Magnus off?

Magnus's theory also explained how Eddie knew he would be at that Orange Julius a few months back, but it did not explain why Eddie would have Gabe's library card delivered to him.

"I'm back," the library assistant said. "I apologize for the wait."

He opened his briefcase on the counter. "This won't take long."

She was bright-eyed, with purple highlights in her hair and a webbed choker around her neck. She wasn't much younger than Natalie, and the thought of his little coffee bean filled him with frustrated longing.

"I'm Mr. Hart." He handed the woman a business card from his case. "Insurance fraud investigator. I'm looking into the murder of a Mr. Gabe Stilman, one of your patrons."

"He was murdered?"

"With a fireplace poker."

She cringed.

"It's a scary world out there," Magnus said. The line served him well and often. "It seems he was researching local criminal activities and attracted the wrong attention. All I need is a list of items he checked out over the last six months or so."

"That's it?"

"If you'd be so kind." He extended his palm.

She took Gabe Stilman's library card, tapped at her keyboard for no more than sixty seconds. The printer behind her came to life and spit out three sheets of paper. "Just that easy," she said, sliding them across the counter.

"Just that easy," he echoed.

An hour later later, he knew the reason for his employer's concern.

Chapter Fifty-seven

0 TO 60 MPH IN 5.2 SECONDS. 0 TO 100 IN 12.3 SECONDS.

Top speed, 178 mph.

In layman's terms, the Maserati Granturismo could blow the wings off a cicada two counties over, light the tails of a million lightning bugs with one stomp on the gas, and probably ratchet the local humidity index a full ten percent at the same time. Bret didn't even want to know how much gas it burned in the process.

He still couldn't believe this was his car.

Well, not yet. Not officially. But he'd signed the paperwork with Viktor, and it was a done deal once the courts finished their tedious procedures.

He finished his Monday evening work at Billingsley Coach Company and settled into the Maserati's red leather interior. Overall, he was satisfied with his newly implemented warehouse policies. Some of the old crew griped about them, but what could you expect? People just liked to complain.

Feeling nostalgic, he swung by Groves Park Road. A few residents snapped their heads at the sight of such a car in their neighborhood. He gunned the engine for their entertainment and slid to a stop at the old mailbox.

"Eli," he called from the driver's seat. "Whatcha up to?"

The older man turned at the front corner of the house, metal clippers in hand. "Trimming these dead tree limbs. They like to scrape up 'gainst the house."

"The place still treating you good?"

"Got no complaints. 'Cept maybe that it's too big and lonely. Wanna move back in with me, say the word. You're more'n welcome."

"Thanks. Some days, I admit, bachelorhood sounds pretty good." Bret smiled and gunned the engine. "Listen, I better head home."

He was driving west on I-40 when he got the call from Detective Meade.

"Detective, how are you?"

"Sure could use a cup of coffee. I wanted to tell you my younger sister and her husband visited your church yesterday and they loved the music."

"Well, good. That's, uh, that's always encouraging."

While Bret injected warmth into the words, he felt cold. How could the Rileys steal money from God's own pockets? Didn't He care? Was He asleep? And while Pastor Teman wasn't a bad guy, if he spent as much time policing the church funds as he did subtly soliciting them, he wouldn't be in this situation.

"Still no word," Meade said, "on Mr. Maggart. His antics may be over. It could be that talking to your wife about that accident years ago lifted some guilt off his chest. Don't worry, though. We're still watching for him. He has charges to face here in Nashville for the situation with young Natalie. How's she doing?"

"The kids love her. She's definitely part of the family."

"How 'bout your golf game? You beaten that boss of yours yet?"

"Billingsley? Just yesterday, out at Belle Meade Country Club, I had him on the front nine, but he took the lead back on the seventeenth hole."

"Belle Meade."

"You ever play there?" Ahead, Bret saw the signs for White Bridge Road. Deepening shades of purple circled a bruised-peach sunset. "It's a nice place."

"For men, yes. White men, to be specific."

"Whaddya mean?"

"You do realize my own parents were involved in the Nashville sit-ins back in the early '70s. They fought for civil rights, and as a black man I'm proud of those things they accomplished. The country club you mention, they don't have one woman or African American as a member. Did you know that?"

"No, not a clue. Sorry, Detective. That's not cool."

"Enjoy it, sure. But don't forget there are others who aren't so privileged."

The words stung. As Bret ended the call, he thought of times past when he and his family felt shoved to the fringes, unable to participate for lack of funds or free time. How could a man like Detective Meade, a government employee, be denied the opportunity to play golf here in the United States? And that was nothing compared to those overseas who suffered for race, class, or gender.

The old Sunday school song played through his head:

"Red and yellow, black and white, they are precious in His sight . . ."

Bristling with indignation, he blew past the exit that angled home. The interstate traffic was light, and he needed a few minutes before facing the demands for homework help, story time, game time, cuddle time, "honey-dos," and bank documents. He could drive back the long way on Highway 70.

His foot edged the pedal down, and the purring engine let out a growl. A surge of power pushed him back in his seat, and his levels of testosterone and adrenaline rocketed. He cranked the Bose Surround Sound and yelled.

He was man.

He was brawny, and he was swift.

If this was the masculine parallel of his wife strutting in her heels and latest fashions, he could understand her need to splurge every now and then. Boy, could he understand. Racing toward the setting sun, he imagined his frustrations peeled away by the rush of sound. He imagined his questions whipped away by the speed. He imagined the spinning lights of a—

Spinning lights?

No, no, no. Bret, you idiot.

The sheriff caught him on radar at 103 mph.

It was no use arguing. What could he say? "Sir, I had seventy-five miles to go before pegging out the speedometer"? He was cited for speeding and reckless driving. Since it was his first moving violation in years, he would not face a suspended license, but the sheriff made him sweat before revealing this tidbit.

Would he do such a thing again?

Nope, he vowed. Not ever. He'd learned his lesson.

He mailed in the hefty check the next day without uttering a word of it to Sara. Best not to worry her. She'd only feel bad, since it was her idea that he keep the car in the first place. The worst would be the spike in insurance fees.

He was man.

He was contrite, and he was ashamed.

Sara found the evidence on Friday, after the check cleared their account.

Traffic Violations Bureau?

Her eyes bulged at the amount. Thank goodness her children were years from getting behind the wheel, but this meant her husband was the culprit.

And it wasn't as if she went spying on him. Of all things, she was searching their online banking for a donation made last month. As a couple, they tried to be wise yet generous, and Family Affair was a local ministry they knew funneled funds directly into the practical and spiritual needs of East Nashville.

For heaven's sakes, Bret. What were you thinking?

She poked her head in on the kids in the downstairs classroom. They were bent over their iPads, Kevin reading an article on the American Revolution, Katie taking a spelling test. Natalie was at the rolling chalkboard, writing a quote from A. A. Milne's *Winnie the Pooh* to accompany her chalk-drawn Eeyore.

"Hi, Mommy," Katie said.

"Hey, cutie pie. Don't mind me," Sara told Natalie. "If you'd like, I can bring in a pitcher of apple juice and some Triscuits."

"Si, senora. That sounds good."

"I want gummy worms," Katie said.

"What'd we talk about last night before bed? 'I want' is the first step toward being selfish, isn't it? It's fine to express your desires, but only if you're ready to hear 'no' as the answer."

"Triscuits work for me," Kevin said, still hunched over his work.

Katie nodded. "Me too."

"All right," Sara said. "And if we do have any gummy worms, I won't be surprised if they happen to squirm onto your plates."

At the large island in the kitchen, she divvied out snacks on the Williams-Sonoma serving tray. She loved the new cookware and cutlery, and was grateful that Natalie showed care with them while making meals. She flashed back to girls' day out with Zoe. They still spent mornings window shopping and afternoons catching matinees at the Green Hills cinema, but with Christmas and Cozumel a week away, they desperately needed another shopping trip.

And why not? If Bret was throwing money into city coffers for his masculine road thrills, she deserved another day glorying in her womanhood.

She was a woman, after all.

Sara delivered the tray to her hungry brood. "Enjoy," she said. "I'm going to visit Zoe, but I'll be back later this afternoon."

She drove straight to the Billingsleys' Tudor-style home on Franklin Road. Jason was at the coach company, leaving the two ladies to plot their getaway at the huge oak dining table. Zoe poured them glasses of white zinfandel and fanned out city maps and fashion brochures.

"Thing is, babe, if we're going to do this, we do it in style."

"Absolutely," Sara said.

"New York City?"

Sara nodded.

"Saks Fifth Avenue? Bloomingdale's?"

Sara sipped her zinfandel. "It sounds almost make-believe."

"Those are for starters. You have no idea. I'll take you places only New Yorkers know about, places where the owners know my name and the comps are divine. Oh, this'll be so much fun." Zoe raked Sara's forearm with pearl-white nails. "I'll book our tickets today. Jason, he has his own account. I have mine. The boys'll be none the wiser, and none the worse for it. You think this Monday works, only four days before Mexico? We tell them we're hitting the area malls for some Christmas shopping, then jet out out of here on the first flight instead."

"Have you, uh, done this before?" Sara asked.

"Countless times. With the time change, we'll hit the Big Apple by nine, shop till we drop around four, fly back, and be snuggled on our sofas by seven."

"You make it sound easy."

"The Big Easy. That'll be our next trip. Trick is," Zoe said with a smoky-eyed wink, "unload the bags from the car one or two per day. Slip the items slowly into your wardrobe rotation. 'Oh, this? I dunno, Bret, I think I found it for half off at that cute little boutique on West End.' Start mentioning material and designers, and he'll trip over all himself to escape the conversation."

Sara chuckled. "I take it Jason's the same."

"Two hetero males. Believe me, they're not interested in this stuff."

Another chuckle.

"Unless, of course . . ." Zoe grinned. "Don't forget to remind me, I know a fabulous, and I do mean fabulous, intimate apparel shop in upper Manhattan."

"Are we really doing this?"

"'Are we really . . .?' Listen to you, Sara. So. Dang. Cute. Whatever happened to prim-and-proper, don't-want-to-break-the-bank Mrs. Vreeland? Please tell me things are going swimmingly between you and your lover boy. If you two can't make it work, what hope is there for the rest of us?"

"My lover boy, if you must know, got ticketed for speeding."

Zoe swirled and sipped from her glass. "And?"

"And so he didn't tell me. He paid the ticket, never said a word. That's just not like him. I mean, we've never hidden things from each other."

Zoe arched a sculpted eyebrow. "Never?"

Sara knew it would be dishonest to push her point.

"Boys'll be boys," Zoe said. "I don't hound Jason about it. Let him have his fun, so long as he lets me have mine." She finished her glass in a final gulp. "Is it ideal? No. But, as they say, all's fair in love and war."

"Oh, it's never been a war between us."

"Lucky you."

"You and Jason seem to get along."

Zoe tossed back her hair and looked off through the window. "Don't be naïve. Wars are fought in lotsa ways. Jason, he's always had a knack for making money, and you'd think we would have a fortune in savings, wouldn't you? But no, we spend it drawing our lines and marking off boundaries."

"I'm sorry. I, uh . . . we can skip the trip if that helps."

"No, babe, my battles are my own. This? This is about you. Unless, of course, you don't think any of it's quite up your alley."

"Shopping in New York City? No," Sara said, "sounds like heaven to me."

She was a woman, after all.

Chapter Fifty-eight

"W<small>ON'T THIS BE FUN</small>, E<small>DDIE</small>?"

"As a kick in the head," he grunted. "Now lemme do my packing."

"Don't be such a grump," Claire said. "You love the beach."

"Whaddya know?"

A good deal more than you suspect, she thought.

It was two days before Christmas and the weather outside was frightful, but her passport on the bed promised sunnier days around the corner.

She opened her suitcase and laid out her outfits, smoothing each blouse, each dress, each pair of knee-length beachcomber shorts. She went with cotton for most items, trusting the absorbency would tame her perspiration in the hotter climate. A pink golf visor would do for walks about town and at the villa, while her beige soft-brimmed hat would protect her on the white sand.

Tropical breezes already blew through her thoughts, and she drew strength from them. She was not afraid. Her mind was made up.

Tonight she and her husband would fly a red-eye to Nashville, join Bret and his family for a mid-morning hop to Atlanta, and take the last big jump across the Gulf of Mexico to Cozumel. They would enjoy five days with their grandbabies on the beach and in the water. They would explore the sights.

And when they returned to America, she would end it. This would be Claire and Eddie Vreelands' glorious, bittersweet, farewell tour.

No more covering, Eddie. That's just the way it has to be.

Who knew how he would react, though? Would he turn violent?

As a precaution, Claire had nabbed his rolled documents while he was out one afternoon at the casino. She rode the city bus to a FedEx Office, made two sets of copies, called Mr. Hart and arranged for him to pick up the first set in a sealed envelope at the FedEx counter. She returned the originals to the paint can, clicked the padlock back into place, and thanked the good Lord that parts were still on order for the security camera so that she could move by unrecorded.

The second set of copies now sat at the bottom of her suitcase, slipped between the liner and the hard plastic shell. They gave her a backup plan and some sense of protection. She would draw on them only if necessary.

Claire's fingers trembled as she zipped tight her suitcase.

Tropical breezes, she told herself. *Enjoy your farewell tour.*

"What's wrong with you?" Eddie said.

She swiped the single tear from her cheek. "Thinking about what lies ahead, that's all, dear." She braved a smile. "Come the next day or two, we'll be splashing in the ocean with our grandbabies. Hard to imagine, isn't it? Christmas Eve in the Caribbean."

"They ain't babies no more. You seen Kevin's picture. And that Katie, she's sure a cute thing, isn't she? Must take after her mother," he laughed.

"They'll always be my babies," Claire said. "Same as Bret. So long as I'm alive, he'll be my little boy." She braced herself for Eddie's biting response.

He gave a vigorous nod instead. "You know, he's done all right for himself, hasn't he?"

"He has."

"Gotta hand it to ya, woman. Batty as you can be sometimes, you've put up with me all these years."

"We've had our good moments," she said.

"And got ourselves a rich son outta the deal."

She lifted her chin. "I loved him just the same when he was poor."

"Now there ya go twisting my words. OK, sure. Doesn't seem fair that he lands in that big amount o' dough, when I'm the one doing best I can to keep us afloat. But just like I drilled into that thick skull of his," Eddie said, tapping the air with his finger, "life ain't always fair. You take the good with the bad. And, Claire, you don't got no idea the things I've done for that boy, do ya? None at all."

"I suppose not."

The way Claire saw it, the stuff she did know was bad enough.

This was it. Last-minute chores before their flight out in the morning.

Bundled against a bitter wind, Bret dropped purifying tablets into the fountain out front. The moss was clearing up at least. Kevin pulled alongside in the golf cart, loaded tied garbage bags from the front steps onto the backseat, and together father and son zipped over crushed shells toward the triple garage.

"Where're your gloves?" Bret said. "That steering wheel, it must be cold."

Kevin shrugged. "Left them in my room."

"Better not forget anything for the trip. You have the packing list I gave you? Good. OK, stop here. I'll get the green bags, you get the black."

They raced each other to the garbage bins. Kevin had two bags to Bret's three. Bret fumbled with the lid to the recyclables, dropping one of his bags. The impact split the plastic and spilled paper items onto the flagstones.

"Finished first, Dad."

"Good work."

Bret gathered his mess, noted a Bloomingdale's bag. Hmm. Wasn't that some store in New York City? He looked inside, found a brand label and a half-sheet ad for day-after-Christmas discounts. Strange.

He completed his work, slid back into the golf cart.

"I told her I was sorry," Kevin said as they neared the house.

"What?"

"Hannah. She came by last week. Told her I shouldn't have pushed her."

"Thank you, Kev. Way to step up and be a man."

He parked the cart. "She hugged me. I gotta go pack, Dad."

"Hey, wait up. She hugged you, huh?"

But his ten-almost-eleven-year-old was through the front door already.

Bret followed him inside and logged onto the PC in the study. Thirty seconds later he had the joint checking info on the screen. He found the Bloomingdale's expenditure and half a dozen others totaling $1,462. The dates indicated Sara had been in the Big Apple only three days ago.

While I was at work? She said she and Zoe were shopping around town.

He wanted to rant and roar, but technically she hadn't lied and the amount she spent was within their agreed limits. Was there more she was hiding?

Look here, though. His citation payment was only eight items up the list.

Let it go, Bret. All's fair in love and war.

Seated at the computer desk, he made calls confirming that Viktor Moroz and his Dobermans would be over to housesit while the Vreelands were gone, that his parents were ready for their flight tonight, that his old warehouse guys were set with Butterball turkeys and $750 Christmas bonus checks.

"You think that's enough?" he said into the phone.

"Enough?" Jason Billingsley said. "Sure as there's snow on Denali, it's enough. That's more than I ever gave you guys."

"Exactly, you cheapskate. Hey, we gonna hit the links down there?"

"In Cozumel? You betcha. Don't worry about bringing clubs, though. I know the manager at the country club and he'll comp us some, no problem."

"Listen. One more question." Bret cleared his throat. "Is it true that Belle Meade doesn't give membership to women or African Americans?"

"Who told you that?"

"Is it true?"

"There's nothing saying one of our black brothers can't play there. Can I help it if none of them do? I'm a businessman, Vreeland, not some activist. But hey, if this is your hill to die on, we can cancel your membership."

"That's not what I'm saying. It's just not right that a man gets the cold shoulder from the very people he serves and protects."

"Your detective friend."

"Yeah," Bret said.

"Well, I agree one hundred percent. Not right. You think I don't have a bleedin' heart of my own? How do you think you got your job with me in the first place? Mr. Storinka, he breezes into town and bumps into me at Rotary. Tells me he knows a good cabinet guy out west I should hire. A month later, here you are."

"You never told me that. So you knew Storinka?"

"Only in passing. Go get ready for some surf and sun. Viva la Mexico."

Chapter Fifty-nine

OVER THE PACIFIC, THE SUN WAS DIPPING LOW AND PAINTING THE COASTAL Olympic Mountains gray and dark pink. Magnus sat in his minivan three blocks down the street from Eddie and Claire's. He saw their porch light came on.

Why was he still here in the damp Northwest? This place was a merry-go-round of memories for him. He had spent his childhood only miles away at Fort Lewis-McChord. He'd killed three different people within a thirty-mile radius of this spot.

And now, thanks to Gabe Stilman's thorough library research, he knew intimate details about Storinka Defense Systems. Thanks to darling, middle-aged Claire, he also had an envelope filled with copies of those original documents.

It was highly flammable stuff.

Literally flammable? Why, yes, with one strike of a match.

Politically and economically? Even more so.

No wonder Bookman paid Magnus to eliminate Gabe Stilman, as a means of suppressing this information. No wonder Eddie Vreeland hid the original papers in an obscure place. A used paint can, to be exact.

It was oh, so laughably amateur as to be genius.

Magnus shifted his large frame in the driver's seat. With no reason to stay in Tacoma, he faced a hazardous journey back over the Rockies this time of year, but it was better than being detected on a flight and taken into custody.

Back 2 Nash, he texted his employer.

Not yet.

Long drive ahead.

Keep eyes on Eddie a few more hours.

He sighed. If Eddie was Bookman, why insist that Magnus extend surveillance on him? What was he up to?

With it shaping up to be another stir-crazy night in this van, Magnus dialed his dear Natalie. "Why, good evening," he said.

"What do you want?" She spoke in a hushed voice.

"Are your antenna still up?"

"Stop calling me every week for no reason. Please."

He grinned. "I like that fight in your voice, mi chica. Don't forget, though, what a man like me is capable of. I know how much you care for little Katie."

"Don't you even speak her name."

"Where is she right now?"

"Packing," Natalie said. "To get as far from you as she can."

"Oh? And where do you think I am?" Headlights crawled close in his side-view, but it was only an airport shuttle van searching house numbers in the dusk. "Do you realize," he said, "I can see you right now if you wave out your window?"

"O.M.G. You're such a liar. This time you can't follow us."

Magnus tightened his grip on the phone. "Don't be so sure."

"We're all flying out of here on long-distance vacation with Bret's and Sara's parents. You're not invited."

"Now who's the liar?" he said. "Bret's parents are in Washington. No matter how far you run, I'm close behind. Don't do anything foolish, you understand? Think of Katie. And keep answering when I call."

"I understand." The fight was gone from her voice. "Adios."

He stared over the dashboard, warmed by their conversation. Down the road, the airport shuttle was stopped. That looked like Eddie handing suitcases to the driver. Yes, and there was Claire climbing through the side doors.

The airport? A long-distance trip?

Magnus reflected on the class ring, the library card, the surveillance, and realized all of it was part of Bookman's plan, mocking him at every turn. Even now, the "few more hours" were so that Magnus could watch helplessly while his employer flew off to deal with Bret, Sara, and the $6,000,000.

Trapped by his own ID issues, Magnus knew there was no use following. He slammed his fists on the steering wheel as the shuttle vanished into the night.

Chapter Sixty

Cozumel appeared below their plane, a small flat island hugged by clear Caribbean waters, natural reefs, and white sandy beaches. Sara gazed down, searching for landmarks mentioned in her guidebook. Situated only miles off the Yucatan Peninsula, it was one of the world's top diving destinations. While the island hosted minor Maya ruins and evidence of sixteenth-century Spaniards, the real focus was on the tourists in the expensive resorts and docked cruise ships.

"Doesn't it look wonderful?" Claire Vreeland said from the seat ahead.

"Fantastic." Sara reached around and squeezed her mother-in-law's shoulder. "I'm so glad you and Eddie could make it. I know Bret's thrilled."

"This time we have together, Sara, it's important, isn't it?"

Important?

That seemed an odd word for her to use.

Sara looked around the plane's cabin, heart swelling at the sight of these friends and family all together. She knew that Bret beside her was as pleased as she was. Most everyone was leaned toward the windows for a view. The Billingsleys were two rows back, Sara's mom and step-dad one row back, Bret's parents one row ahead, and the Temans ahead of them. Kevin and Katie were across the aisle in the middle seats, with Natalie on the end.

Thirteen people in all. Total trip budget of $25,000.

Absolutely worth it for a trip of a lifetime.

She realized, of course, that the tropical setting couldn't dissolve the tensions between Bret and his father, Bret and the pastor, Claire and her husband, not to mention the recent barrier between Sara and Bret. For the time being, though, the natural beauty and the anticipation of the next few days served as a buffer. It would take some time for everyone to settle in, reacquaint, and let go of concerns from home and work.

Sara said, "You're right, Claire. This is important."

The plane landed as a molten-red sun spilled over the peninsula. Sara noticed that here in December the weather was pleasant and warm even in the early evening. The Billingsleys warned that gnats and mosquitoes would be out "in biblical numbers," and they whipped into view travel-size bottles of repellant and sunscreen for the coming battles with nature.

"Why's 'biblical' so often a negative adjective?" Pastor Teman asked Sara and Bret as they shuffled through customs. "God gets the raw end of the stick."

"Guess most people don't read the Book all the way through," Bret said.

"There are all those plagues," Sara said. "And the whole deal with Job."

"Now there's a guy who got the raw end of the stick, Pastor."

"And got everything back, if you recall. Twice as much as before."

Sara frowned. "Well, he certainly took a beating to get there."

"We live in a different age," Pastor said. "We're under grace, and our adoption's been sealed as the children of the King."

The Mexican customs official waved him forward, unimpressed.

Three taxis took the hungry, travel-weary group into San Miguel, darting in and out along the airport boulevard, skirting the piers and beachfront shops, turning down side avenues. At last they arrived at their private, six-room villa.

"We're staying here, Daddy?" Katie bounced on her toes.

"This is cool," Kevin said.

"You two don't ever run short on words, do ya?" Eddie gave his grandson a medium-force jab in the arm, and Sara watched for the reaction.

"Mostly Katie doesn't," Kevin whispered to his grandpa.

Eddie threw his head back and laughed. "Vreeland male, through and through. Yep, you and me, we're gonna get along."

Kevin beamed.

Sara and Bret exchanged a glance but said nothing.

The villa was magnificent. Palms surrounded the two-story, white-stucco structure that boasted arched doorways, covered terraces, and stone flooring to keep things cool. The furniture was upholstered in rich traditional colors. Terra cotta pottery and local crafts graced the living area. A curved outdoor staircase led down to a tiled pool in the fenced backyard, where bougainvilleas and banana trees muffled the sounds of a rock fountain and waterfall.

"Room numbers and keys." Bret divvied them out, while Sara handed over folded towels and bath soaps from the villa owner. "All the couples are together. Natalie, you and the kids'll share a room if that's OK."

"You joking?" Natalie said. "We're in Cozumel. Do you think I'll complain about a thing?"

She sounded more carefree than any time since her captivity.

Moments after arrival, Zoe had slipped into an orange gauze sarong, and it billowed around her ankles in the warm ocean breeze. She winked, flicked a glance at Sara's tan pumps. They both wore items from their recent outing.

"Who's hungry?" Jason called out. He threw an arm around his wife's waist, and she rolled her eyes as he pulled her close. "I say we meet back here poolside in thirty, then we stretch our legs through town, and Zoe and I treat you to your very first meal in Meh-hee-co."

"The royal treatment," Zoe said.

Eddie also threw an arm around his wife's waist. "Now we're talkin'."

A half hour later, plus eleven or twelve minutes in honor of the more laidback culture, the group stretched their legs through the streets of San Miguel while the Billingsleys acted as tour guides. They pointed out mailboxes ("Aren't they cute?"), hat stands ("Get a jipi hat while you're here, but barter, don't just pay the price it says"), smoothie shops

("The liquados are awesome"), and signs for public restrooms ("Always good to recognize those in a foreign country").

They greeted every local with a "Que paso?"

"Our Spanish," Zoe said, "isn't even that good. But so what, right? You try, and at least you sound like a cultured tourist instead of some barbarian. Makes a difference. Natalie, trust me, babe, you'll be very popular."

"Tough part for me," Jason added, "is slowing down, way down. I like things chop-chop. Time is money in my world. But here? You take your time and get to know a person. None of those rushed meet-n-greets we do in the States."

When Sara caught Pastor Teman's eye, he shrugged.

"Here we go. Pepe's Grill." Zoe gestured to a second-story restaurant with windows facing the pier. "Some fabulous lobster, prime rib, and my favorite, the shrimp Bahamas flambéed right at your table with bits of pineapple and banana in a yummy curry sauce. You have no idea. My mouth's watering already."

Bret smiled at her enthusiasm.

Sara took his hand, and together they trailed Zoe's wispy sarong up the stairs. Her calves were lean, unnaturally tan.

Two hours later, thirteen overfed tourists waddled along the starlit bay with the sounds of guitar trios fading behind them. Most of the adults had ended dinner with café Maya, a mix of coffee, vanilla ice cream, and liqueur. Their pace was meandering and their voices loud.

Sara nuzzled against Bret. He took her hand in his and they dropped back from the chattering group.

"It's strange seeing my mother with my stepdad," she said. "I mean, I hardly even know him. It's fine. She looks happy. I, uh, I just don't have a lot in common with her, never really have."

"She's reserved, but she's always seemed nice."

"And your mom? Hon, she's a doll. Have you spoken with your dad at all?"

"On the plane," Bret said. "But not about the ties to Storinka. Not yet."

"It's good just letting him be a grandpa, I suppose. Please don't let him breed his attitudes into our son, though. Kev, he's so impressionable at this age, and some of the stuff Eddie said at the dinner table. . . . I want Kevin taking his example from you, being respectful and fun and honest."

"Honest." He nodded. "Sure thing."

Sara hoped he would take this chance for some quiet confession about the ticket. If he came clean, she would do so about her excursion with Zoe.

He said, "Tomorrow's the big day with the kids and grandparents, isn't it? Snorkeling and swimming with dolphins at that inland lagoon. What's it called? Laguna Chuckakabob?"

"It means 'little sea.'" Sara giggled. "And it's Chankanaab, you dork."

"That's when I'll talk to my dad." Bret's voice deepened, his grip tightened. "And I better get some straight answers from him."

Magnus needed to get to Nashville. When the Vreelands, both junior and senior, returned from this little escapade of theirs, he would be waiting.

Don't you know? If you try to escape, there's a price to be paid.

He knew it wouldn't be easy buying a used car from a private owner on Christmas Eve, but the minivan would never make it over the Rockies in the snow. Thanks to Craigslist, he located a $4,495 Honda Accord on Tacoma's west side. He talked the price down to $2,995, sensing the man, his wife, and three kids were desperate for holiday cash. He gave them $3,000, let them keep the extra five dollars, and tossed over the keys to the minivan.

"For you," he said. "I used to dream of a quaint little family like yours."

I am Magnus the Generous.

He ran a quick errand at FedEx, and by 1:15 P.M. he was headed down I-5 to I-84, which cut east into Idaho and Utah. He used the time to make some calls, digging for the dates of the Vreeland family's getaway so he could chart his course and arrive beforehand.

Viktor Moroz was the first one he tried, but the man was belligerent.

"My dealings with you are over. I told you this before. And don't think you can come onto the estate while they're gone. I like the Vreelands. I am guarding the place with my dogs."

Loyal, protective Viktor.

With his next call Magnus got the receptionist at Billingsley Coach Company. She greeted him in a syrupy accent. He told her he represented a West Coast coach dealer and wanted to speak with Bret Vreeland.

"Mr. Vreeland's not in," she said. "Y'all want to leave a message?"

"Ahh, so he's left on his trip already? Bet you're jealous."

"I've been there," she said. "To Cancun anyway, close enough. They don't fly back till Wednesday, but if you like, I can transfer you to his voicemail."

"No," he said. "I'll catch him when he gets back."

Barring breakdowns or black ice, Magnus Maggart would do just that.

Chapter Sixty-one

CHRISTMAS DAY IN COZUMEL. THE WATERS AT CHANKANAAB NATIONAL PARK shimmered like a tiny ocean, landlocked, but fed by the sea through a subterranean tunnel. The Vreeland children and their grandparents made their way past restrooms, lockers, and snack shops. Sunbathers stretched out blankets and towels. Snorkelers staked out early spots beneath large thatched shelters.

Claire tugged on Eddie's elbow. "For all the world, don't they—?"

"Gosh, what now? It's too early, too bright, and me, I'm just about wiped out after all night and day on them flying deathtraps they call airplanes."

"Those palapas," she tried again, "they look just like umbrellas in a drink."

"Now you're talking. A pick-me-up's what I need."

"Oh, Eddie. Don't start."

Katie bounded alongside them, a Care Bear pack swinging from her arm.

Claire wished she could bottle some of that endless energy. She would need the strength to savor every moment of these next few days as one happy family, and need the strength to complete this farewell tour.

"Grandma," Katie hugged her leg, "Merry Christmas."

"Well, look at you, darling. Merry Christmas."

"Grandpa." She hugged his as well.

"Li'l lady, what's got into you this morning?" he said, flipping on the smile.

Eddie seemed truly enamored with his grandchildren and that was something, wasn't it? Her Eddie had his good side. He could be a real charmer when he wanted to be.

Claire tapped the brim of Kevin's hat as he caught up, small arms loaded, conditioned soccer legs poking from long swim trunks. "Got your arms full, young man. Thanks for carrying all that stuff."

"Ants carry like a thousand times their body weight."

"I'm not an aunt," Claire joked, "I'm your grandma."

He laughed out loud.

And to Claire that felt good. Was it prideful of her to feel so? Even as a young girl, she loved putting smiles on people's faces, but many days, standing at her living room window on S. Bell Street, she thought she had lost that ability.

Bret and Sara approached with Natalie and Sara's relatives. Christmas greetings were exchanged, and the setup of chairs and towels decided.

Next, Bret gave the rundown for the day. The Billingsleys, he said, were on a scuba diving expedition since they both had certification. The Temans were enjoying a leisurely day at the town's gift shops and waterfront.

"But not us. We're all set for Dolphin Discovery in an hour."

"And the sea lion show after that," Sara said.

"Can we touch the dolphins?" Katie asked. "Do they bite?"

"Girls." Kevin looked up at Eddie and they shook their heads in shared exasperation. "It's not like they're sharks, Katie. Don't be dumb."

Bret said, "Shoot, Dad, how about some positive reinforcement here?"

"What? Now I'm in trouble? He's your kid."

"And your grandkid," Sara and Claire said in unison.

"Sorry." Kevin extended a bottle of sunscreen. "Here, Katie."

"Thanks."

"Dolphins. One hour." Bret tapped his wrist. "Should be lotsa fun."

"Lotsa dol-fun," Claire said.

Bret's green eyes caught the sunlight as he pivoted her way. He grinned, gave her a hearty embrace, nearly lifted her out of her sandals. She slapped at his back where old high school muscles still seemed present. He set her down, and while most everyone else headed for the turquoise waters, he told her how much he loved and missed her, how sorry he was for her struggles.

"They're mine to bear," she said. "But I've . . . well, I've made a decision. No more, you hear? No more. Eddie's done things, Bret, things I can't excuse."

She saw those emerald eyes harden.

"I'm with you, Mom. You do whatever you have to do." He called over his shoulder. "Dad? Yeah, over here. Can we go walk a minute?"

Bret and Eddie walked on shaded paths amidst botanical gardens that surrounded the lagoon. They seemed to be the only ones exploring this area. Despite the rising heat, the breeze from the Caribbean kept things bearable.

"Dad," Bret said, "it's great seeing you interact with our kids. They love you, and Kevin seems to hang on your every word."

"They're my blood, aren't they?"

"What I'm asking is for you to tone it down. The whole thing about women, the negativity, all of it down a coupla notches."

"Sure. You say the word, it's done. Done deal, Bretski."

"Please be an example to him. Give him a reason to hang on your words. You and Mom, your relationship's been up and down, and I'm just gonna say it, Dad, I know that you've hit her at least once. When I was just a kid. That's not the sorta behavior or attitude I want my son growing up with."

"Ah-ho, so now you're my judge, is that it?"

"Kev's had problems with bullies in the past," Bret pressed on. "We're raising him to be a kindhearted boy, while still teaching him to be aggressive in the right moments, like in his soccer games, and—"

"Nice picture, by the way. The one you mailed us."

"Yeah, thanks to Sara. She sent it."

And thanks, Bret realized, to a gift certificate from an anonymous donor at Sip Café. They knew now it was Theodore Hart, AKA Magnus Maggart, and that called into question the goodness of the gift. At the time it seemed like a blessing from God, but looking back Bret wasn't so sure how to read that situation. There was a verse in Psalm 68 that talked about receiving gifts even from those who rebelled against you. Did this situation qualify?

"Listen, Dad," he said. "I love you. You're one of those guys who always found a way to get things done, who could make stuff work, come up with a new angle. Growing up, we didn't have much in the cupboards. Things were tight. But at least you hung around when some fathers would've bailed."

"Sure, I know I'm not perfect. But your mother, I do love her."

Bret had to hear this for himself. "You still drinking, Dad?"

"Here ya go, back on your high horse. I don't see what business that—"

"I love Mom too. It's my business."

Eddie halted.

Bret saw over his shoulder the recreation of a Maya structure that hinted at life long ago, deep in the jungles and atop limestone cliffs. Nothing but ruins now. Crumbled temples reclaimed by vines.

Bret faced his father. "When you were sober, you were the man I looked up to. Drunk, you made me scared of getting married. After Sara went through her stuff with Alex Page, I knew she needed a man who wouldn't hurt her. I was head over heels for her. I didn't wanna be showing up late at night with beer stains on my shirt and all my money gone. I was scared to death of messing it up."

"And you blame that on me?"

"I'm saying I want the best for both you and Mom."

"Well, thankee you, Mr. High-and-Mighty."

"Please, Dad." He spread his arms, palms out. "I want my son to look up to you. Right here and now, this is a second chance for all of us. Maybe a last chance for some."

"You done yet?"

"No." Bret stepped closer. The uneasiness in his gut fermented into something sour and hard-edged. His fists hung at his sides, and a large part of him wanted to mete out justice on the spot. "Deal is, you lay a hand on Mom again, I'll make sure that she gets free of you and that you get nothing but breadcrumbs, your Oldsmobile, and supervised visits with your grandchildren."

"Well, hot dog. What a deal."

"I'm not kidding, Dad."

"Son, you got no idea the things I've done for you. And this? This is my thanks? All that money at your fingertips, and you turn mean and self-righteous."

Bret's chest bulged against his T-shirt. "Did you know Ivan Storinka?"

"Who?"

"The guy who willed Sara the money."

"Can't say that I did."

"Maybe not personally," Bret said, "but did you ever work for him in the Seattle area? You two ever talk on the phone?"

Eddie started walking again. "Might've done a job here or there. Me and Gabe, we loaded containers. Tough work, but good pay."

Bret wanted to ask where all that "good pay" went, but stuck with his line of questioning. "When was this?"

"I dunno. 'Ninety-seven, maybe 'ninety-eight, through two-thousand-two."

"And did you ever talk to Mr. Storinka on the phone?"

"Done asked me that already."

"You didn't answer."

"Say, what's the point of all this? The past is the—"

"Dad."

"No, Bret. Never."

"You didn't arrange for him and one of his henchmen to run down Alex?"

"The accident out on Route Four-Ten?" Eddie tilted his head. "What're you getting at? That truck driver, he did his time, but that was for driving past his allotted hours. Reckless of him, yep. But a henchman?"

"Theodore Hart did his time. But he also goes by Magnus Maggart. I wanna know if you paid him, or Storinka, or whoever, to get rid of Sara's fiancé so that I could have her for my own. You knew how much I loved her, and—"

"Bretski, what is this nonsense? I hear you babbling and it's all Chinese to me. I've made my share of mistakes trying to bring home money for us. Thought I could hit the big time. One right card. One more roll. Gimme my lucky number. But it never happened and here I stand, still paying off a second mortgage, driving a beater, and hoping you don't never have to go through the same. This new turn of circumstances, believe me, I'm happy for you. Want it to last. Don't you ever judge me for doing what had to be done. Please. That's all I ask."

"So Magnus lied. You had nothing to do with Alex's accident?"

"Son, I swear it up, down, and sideways. I had not a thing to do with it."

Chapter Sixty-two

SUNDAY. DECEMBER 26 AT SARA AND BRET'S REQUEST, FAMILY AND FRIENDS gathered by the pool in the villa's backyard. It was an informal 10:00 A.M. service, an observance of the season even in this sunny, faraway land. Banana tree fronds whispered in the wind.

"Pastor, you sure you want me to sing?" Bret said. "A cappella?"

"We would all love to hear something from you."

"Absolutely," Sara said. "Why don't you stand on the stairs so the sound will carry better?" She was proud of him as he mounted the curved white-stucco staircase and sang out in his strong yet intimate voice.

A few joined in. Most basked in the sunlight and the sounds.

"Thanks," Pastor Teman said, as the music concluded. Over cargo pants, he wore a white guayabera, a loose-fitting shirt with folds and pockets that he must have bought during yesterday's shopping. "We'll keep this short," he told the gathering, "but you can imagine how difficult it is for a pastor to be away from his flock at Christmastime. My assistants are covering in my absence, and it's nice to be here with all of you."

"Nice for us too," Claire said.

"As long as we pass around the sunblock, there's no big rush, is there? This is Meh-hee-co, after all. Isn't that right, Jason?"

"That's right," Jason said. "Give 'em hell."

The gathering froze, and Sara groaned.

"Uh . . ." Jason tried again with equal gusto. "Give 'em heaven."

Pastor smiled. "I take it we're not all regular churchgoers, and that's all right. I like your enthusiasm. The tension between heaven and hell, it does get hazy at times, but we have a Heavenly Father who provides for His children. And through the birth of His Son two thousand years ago, He put a plan into action that allows each one of us, even those lost from Him, to be fed with this Bread of Life. Yes, even you, Mr. Billingsley."

"Hey, now there's some good news," Jason played along.

"Exactly right."

Zoe bumped her husband's hip. "Would you let the man finish?"

"Finish?" Pastor said. "I'm just getting started."

Jason turned serious. "Uh, Bret and I have an eleven-thirty tee time."

"Shh." Sara put a finger to her lips. "You're only dragging it out longer."

"In the sixteenth chapter of Exodus," Pastor said, resting a hand on his stomach, "we see an early example of this heavenly bread. The Israelites were without food in the wilderness, worried they'd starve. I'm sure it's hard to imagine in the current setting, but we've all been there, haven't we?"

Sara nodded. She thought back on her family's years of week-by-week existence, and felt a twinge of guilt. While she was grateful for what had happened, there were still so many who struggled day by day.

Lord, why're we the lucky ones?

"So God rained down manna for His people," Pastor Teman continued. "Each morning, it appeared on the ground, thin and flaky, white like coriander seed and sweet as honey. There was some work involved. The Israelites had to go and gather it. But each family had exactly what it needed. In the same way, God gave His Son as the Bread of Life, sent down from heaven to take care of our needs. In the same way, God heard Bret and Sara's cries. They worked. They obeyed. He gave riches they never expected, and they have remained selfless and faithful through that process. Here we all stand as a result."

Selfless? Faithful?

Sara imagined her taxi rides through Manhattan, her whirlwind New York shopping with Zoe. Not only did she spend enough money to sponsor and feed their Haitian family for five years, she hid the entire incident from her husband.

Of course, he was no angel, was he? Mr. Speedy Gonzales.

She tried to catch his eye, but Bret slipped on his shades to block the brightness of the radiant sun.

Magnus used snow chains when necessary, and by Sunday evening he crossed the Continental Divide in the used Accord. His communications to Bookman had gone unanswered for nearly three days, and he assumed Eddie Vreeland was in a distant land, unable to send or receive texts. Not that it mattered much now.

Magnus passed a rustic motel, the Slept-Away Inn. The sign said "family owned" and he turned around. Although southern Wyoming's windswept, snow-dusted hills were more navigable than the Rockies, they were still too cold for a night in the car, and he needed some sleep.

The motel faced an empty pool surrounded by chain-link. There were only two cars in the lot. Seemed safe enough. He paid cash, completed the handwritten registration, and got a key to a room decorated with brown and orange curtains and matching bedspread. What did he care? He had a place to rest, and there were no clues to his location for the electronic credit-card sniffers.

But soon the authorities would have clues about Bookman.

On Friday, before driving off from Tacoma, Magnus had stopped back in the same FedEx Office where he picked up the copied documents from Claire Vreeland. He packed and sealed a box, found the address on his phone. Due to holiday weekend and weather, the package would arrive on Tuesday.

"Fine," he told the woman at the counter. "Send it."

Wouldn't Detective Meade be shocked when he opened his belated gifts?

Blood-dotted boots.

Threads from a red flannel shirt.

And a date-stamped recording of Eddie Vreeland entering a certain friend's house along the shores of Lake Meridian.

Happy holidays, Detective. And ho, ho, ho.

Gloating, Bret stood in shorts and flip flops on the second-floor terrace outside his room. He swatted away a small cloud of gnats and grinned.

OK, so he didn't win Sunday's game.

Forget about that. Old news.

Here on Monday, as clouds rolled in and a warm rain fell, he took the game from his boss at the fourteenth hole and held on for a two-stroke victory at Cozumel Country Club. Jason said Bret's childhood near Seattle gave him an unfair "rain handicap," and Bret said Jason was the one who was "all wet."

Tomorrow was the last full day of this trip, with an outing already mapped out to the Maya ruins at Tulum. Taking into account ferry and bus rides, it would last all day, which meant Wednesday Bret would fly home as reigning champ.

"Marco," Kevin called out in the pool below.

"Polo," Eddie echoed. He ducked under the surface and swam off.

In the shallow end, Bret's mother spun Katie around, producing nonstop giggles. Natalie reclined nearby with legs bent at the knees and dipped into the water. She was such a godsend for the kids. It was tough to see her still hiding those scars, but her eyes shone brighter and she seemed less edgy.

Citronella torches fended off mosquitoes along the yard's perimeter. The light of the flames hopped about on the waterfall, playing tag in its current.

Zoe was out there.

Bret watched her tug at a wide, green, banana frond and roll drops of the earlier rain into her mouth. She wore a yellow bikini, tied at the sides, almost fluorescent against her bronzed skin.

"Honey, you won't believe it."

He flinched at the sound of Sara's voice. He spun back through the arched doorway and met her as she closed the door from the hall. "Believe what?"

"I just . . . Are you all right?"

"Sure," he said, pulling her close. "I beat Jason today. Did you hear?'

"Three or four times."

"It's no small feat."

"And neither are yours. You just stubbed my toe with your flip flop."

"Oops." His arms encircled her waist. "C'mon. I wanna give you a kiss."

"I'm sure you do." She gave his bare chest a playful swat. "Look, I'm trying to tell you the latest, so hold your horses."

Bret fell back onto the bed, face-up, arms crossed behind his head.

Sara propped herself on an elbow beside him. "My mom and I, we walked all around town this afternoon after the downpour. Everything smelled fresh and clean. We had a wonderful time together, best in ages, even did some shopping at that new Chedraui mini-mall only a few blocks away."

"That's good. Glad to hear it."

"Don't you rush me, Mr. Hot-to-Trot." She gave him a peck on the lips. "So we were bartering with this shopkeeper over the price of a hammock, and he's not budging, and then this elderly lady steps in and says a few words to him. Next thing we know, we're walking out with the hammock at two-thirds off."

He lifted both eyebrows. "Now that's a deal."

"Still not done. As a way of thanking the lady, we ended up having liquados with her. Mango? Absolutely delicious by the way. And she tells us she's a missionary who has worked for years throughout the Caribbean—"

"Boy. Sounds rough."

"Including Haiti, Bret. She's been in the trenches with the earthquake victims, particularly the orphans who have nothing at all."

He decided to keep silent.

"She gave me her card, told me she would love to have us come work with her sometime. It's a thankless job, she said, but the kids make it worth it. Don't you think it would be amazing for Kev and Katie to see something like that?"

"Yep. Great," he said. "Listen, sweetheart, you caught me with my mind on other things, but we should definitely talk more about it later."

Sara faced him, crossed-legged on the bed.

"What?" he said.

She brushed hair back over her ear. He saw her eyes cloud over.

"Don't do that, Sara," he said. "The waterworks, that's not fair."

"What's going on with us?" She sniffed. "This was our dream, a trip to Mexico, and now that we're here, we barely even look each other in the eye."

"Who says anything's going on?"

"You're not the same, hon. We're not the same."

"And you can't guess why?" Bret said. "C'mon."

"Why what? I, uh . . . what're you saying?"

"Bloomingdale's." He stood to his feet. "That ring any bells?"

"That's what this is about? Hon, I kept under our limit."

"By thirty-eight bucks."

"Oh, so you have it all tabulated in your head. Thanks for keeping such an eagle eye. Heaven forbid we step one inch from our precious budget. And you planned to tell me about your speeding ticket when exactly?"

"A ticket," he said. "Not an out-of-town trip."

"You make it sound worse than it was."

"Where were the kids during all this? You leave Natalie to babysit while you run off to meet some guy?"

"Some guy?" She rolled her eyes. "I was with Zoe, if you must know."

"Zoe," Bret said. "So do she and I get to run off on trips together now?"

"That's hardly the same thing. Are you saying that appeals to you, the whole fake-tan, fake-boobs look?" Sara stared up at him with her almond-shaped eyes. "You know, I love her to pieces, but there's only so much a person can do to cover their issues. You're telling me Jason's the faithful, satisfied hubby?"

"Stop." Bret threw his hands into the air. "I'm not gonna do this."

"You know, after eleven years I'd like to think we can trust each other."

"Ah-ha. Got it." He wrestled into a T-shirt. "Trust each other."

"Isn't that the way it should be?"

"That's what you say. But where are you? Off spending money right and left, making up for lost time. How should I know what else goes on? Meanwhile, I'm busting my hump at the coach company, same as always, so that you can—"

"You're out playing golf with Jason every other day. You're on salary. Whatever happened to the sixty-hour work weeks? No, it's not the same, and if I hadn't been working at the clinic, taking care of patients like Mr. Storinka for the past seven years, we wouldn't even be here right now. We'd be staring at our bank balance with our usual post-Christmas funk. You want to go back to that?"

He knew it wasn't meant as a threat, but it sounded that way.

"What I want," he said, grabbing his wallet, "is some air."

Chapter Sixty-three

Bret slammed the door on his way out. Rhonda Teman peeked from her room down the hall. He lowered his head and stormed past, took the villa stairs two at a time. His flip flops slapped against cold stone. At the bottom, his knee jarred one of the terra cotta decorations, but he caught it before it struck the floor.

"Daddy, what's wrong? Why're y'all fighting?"

He turned to find Katie's blond curls plastered to her small head, her round eyes full of tears. "What is it," he said, "with you women and your waterworks?"

Kevin joined his sister in the archway. "Dad?"

"You're dripping water all over the floor," he snapped. "Go dry your hair, both of you. It's late. You two should be in bed."

Bret strode from the villa into the darkness of San Miguel.

He wandered the streets, heart pounding, pulse thumping at this neck. By the time the reigning golf champ dipped into a local bar where he was certain no one would find him, he felt defeated. What did beating Jason prove? That Bret could ogle the man's wife? And what was he thinking, yelling at Kevin and Katie? For that matter, what sorta classless bum threw out accusations while his wife talked about helping orphans in Haiti?

"Cerveza," he told the bartender in his garbled Spanish. "Dos Equis."

The short, large-mustached man popped the cap from a bottle.

Bret took a swig of the beer. He glanced over his shoulder, realized he was the only Caucasian in the bar. Which was fine with him. No one in this local dive knew him. He took another swig, wiped the residue from his mouth.

What were you thinking, Bret? Real mature of you back there.

But Sara lied to him. She told him she would talk to him before going out and spending money like that again. Not only did she skip town, she left their children behind to do so. Was she telling the truth about being with Zoe? How could he know? If she deceived him to run off in the first place, how did he know she wasn't deceiving him about her actual travel partner?

Even in his anger-stirred imagination that seemed far-fetched.

Or was it? Didn't she still have a picture of Alex Page hidden somewhere?

He recognized, of course, that Alex was dead and that the picture was her way of still mourning his loss, but that neither soothed his current frustrations nor excused his actions at the villa.

"What's going on with us?"

Good question.

He lifted the bottle to the light over the bar, judged it to be a third empty.

Bret knew couples who damaged their trust on a daily basis, but this wasn't about other couples. He and Sara were close, always had been, and even small indiscretions were cracks that could threaten the whole structure. A pile of money in the bank didn't change the underlying issues, did it?

He drank past the half-empty line, but if this was meant to numb his head it was going to take another two or three beers.

He thought of crumbling ruins, taken over by thorns and vines.

Thought of his dad's years of boozy breath.

Of his wife's deflated tone.

His kids' worried looks.

"Uno mas?" the bartender offered.

Bret gripped the bottle, felt the label shred in the condensation. He could hide out here all night, be back before sunrise. Everything would look different in the morning. A few drinks wouldn't ruin him. Whether it be alcohol or money, it was all about moderation and balance, wasn't it?

Yep, he knew this to be true.

And also knew in this moment it was his way of justifying his actions.

He shook his head. No, he wasn't going to do this. He plunked down a handful of pesos, muttered "Gracias," and headed back to the villa.

Most of the bedroom lights were off by the time he arrived. It was late. Bugs hummed beneath the palm trees. He slipped through the front door and found Zoe alone on the living room divan, still in her bikini. The wraparound was tied low, a few inches below the jewelry at her belly button.

"Bret? Oh, good, I was so worried. We were all worried."

"Where is everyone?"

"Early to bed, early to rise. We're doing the Tulum ruins in the morning."

He met her smoky gaze and looked away. He'd barely finished one drink, but it seemed he couldn't think straight. He moved toward the stairs, figured he would find Sara still in tears or in an uneasy sleep. How could he face her? How could he trust himself not to hurt her again with his words?

"You OK?" Zoe said.

"Fine."

She crossed one tan leg over the other and stretched an arm along the back of the divan. "Come. Sit. You look like you need to talk."

"I, uh . . ." He shifted his weight. "I messed up."

"With Sara?"

"Mm-hmm."

"Oh, she's such a doll. A man like you, you're bound to mess up every now and then. It'll all blow over. These things always do."

"Did she say anything to you?"

"You going to sit down? Please, Bret. You're making me nervous."

Bret propped himself on the edge of the divan, head in his hands. Zoe touched his arm, her fingers warm and electric. The current ran through his body. He closed his eyes and felt the stillness of the villa settle around them, offering an intimacy that both worried and thrilled him.

Lord, what am I thinking?

"It's nice out by the pool," Zoe said. "Just the moonlight. The breeze. If you want to talk, we can go out there."

He shook his head.

"Or," she added, "I mean, who says we have to speak a word?"

She nudged against him, fingers tracing the skin on his arm. His every pore, every nerve, was on alert, and he realized how easily he could take her hand and guide her into the backyard shadows. Her nearness created a heat that peeled away his lethargic depression.

"You know," Zoe said, "Sara doesn't trust me. Not when it comes to you."

"Whaddya mean?"

"Oh, it's women's intuition, I guess. She just . . . she just senses it."

Bret's head was spinning again. "Listen, I've gotta go up and talk to her."

"You don't feel it, Bret? The energy between us?"

Feel it? Shoot, Zoe's energy crackled in this nighttime air, buzzing with her carefree, no-children, no-worries attitude. She represented a freedom of responsibility no longer available to him as a committed husband and father.

Committed husband?

"Zoe. No." He stood, his shoulders squared.

"What, babe?"

"This. No. We're not doing this."

"Doing what?"

"Your husband, he's my boss and I could lose my job."

"Jason the angel? That what you think? Trust me, you won't lose a thing."

Forgive me, Lord. Everything that matters, I could lose it all.

Bret stepped away from her. "I can't turn my back on my wife, on what we have. That's what's real. She and the kids, they're what matters."

Zoe wore a pout. "I'm only trying to be a friend."

"Right. The way you were when you ran off to New York with her."

"A girls' day out."

"Listen, call it what you want, but this isn't gonna happen. Please honor what Sara and I have together. It might seem old-fashioned or narrow-minded or whatever, but I'm not throwing away eleven years just like that. No way."

"I wouldn't want you to, Bret. Seriously? You and Sara, you give me hope that real love is out there." Zoe stood and leaned close to kiss his cheek.

"Nope." He pulled away. "That's it, Zoe. Goodnight."

Chapter Sixty-four

"COUPLE WEEKS AGO, CLAIRE, WHO WOULDA THUNK WE'D BE STANDING here?"

Who would've "thunk" a lot of things? she said in her head.

Claire Vreeland felt woozy after the ride across the Cozumel Channel and the bus journey south along the coastline to Tulum, but the archaeological site more than made up for her physical discomforts. Even Eddie was impressed with the ancient walled city, its crude stone temples, and El Castillo, a large castle-like structure rising from a cliff that jutted over the waters of the Caribbean.

Most everyone from their group was on this expedition.

The Temans, they were an awfully nice couple. They strolled hand-in-hand and carried bottles of Coca-Cola that they sipped from with straws.

Sara's mom and stepfather snapped pictures of each other and wore matching sunglasses with dolphins jumping from the corners. So adorable.

And my, the Billingsleys were quite the pair, weren't they? Jason made it clear on the bus that he was bored to be here again, and he shuffled about with eyes glued to his fancy-dancy phone. Zoe paraded about in khaki shorts and a tight white tank top, and gave Natalie her own guided tour.

Natalie wore a long, flowing skirt over her blue one-piece swimsuit. She expressed hopes of swimming afterward at Tulum's less-crowded beaches.

All of this Claire observed from behind her wraparound "granny sunglasses," as Katie called them, the same way she watched life pass by from her window back home. She wanted the best for all present, but most of all she wanted Bret and Sara, Kevin and Katie to be happy.

Last night's raised voices? Those worried her.

Despite being nothing compared to her lifetime of skirmishes, bruised arms, and black eyes, she hated to hear any conflict between her loved ones.

"Bret, he made a mistake skipping this place," Eddie said.

"He told me at breakfast that he'd had enough of ruins. I think," Claire said, "he and Sara wanted time with the kids, this being the last day and all."

"They can do that anytime. Tellin' ya, big mistake."

"Least we're here together, Eddie."

"What of it?"

"Might be the last chance we get to do something like this."

She thought of the documents in her suitcase and the duplicates already surrendered in an envelope at the FedEx Office. She wasn't certain just how long these things took, but she knew it was only a matter of time. A crime was a crime, and there were no two ways around that now, were there?

"The last chance?" Eddie hopped onto one of Tulum's stones and struck a pose. "You think we can't go traveling anytime we want? We can, Claire. That your wish? Why didn't you say so years ago?"

"Don't be foolish, dear. Such things cost money."

"And who do we know with lotsa money, uh? Yep, that's right. Don't gimme that look, like you ain't ever thought the same. I got it all worked out."

Her skin prickled in the heat. "Got what worked out?"

"If I told ya, I'd have to kill ya."

She looked away.

Nearly choking with mirth, he jumped down and planted a kiss on her cheek. "Always the worry wart. Woman, you need to get you a sense of humor."

"I'm a grandma not an ant," she mumbled.

"What's that you say?"

"You may not believe it, but I made Kevin laugh the other day."

Eddie stood up straight. "I . . . I'm sorry, Claire."

She sighed. "Did you pass gas?"

He chuckled. "See, now what business do I have sayin' you can't be funny." He peeled off her wraparounds, met her eyes with his. "Me and Bret, we talked the other day at the lagoon, and we both know I done a lotta things I regret. A lotta things I wanna change. But this much is true, Claire, I never once regretted marrying you." His eyes blurred in a rush of emotion. "Not once."

Sara awoke to a tray of fresh-squeezed orange juice, hot coffee, fresh fruit, and eggs scrambled with chopped onions, green peppers, and tomatoes.

"Huevos mexicanos," Bret called it.

"Looks delicious."

"Looks can be deceiving," he said. "But I hope you're right. Kev made the coffee, Katie poured the juice, and I did the slice and dice. Don't mind the finger."

"Honey," she said, sitting up. "Does that hurt?"

"Me man. Me tough." He propped himself on the edge of the mattress, smelling of chlorine and coconut oil. He fed her the first bite with a fork. "Eat up now. We got places to go. It's our last day to get our crazy on." He twirled his wrists, snapped his fingers. "And catch some island fever."

"Someone's got a fever."

"'And the only cure is more cowbell.'"

She couldn't help but grin at the old *Saturday Night Live* line, but a few snippets of humor didn't erase the events of last night.

"What's really going on, Bret? Is this supposed to smooth things over? You dart out of here after dark, no one knows where you are, and you leave me with both the kids in tears. I find out Zoe's gone looking for you, and that doesn't exactly help the thoughts running through my head. The breakfast. The coffee. I appreciate all this, but we still need to talk, don't you think?"

"Agreed," he said. "That's the point. Everyone else, they left at the crack of dawn on that outing to Tulum. It's just you, me, Katie, and Kev. I was wrong, Sara. Please forgive me. I already apologized to the kids, and we swam in the pool and made the breakfast together. We let you sleep in, but, c'mon, even a princess has to get up sometime." He smiled. "I don't care where we go, what we do, as long as it's the four of us, and as long as you and I get to dance together on the sand. Deal?"

His Blackberry vibrated on his nightstand.

"Please don't answer it," Sara said. "Can't you call back later?"

"Yeah, OK. I'll just . . . hmm. It's Detective Meade."

Bret didn't have the heart to break the news to his children. Sara said they would find out soon enough, and neither Bret nor Sara could think of a reason to sour the kids' last few hours with their grandpa as a free man.

Why did this have to happen now?

Just when Eddie Vreeland was showing a desire to change.

Bret knew his father could turn violent, especially when under the influence. He long suspected Gabe Stilman was a gambling buddy and a bad influence at best, a partner in dockside crime at worst, and he could think of a number of scenarios that would put the two men at each other's throats.

Criminal homicide, though? A brutal, cold-blooded murder?

Detective Meade said Eddie Vreeland would be charged, handcuffed, and arrested upon their connecting flight's arrival in Atlanta. He would later be extradited to supervising authorities in the state of Washington, where he would stand trial. If convicted, he would very likely spend the rest of his life behind the bars of a state penitentiary.

"Do you think he did it?" Bret said.

"In my job, there's not a lot of time for conjecture, Mr. Vreeland, but the evidence I received is compelling. It was FedExed to me from Tacoma. From your mother? Does she suspect or fear him? If so, she may have thought of me as her safest connection due to my acquaintance with you."

"So why are letting me know? I could tell my dad to stay put in Mexico."

"Would you do that?"

"No," Bret admitted.

"And what would happen to your mother?" Meade's voice softened. "My hope is that you know something we can use to help see him acquitted or to lighten his sentence. If you think of anything, you let me know."

Bret spoke to his mother about it after her late return from Tulum.

Yes, Claire said, she had turned in evidence at FedEx, and even though she was having second thoughts after Eddie's words and actions today, it was too late. It was in the good Lord's hands now. Justice must be served.

Chapter Sixty-five

Viktor the housekeeper, dog keeper, bodyguard, executor, and trustee left the secluded Vreeland estate at dusk on Tuesday and returned after nightfall. Gas lanterns illuminated the pillared entryway. He stopped his Mercedes convertible, powered down his window, and punched in the code at the gate.

Magnus darted from the shadows of the limestone edifice and shoved the barrel of his Kimber Super Carry into the Ukrainian's squat neck. He told him the caliber of his weapon's bullets and the damage a .45 shell would do to his thick Ukrainian cranium.

"Ukrainium," Magnus joked.

Viktor stared ahead through the windshield.

"I've been absent since late October, but you still should've paid better attention, Viktor. I got into town last night and I've waited all day for this opportunity. And to think you were once a bodyguard."

"Housekeeper."

"Where's your gun?"

"I no longer carry a—"

Magnus pistol-whipped the man. "Your gun."

Blood trickled from Viktor's angular cheek. He reached for his jacket.

Magnus stopped him and drew out the Walther PPS. He ejected the clip into the dirt, tucked the firearm into his waistband. He hit the power lock on the armrest and opened the back door. He slid into the Mercedes, drew his gun through, and had it back against his quarry's neck before he could counterattack.

"Drive on through the gates."

They were closing automatically. Viktor said, "I will not take you in there."

"Then I'll kill you and drive through myself."

"You don't know the combination."

"Then I will torture you for it, kill you, and drive through."

Viktor was stoic as the gates came together. "Either way I die." He pulled the keys from the ignition and tried to loft them left-handed over the wall.

Magnus jutted his free arm forward, inhibiting the throw, so that the keys struck this side of the wall and jangled into the dirt.

He said, "You're a very brave housekeeper, and I admire that. We've known each other for years, brushes here and there, and you know I don't make idle threats. I'm already cranky. It's been a long drive to get here."

Viktor reached for his ankle and drew a knife, but the angle was all wrong, from the front seat to the back with the steering wheel in his way.

Magnus shot him through the thigh.

By the time Magnus was done, Viktor had multiple wounds and a final round through the back of the head. For the mess and delay, Magnus was rewarded with the gate code, basic estate layout, the Vreeland's flight info tomorrow, including their group's prearranged transportation in two rented limos.

The Kimber was not quiet. Surely, a neighbor had reported the noise. Magnus considered driving onto the estate, but he would only trap himself with the evidence for when the police arrived. To further discourage that option, Dobermans appeared wraithlike behind the gate, snarling, with teeth bared.

He wedged the corpse below the level of the passenger window and took the wheel. He was seated in his victim's blood. Keeping his speed steady, he crossed the stone-sided bridge and passed his Accord a half mile away.

He needed to clean up. Needed another vehicle.

The Nashville skyline glimmered in the cold as he drove into Germantown. He still had keys to his black Dodge Charger and to the apartment at which it was garaged. The dwelling was paid through the end of the year, under the name Theodore Hart, and that meant it was on the local authority's radar.

After his mind-numbing weeks of watching Eddie Vreeland, he knew there wouldn't be any cops still assigned to the place. To be sure, he circled twice.

It was late. No signs of life.

He had his backup plan.

Chapter Sixty-six

WEDNESDAY. 5:57 P.M., EASTERN.

Claire Vreeland had no words for her mix of relief and deep despair. She would never forget this moment. Her Eddie. Oh, if he only knew. She watched him tromp up the tunnel leading from the aircraft into the terminal in Atlanta. She pretended to readjust her carry-on luggage.

He pulled further ahead.

Coming alongside Claire, Bret shouldered her bag and took her hand. Neither of them said a word as Eddie turned the corner, just out of view. She heard Sara behind them, telling the kids to stay close and not rush her. None of them wanted Kevin and Katie to see their grandfather taken away in handcuffs.

The truth would come out soon enough, wouldn't it? No reason to leave that image in their impressionable minds. No reason at all.

"Federal law officers," a gruff voice said.

"What is this?" Eddie's laugh was hollow. "No, you got it all wrong."

"You are under arrest for the murder of Gabe Stilman. You have the right to remain silent . . ."

Claire collapsed to her knees there in the tunnel. She squeezed Bret's hand, her head falling forward as the years of abuse and loneliness and courageous façade wound through her thoughts. She had carried her burden daily, tried to be Christ-like the best she knew how. She gasped, realized she had been holding her breath, and the sobs gushed from deep within.

Bret was still holding onto her. Sara knelt beside her. Their arms cradled and supported her.

"Go around," someone snapped at the bottlenecked passengers.

"Grandma?"

Kevin was here. And precious Katie.

Claire held onto them as her sobs grew louder and the teardrops fell.

Chapter Sixty-seven

MAGNUS HAD LESS THAN AN HOUR TO WAIT. HE SAT ALONE IN A CROWDED Shoney's a mile north of Nashville Int'l Airport. His plate of sweet potato fries was nearly empty, same with his cup of Sprite.

"You need a refill on that, doll?"

He glanced up at his server. "That'd be swell."

As she hurried off, he stared over the dinner crowd, seeing no one, seeing everyone. He felt superior. He felt cocooned. It was true, then, that Bookman was out of the picture, removed like a mismatched puzzle piece. Magnus had confirmed it through a short call to Natalie. She might have lied, but what would that accomplish? Thanks to his lessons, she knew firsthand not to test him.

Too bad Magnus didn't know Bookman's identity weeks ago. He could have better manipulated the situation with the Vreelands and avoided a cross-country trek in the dead of winter.

But thanks to his assignment from Bookman, he knew of the Vreelands and their fortune. With the papers from Claire tucked into his briefcase, he could extort some of that fortune by threatening to ruin them in probate court. He didn't need Bookman's money. Anyway, he still had $16,411 in his expense account.

I did my time in the state pen. Your turn next . . . boyo.

The waitress set down his refill. "Here you are. Anything else?"

A few newcomers squeezed by, and the waitress leaned forward to avoid being trampled. Magnus pushed back in his chair to avoid a public spectacle, annoyed by the masses and their herd mentality.

"If I could get the bill, please," he said.

He sucked down the second cup of Sprite. At 7:05 P.M., he paid at the front register, left a twenty percent tip so as not to appear stingy or extravagant.

The key was to not be remembered.

His pulse raced. He felt lightheaded. He told himself to stay cool and calm.

He drove the trusty Charger to the airport, locked up, and headed with briefcase in hand to the main terminal. The Arrivals board indicated the Vreeland's flight from Atlanta was on time, arriving at 7:28 P.M., Central.

Moments after the plane's arrival, he called Natalie. Texting would be easier perhaps, but he preferred to hear her voice with its combination of intelligence, fire, and fear.

"Hola, my little coffee bean. Are you off the plane yet?"

"Waiting for the doors to open."

"We have rides home arranged for you," Magnus said. "The limousines are idling outside Baggage Claim even now. Your job, Natalie, is simple. Make sure everyone else gets into the front limo, while you and the Vreelands fill the one in back. I will be there, so don't do anything foolish. Are your antenna up?"

"They're up." There was that intelligence.

"I'll see you soon. And don't let anything happen to little Katie."

"Never," she said. There was that fire.

"I'm counting on it, Natalie. How could you live with yourself if you did?"

He ended the call. He stared off. His head felt hot.

Sara's eyes followed the baggage carousels as they wound around like shiny fish scales. She stepped closer to Bret, held onto his arm. In Atlanta, her mom and stepdad had parted ways with the group and caught a westbound flight. She missed them already. Especially her mom.

The Cozumel trip, in many ways, was everything Sara dreamed it would be, with unforgettable views, incredible weather, unique experiences, and deep connections, but now that it was over she just wanted to be home.

And this turmoil over Eddie?

My, what a traumatic way to end things.

Claire seemed ten years younger after her emotional release in the passenger tunnel, but her eyes were still red. Bret's face was crestfallen. He loved his mother, and during the layover in Atlanta she told stories of things endured at her husband's hands. He fumed at his own lack of action.

Sara reminded him he was too young then, what could he do?

He said, "But I swore I would never again sit by while someone suffered. And it was happening under my own parents' roof."

"Once every other month, though. Sometimes longer in between."

"Yeah, and what of it?" he said. "That makes it OK?"

"Eddie was careful to hide it, and Claire was a master at it. You're not the first person to find out stuff like this, but sadly he had to kill a friend before she got the courage to do something. She's here now, though. And she needs you."

He nodded. "We need to help her get back on her feet."

"You know, hon, she ought to just live with us. We have enough room."

Another nod. "Thank you, Sara. Any other way just wouldn't feel right."

One by one, the bags came around. Bret and Kevin gathered their family's luggage. The Billingsleys were ready to go. Within ten minutes, the last piece arrived, an oversized blue and white sack that Natalie slung over her shoulder.

"We should have two limos waiting," Sara told everyone. "Viktor called yesterday evening, said it was all arranged. Simply up to us to tip the chauffeurs."

Their ragtag group lumbered outside. The night was black, the air crisp.

"Cool." Katie pointed at the sleek Lincoln Town Cars. "Can I ride up front?"

Natalie took her hand. "In a limo, you ride in the back, silly girl."

"Why do I always have to ride in back?"

"It's fun," Kevin said. "There're mirrors and couches and stuff."

Natalie veered toward the rear limo, dragging the kids in her wake. Sara and Bret followed, with Claire between them. Sara figured it made more sense for all those headed to the estate to do so together.

They said farewells to the Billingsleys and Temans who climbed into the front limo. Jason told Bret to be at work in his office "come first week of January, champ," and Pastor told him to be leading worship on stage next Sunday and "every other Sunday till Kingdom come."

The trunk of the second limo clicked open.

"Good evening," the chauffeur said. "The Vreelands?"

"That's us." Bret gave the man the Belle Meade address.

Lean and suave, the blond chauffeur dipped his hat. He smelled of cinnamon. Sara and Natalie followed the kids into the car's spacious interior. Claire was unsteady but made it inside. Lights ran along the ceiling, the floor, the wet bar. A combo TV/DVD player captured Katie's interest.

Bret showed up a moment later. "Shoot, I tried to help, but the chauffeur insisted that he load our luggage."

"And the problem is?" Sara slapped at him. "That's how it works, hon."

"Guess I like doing some stuff for myself, thank you very much," Bret said.

"You know, you'd make a good servant and a rotten king."

"God's the king," Kevin cut in. "The King of kings."

The driver seemed to take his time with the loading duties. He closed the trunk and moved to his seat in the front. The moment he shut the door, the lights in the back dimmed to a midnight blue. The limo inched forward, silky and smooth as it rode the speed humps that led from the loading zone.

"And we're children of the King." Katie's eyes reflected the lights. "Sunday school teacher, she says that's why we have a big house and fancy cars."

Sara wasn't sure how to respond to that. She expected Bret to speak up since he wrestled with these issues often, but he seemed drained from the upheaval and revelations of the past few hours. Instead Claire's voice, still hoarse from the incident in Atlanta, turned everyone's heads.

"Shouldn't we take a look at the Son of the King, God's own Son?"

"Jesus," Katie said.

"He never owned a house, did He?"

"Nuh-uh."

"No, and he never traveled far from His childhood home. He lived mostly off donations, and he hung out with smelly fishermen, didn't even have a pillow to lay his head on. Imagine that."

"I need my pillow," Katie said.

"I can sleep anywhere, anytime," Kevin bragged.

Sara smiled at that fact, a recent change due to his surgery. And thank God for it. She turned her gaze outside as the limo eased into the evening's traffic on I-40 West. The divider window at the front of the passenger area was darkened, affording privacy to those in the back. An intercom was situated below.

"Just remember," Claire told her grandkids, "being God's child doesn't mean you always have it easy or get more toys and nice things. Doesn't He love His children in Africa and China? Or Thailand? Of course He does, but many of them don't have a radio or a TV. Some don't have food to eat or cars to drive in. And many of them love Christ all the same."

"Maybe because He didn't have a pillow either," Kevin said.

"Yes, Kev, I do think that's part of it. My, oh my, what a smart grandson."

"Me too," Katie said.

"And a smart granddaughter." Claire linked hands with each of them.

Next to Sara, Bret shifted about in his seat.

"Do you remember Pastor Teman talking about manna from heaven?" Claire said. "He mentioned that Jesus is our Bread of Life. Well, Jesus told us to pray, 'Give us this day our daily bread.' We don't have to worry about weekly or monthly bread. Just daily. That's all we need. And do you remember what happened when the Israelites tried to gather manna for more than just one day?"

Katie shook her head.

"I know that part," Kevin said. "It got rotten and full of maggots."

"Who wants maggoty bread?" Claire said. "Yucky, huh?"

"Yucky," Katie agreed.

"We ought only gather what we need day by day by day, instead of hoarding things. That way we trust God instead of trusting only in ourselves."

Bret was still fidgeting, looking left, right, back over his shoulder.

"Lose something?" Sara said to him.

"And where is the Child of the King now?" Claire said to her grandchildren. "He's gone to prepare a place for us, and He's had a good deal of time to do so, don't you think? Heaven, oh my. That's where my hope lies."

"Not to change the subject," Bret said, "but right now I'm just hoping this chauffeur gets a clue where he's going. He pulled off at Fesslers Lane, which leads into all the industrial stuff. This is definitely not the way home."

Chapter Sixty-eight

FROM THE FRONT SEAT OF THE VREELANDS' LIMO, MAGNUS MAGGART WATCHED the other limo go its merry way from the airport. Those passengers didn't interest him, although Zoe Billingsley was hard to ignore, the way she preened and flaunted her wares. Of course, it was true in the world of insects and arachnids that the females often lured in their partners only to devour them soon after.

I am Magnus, and I master my desire.

When the blond chauffeur slid in behind the wheel, Magnus told him to get moving. He thought of Natalie seated behind him, and he imagined getting back to the estate where he could savor his time with this family and their live-in tutor.

Welcome home from your escapade.

After last night's mayhem he had cleaned his Kimber thoroughly, wiped away every bit of body matter. He cradled it now in his palm where it glistened.

"Are you all right over there?" the chauffeur said to him.

"Why're we . . . turning?" Magnus asked. "I told you . . ."

"You told me you would kill me if I didn't do as you said. You told me to drive them to their address in Belle Meade."

"But none of this is . . . this isn't the right way."

"Trust the limo driver to know where he's going, would you?"

Magnus tried to sit up straight, but his large frame seemed to collapse around him, his bones dissolving, his muscles wobbly. He felt heavy, so heavy, and that heaviness pushed him down into the seat cushions and flattened him. He was a blob of tissue trying to hold steady a heavy piece of metal in his lap.

"I think I'm going to . . . to be sick."

"No, it only feels that way," the chauffeur said. "Don't worry, I've tested this particular cocktail more thoroughly than the injection you got from me a few months back. This one should last ninety minutes tops."

"You . . . injected me with something?"

"No, Magnus, you took it orally. In your Sprite refill."

Magnus thought of the jostling restaurant crowd. The sweet liquid. The beginnings of the headache and the grogginess. He tried to say something, but his tongue flopped like a fish against his teeth and his gums.

"How do you know my . . .?"

"Your name? Don't worry, boyo. I've watched your every move. And here we are all together, just the way it was over twelve years ago. You. Me. Sara."

"Sara," Bret said, "there something's off about this."

He pressed his face to the tinted glass. This industrial section of town was poorly lit, and the overcast December evening offered no help. No moon. No stars. Only blackness. He tested the window controls, discovered they were locked, probably from the cockpit up front.

"Perhaps the driver's low on gas," Sara said. "Any nearby stations?"

"This time of night? This area of town? Nope. Hey, Kevin, press that intercom button. See if it works."

"Nothing, Dad."

The vehicle rounded a corner onto Lebanon Pike.

"Look," he said. "There are signs for Mount Olivet Cemetery."

"Don't say that, Daddy." Katie hopped into his lap. "You're scaring me."

"We're getting closer to the river. Listen, everyone, this chauffeur's probably lost or something, but the fact that he's locked our windows and doors and won't answer the intercom, it doesn't feel right. Did anyone recognize him? Could it be Mr. Hart, the one who drove that black Charger and harassed us?"

"Theodore Hart was big-boned," Sara said. "This guy's close in height but leaner. Honestly, most of my attention was on the kids and getting home."

"He had bottle blond hair," Claire noted. "Not natural at all. A disguise, if I had my guess. When I looked his way, he dipped his cap so I didn't see his face."

"You think they want a ransom, Dad? How much?"

"Don't even joke like that. Not funny."

Huddled in the front corner, Natalie sank deeper into the leather couch. She had her own memories to deal with, and Bret didn't want her slipping back into that reserved behavior she had shaken free of in Mexico.

"OK," he said. "Quiet everyone. I'm calling Detective Meade."

Magnus Maggart had almost no control left of his body. He was a piece of machinery, defective, unplugged. His mind, however, was still churning.

"Who are . . . you?"

"Bookman," the chauffeur said. "You should know that."

"Book . . . man. In jail."

"I'm telling you, it's almost painful watching you try to speak, but if you're talking about our man, Eddie Vreeland, he's nothing. He did the odd job here and there, small-time deals, turned a blind eye for a bribe. He made a great fall guy, though. Prop 'em up and knock 'em down. Let him take the blame."

Bookman guided the limo over a mound of gravel and old asphalt.

"Hang in there," he said, "and you'll understand. We'll be pulling up to the factory any moment now. It's not much to look at these days, but two, three years ago, Storinka was a round-the-clock manufacturer here in Nashville. Mismanagement, underhanded deals, those are the reasons for its local decline. Here we go." The chauffeur waved his black cap at the window. "Practically abandoned. A perfect place for some dialogue with the Vreelands. Here, let's see what you brought along for us in your briefcase."

"You are . . . dead man."

"And that's a threat, I suppose? I don't think I have much to worry about from just now. I've tasted that chemical concoction myself, and it packs a wallop. Go on. Take your best shot, Maggart. I'm sitting right here. Take it if you got it."

The Kimber rested on Magnus's lap, a flat stone in a thick bog.

Sinking slowly. Slowly.

Or was it the vehicle that was slowing?

"About time for you to get out," Bookman said. "I've kept tabs on your phone, followed you, let you do your thing, but in the end you gave me the very info that sealed your death warrant. You were the one driving that day, you told me. You were a hired killer."

By great effort, Magnus said, "I killed you . . . already . . ."

"Not me, boyo. Someone similar, someone who could disappear without many questions. But yes, you meant to kill me. For that you will suffer."

Bret checked his Blackberry. 8:03 P.M. Despite this reasonable hour on a Wednesday evening, there was no response from the detective. Maybe he was tired of the Vreelands calling any old time, treating him like their own private eye.

Bret hit Redial.

"Keep trying the doors, the windows, the intercom," he said.

Sara elbowed him. Tilted her head toward Natalie. Their college-aged tutor and family friend was tucked into a ball on the limo's far seat, knees pulled to her chest, shoulders quivering.

"Katie," Bret whispered to his six-year-old in his lap. "Looks like Natalie needs some hugs from her little sister. Think you can do that?"

"Mm-hmm."

While Katie and Claire moved to embrace Natalie, Kevin continued his search of the vehicle. He stopped and pointed up.

"Dad. What about the moonroof?"

"So dark out that I hardly noticed it. Good thinking, bud."

"It . . . it works. It's opening."

"No, Kev," Natalie said, her head snapping up. Her nose stud glowed in the interior lighting. "Don't go out there. He'll hurt you."

"Who? Whaddya mean?" Bret leaned forward. "Do you know who it is?"

Natalie's hazel eyes widened.

"C'mon, you know how much all of us love you. If there's anything you can tell us that'll help, this is the time to spill it." He paused. "Is the chauffeur someone working for Mr. Hart? Or Magnus? I see it in your eyes, Natalie. Just tell us. If he's threatened you, what difference can it make at this point?"

Natalie held Katie to her chest and mouthed, "Her."

Bret and Sara shot forward, arriving on their knees beside the couch. They ignored the vehicle's braking, leaned closer to Natalie for an explanation.

"I think he's after your money," she said. "I'm not certain. Maybe both the money and me. But he keeps calling, making threats about what he'll do to a certain young girl if I don't cooperate. I haven't known what I should do."

Bret thought of Natalie's occasional cell phone calls at the estate, followed by irritability and isolation. How many times was she forced to relive those nights of captivity? To sense her attacker lurking around the corner? Or worry that her mistakes might cause Katie harm?

"Wait," Sara said. "I think we're stopping."

Kevin poked his head through the moonroof. "Yep. Stopped."

"Down, Kev," Bret told him. "If he gets out, he might see you. And if it's nothing but a short wait for a stoplight or traffic, I don't want your head out there when we start moving again."

"It's an old parking lot, Dad."

Bret held up a hand. "Hold on, everyone. Listen."

A door clicked open with a solid yet muffled sound.

Sharp tingles spread through Magnus's toes and his fingertips. The painful sensation indicated a swing back toward normalcy. He wasn't there yet, but if he held on a few minutes longer his limbs might regain some function.

"You meant to kill me . . ."

Magnus was certain he knew this man, the details there in the back of his brain somewhere, a box to be pulled from the attic and sorted through.

"For that you will suffer . . ."

How? Magnus wondered. When? Where?

"Oh-ho, here we are," Bookman said. "The old Storinka factory."

Magnus figured he drank the chemical cocktail in his Sprite around 7:00 P.M. The dash clock read 8:15 now. Over an hour had passed, and the worst of his symptoms should have peaked by now. Indeed, the tingling in his calves and forearms suggested he was on the mend. Only a few minutes longer and the gun in his lap would turn from flat stone into deadly steel once more.

The limo came to a full stop.

"I'd ask you to get out, Magnus," Bookman said. "But I doubt you could."

"Who . . . are you?"

"Bookman. Like I told you." The man known as Bookman, the man who was not Eddie Vreeland, marched around the front and opened the passenger door. "Think about it, M-and-M. I told you on the phone that 'Bookman' wasn't exactly a brainteaser."

Magnus felt his arms being lifted, his heavy frame being hefted from the seat. He was still a tingling mass of bog slime, formless, with only hints of life.

"Did you even try? Think. What item can be found in any book?"

Magnus was laid out on the ground beside the limousine, where the headlights revealed a parking lot of cracked asphalt and weeds. Further on, lights illuminated the old CSX train trestles that crossed the Cumberland River. Face-up, he lifted his head. Wiggled his toes. Focused himself on survival.

"Here's your last hint," Bookman said. "In Ukrainian it's called a 'storinka.'"

As Magnus fielded this clue, his employer dropped the Kimber handgun beside him. The metal glinted only inches from Magnus's nose. The mouth of the large-caliber barrel was black.

"Does this scenario seem familiar?" Bookman asked. "You once aimed your eighteen-wheeler and killed a man. You took money and carried out orders for a cold and ruthless man. What does that make you, Magnus? Or do you prefer Theodore Hart? Does it matter in the end?"

"I am . . . Magnus . . . Maggart."

"Fine. Here's what I'm going to do, Maggart the Braggart. I'm going to drive to the end of the lot, turn the vehicle around, and come barreling back at you. Can you stand to your feet? Can you find the dexterity to handle your weapon? Are you strong enough to survive? Let's find out."

I will rise. I am strong. Natalie, you and I can teach others.

Chapter Sixty-nine

"O<small>H, MY,</small>" B<small>RET'S MOTHER WHISPERED, HER FACE PRESSED TO THE SIDE</small> window, "I can see the chauffeur's blond hair. He's dragged something from the front seat."

"Can you see what it is?" Bret said.

"I'm trying, dear. It looks, well, it looks for the life of me like a body."

In Bret's hand, the Blackberry indicated a return call.

"Detective?" he said.

"You all right, Mr. Vreeland? I would've seen your call earlier, but you caught me in the middle of Wednesday prayer meeting."

"We can use some prayer ourselves." Bret collected his thoughts. "We, uh, we just got home from Mexico, and now our airport limo driver's lost over by Fesslers and Lebanon Pike. He's got our door and window buttons locked so that the whole family's trapped in here. I can see, yeah, it looks like we're at an old factory. Says . . . says 'Storinka Defense Systems.'"

"Near the police impound lot. I know the place. Look, I'd like to apologize for the end portion of your vacation. I hear your father went without a fight at the airport, but naturally he denies all charges."

Bret quieted his voice. "My mom told me some of it, and she has a stack of receipts and manifests, all the stuff linking him and Gabe Stilman. Same stuff that you must've got. Speaking off the record, my dad might be guilty."

"You lost me," Meade said. "I never got any paperwork."

"But didn't you say it came from Tacoma?"

"A FedEx Office. It was a box of clothing items and a DVD."

Bret tapped his mother's shoulder. She was still at the window, glued to the goings-on outside. "Mom, didn't you tell me you gave copies of your evidence to a detective? Was it to a Detective Meade here in Nashville?"

"Meade? No, it was an investigator. An insurance man named Mr. Hart."

"Mr. Hart?"

"Yes. Met him at our place in Tacoma."

"Big, strong bulky guy?"

"Why, yes."

Bret pointed through the tinted window at the large form stretched on the pavement. "I know it's dark, but can you tell me if that's the same guy?"

She squinted. "Certainly could be Mr. Hart. Same size and build."

"Wait," Sara said. "Let me see. Do we know if it's really him?"

"It's him," Bret said into the phone. "Magnus Maggart. He's hurt or dead. You think he sent you that evidence, Detective? Maybe he was trying to frame my dad, using my mom to help without her realizing it."

"If so, that would call your father's charges into question," Meade said.

Bret watched the chauffeur hovering over the body. Boy, a part of him wanted to go out through the moonroof and pound fists into the face of Magnus Maggart, demand explanations from him. Another part was simply grateful, like Sara, that their family was unharmed. Magnus had come too close for comfort.

"Mr. Vreeland, you have your Glock on you?" Meade said. "You carrying? Probably not, since you just got back from your trip. In that case, leave him where he lies. Tell everyone to hold tight till I get there. I'm ten, maybe twelve minutes away."

Bret ended the call, turned to deliver the news. He was interrupted by a slammed door and the car's gunned engine. The sudden power threw him against the backseat. The limo careened over the asphalt, gained speed, skidded to a sideways halt, and turned back the way it came. This time there was no let up on the accelerator. Bret realized the chauffeur was aiming the wide nose of the Town Car at the man lying down.

Magnus, apparently, had forced himself into the limo back at the airport, probably waving his gun about and issuing threats.

No wonder the driver was angry.

The limousine charged onward, a hurtling hunk of steel.

Magnus drew on every ounce of willpower, channeled it into physical strength, and inched his drugged body toward the foliage at the edge of the lot. He clutched the Kimber to his belly.

Headlights bore down on him.

Hypnotic. Blinding.

He rolled into a prostrate shooter's position. He thumbed off the safety, aimed through the brightness toward where the driver's seat should be. His muscles were strands of sea kelp, rubbery and pliable. The smell of salt and fear on his skin invigorated him.

He pulled the trigger three times.

The Town Car veered away, two rounds zinging off a side panel, the third skimming off the hood. Dirt and pebbles spat at Magnus as the car roared by.

This was madness. Bret's loved ones were trapped in this limo, caught in an escalating game of do-or-die. He knew Magnus was armed with a minimum of five more rounds, and whoever this hotshot chauffeur was, he seemed intent on using the car as a weapon. In legal terms, it would be "vehicular homicide."

Poor Sara. Early in their marriage, she had fought those old nightmares on a regular basis, and she didn't need this.

At the far end of the old lot, the limo skittered over patches of broken pavement. The rusted ironworks of the trestles rose in the darkness ahead, stretched high over trees, rock, and river to Shelby Park, the Vreelands' old East Nashville stomping grounds.

"I've gotta do something, Sara," he said.

"What?" Her face was grim. "Honey, be careful."

"At least we know the driver's on our side now, so your safest bet's staying in here. If I can get to Magnus, he doesn't seem to be at full strength."

"You can do it, Dad," Kevin said. "Go."

"I'm going. You put your arms around your sis and hold on, OK?"

Kevin nodded, covering Katie even as the limo's tail swung around and everyone grabbed for a handhold. The tires squealed in the fight for traction.

No hesitation, Bret. Now.

Before his wife or daughter could stop him, before his mother could plead her case, Bret gripped both sides of the moonroof opening, squeezed his shoulders through, and propelled himself from the car. He tumbled over the side, struck his hip on the door handle, tucked his head as he landed on hard ground. He hoped the headlights had obscured Magnus's view of his maneuver.

The limousine gunned for Magnus again.

Bret made his own approach by darting up a slope through vines and scrub growth, finding a berm that ran behind the foliage. He sprinted along it. His eyes scoured the ground for a weapon.

There. A fallen tree limb. The length of a baseball bat and twice as thick.

It would have to do.

Magnus knew Bookman was toying with him, just as he had for months. Twice, the powerful Town Car roared by and missed him while Bookman leered from behind the glass. Magnus's muscles were regaining strength and he needed to act now. No playing around. No mercy.

At the far end of the lot, the limo prepared for its third pass.

Magnus had five rounds left. If he stared this charging bull down and put the bullets between its eyes, so to speak, he could end this.

And if done right, the car would slide to a halt.

He would open the back door and take Natalie's hand.

Ask her to join him on a journey of higher education for the strong.

The Bible thumpers got it all wrong with their ideas of the meek inheriting the earth, of men in rags getting the front seats at their church gatherings. The strong gained nothing by propping up the weak. They only weakened themselves. The real idea was to purify the gene pool, leave the healthy, the wealthy, the wise.

Get tough or get gone.

And that goes for you, Bookman. Bye-bye.

The limo charged, its tires churning, engine shrieking.

Magnus lined up his first shot, let out his breath, counted one-one-thousand, two-one-thousand, and squeezed the trigger. The left headlight went out in a spray of tinkling glass. His second shot took out the front windshield, finishing the work of an earlier round that skimmed off the hood.

Bret watched the first two shots strike their targets and knew if he failed now, Magnus would kill the driver. The car would careen out of control, with potential injury or even death to those within.

Dear Lord, no.

The cry came from deep in his chest, a heartfelt yearning. Everything important to him could be torn away in an instant. Why hadn't he kept them in his prayers more often of late? What'd happened to his daily communion with God? So quickly the cares of the world had crowded in.

I am weak. I need Your help now more than ever.

He raised the tree limb over his right shoulder, aimed his body down the slope at a sharp diagonal. Gaining speed, he started his back swing, but the shift of weight found him plowing through a patch of loose rocks. His feet lost traction. As he pitched forward, club still poised, his enemy rolled over and spotted him.

The car was close now. The remaining headlight blazed. Magnus looked left and high, let his peripheral vision fill in Bookman's form behind the steering wheel. This time he wouldn't miss. He would blow the man's head to bits.

One-one-thousand . . .

From behind, rumbling stones diverted his focus.

He twisted onto his back, found the solid shape of Bret Vreeland plummeting toward him. Magnus raised his weapon and fired. The barrel flared. The sound was deafening. The .45 ACP round tore a hole from Bret's thigh, blowing out chunks of tissue and bone.

Magnus had no time to congratulate himself before a thick wooden limb in Bret's hand completed its arc and clobbered his skull. Bret thudded to the ground beside him, as colors flashed across Magnus's vision and spun into blackness.

Magnus heard the limo's racing engine. Heard tires bearing down. The first touch of rubber pulled the skin from his scalp.

Bret landed hard, spun away, shouted in agony as pebbles ground into his gaping wound. In so doing, he avoided the Lincoln Town Car as it completed its mission and smashed into the body beside him. The long, low vehicle dragged the hulking form of Magnus Maggart across the pavement in a tumbling, wet, thumping mess. When at last it came to a halt, the body was unrecognizable.

If Bret hadn't rolled clear, would he be a part of that mess?

Did the driver not see him here?

Tired at last of its rampage, the limo with its one good headlight made a slow turn through the lot and came to within ten yards of Bret's position. The chauffeur stepped out. He picked up the gun left in the wake of his victim.

"The man deserved it," he said, nodding toward Magnus's corpse. "That was a long time coming."

Bret gritted his teeth, tried to sit up.

"You in pain?" the driver said.

"Not . . . too bad."

"You will be soon enough, boyo. That leg looks none too good."

Bret's thigh oozed blood, and he spotted bone chips in the mangled stew. Beyond the driver's shoulder, Sara crawled through the moonroof. She slipped her hips over, slid to the ground, and rushed to his side. Her face went white.

"Don't let the kids out," Bret called to her. "Or my mom."

"What happened, hon?"

"Magnus, he's dead. And my leg, it's not good, but I'm sure . . . Urrrrgh." The first full wave of pain radiated outward. "Please. They can't see this."

Sara called 9-1-1, explained their situation and location.

"Detective Meade's also . . . on his way," Bret said. "Any minute now."

The driver stood behind Sara. "Help's good, but let's be sure we're all on the same page here. I protected you by running down a lunatic, is that clear? And one other thing." He removed his cap. "Sara, I think you and I need to talk."

Chapter Seventy

SARA VREELAND, IN TIMES PAST, DREAMED OF ANOTHER MAN. SHE WOKE FROM images of his body scraped across hard stone, smeared by spinning tires, too shattered to be put back together again. Sometimes she woke in tears. Sometimes in a cold sweat. These incidents declined in number as time wore on and as Bret came alongside to walk her through the grief of the man she once loved.

Less often, she dreamed of the other man as he was on their dinner dates while they were engaged. He was dashing in his Italian suits and ties, light brown hair slicked back from chiseled, almost Slavic features, eyes an icy blue.

"Alex Page," he introduced himself to her that first time.

"Short for Alexander?" she asked.

"Just Alex. Alexander's too pretentious."

"Alex it is."

And here now, after twelve years and eight months of mourning what might have been, after eleven years and five months celebrating and learning to appreciate what was, Alex Page stood before her.

He was a ghost in the darkness.

No, he could not be real.

"Sara, I think you and I need to talk."

It was his enunciation of her name that tore away the veil. The chauffeur's voice was deeper now than during his brief greetings at the airport. His cap was off. His hair was dyed blond, impossibly so. There was no disguising, though, the angles of his face and those eyes.

Sara's and Alex's gazes locked, and in a flash from the past, he cocked his head to the right as though admiring the work of a master sculptor or painter.

She froze. She was the statue.

And then his adoring glance brought her back to life, as it had long ago.

She cried out, a wrenching of heart and soul that tore from her lungs and throat and threw her forward.

"My Sara, I love you. Please allow me to explain."

"You're dead," she said. "No. Don't do this."

"I'm still here." He spread his arms, gun in hand. "I want us to be together."

"You're talking to my wife," Bret said. His breath was labored.

"Allow us this moment, if you would, Mr. Vreeland."

"It's you?" Sara said. She shook her head. "No, no, no, this is not happening. You're crazy. Where have you been all these years?"

"That truck was intended to hit me in April of ninety-eight, that is true, but my father's housekeeper warned me beforehand."

"Your father? You never even introduced me to him."

"But I'm told that he loved you, Sara. He gave you everything."

"Storinka?" She swallowed. "Ivan Storinka was your father?"

"Storinka, yes. In Ukrainian it means 'page.'"

On the ground, Bret tried again to sit up. "What's going on?"

"Good evening, I'm Alex Page."

"Alex . . .?" Bret's eyes jumped to Sara.

She nodded. This was too much. She helped her husband remove his shirt, took a small branch from a nearby tree limb, formed a tourniquet around his thigh. She tried not to pay attention to the details of the wound but to the larger issue of blood loss. She used the stick to tighten the tourniquet.

Oh, Lord. Help us.

She could hardly breathe. Her entire world was in need of a tourniquet.

"Good work," Alex said, looking over her shoulder.

Bret stretched out, eyes screwed shut. "Urrrgh."

Sara held his hand and looked up at this man behind her. Despite his ridiculous blond hair that must be part of his new persona, he was handsome. No doubt about that. His eyes were piercing, and he still had that confidence and "it" factor that attracted her from the start.

"Would you please put that gun away?" Sara said.

Alex Page ignored the request and jumped back into his explanation. "I was Storinka's only son," he said. "His wife, his ex, was barren, but I was born to one of his lovers. I came to America before he ever thought of doing so. I created my own identity, free of him, free of connections to my past."

"And when he moved here, you joined forces in his company."

"Exactly, Sara. He mentored me, hoping I would take it further."

"And no one knew."

"Some knew. Some of his old rivals who were against this merger."

"And they're the ones who wanted you dead? Help me fit this together."

"The truth is even uglier." He flicked the gun's safety off and on. "My father ordered my death when I refused to continue with the company. I didn't want that life anymore. I was done with it. I knew details that could compromise him, and he was especially furious that I fell in love with a certain working-class American girl. He still clung to old ways of thinking from his homeland. He had survived so much and fought so hard to establish himself and his business from scratch."

Sara brushed a hand through Bret's hair. He was in a cold sweat. When would help get here? Were they having difficulty finding this obscure location?

"Bret? Sara?" It was Claire's voice from the limo.

"Stay in the car with the kids," she said. "Just a couple of minutes, please."

Claire ducked out of sight.

"You're a beautiful mother," Alex said to Sara. "I knew you would be."

She ignored that. "Did your father know you were still alive, Alex?"

"Why would he deserve that?" Alex's eyes gazed off. "Like everyone else, he believed I was killed that day. Viktor, his housekeeper, was my one confidant."

"Viktor Moroz?"

"He told me that, yes, my father's guilt was real, even though he publicly denied his part in what happened. From Viktor, I learned about your connection with my father and his decision to include you in the will."

Bret's groaning grew louder.

Sirens sounded in the distance.

"So it's true," Sara said. "He was paying me for what he did to you."

Alex nodded. "But don't you see, Sara? You and I can now live this life together, with the money, the estate, with each other."

He was speaking her old fantasies. To hear him voice those desires gave them warmth, breathed new life into them. Could this be the way it was meant to be? But she had two beautiful children now, and a man whom she loved.

"I was at your funeral, Alex. Bret was too."

Bret grunted at the mention of his name, his face contorted in pain. "Who was in that casket?" he managed to get out.

"I'm told it was a closed casket," Alex said. "But one of Storinka Defense System's dockworkers was inside, a fellow who flapped his lips far too much about armaments headed overseas. His name was George Stilman, son of Gabe Stilman. He and I were very similar in size and basic description."

"And who else knows he got run down in your place?"

Alex swallowed. "Only Viktor and I. Viktor caught wind of what they had planned for me on that lonely state road. They laid out a thin nail strip as I came home from a meeting in central Washington. When I pulled over to change my tire, they would run me down as though it were an accident. Viktor intervened. He sent George ahead of time, so that he would be there to help me with my car. While I took George's vehicle home, he stayed to do the repair on my Infiniti. Theodore Hart plowed him over minutes later, made mincemeat of him, and everyone was convinced I was the one who died on that road." He jerked his chin toward the body of Magnus Maggart. "Seems only fitting, doesn't it?"

"What about this George Stilman?" Sara said. "Didn't anyone miss him?"

"The same day at the Seattle docks, completely unrelated, word spread that he had been in a mishap and got crushed beneath a container as it plunged into the sea. His body, rest his soul, was never recovered."

"You mean, to protect yourself you threw another man's life away?"

Alex sighted the gun, aimed the barrel at the nearby foliage. "If you want to see it that way, Sara, but he was already going to face consequences for his big mouth. His behavior on the docks was not wise. I used it to my advantage."

"At least tell me," she said, "where've you been all these years."

"I'm here, Sara. I love you. That's never changed."

"Where, Alex?"

"I know that you care for me," he said. "Our love was real."

"My husband's lying right here. Don't you have any respect?"

Alex touched her shoulder, and that single connection shot through her being, reawakening all those longings, those lost dreams. He said, "Bret was brave. He saved my life, perhaps all of yours too. Let him go, Sara."

"What?"

"He's lost a lot of blood. Come with me. We can start over."

Jesus, help me. I've let my mind get crowded with all this stuff, the estate, the feeling I'm worth something. You are where I get my worth. You alone.

Sara tightened the tourniquet another notch, saw Bret's face whiten. The blood at the wound had stopped oozing, which only provided a clearer image of the massive cartilage and muscle damage, not to mention splinters of bone.

Please let my husband live. Lord, that's what I want.

"Alex," she said, "these words would've meant something to me years ago. Even six months ago they would've caused me to struggle. But this is crazy. No, I love my husband. We've tasted what it's like to have everything I lost with you, and it's only clouded things between us. It's stuff. Just silly stuff."

"Sara." Bret grimaced. "I love you, for . . . richer or poorer."

"I love you too."

The sirens grew louder.

"A touching picture," Alex said. "But it will be for poorer, Sara, if you can't find it in you to follow after me. You must find the strength to get what you want and put aside these obligations."

"I want my husband." She cradled Bret's head on her lap.

"Understandably," Alex said, "but don't tell me you never cared for me. I see it in your eyes. You still have the same heart. You and I can be happy together. I can raise these children as my own. We can share my father's estate."

"Oh, is that what this is about?" Sara said. "The will?"

"Don't be foolish."

"You left me to go on without you, and now you want me back when there are millions of dollars involved."

"No, that's not it at all. I couldn't risk your life by coming back out into the open. Instead, I carved out a new life for myself a second time around. I even married. It was not happy. I don't need the money. I still have many ties that suit my lifestyle and needs. I want you, Sara. I want the one love of my life. I want what was taken from me by a hard, embittered father. I want you."

"And I want you too . . ."

His icy eyes brightened.

"To leave me and my family alone."

His voice chilled. "You make this choice, Sara, and you lose the estate. Lose everything." He removed a thick manila envelope from beneath the shirt at his back. "You see this? Gabe and Eddie, they gathered evidence of Storinka's illegal dealings. Bret's mother, she found and copied it, and Magnus got a hold of this set here. Maybe Gabe knew about his son's death in my place, maybe not. Either way, they hoped to bring down the entire empire. This evidence gets into the hands of federal prosecutors, and they'll come after every penny owed to the Pentagon for unfulfilled contracts and back orders with Storinka Defense Systems. And your testamentary trust? You'll lose it all. I did away with Gabe myself to be sure he never said a word, but I'm not above using this if I must."

"You mean, Eddie never did kill anyone?"

"Eddie's a pathetic little man who tried to conceal this evidence so that his son and daughter-in-law could keep their fortune."

"That was his secret? That's what he was hiding? He did it for us."

Alex jabbed the gun into his waistband, pulled a lighter from his pocket. The lighter flared, went out. Flared, went out. "We torch these papers, and you and I can enjoy life as it should've been. I'm part of the deal. I always was."

"This is crazy, Alex. This isn't love."

"Love is crazy."

"Love is stronger than crazy."

"What's it to be, Sara?" The lighter flared again. "Your choice."

Chapter Seventy-one

CLAIRE VREELAND HEARD EVERY WORD THROUGH THE OPEN MOONROOF. SHE was huddled with her grandbabies in the confines of the limousine. Natalie was beside them. Only twenty yards beyond their window lay the dead man who she heard had once tormented poor Natalie, and the relief was evident in the young woman's eyes. Claire was careful to keep Katie's eyes shielded from it all. There were some things even an adult was best not seeing.

Was this true, though, that Eddie was innocent?

Was he framed all along for Gabe's murder?

If so, the papers in Claire's suitcase in the trunk would spell trouble only for Bret and Sara. Her evidence could tear away the luxuries they now enjoyed. That wasn't fair to them, was it? My, oh my. For years, Claire had covered for her husband. Now, she decided, it was time to cover for her son and daughter-in-law.

I'll burn those papers myself, she decided. *No one'll be the wiser.*

What about Eddie? What to do with him? It sounded as though he would be cleared of all charges and allowed to come home. He wouldn't be going to prison, after all.

But to rehab?

If she had any say. She was done enabling him.

To counseling?

Most assuredly, yes. This marriage might yet work, but she would never again suffer his hands upon her.

A tiny voice startled Claire from her thoughts.

"Kevin, where are you going?" Katie said.

Claire glanced up in time to see her grandson's legs scissoring out through the moonroof. She reached for him. "Kevin, no."

But he was gone.

Bret's pain worked in stages.

The first stage left him stunned and groaning on the asphalt, his thigh blown open. His wife rushed to his side. The driver waved a gun. All of it was blurred and distant, disconnected from reality.

The second stage introduced him to a slow-burning fire at the edges of the wound that worked its way down into meat, gristle, and bone. During this stage, his senses sharpened. He heard the skittering of insects in the dirt and the drops of his own sweat into the earth. He smelled the residue of gunfire, the coppery odor of blood. He saw Alex Page toting Magnus's Kimber semi-automatic.

The third stage was agony. The fire in his destroyed thigh exploded outward with volcanic fury, raining down drops of burning lava. He couldn't think. Couldn't focus. He writhed on the ground.

Voices.

Alex and Sara.

An envelope of papers, of evidence.

A choice between right and wrong, past and present, justice and lies.

When it came to standing for the truth and for love, there was always a choice, wasn't there? Each person had that power.

"Don't . . . do it," Bret said.

Sara leaned close, her eyes full of compassion and confusion. "What?"

Although the emergency vehicles weren't yet visible, amber lights spun through the winter-stripped branches. Help was close. Would they be able to save his leg? Would he bleed out here in this abandoned lot?

He said, "Don't . . . burn it. We don't . . . don't need it."

"The man's delirious," Alex Page said. "A bunch of mumbo-jumbo."

"No, he's right," Sara said. "We can't keep what's not ours. You want me to choose? All right. I choose Bret."

Alex stepped closer. "And a sorry choice, by the look of him." He lifted his foot and pressed it down into the exposed meat of Bret's thigh.

Bret yelled out. The fire engulfed his skin, his thoughts.

Sara clawed at Alex, tried to shove him off, but he merely chuckled.

"I'm a nobody," he said. "A vapor. I don't exist without your love. Give that to me, or I'll leave you with nothing and no one to love."

"I love my husband." She threw her weight against him. "I love my kids."

Alex pressed down harder.

"Urrragggh!"

Bret's eyes shot open. His mouth gaped in an endless scream. He could do nothing, say nothing. He was at the mercy of this madman.

"Listen to him, Sara. You dear man's dying."

"Bret is my man," she said, "till death do us part."

"And then will you be mine?"

"Never."

Bret watched his wife pound her fists against her former fiancé's chest. She grabbed at his foot, tried to dislodge it. Tears spilled from her cheeks, landing hot and heavy on Bret's arm. Alex reached for his pistol again. Sara tried to reach around and catch his wrist, but he swatted her away.

"So be it," he said. "'The Lord gives and the Lord takes away.'"

She yelled, "Don't do this, Alex."

Sirens blared, and an emergency vehicle followed an unmarked sedan onto the far corner of the lot. Alex dropped his gaze to Bret's pain-ridden face. Bret saw the gun angle toward his own head. This was how it would end, and he could do nothing to stop it. He wriggled beneath the man's foot, but every moment was torture.

Please, God, don't let him do anything to Sara or the kids.

Behind Alex, a small form flew down the same incline Bret had traveled minutes earlier. It was Kevin. He must've crept from the limo in the darkness.

Like father, like son.

Bret watched his ten-year-old plant a leg into the soil. Using all the force he employed on the soccer field, Kevin whipped his right leg around and drove it all the way through, as though firing a goal into the net. The kick cut Alex's right leg out, took the left one with it. He cursed, buckled. The gun fired a round at the heavens, as he landed hard on his back and his packet of papers fluttered from his hand. Kevin also slipped and fell.

Gasping, Alex fumbled with the gun and lifted it once more.

"Sara," Bret yelled. He tried to rise up. "Watch out."

"Drop your weapon," Detective Meade shouted. He was shielded by the open door of his unmarked vehicle, his sidearm resting on the frame. "Put it down on the ground. Do it now."

Alex took aim at Sara's chest.

A pair of rapid-fire gunshots bellowed over the parking lot of the abandoned Storinka Defense Systems factory. Hemmed in by earthen berms and iron train trestles and cold asphalt, the sound deafened and disoriented Bret. He tried to rise to both knees, but his last vestiges of strength gave way and he pitched onto his side.

Sara? Kevin?

Within arm's reach, Alex Page lay dead.

Detective Meade rushed forward, weapon still drawn. He approached the body, made certain there was no danger.

"Where were you?" Sara cried. "I tried to keep him talking, but he was going to kill Bret. Get those paramedics over here."

"Right away." Meade looked down at Bret. "And what happened to you?"

"I . . ." He groaned. "I think my golfing days are over."

Sara and Kevin moved aside as EMTs prepared Bret for transportation to the hospital. Claire and Katie joined the throng, lingering near the back. Bret bore most of it in silence and tried to avoid worrying his family. They would have other things to deal with soon enough, other battles to fight. It never really ended, did it? Day by day by day, they gathered their manna. Day by day by day, they lived for a treasure that would not fade.

As Bret was loaded onto a gurney, he said, "As for me and my house, we will serve the Lord." He closed his eyes, managed a weak smile, and they carted him away.

A Yell and a Whisper

behind his quivering lips, the accuser grinds his teeth and curses those who are committed to the one, wondering what they see in him, what makes him so desirable

the situation offers no explanation, and so he roams another day

"i'll find others, many others, and grind them down"

blue and green, ever-spinning, the earth reflects celestial lights and dying suns, but most irritating of all reflects the beauty of the one who spoke it into existence, the one whose finger-snap sent forth an expanding canvas of energy, dark matter, planets, and meteorites, and creatures fashioned in his very image

"look at them," the accuser says, "the whole disgusting lot of them"

from the globe's surface, from huts and hovels, manors and mansions, fingers of light stretch toward the sky, prayers of the tired, the broken and weak, prayers of the destitute, sick and abused, all of them reaching, ever beseeching the one

"why him, always him?"

the very thought produces another headache, all this childish reverence for one who refuses to be made visible

"show your face, why don't you?" the accuser yells

"i do," the almighty one whispers, "each and every day"

"ha, that's not what they say"

"they say a lot of things and mean only some of them, but there are still those who resist, those through whom i show my love"

"and for the rest there'll be hell to pay, on that you can bet your life"

"i already have," says the one, "so that they don't have to pay"

with that, the conversation ends

Chapter Seventy-two

May 2011

THE VREELANDS WATCHED HIM RUN.

The three-year-old stallion was fit and well-groomed, but Animal Kingdom wasn't the most impressive horse on the track at Churchill Downs. He had never raced on dirt, and according to the sportscasters, his jockey had been injured the previous day during training.

Enter Johnny V.

Jonathan Velazquez was a veteran, well-known and respected. He was riding in his thirteenth Kentucky Derby. He had yet to win this race, and two years in a row he was scratched from the list due to his mounts' last-minute physical ailments. This year he was listed to ride Uncle Mo, one of the early favorites, but when the horse came down with gastrointestinal problems, Johnny V was left without an animal for the third time in his Derby career.

The decision to put Johnny V on Animal Kingdom was hurried and desperate, and odds-makers showed little respect for the new pairing.

Here at the 137th Kentucky Derby, a record crowd of nearly 165,000 watched the humble-looking horse enter Gate 16. With a mile and a quarter to run, he would have two minutes to prove what he could do.

Johnny V focused forward, eyes staring between the horse's ears.

The gunshot cracked.

The gates burst open, unleashing thundering horse hooves and flowing tails. Animal Kingdom moved along the outside of the pack, held back, and waited. With a half mile left, he inched forward. With a quarter mile left, Johnny V used the crop to urge him onward at greater speed. The strange pairing, the unknown horse and unlucky jockey, moved past the fifth- and fourth-place horses.

They accelerated and closed the distance.

Third place. Second place.

Other favored horses fell away, and Animal Kingdom crossed the finish line with a full length to spare.

Together on the sofa, Bret and Sara Vreeland stared at the TV, both afraid to say a word. They too had tasted of heartache and rapture. Yes, they had been tested, prepped, and purified.

And there the great horse stood.

Victorious, just like that.

Bret muted the TV and massaged his hip, where the stump of his leg protruded from gym shorts. He owned a prosthetic and a wheelchair, but most days he preferred the simplicity of crutches. He never questioned that decision to dive at his enemy. It was not in his DNA to sit by and be silent. And it had possibly saved the lives of his family.

Plus, he still had his guitar. He still had his voice.

As predicted, probate court took everything to cover arms manufacturing contracts between Storinka Defense Systems and the U.S. military. Per the limitations of a testamentary trust, the cars, the estate, all of it was gone. Even Viktor Moroz was gone, his body discovered in Germantown in the trunk of his own car, the bullets matching the caliber of Magnus Maggart's Kimber pistol.

The Vreeland family was back at 724 Groves Park Road, but at least it was paid in full. Eli Shaffokey lived alongside the garage, his camper plugged into an outlet and his water hooked up to a hose. The Dobermans once belonging to Viktor now guarded the backyard, more bark than bite. Kevin and Katie loved them.

Eddie Vreeland was a free man once more, but he and Claire had a long road of counseling and recovery ahead.

The kids were back in public schools.

Natalie Flynn was reenrolled at Trevecca Nazarene, finishing her degree.

Though Bret still enjoyed his higher paying job at Billingsley, he punched in every day just to see the smiles on his old crew's faces. He switched his country club membership to a different location, one at which he and Detective Meade could share tee times. Of course, his game would never be the same, but he had no problem driving the cart. Being a caddy wasn't so bad.

Sara worked part-time at the sleep clinic. Although she and Zoe shopped together on occasion, things weren't quite the same.

Sara still owned the sapphire necklace.

She did not, however, own the 3 × 5 photo of Alex Page. Without ceremony, she tore it to pieces and let it go.

The Derby was over, the post-race commentary just beginning. Bret felt Sara's hand slip into his, and he gave it a squeeze. They sat in silence until his phone rang on the arm of the sofa.

"Pastor Teman. Yeah, what's up?"

"Are you ready for some news? Is Sara there?"

"She's here." Bret put it on speaker. "I think we're ready for anything."

"That's good, because here's the latest. The street date for your album is three weeks away, but guess whose first single just cracked the Top Ten on national charts? Churches across the country love 'Passionate People,' and the presale numbers are through the roof. Get ready, Bret. You too, Sara. A wheelchair's not going to stop what God wants to do. I know that's easy for me to say, isn't it? But I truly believe that you and yours will have opportunities to minister in places you never imagined."

"Wherever God leads," Bret said.

"To Hawaii or Haiti," Sara agreed. "To the rich or the poor."

"Or all of the above. Either way," Pastor Teman said, "I believe you're one step away from something wondrous."

Acknowledgments

Jonathan Clements (Wheelhouse Literary Group) — for climbing into this lifeboat with me when there wasn't a sliver of land in sight.

Art Ayris (Kingstone Media Group) — for steering this particular ship of faith and inviting me to climb onboard.

Cari Hawks Foulk (Wheelhouse Literary Group) — for studying the tides and reading the currents.

Steve Blount (Bay Forest Books) — for guidance to keep the ship afloat.

Ray Blackston (friend and author) — for letting me know the vessel was trustworthy.

Mona Gambetta (The Gambetta Group) — for cover art that blew my expectations out of the water.

Andrea McCarthy (Bay Forest Books) — for a book trailer that captures the tension and excitement I hope is found within these pages.

Carolyn Rose Wilson (wife of 21 years) — for encouragement, patience, love, research help, backrubs, and laughter as we share this adventure together.

Cassie and Jackie Wilson (daughters) — for many fun times together, whether floating in the Dead Sea, playing Stratego, or getting driver's licenses.

Barbara Guise (grandmother) — for showing what it means to work hard, love your spouse to the very end, and for helping with a fantastic home for our family.

Matt and Heidi Messner (brother-in-law and sister) — for showing what it means to serve faithfully and with joy, and for sharing cruises, hikes, beach walks, award-winning drinks, and Sunday services.

Shaun Wilson (brother) — for hanging on while others let go, for speaking softly when a loud voice was the norm, and for facing the wolf spider brigade with me on only one of our dozens of trips together.

Deborah Mart (mother-in-law) — for joining us in our travels, artistic dreams, and conversations about money and the lack thereof.

Robert Guise (uncle) — for retreats together at your cabin in the Sierras, where I can fish and write, laugh and eat elk.

Keith Monaghan (brother-in-law) — for reading my books, coming up with marketing ideas, and offering computer advice when I thought I was sunk.

Louis and Jamie White Harrison (friends and family) — for sharing Easters, Christmases, books and movies, enchiladas, taco soup, and UFC fight nights.

Sean Savacool (friend and family) — for talking books, life, and faith, and for following after God in your relationships and music. Go, Eastern Block!

Matt Bronleewe, Kevin Kaiser, Chris Well (The Council of Four) — for friendship and book-talk, mostly healthy snacks and drinks, and shared hopes and dreams.

River Jordan (friend and author) — for your example of community, prayer, and great writing, and for killing off scorpions for a mighty good cause.

Tom Hilpert (New Joy Fellowship) — for spiritual challenges, story brainstorming, and a mystery series deserving shelf space of its own.

Charliy Nash (sleep apnea sufferer) — for providing details of your own clinic experiences, not to mention your own thought-provoking short stories.

Ken Sircy (Sentry Insurance) — for helping cover us in practical matters, while also sharing my love of books, coffee, basketball, and family.

Erin, Brad, and Lesa at Roast, Inc. (coffee roasters) — for excellent coffee, granola, conversations, and the space to meet friends and write tales.

Steve Garrett (New River Fellowship) — for taking time to talk, and for loving Jesus without pretense or apology.

Fred and Theresa (Teen Challenge, Club 517) — for welcoming me with open arms in Eureka, California, and for giving your lives to change the lives of others.

Dave Ramsey (radio host) — for welcoming us into your home for a fundraiser, and for years of honesty and humor on the airwaves while offering practical financial advice. No credit cards in this home.

August Burns Red, The Black Keys, The Book of Eli Soundtrack, Eastern Block, Matisyahu, Matthew West, The Social Network Soundtrack, and Underoath — for sonic energy while I wrote into the late-night hours.

Friends and Fans (you know who you are) — for reminding me to keep writing, pondering, and enjoying this journey day by day by day.

Father God — for creating beauty and mystery.

Jesus the Son — for sacrificing beyond anything I deserve.

Holy Spirit — for comfort, counsel, and conviction like no other.